THE SOUND OF MY SOUL

A Visionary Novel

By

Patti Williams

*The soul speaks to us through our feelings.
To find our passion
we must listen, follow, and trust
that which our soul declares.*

The Sound of My Soul
A Visionary Novel

Published by
Favrile Imprints
P.O. Box 225
El Verano, CA 95433

Edited by KC Moffatt
Book cover illustration by Chase White

PattiWilliams.com

First print edition, September 2016

ISBN-13: 978-0-9981191-0-6

Printed by CreateSpace

Dedication

To my Mother,
whose encouragement gave me light
even in my darkest moments,

To Angels everywhere,
who always encourage us if
we take the time to listen,

and
To the Seekers of our era,
may you find the sound of your soul
and share it with the world.

I am not a mechanism, an assembly of various sections.
And it is not because the mechanism is working wrongly, that I am ill.
I am ill because of wounds to the soul, to the deep emotional self,
and the wounds to the soul take a long, long time, only time can help
and patience, and a certain difficult repentance
long difficult repentance, realization of life's mistake, and the freeing of oneself
from the endless repetition of the mistake
which mankind at large has chosen to sanctify.

D. H. Lawrence
Healing

PROLOGUE

A New Life Choice

Every life has a beginning; every soul has a choice.

Excitement shivered through Lo-ahn as she stood on the edge of the Ring of Destiny. The path of her next lifetime was not a decision to take lightly. Her Council of Elders had summoned her to decide together the purpose of this incarnation. Today, she would be reviewing several choices, like a dress rehearsal, to make her final decision before returning to Earth in a new body.

Behind her was Soulara, her guardian angel, always with words of encouragement and enlightenment, whose nurturing had given Lo-ahn the confidence to want to return to life again. She knew that only in a body could she advance in her quest for unity with the Oneness, the purpose of all life.

She wondered what her choices would be for this lifetime.

When she had met with her council after her previous lifespan, they had agreed on her focus during her time between lives. The gathering today was a sign that she was ready for the next level.

Lo-ahn turned toward Soulara for one last look of reassurance.

Soulara had been with her since the beginning, and Lo-ahn acknowledged her Guardian Angel with thanks for her constant care and guidance.

As they entered the circular enclosure of the elders, Lo-ahn raised her eyes to the open vaulted ceiling as rays of light sprayed gently around her. She reached out to receive the energy, feeling as if she were reconnecting to the Oneness.

With Soulara hovering nearby, Lo-ahn came to the middle of the room, pausing in front of a crescent-shaped table where her five elders were waiting. They had each spent many lifetimes on Earth, rising to become masters and trusted counsel to those preparing for a new incarnation.

Three of the elders were clothed in long purple robes; the other two were dressed in white. The colors signified attainment of the two highest levels in the rank of masters.

She recognized four of them from previous sessions. Her consciousness leapt as she acknowledged Islea at the end of the table. Many incarnations had passed since Islea had attended her council, and Lo-ahn knew this higher presence meant an important lifetime was upon her.

As Lo-ahn received their telepathic communication, she felt as if all of them were speaking to her simultaneously, yet the information was clear.

"In several lifetimes, you lived a rather solitary existence, choosing not to get close to others. There were also other lifespans when you wanted to be in control, not submitting to others, because of even earlier submissive lives where you ignored your own basic desires.

"You have held yourself to a high standard of perfection and judged others when they did not meet your expectations. This lifetime will be a chance for forgiveness of both yourself and others, allowing compassion to pour forth. This will be the key to your success."

Lo-ahn nodded, remembering the past appraisals of her council.

They continued, "This will be an opportunity to learn about balance and to open to relationships with family and others. Remember, when making your choice, consider both the body's genetic inheritance propensities and your karmic pattern. Choose the body you wish to inhabit with these factors in mind." The instructions were both caring and firm to ensure she understood what was expected of her.

She felt the love and compassion of these elders as she listened to their parting words. "We are always with you whenever you desire our help. You may proceed." They gently disappeared from her vision and Lo-ahn nodded to Soulara, indicating her readiness to enter the Ring of Destiny and begin the choosing process.

Space shifted as an intense light surrounded them, pulling them inward as if through a funnel. Banks of shimmering translucent glass-like screens were arrayed around them like a circular three-dimensional movie theatre.

In the center of the ring, a scanning device with a mass of crystalline lights pulsated, awaiting Lo-ahn's commands. Here, Soulara showed Lo-ahn how to use her thoughts to maneuver and peruse the images appearing on the screens. The luminosity surrounding them subsided, and a concentrated energy force balanced Lo-ahn's apprehension, calming her.

Stillness encompassed Lo-ahn as she took her place at the control station. As if a switch had been flipped, the screens came alive with action, colorful images, and the sounds of everyday life on earth.

Lo-ahn hovered, turning in a circle, watching the panorama of people, places, and events of the three potential paths before her. She mentally operated the display as she watched a series of scenes unfold, traveling through time on lines that converged, showing her possible developments of each future life.

Most of the scenes showed only the childhood and early adulthood for each body, as the influence of the soul during those formative years would impact all future paths, leaving open the ultimate outcome of each existence. Lines of energy glowed like colored guideposts, showing important turning points and crossroads in time.

"You've given me three very appropriate choices," Lo-ahn acknowledged.

"Take your time and experience each body to see what best suits your goals for this lifetime," Soulara said.

Lo-ahn focused on one of the monitors where a couple showed delight at the birth of their daughter. A montage filled the screen showing the child as it matured from babyhood to early adulthood. She looked at Soulara, choosing her words carefully. "She's an only child, and the family is very wealthy."

Soulara nodded. "What else do you see?"

Turning back to the monitors, she watched the little girl playing alone in her bedroom. Hearing the sound of arguing in the other room, the girl stopped what she was doing and listened, a frown dancing across her tiny brow. Lo-ahn halted the action and entered the picture to experience the unfolding drama, feeling the physicality and emotions of the scene.

Coming out of the scene, she spoke as if to herself. "She seems isolated and…" Lo-ahn hesitated. "I don't know exactly what." She focused again on the screen and the look on the girl's face. "She seems to have no feelings."

"Remember, each choice brings a challenge."

"Yes, I see that." Lo-ahn turned to the next monitor where a young child lay in a hospital bed in what appeared to be a sanitarium. A doctor took her pulse as her worried parents looked on. Lo-ahn saw the love from the parents, particularly the mother.

As the child matured into a teenager, she was smaller than her classmates with less energy. Often she stood by the sidelines, not participating in everyday school activities. A young boy showed her kindness. When he asked her for a date, her father forbade it. Slipping into the drama, Lo-ahn shuddered as she felt the fear the girl had of her father.

Returning to the controls, she glanced at Soulara. "She has a need for forgiveness, one of the traits my Council wanted me to develop." Her voice quivered. "I'm uncertain about her." She turned to another display. "There's one more to review."

This time, she moved into the scene and followed the action of the girl as a toddler through to her teenage years. Lo-ahn projected her thoughts to Soulara. "The outcome is unclear, yet her mind is strong and determined to succeed. This is exactly what my Council of Elders wanted me to experience in this lifetime."

Soulara nodded her approval.

Leaving the action and turning in the circle one last time, she made an appraisal of each life, excitement about her choice surging through her. Eager to share her decision, Lo-ahn looked from Soulara to the screen. "That one. Sallie Jane Whitaker." She liked the sound of the name. "I choose the body of Sallie Jane Whitaker."

"Tell me why you've chosen her body rather than the others presented to you."

"Her body is strong. She has a good intellect, which will allow me to reason things out rather than relying on others."

"You realize the challenges of that trait?"

Lo-ahn nodded. "She will want to lead rather than follow, which can give rise to conflict that may cause her to turn away from others, rather than stay and lose her identity. She won't want others to tell her what to do."

"What about the other life choices? Take one last time to experience each of them so as to be certain."

Lo-ahn looked at the image of the young girl who lived in luxury.

"She will become a woman of substantial means. I fear having too much money will cause me to become complacent and not take action."

"There's something more."

"Yes, there is. There is a sense of despair arising from her isolation." She hesitated a moment and looked toward Soulara for guidance. Soulara acknowledged her reasoning with a nod and urged Lo-ahn to continue.

Lo-ahn looked at the second image. "For this body, health issues will play a part, at least in the early years." Lo-ahn touched the image on the screen feeling again the physicality of the sickened body. "Between her fragile nature and the intimidation of her father, I wonder if I would succeed." Lo-ahn hesitated.

Soulara gently nudged her. "What about your soul group?"

"Fe-sol and Garand are also looking at the same images. We have an agreement to work together in this lifetime." Lo-ahn stopped and sent her thoughts to connect with them, opening up to hear them as they too made their choices.

Feeling their resonance in harmony, she turned to Soulara. "They both agree." She pointed to the screen, which showed images of a family. "This also means we will be able to resolve old issues."

On the screen was the teenage girl, Sallie, dropping a pile of schoolbooks on a kitchen counter. Lo-ahn walked to the monitor and merged with the young woman as she began the process of cooking dinner, a wry smile draped on her face.

Leaving the scene, Lo-ahn glowed with excitement. "My Council of Elders wants me to work on learning the true nature of family and community. My need for control and desire for perfection will be most tested by the physical patterns shown for this particular body. In addition, Fe-sol and Garand want to work on shared decision-making. I will need to stand up for myself without turning away."

Lo-ahn reflected upon a previous incarnation where she had been the wife of Fe-sol, with Garand as her father-in-law. She remembered the stiff, high lace collar, tight bodice, and full heavy clothing required to impress others of the merchant class. Fe-sol and Garand enjoyed parading their new wealth within the community, commanding her to their lifestyle.

"Because of their demands and my inability to make my own decisions, I cut myself off from my emotions. This will be a good incarnation to make the necessary changes for advancement. I believe Sallie will provide the best setting to help me meet those challenges. Because we missed making that family connection in our last lifetime together, all three of us wish to make amends and create a new outcome this time."

Nodding her acceptance of Lo-ahn's choice, Soulara sent her approval through waves of love and compassion toward her charge. "What do you think will be the most significant aspect of Sallie's life?"

"I know the outcome isn't clear to me, so I might exercise my free will. Yet, the combination of her body and my soul will provide the ability to learn about trust and being in relationships with others. Her strong mind will help her succeed."

Soulara nodded. "This time you will have several chances when you are young to resolve these issues. If you ignore them, you will be sent further opportunities, although your misfortunes will escalate until you must listen."

"I hope this time I will make the decision which allows for consensus and family."

"The outcome is unknown. You must make your decision based on the limited glimpses from the Ring of Destiny. Trust that what you have learned here will assist your choices when you are incarnate. Free will is absolute once you enter a body. It is up to you to develop your faculties so as to remember what you set to accomplish."

Soulara paused to allow the information to imprint Lo-ahn. "You will get additional instructions from the Place of Recognition so that you can recognize signposts and important people when they come into your life."

"Yes, I'll go over the memory triggers so I can identify the turning points as they manifest."

"The signposts will come in various disguises: a random thought from a stranger, a friend who wants you to meet someone, a feeling in your body that says to pay attention, among others. Listening with your heart will help you on your journey."

Lo-ahn nodded, then gave her guide a conspiratorial look. "There was also a shadowy figure in the background that I hope is my soul mate, Varan. Perhaps this time, we can be together." Lo-ahn's delight was evident at the prospect of this new life.

Soulara smiled and went on, "As you go into this life, you will forget everything your soul knows from this dimension so your experience will come truly from your own personal will. Your unconscious mind will hold the key to your spiritual memories. As well, it is important to join the physical aspects of this body with the spiritual qualities of your soul.

"Remember, I will be with you, and you will have other guides as well. We will come when we are needed. You must ask for our help. We do not interfere until you make a request. Always, though, I will be near, whispering love into your ear."

PART I
Forgetting

Our birth is but a sleep and a forgetting:
The Soul that rises with us, our life's Star,
Hath had elsewhere its setting,
And cometh from afar:
Not in entire forgetfulness,
And not in utter nakedness,
But trailing clouds of glory do we come
From God, who is our home:
Heaven lies about us in our infancy!

William Wordsworth
Ode on Intimations of Immortality

CHAPTER ONE

A Perfect Life

The satisfaction of the life Sallie had created permeated her being.

My perfect life, she thought. As a small bubble of joy began to rise in her body, Sallie cast it aside. *Too much to do. Perhaps later. Focus. Right now, I need to focus.*

Reviewing her agenda in her head as she power-walked in the grey dawn light, Sallie's mind raced, winding through the coming day like a tightly strung watch ticking off the minutes with precision. Her focus was so complete that she missed the sounds of spring echoing across the wide streets, neatly manicured gardens, and designer homes of her affluent Las Rosas neighborhood.

Sallie's body tingled with a prescient feeling that reminded her of an old childhood rhyme. *Step on a crack, break your mother's back.* Finding herself watching the cracks in the sidewalk, she absentmindedly reverted to her old childhood remedy of alternating her pace so that she stepped over the breaks in the concrete, first with her left foot and then with her right, often taking small, mincing steps to keep in sync.

The change in tempo exacerbated the minor difference in the length of her legs so that her slight limp, usually imperceptible when under her control, became more noticeable.

Her mind turned to the snippets of conversation she'd heard whispered around the office the day before. *Peter Samson buying the business! It can't be true. Mike would tell me for sure.*

Sallie did her best to dismiss the idea as mere rumor, at least until she had a chance to discuss the issue with Mike. Over the years, he had become like the father she'd always wanted, trusting in her competence and fostering her ambition. *Surely he would consider me before a stranger if he's looking to sell. Wouldn't he?*

As she approached her cul de sac, the early morning light cast a beam on the spacious front porch of the Craftsman bungalow she had so meticulously renovated. She slowed as she approached and gave her home a critical look, liking what she saw. *Every day, in every way, I create my perfect life*, Sallie's mantra, chanted repeatedly over many years, flashed unbidden through her mind.

Sallie waved to her neighbor, Jean, then turned to her front yard. Anchored by pistache trees, the garden was a mix of early California and English Country. California native plants, still in their dormant state, nestled comfortably against antique roses just beginning to sprout their deep green leaves. *The whole definitely is more than the sum of its parts.*

A flash of brown caught her eye and she turned toward the corner of the yard to investigate. *Another dead rose bush? That's the third this winter.* She hurried over to probe the soil with her finger.

Sallie might have taken the death of her rose bush as a sign, as signs are everywhere. Like little nudges on the fabric of life, Sallie's guardian angels had been sending her these messages, often occurring in threes. This morning, however, she was oblivious to their guidance and saw only a problem to solve, mentally adding another item to her already full agenda: call the gardener. Ticking off her priorities for the day, Sallie flicked the dirt from her fingers and walked up the steps to her porch.

The air was still and a quiet peace descended upon her. She let her eyes glaze, as if to catch a thought from an unseen visitor. Next to her, a small set of silver chimes tinkled softly in her ear. She tilted her head to catch a remembrance of something past, something she had somehow forgotten.

Reaching up to touch the chimes, she frowned as she looked out from her porch to ascertain what might have stirred the air. *There's no wind. What is it? How did they chime? Have I forgotten something?* Her rational brain kicked in and she shrugged, heading inside and going straight to her desk to complete her to-do list for the day.

In the kitchen, Sallie put the kettle on the stove for tea to begin her morning ritual, then opened the refrigerator door to find breakfast. She stared blankly for a moment, her mind still on the day ahead, then snapped back to the task at hand. *I'll make some muffins for the office,* she thought, taking out milk and eggs.

As she turned to put the items on the counter, she noticed her answering machine blinking to signal a new message. She hit the button and was greeted with the voice of her brother, Mark.

"Hey, Sis. I know we haven't talked in a while, but, it's… uh… it's about Dad. Oh, there's nothing wrong. He's okay. It's just… uh… he's getting older and we, that is, Nancy and I, we think he should… uh… I mean, we want to talk to you about what to do. Give a call when you can."

Old memories from her childhood flashed through her mind: her mother's soft voice telling her a bedtime story, her baby brother resting softly in her arms, her father entering a room causing her to jump to attention. A frown creased her forehead as her mind pushed back

16

against the onslaught of these long forgotten moments.

She picked up the phone and started to dial the number, hesitating on the final digit. At that moment, the tea kettle began its incessant whistle, commanding her attention. Sallie carefully placed the phone in its cradle and turned back toward the more pressing demands of the day.

Pouring a cup of tea, Sallie took a sip and wandered over to the secretary desk in her living room. She lowered its writing top and pulled a dusty stack of old photographs from a small drawer. Flipping through them, she paused on a grainy image of three figures on a Little League field. Her father held a bat in one hand and had the other around her brother, who stood with his hand in the air, a ball in his glove like a trophy. They both beamed with excitement. A younger version of herself stood in the background against the dugout fence with a forlorn look on her face. Sallie frowned and shoved the photos back in the drawer, slamming it shut.

An hour later, carrying her attaché case and a basket of fresh-baked apple muffins, Sallie left for her downtown Las Rosas office. With the warm sun dancing a beat on her shoulder, she walked with a brisk stride, holding herself high to mask her slight limp.

Her first stop was Anne's Book Nook, her favorite haunt in town. As she rounded the corner, Sallie's eye caught a display of angel books in the front window. She put her face close and rapped to attract Anne's attention. Her best friend's face lit up as she opened the door and welcomed Sallie inside.

"Hey, look at you," Anne said, her eyebrows raised over her dark framed glasses. "You've got on your power suit and focused look today. What's up?"

"My top client. Seems he's looking for a commercial building in town for his business."

"Sounds big."

"Only the biggest transaction of my career." A small crease darted between Sallie's eyes.

"Why the frown, then?"

"It's my first commercial project. I'm more at home in residential, working with families."

"You're never one to rest on past laurels. I'm sure you'll succeed in this, just like everything else."

Sallie gave a lopsided smile as she changed the subject. "More importantly, how's Matt? Today's the big day."

"Yeah, could hardly get him to go to school. He's as nervous as any big league ball player on opening day."

"Well, it *is* opening day, Little League style. And, the Trojans always do well." Sallie glanced at her watch. "Oh! Sorry, hon, got to run." She paused as she turned toward the door, nodding at the window display. "Angel books selling well?"

"People are always interested in angels. The idea of an unseen helper is enticing."

As she touched the doorknob to exit the store, Sallie's eye caught a beam of light shining through the window on one of the offerings. As if of its own accord, her hand reached toward the book. *There's something I must remember*. Time slowed down and her vision blurred. She frowned and closed her eyes, straining to summon the memory of something long forgotten—something important.

Anne touched her sleeve. "You okay?"

Coming out of her reverie, Sallie looked at her friend. "That was odd, like déjà vu. I can't shake this feeling that I've forgotten something." She gave a shake to clear her head. "Oh well, I'm off. See you this afternoon."

As she approached the cream-colored Spanish style two-story building, Sallie smiled at the swinging sign. *Michael Caldwell & Associates. My name will look good up there someday*, she thought. *Mike's told me I'm his best agent.*

Through the tall double doors, she entered into a spacious lobby, two stories high, with dark wood paneling. There was a seating area for customers with a deep Persian rug of burgundy and green in a traditional design, as well as a built-in reception desk, behind which Julie was hanging up the phone.

Wrinkling her nose at the acrid smell, Sallie gave a quick smile. "Smells like the floors were cleaned with pine tar. Perhaps we should leave the front door open to air things out."

Julie nodded as Sallie propped open the door. "Thanks, Sallie. I was almost used to it."

Sallie strode to the front desk and placed her basket on the counter. She pointed toward the contents. "Fresh-baked apple muffins. Tell everyone to help themselves."

"Looks delish!" Julie grabbed a muffin as she handed Sallie several slips of paper. "Here are your messages." She hesitated, and then sputtered, "There was one from your brother. Asked you to call. I didn't know you had a brother."

"Thanks, Julie," Sallie grabbed the messages, giving a slight shake of her head to maintain her composure. *I've left that behind. No need to reminisce.* She turned to the doorway marked "Staff Only," entering a large open office filled with dark mahogany desks, file cabinets, and dividers allowing each agent privacy within their own area.

At the far end was a private corner office with tall glass panels and a sign on the door with the name "Michael Caldwell." The glass panels were covered with sheer linen curtains, which, when closed, were a sign Mike did not wish to be disturbed.

Her earlier premonition returned and a chill passed through her arms. She shivered and brushed it off with an unconscious flick of her hand. Sallie considered probing Mike for some hints about his long term plans for the business. She glanced toward his office. *Perhaps later,* she thought, noting the closed curtains and the animated silhouettes of Mike and another person in what looked to be a heated discussion. It was probably about the shopping center. If he managed to seal this deal, it would make the numbers for the year—and beyond. Not many real estate brokers got the chance to build a shopping center, let alone manage it upon completion. Retirement money, he had said.

Sallie's status as a high producer had earned her an enclosed office with plantation-shuttered windows. As she walked purposefully in that direction, her assistant, Gail, stood on tiptoes to see over her partition, a perennial worried look on her face. She was solid and dependable with an efficiency equal to Sallie's, taking care of the myriad details necessary to maintain the focus of the business.

Waiting until Sallie was close, Gail whispered, "There's a problem with the Watson escrow." Sallie raised an eyebrow as Gail continued, "Seems Jim doesn't want to lift the final contingency."

Sallie nodded and accepted another pile of message slips and stepped into her office, closing the door behind her. She settled into her comfortable office chair and placed her messages in precise piles in front of her. Picking up her telephone earpiece, she started punching numbers. Several phone calls later, all transactions were back on track. Dropping the earpiece back on the desk, she heard a knock at the door and looked up to see Mike's face in her doorway. Fatigue lurked behind his eyes, though his smile was as steady as ever.

"Got a minute?"

"Sure." Sallie motioned to the chair next to her desk and turned to give him her full attention. After almost a decade of service in his office, Sallie admired him for his decisiveness and ability to consider the various needs of both experienced and novice agents, all while running the number one real estate agency in town.

"How's the Watson escrow?"

"The last contingency has been removed and it's back on track."

"It'll close by the end of the month?"

Sallie nodded. "It should close by the end of next week."

"All right! That makes our numbers for this month." Mike pounded his fist into the palm of his hand, sounding ecstatic.

"Yes, I know."

"That's what I like about you." Mike gave a sharp nod. "You're always looking ahead." He steepled his fingertips. "I heard you have a new client."

"A new-old client. I sold him a home in town last year. His company just went public and he's looking for a larger complex for his business."

"A commercial transaction?"

She nodded.

"You close this one and that vice presidency is yours."

A jolt of excitement ran through her. She had waited a long time to hear those words. Yet, the thrill was tempered by a rising anxiety. "You know I'm not as comfortable with commercial transactions."

"I'll be there for the details."

"You've been really good to me, Mike. That means a lot." As they shared a smile, the rumor about Peter Samson again sprang unbidden into her mind, causing her stomach to lurch. Maintaining an even tone of voice, she asked, "Anything new on the horizon with you?"

"Oh, just the same ole, same ole."

As Mike rose to leave, Sallie continued, "I assume you've heard the rumor going around…"

"I've never known you to listen to rumors," he said. "Why start now?"

As he walked to the door, he turned back to her. "Oh, by the way, stop by my office before you leave today? I need your countersign on another bank transfer."

"Sure. Let me get a couple more things done here and I'll drop by."

The clock tower in the square adjacent to her office chimed the quarter hour. Sallie had just enough time to go home, change, and get to the ball field to watch the game. Spotting Anne in the stands, she waved and found her way to a seat in the bleachers just as Matt threw the first pitch over the plate.

"Strike!" the umpire called.

"All right!" Sallie said, slipping an arm around Anne. "Looks like Matt is right on today."

"You're on time! Client meeting go well?"

She nodded. "He and I are definitely on the same page."

"Once you get in your groove, no one can stop you." Anne turned back to the game. "Come on, Matt! Keep it up!" She shot Sallie a conspiratorial look. "You know, I heard through the grapevine that Jeff Owens wants on your dance card. What gives, Ms. No-One's-Good-Enough-For-Me?"

"Wow, word sure gets around fast." She lowered her voice. "I'm not interested. There's just something about him."

"Okay, girlfriend. Give."

"It's just my, uh, intuition."

Unable to fully articulate her objections, Sallie's mind drifted back to a recent encounter with him at Luigi's Italian Deli. She and Gail had been waiting in line for service and he had come up behind them, leaning over her shoulder and whispering in her ear, "Damn, you're looking *fine* today." Sallie shuddered and brushed the hair near her ear as if his touch still lingered. She remembered the smug pushiness in his tone as he made a pass at her. "How about me and you go to dinner at

Chez Panisse? I know it's your fav." *How did he know my favorite?* His words after she rebuffed him still echoed in her mind. "Whatever babe, don't get your panties in a twist. Just wanted to show you a good time." *Well, if that's true, he can start by leaving me alone.*

Sallie sighed and gave a shrug. "He's just a little too, well, *forward*. Besides, Gail told me he's hooking up with Connie Sanders, not that he'd admit it."

Anne laughed. "Well, just keep in mind you've been single for over ten years now. At some point, you need to get back on the dance floor."

"You know my motto: 'Better to be single forever than married to the wrong man.' "

"You're just looking for Mr. Perfect." Anne glanced at her friend to see how far she could push it. "At some point, you have to let someone into your life."

"You're the only one I know who's making a marriage work. I'm holding out until you clone Joe."

"Like I said, no one's perfect," Anne laughed.

One of the Trojans hit a home run and Matt raced home from third. Sallie and Anne jumped up cheering. The Trojans clinched the victory, with Matt as the winning pitcher.

Sallie and Anne hugged each other. "They're on their way to the championship," Sallie boldly predicted.

"Let's not get ahead of ourselves, my friend," Anne chuckled. "There's a lot of baseball left this season."

Sallie nodded. "I know, you're right. It's just fun to dream."

As they left the ballpark with Matt between them, Sallie's cell phone buzzed. She looked at the screen. "It's Gail," she said, a puzzled look on her face. "Let me take this." Sallie listened, and her face went pale. She hung up the phone and looked at Anne.

Anne took in her dazed expression. "What is it? What happened?"

"It's Mike. He's had a heart attack."

"What? Where?"

"At the office. About a half hour ago. Gail heard a sound, a thud, and found him on the floor in his office. He's at Mercy."

"I'll take you." Anne grabbed her arm and turned toward the parking lot.

The funeral cortege wound its way through the narrow lane of the cemetery that served the community. There had been a huge turnout at the church, and the mourners descended upon the property, working their way to the lone oak tree at the back where the casket was being put in place.

Exiting the limousine, Sallie helped Mike's wife, Carol, and his teenaged daughter, Lisa, to the site they had picked out for Mike. As she led them to their reserved seats, she surveyed the people who had turned out to pay their respects. There was the office staff and several of their spouses, other real estate professionals who were part of the County Board where Mike had been President, as well as members of the Chamber of Commerce where Mike had also served. At the far end of the crowd, she spied Peter Samson, along with his entire office staff, a mourning-appropriate visage on his face. *What's he doing here?* she wondered, bitter at the reminder of words left unsaid.

As the speakers took turns sharing fond memories of Mike, Sallie stared vacantly at the casket listening to Lisa sob against her mother's shoulder. Carol put an arm around her daughter, her face contorted yet controlled. When the ceremony was over, Sallie stood up and put a bouquet of white roses on top of the casket. The mourners began to disperse and Sallie followed, leaving Carol and Lisa to a last quiet moment alone.

A short distance away, Sallie acknowledged mourners who knew Mike professionally and offered their regards to her and his family. A broker, whom she recognized as being part of the County Board, came up to her, shaking her hand and speaking quietly, "Sallie, just wanted to let you know we think you're the logical choice to take over Mike's position as County Board President. I'll call in a week or so." Sallie nodded silently and offered a tight-lipped smile.

The owner of the shopping mall property touched her gently on the shoulder to get her attention. "We need to discuss the arrangement we had with Mike. Perhaps you can take over. No rush. We know you have a lot to deal with right now."

"Yes, of course. We'd like to keep that project on target."

As she worked her way through the crowd, Sallie's responses were appropriately professional, yet devoid of the usual passion she offered to her clients. Once the crowd had thinned, Sallie looked back toward the casket where Carol stood with an arm around Lisa. Carol gave her a nod, and the three of them walked back toward their waiting limousine, talking briefly with friends who came to give their condolences, many of whom Carol invited back to the house for the wake.

As Carol and Lisa were settling in, Sallie gave one last glance around. Just as she was about to slip into the car, she noticed a slender man in a brown suit heading toward her. He didn't look familiar, though it was clear from his determined walk that he knew who she was. *Who could that be?* Sallie's brow furrowed as he closed the distance between them.

"Good morning, Ms. Whitaker." He shook her hand and offered her a business card. "I apologize for interrupting you at a time like this. I'm Norm Phillips from the State Department of Real Estate. I'd like to meet you tomorrow at your office to examine your books."

Shocked, Sallie frowned at him. *Does he know how inappropriate he is?*

As if to answer her unasked question, he offered, "I know this isn't a good time. Mike and I had an appointment scheduled for today. I drove down from Sacramento this morning. I didn't hear the news until I had already arrived…" His voice trailed off as his mouth settled into an apologetic smile.

Regaining her composure, she put out her hand to take his card. "Our books are always open to the Department. Mid-morning?"

He nodded. "So sorry for your loss." He turned and walked away, leaving Sallie with an unsettled feeling. *I wonder what he wants.*

The limo driver touched her arm, breaking her reverie. "Ready, ma'am?"

She nodded, turned abruptly, and slid into the car.

The finality of sudden loss hung heavy in the air as friends and family arrived at the Caldwell house, laden with food offerings for the grieving family. Carol's hospitality was as impeccable as ever, yet her eyes were vacant, devoid of their usual sparkle. Sallie watched with compassion as the older woman went through the motions of accepting condolences with grace. *She's stronger than she knows*, thought Sallie.

At last, Carol said goodbye to the final guest and collapsed on the couch. Sallie sat down beside her and put a gentle arm around her, smoothing her hair. Carol crumbled under the soft strokes, weeping into Sallie's shoulder with deep, heaving sobs. After a few moments, she straightened herself and wiped her face roughly.

"It's just such a shock." Carol sniffed. "He took care of everything."

"You know I'm here." Sallie's voice was soft as she handed Carol a tissue.

Carol turned to Sallie, blotting her eyes. She nodded and offered a weak smile. "I know."

They sat in silence for a while, both lost in their thoughts. Finally, Carol took a deep breath and let it out slowly. When she spoke, her voice was steady. "I know I shouldn't have let him, but he did everything. From the beginning, he told me not to worry."

"Let's just take things one at a time," Sallie said. "We're friends, you know. Friends help friends."

Carol gave her an appreciative nod. Sallie looked at the dirty dishes haphazardly scattered around the room. "I'm going to start by cleaning up." She stacked several plates, rising to take them to the kitchen.

"He was just so secretive. I sometimes felt as if I didn't know him at all." Carol touched Sallie's arm. "He had a stepfather, did you know?"

Sallie frowned and shook her head. She set the dishes back down on the coffee table and sat down.

Carol spoke in a quiet voice, as if to herself. "I don't know why I let him handle our finances. I guess it just seemed like the proper thing to do. I never really knew much of the details of his upbringing. He never wanted to talk about it. Only Caldwell wasn't his real name. He was born Mickey Ray Schmidt. He and his younger brother were illegitimate and then his mother married Caldwell. His stepfather might have been abusive... Mike would never discuss it."

Sallie patted Carol's hand. "Right now I'm more concerned about you. What can I do to help you?"

"Well, there's a letter. I was wondering how to respond."

"Let's look at it together."

Carol went to Mike's home office and returned with an envelope. She turned it over in her hands a few times before handing it to Sallie.

Sallie's brow furrowed as she noticed the official seal on the envelope. She pulled out the letter, her eyes widening as they flew down the page. When she again met Carol's worried gaze, she sat there dumbfounded for a moment before she found her voice.

"This is a notice of foreclosure."

Norm Phillips was ensconced in the conference room with the files he had requested. Sallie had spent a good part of the previous day with the staff with two goals in mind: keep the business going, and keep the rumors from flying as to why Phillips was reviewing all of their documents. Most of the concern was regarding whether the company and any of the agents would be found out of compliance with state regulations. The State Department of Real Estate was quick to suspend licenses and assess fines for the slightest misstep.

Sallie glanced into the conference room one last time to assuage her anxiety, and then headed back toward her office, trying to push down a nagging flutter in the pit of her stomach. *He'll never find anything wrong. If there's one thing I know for certain, Mike was scrupulous with his office files.* But how could she be so sure? She still didn't know what to make of the foreclosure notice. Carol had given her full authority to gain information and that was what she intended to do.

Sallie paused at Gail's desk and handed her the letter. "For your eyes only."

Gail's eyebrows flickered at the seriousness of Sallie's tone. "Of course. And I have something for you." She handed Sallie a phone message with Peter Samson's name and number, requesting her call. Sallie nodded curtly and retreated to her office, closing the door behind her. She picked up the phone and dialed his number.

Samson picked up quickly. "Sallie, thanks for returning my call so promptly. I'd like to meet with you." He paused. "Soon."

"What is this regarding?" Sallie was brusque.

"I'd rather talk in person. Today, if you're available."

"I'm not certain I have time if I don't know what you wish to discuss with me."

"Mike and I were negotiating the sale of his business."

She stiffened at his response. "Yes, of course. This afternoon. Where?"

"How about Le Bon Séjour at five?"

"I'll be there."

Sallie's eyes misted with fond memories as she approached the front windows of Le Bon Séjour. The restaurant had been a preferred haunt of the office, and many deals had been struck within its elegant French-Vietnamese setting. As she pulled open the double doors leading into a small entryway, the smell of pork rillettes filled her senses, reminding her of late Friday nights when Mike would take the office to celebrate one closing or another. The memory caused her to step back and release the handle. *I shouldn't be here. Not now.*

Kim, the owner, saw her and hurried to open the door, extending her hand in welcome and pulling Sallie into the dim interior entryway. "So sorry for your loss." She put both her hands around Sallie's. "I am at your service now, as always."

"Thank you. You've always been a true friend to us."

The restaurant was divided into small rooms, each decorated with restrained elegance, a combination of French sensibilities with Asian simplicity. Kim bent her head toward the interior of the restaurant. "He's in the small room in the back. Your favorite." She turned and led Sallie toward the private space, closing the door after her.

The room, decorated with antique Asian furniture, held a round table for ten and a small seating area with a love seat and a chair. A small buffet stood in the corner, set with a bottle of wine and two glasses. Peter hurried toward her with his hand outstretched.

"A pleasure to meet you."

"Your reputation precedes you."

"May I interest you in a glass?" Before she could answer, he moved to pour the wine. She noted the bottle was one of her favorites. Handing her the glass, he motioned toward the seating area. "Please, let's talk."

Sallie sat in the middle of the couch. Peter perched opposite her on the arm of the chair so that she had to lean back to look up at him. Wasting no time, Peter started, "First, I must express my condolences for your loss." Peter took a quick sip of wine and continued. "I know it's an awkward time, so let me get right to the point. Mike and I had a hand shake agreement for me to purchase his business."

"Oh."

"Yes. We had verbally agreed on the terms."

Sallie gritted her teeth, trying to maintain a calm presence. "Since when did you want to get into residential? I thought you were only commercial."

"We are. Only commercial. And will continue to be. Mike wanted to retire and we were just negotiating which of our lawyers would draw up the contract."

"And which one got the job?" Her voice was quiet and composed, yet her mind was reeling. "I'm not certain what you want from me."

"I have the terms of our agreement here." He pulled an envelope from his chest pocket. "I'm asking you to review it with his wife and let her know I would like to continue the sale."

Sallie rose and put her untouched wine glass on the coffee table. She took the envelope from Peter and walked toward the door.

"What are you going to do?"

"I'll do what you've asked. I'm going to talk with Carol."

He gave a satisfied nod. "The terms include a vice presidency for you."

Sallie gave him a small nod and tight-lipped smile, then took her leave. Without looking back, she strode down the hallway to the ladies room. After checking the stalls to make sure they were empty, she leaned against the sink and clenched her eyes shut, taking a deep shuddering breath. After a moment, she opened her eyes and stared at her reflection in the mirror. *What has Mike done? What did I really mean to him?*

She thought back to the night she had first met Mike at a Chamber of Commerce welcome event for newcomers to town. From that first handshake, their conversation had been warm and engaging, as if they had known each other for years. She had instantly been drawn to his ready smile, his direct gaze, and his ability to put people at ease, giving his full attention to whomever was in front of him.

Over time as their acquaintance blossomed into a deeper friendship, Sallie had come to admire his ability to mentor and care for people within his business family. When he offered her a position within his firm, she had jumped at the chance and never looked back. He had always told her that she was his best agent, and she had worked even more diligently to live up to that reputation.

A rush of grief at the loss of her friend threatened to overwhelm her. Yet, below it, there was something even harder to face—a burning sense of betrayal. *Why didn't he talk to me about buying his business?* Her head drooped onto the counter, resting on her arms as her tears flowed freely for the first time since Mike's death. *Now I'll never know.*

The next morning, Sallie arrived at the office and found Inspector Phillips seated in the conference room, writing on a legal pad. All of the bankers boxes were stacked against the wall. Walking past him, she headed to Mike's office at the end of the hall. *When will he be out of our hair? I need a moment to think.*

Gail stood up over her cubicle. Sallie nodded to her, and Gail followed her into Mike's office, closing the door behind her as Sallie drew the curtains shut. Gail looked at her with concern.

"Don't worry. Everything is going to be fine. I have it all under control." Sallie's tone conveyed more confidence than she felt, but it was what Gail needed to hear.

Gail breathed a sigh of relief and smiled. "That's what I told everyone."

After Gail had caught her up on the latest developments, Sallie sat in Mike's chair, turned on his computer, and scanned the property records. She had just opened the shopping center file to reacquaint herself with its particulars when Phillips knocked on the open door.

"May I come in?" he asked.

Sallie closed the files on the computer, leaving only the wallpaper. "Of course." Sallie jumped up, waving him to take a seat opposite her.

Phillips dropped a stack of files on the right side of the desk as he sat down. Taking a handkerchief from his pocket, he took off his glasses and cleaned them. "I must say, your files are in much better shape than I've usually encountered."

Sallie nodded. "Yes, that's been one of our priorities. Mike set up a system early in his business, and we've always expected staff to follow."

"Well, then, let's begin," he said. Taking the top file and putting it in front of him, he opened it and took out a piece of paper, turning it so she could see it. "The Department has a few suggestions you should be following. None of these are significant and should require only minor adjustments to your method." Sallie recognized that he followed the state regulations with precision.

Phillips took his time, meticulously going through the files, taking each folder from the top of the stack on his right and turning them over on a new stack on his left, until there was one folder left. Sallie's expression remained patient, even as her mind raced. *Enough already, let's wrap this up.*

"There's just one more item," he said, his jaw setting into a judgmental line as he opened the last file. He handed Sallie a paper, which she recognized as the form used to transfer funds between their escrow and house accounts. "This is your signature, is it not?"

"Yes." Her voice was clear. *There's nothing wrong with this transaction.*

"Do you recognize the account number to which the funds are being transferred?"

Her eyes swiveled to the corner of the form and widened for a second before a frown creased her forehead. She did not recognize the number. Her mouth opened, but no words emerged. *What has Mike done?*

"I also could not find any information on this account. So I called the bank. There are two accounts titled as trust accounts, one with his home address and the other with the business address." He stopped to scrutinize her face. "Somehow, I think you were unaware of this fact."

Her expression hardened. *It's none of your business what I know.*

Phillips continued, "It appears he would deposit some checks—not all, mind you, just a few of them—first in the home address account, then, within the three-day limit allotted by law, into the 'true' trust account. I've found three such instances."

He picked up one of their internal control forms that showed all incoming checks deposited in their escrow account. "This check is dated the 12th." He then showed her the bank statement for the official escrow account. "A check was deposited into the official account on the 15th."

She looked at the paperwork. His assessment was accurate. Mike had used escrow funds for his own benefit. She folded her hands together, pressing hard to control her shaking.

"As you can see, this is a very serious issue. I will say this, the fact that he deposited the funds within the three-day limit means he technically was within the law. However, this doesn't lessen the impact that he utilized funds for his personal benefit that were not his to use." He stopped and looked at her. "And, it appears as if you have colluded with him to help hide his theft. Your signature indicates your knowledge of the accuracy of this accounting."

Not hiding her distress, her voice held a plaintive note. "I need to go through all these files with our bookkeeper before I say anything."

"Did you not look at the dates before you signed off on this report?" Sallie stonewalled him.

Noting her reaction, his voice softened. "Your license will be suspended until the investigation is complete, which could take several months. Someone else will return to review these files and another seven years back."

Sallie found her voice. "No, there must be something else I can do. Please. His widow needs my help."

"You may not operate as a real estate broker until this investigation is complete." Phillips stood up. Sallie looked up at him, then stood to face him. "I will be making my report to the Department in the next couple of days. You will have an official letter within the week."

Sallie nodded, reeling from this unexpected blow. She stared blankly as he gathered up his files and took his leave. After he had gone, she collapsed into Mike's massive chair. A new mantra began to play in her mind. *I must prove my innocence.*

The moment Phillips was out the office, Gail came running in. "Is he finished?"

Sallie looked at her with glazed eyes.

"What's wrong? Sallie?" Gail strode to the desk, leaning over to get Sallie's attention. She snapped her fingers in Sallie's face. Sallie jerked awake and gave Gail a direct gaze.

"Mike must have had more stress with the shopping center than we thought." Sallie put her head in her hands.

Gail gasped. "Oh, I almost forgot! The shopping center. They want you to call." She handed Sallie a message slip.

"I hope they're not going to pull out."

"It didn't sound good."

"What else can happen?" Sallie's words hung in the air, as she swiveled to pick up the phone. *What next? What next?* Sallie punched Carol's number.

When Carol answered, Sallie said, "Can you to come to the office right now? There's something important to discuss." She listened to Carol ask for an explanation. "No, it's office business. It's now your business."

Sallie placed the phone back on its cradle and turned to Gail. "Would you make us some tea, please? I need to call Mike's attorney and I'd rather tell you and Carol everything together." Gail nodded and hastened out the door.

Sallie looked through Mike's contacts until she found the number for Fred Meyer's private line. She took a deep breath to compose herself, then dialed.

After a single ring, a gruff voice answered. "Who's this?"

"I apologize, Fred. It's Sallie Whitaker from Mike Caldwell's office. I realize this is your private line. Something important has happened. I need to talk to you. Today. In person."

"What are the particulars?" his voice was businesslike. Once Sallie had given him a quick summary of the current situation, they settled on an appointment for the end of the day.

Carol arrived moments later, and Gail ushered her into Mike's office, shutting the door behind them. Sallie filled them in about the conversation with Phillips, giving Carol details of the law regarding escrow accounts. Once they were finished, Sallie sighed. "We need to tell the staff. Right now."

"What are you going to say?"

"I'm not certain. I'd like to say the minimum until I get a chance to talk with Fred. As Mike's attorney, he knows this business the best.

Perhaps he knows how to solve this."

Once Gail had gathered the available staff in the conference room, Sallie stood at the end of the table and went through the audit just as Phillips had done.

"Now, one final item." She took a deep breath to find the words. "His investigation uncovered an irregularity. I need to review our files with Fred before saying too much. The upshot is that he's holding me responsible and…" she hesitated, not certain what to say, then straightened her back. Her voice grew stronger as she continued, "What he has told me is that I cannot… work… that is, he doesn't want me to participate in the business until… until another audit is done."

There, I've said it. She dropped in her chair as the staff all starting asking questions at the same time.

Gail stood up and put her hand on the top of Sallie's chair. "Look, let's let Sallie talk to Fred. Then we can reconvene when we know more answers." Gail shooed the staff out the room, then turned to Sallie and Carol. "What are you going to do?"

Sallie's eyes went between the two of them as she focused on the task before her. She opened the file folder on the table. "Gail, can you get me the back-up for these three transactions?" She checked the clock on the wall. "I'm meeting Fred in thirty minutes."

"Right away." Gail sprang into action, closing the door behind her.

"What does it all mean?" Carol asked. "You have to start real simple with me. Remember, I don't know your business."

Sallie turned, wanting to tell Carol not to worry, that everything would be okay. As she opened her mouth, Sallie realized that here was her new boss, the owner of the business. Here also was a good friend, one who was in mourning. Not wanting to arouse her fears prematurely, she said, "Look, I'm not totally certain what Mike did, and I'd rather wait to tell you until I know more. What I do know is he possibly put money into an account that might have been a mistake, and I countersigned his deposit as required by law."

Carol frowned. "A mistake. Didn't you know it wasn't right?"

"It looked right to me."

"Then what happened?"

"Let's talk after my meeting with Fred."

Carol nodded. "You will tell me the truth, won't you?"

"Of course."

Sallie had never before had a reason to visit Fred's office. Mike had always handled the company's legal affairs, and she hadn't felt a need to interfere. As she entered the office lobby, her eyes widened with surprise at the apparent chaos of the space. Fred's legal work was so fastidious that she had expected his working environment to be the same. Instead, stacks of files covered every surface, some almost neatly organized, others appearing as if they had been thrown together in a hurry.

The secretary's desk was empty and the room was quiet, with open doors leading to an office on the right and a conference room on the left. As she opened her mouth to call out a greeting, she heard a voice in the office. "Sallie, is that you?"

"Yes," she answered, a little too loud.

"Give me a minute. There's coffee in the conference room. Make yourself comfortable."

Sallie entered the light-filled room and walked toward the window, taking in the setting sun and manicured landscape below. Wildflowers covered the low foothills in the distance. *On another day, I would like the view.*

Fred bustled in with several thick files under his arm. The portly man spoke quickly as he made his entrance, conscious that his time was counted by the minute. "Mike and I were together a long time. Over two decades by my count."

Sallie turned and extended her hand. "He always spoke highly of you, said you were the best. I hope you will continue our relationship."

"Of course." He nodded toward the table. "No coffee?"

She shook her head. "Unfortunately, this is not what I would have hoped for our first conversation."

They both sat and Sallie pulled out her file, going through the paperwork. After her explanation, Fred sat back in his chair, giving her an appraising look. "Did you not know what you were signing?"

"Look here." She pointed toward the first entry. "The form says 'Caldwell Escrow Account,' then there's the account number after it. When I signed it, there was no account number. I didn't know he had two accounts."

"I see." He studied the paper, then looked at the second one. It also had the same title, yet this one was the business account. "Didn't you sign this one, too?"

"That's the issue to me. I've been thinking about that signature. I even went and looked at my calendar to see what I was doing that day." She hesitated, as if replaying those scenes would give her clarity. "It seems that on all three, and this is the best I can recollect," she took a deep breath, "I must have been in a hurry and signed without the account number nor the amount listed. I remember he said something to the effect of not to worry, he'd fill in the details later."

Fred put his hands on his ample chest, leaning back in the chair. "I see. Is there anything else?"

"Well, the day he died, the same thing happened. This is how I realized what might have happened on the other two."

"What happened to the funds on the day he died?"

"He had gone to the bank that afternoon. Everything was in order."

"Thank goodness."

She nodded. "Yes, thank goodness for that."

"However," he said, "It's still a problem on all three. And you do look as if you are guilty."

She gulped. "I know. Believe me, Mr. Meyer," she got very formal, "I didn't know. I didn't know about the second account, and I didn't know about him putting the funds into a personal account."

"I believe you; however, it might not matter to the State Board. You know the law on this matter, about having an escrow account, how to do the accounting, the three day law, and all that."

"Yes, of course."

"Of course you do. I just had to ask."

She nodded. "What now?"

"Get me copies of all the files. Who, what, when, where, how, you know the drill. Then, let's talk again."

Pulling into her driveway, Sallie dragged herself from her car and shuffled to the front door, not even noticing her newly budded roses beginning to show their colors. Robot-like, she entered her house, dropping her attaché case on the floor. She turned to close the door, but instead stepped back out onto her porch.

Her vision narrowed to a small dot on the horizon extending beyond the limits of her sight, temporarily blinding her to the late afternoon light outlining the garden in shadows. The entire timeline of her life lay in a corridor before her, and the past decisions leading to this moment flashed through her mind. She could not breathe, nor think, nor feel her body.

A rage of white heat arose in her, moving swiftly through the ink-dark shadows, like a ball of fire traveling at the speed of light and wiping away all that mattered most to her. Beginning to sway, she put out a hand for one of the columns, willing her previous existence to return. The carefully constructed layers of her life peeled away, much as the roses in her garden would open and age, each petal slowly dropping into the dirt until all that was left on the tall stems was the center sepal.

"Control yourself. Control yourself," Sallie muttered to herself. "Control yourself." She closed her eyes and rocked back and forth, willing herself to find her center, willing herself back into her body. She put a hand to her face, rubbing from her neck down the side of her body, finding the limits of her physicality, and opened her eyes.

She rubbed her trembling arms, as if that gesture could erase the feelings coursing through her body. Willing herself to move, she counted the floorboards of the wooden decking beneath her feet. The porch spanned the width of the front of her house and she moved with jerky movements from one end to the other, weaving through the colorful furniture covering its broad expanse.

Words filled her head, single words she found unable to put into sentences. *Abandoned. Again. Betrayed. Again. Trust. Again. Again. Again. What is this word 'again'? What does it mean? Why does it sound so foreign? As if it were a foreign language? I've always pulled myself up. All by myself. Find what I want. Then, I begin to trust I have created something. Then, it's gone in a second. It's what I get for trusting others.* Defeated, Sallie crumbled onto the chaise and remained there until long after the sun had set.

Talk of her misfortune spread like a windstorm. As Sallie's carefully structured persona dismantled, she retreated from the outside world. Even cleaning her already fastidious home didn't quell the anger bottled inside. She clung to her new mantra, repeated in endless succession: *I must prove my innocence.*

While time marched on, cruel in its indifference, Sallie unraveled. She wandered with an unfocused gaze through her now disheveled house. Most days she spent watching old movies on television, not even bothering to dress for the day. Telephone calls were left unanswered. She ignored her brother's repeated messages.

When the weekly newspaper arrived on her doorstep with the headline "Caldwell Postmortem: Local Realtor License Suspended," Sallie pitched the newspaper toward the coffee table, ignoring the pages as they slid off the edge and fluttered to the floor. *What are they doing to Mike's legacy? All the good he did. All that he was to others. It's just not fair. Why Mike? Why me?*

She ignored the paper for several hours, then gathered it and sat down, reading and re-reading the article, attempting to make sense of the circumstances of her life. *Just because he took three days to put some funds in the escrow account. It's not near what others have done. He didn't keep the money. He didn't steal. I didn't steal. Why?*

Sallie felt as if she were a child again, out of control. This was new territory for her and emotions long forgotten from her childhood rose up to disturb her awareness. *I've worked so long to create the life I wanted after Mom died. I want to be my own person, not at the whim of men like my father who want to bend me to their will. Not at the whim of any man who wants to make me feel guilty.*

She pushed these unwanted feelings and memories away. Yet, never far from surfacing, they bubbled up and over the top of her consciousness, like yeast-filled dough left too long on a warm oven surface. Her memories of childhood were dim. When asked, she would say, "We moved a lot; my mom died when I was young; I had a younger brother I adored; I loved school; reading was my favorite pastime; and then I went to college."

Slowly, though, raw, unpolished impressions emerged. Colorless, like faded pressed flowers from a long ago age; fragile, washed-out, pale reproductions of their former selves. It had to be that she would find these memories.

When she thought about it, her heart would throb, like a fragile bone that would crack if touched, reminding her of how her arm hurt when she broke it as a child. She recalled hearing the snap as she fell from the parallel bars to the schoolyard asphalt. Stunned, she'd felt the radiation of pain and knew she was injured. Her subsequent tears were more from the fear of being punished for wrongdoing than a manifestation of the throbbing she felt.

Her heart echoed this pain as she allowed the old memories to surface. She had pushed them down, those memories. Down until she thought they, and her childhood, no longer existed. When she felt that old familiar tug of pain, they arose. Like waves upon the beach, her recollections began their relentless pounding on the sands of her consciousness.

For the first time since she was young, Sallie cried for help. *What did I do wrong? What do I need to do now? What do I need to do? Someone help me. Please. Help.*

CHAPTER TWO

Soulara: An Uncommon Conversation

Hearing Sallie's cry, Soulara resonated a song of joy. Though she had always whispered in Sallie's ear the spiritual clues for her success in life, it had been many years since Soulara's voice had been acknowledged. Sallie's call for help was her call to action.

In the beginning, once Lo-ahn had made her choice of a physical body, she and Soulara were joined in a swirl of light and sound. An arena of possibilities, mutual perceptions of commitment, and playful dreams of realization—all this and more—surrounded them as they prepared for Lo-ahn's journey into life. Images, colorful and translucent, were carried on beams of celestial light that imprinted Lo-ahn and Soulara's mission and infused them with their place in the Divine Plan for continued expansion of the universe.

A choir of angelic beings had sung Lo-ahn's soul into consciousness as Sallie, and each note of its song reflected a possible outcome in her coming life. Soulara's connection with her was etched in the joint mission each chose to complete. An interconnected partnership, celebrated through resonance and joy, their journey together symbolized the notion "as above, so below." The phrase affirmed that all above in the realm of the Spirit world would be reflected below in Sallie's domain of Earth and vice versa. Sallie experienced the reality of Earth while Soulara's knowledge encompassed the ethereal space of light. In this partnership, a new awakening of self could emerge for both of them.

As Sallie fell into a deep sleep, Soulara gently lifted her for the journey to the Temple of Learning to discuss the purpose of this challenge. They slipped through the dimension separating their domains, Soulara gently caressing Sallie in reminder of her perfection, her lovability, and her ability to be.

In her dreamtime, Sallie journeyed for resolution, as the answers to her questions would come forth when her mind was quiet and her interest was piqued. As they alighted at the entrance to the temple, Sallie's eyes opened and her consciousness began to scan the horizon while her memory gradually returned. From atop the highest hill on a promontory point, she breathed in the smell of the ocean, rocks, and dense thicket of foliage that formed the coastline, a favorite setting of her imagination.

A deep sigh emerged from Sallie's lips as she began to recognize her surroundings. She circled the temple, touching each of the twelve marble columns as she went. Soulara, standing near, allowed her to settle into her environment. As Sallie continued along her path, ancient archetypes took over and she began a ritual from a long past age hiding within her unconscious self. She stopped at the doorways that faced each of the four directions to acknowledge the elements that gave vitality to her soul.

Facing east, she began the ceremony as the barriers to her

remembering fell away. Sensing the touch of the air upon her skin, she lightly brushed over her body and lifted her arms high into the sky, acknowledging its cleansing effect as a feeling of compassion and unconditional love enveloped her.

Moving to the south, Sallie closed her eyes and stretched her face to the sun, feeling its heat penetrate to the marrow of her bones. She put her hands together as if in prayer, rubbed her palms back and forth until they felt hot, and then gently touched her face. Opening her eyes, she observed the rays of light as they descended upon her, radiating outward and covering her with warmth and clarity. She brushed her body with her hands, flicking away all negative energy, allowing for release of the anger and resentment that had recently made her feel so heavy.

In the west, the taste of the salt in the air from the water below flowed gently over her lips and touched her face. Running her tongue over her lips as if she were absorbing the nourishment of the water, she allowed the fluidity of the moment to infuse her and began to release her attachment to her circumstances.

She turned toward the north and smelled the fecund earth, feeling its slow steady rhythm, moving her hands in a circular motion as if pulling the earth energy into her nose and releasing all that was unnecessary to her soul's purpose. She stamped purposefully on the land beneath her feet, grounding and stabilizing her body. The movement infused her with courage and expelled her fears.

Approaching the center of the temple, she looked up at the covered rotunda with its tiny mosaics interwoven into a mandala of brightly colored precious stones, each reflecting the four directions. She nodded her acknowledgement of their purpose in her life.

Settling on the bench that ran around the inner edge of the structure, Sallie sighed deeply as she began to experience the peace of her true existence. Soulara bowed to acknowledge Sallie's significance and the

45

pleasure she had in knowing her. Their conversation, a dialogue without words, ensued as they merged, mind to mind, heart to heart, to share their perceptions and knowledge of the purpose of her recent trials.

A small smile played on Sallie's face as it began to relax. "It seems I have forgotten you and this wondrous place of healing."

"I was there at the beginning when your soul made the decision to return to a new life. I assisted you in determining your purpose and your life mission, as well as the challenges you would undertake. I have been with you always, waiting for your call, for I am unable to intercede on your behalf unless you ask."

Sallie was attentive, focusing to draw out the memories. "It's all so familiar, as if there's never been any separation between us."

"I carry the memory of all we have put into action. Even as your mind forgets when you come into birth, I softly whisper to you, providing ongoing love, support, and guidance. When you find your life in flux, it is only because you have forgotten who you really are. Calling to me is the beginning of remembrance, a sign you are on your true path."

Rising from her bench, Sallie looked to the northeast with its rugged peaks running jagged along the rocky shore, now turning brown with the beginning heat of summer. Chaparral, nestled into crevices, gave a range of colors from shiny green to rusty orange, shading into a dull brownish-tan.

She turned to face her guardian angel. "I have been betrayed again. By a man whom I respected. I thought he…" her voice choked as feelings overwhelmed her. She took a minute to let them settle, then added quietly, "I guess… I'm just sad, hurt, and angry."

Soulara caressed Sallie with her voice. "Do you think this is an accident?"

Sallie looked away and replied softly, "No." She turned back to face Soulara and smiled. "Otherwise I would be saying I had little power in my life."

Soulara nodded at Sallie's insight. "Have you considered that your chaos is a call to new consciousness that summons you to another future?"

"I was happy with my life. I couldn't have asked for more."

Soulara was quiet, allowing her charge to reflect on what she had said.

Sallie's voice was forlorn. "I guess that life is gone, isn't it?" She looked away, again willing her emotions to subside. "It's just I have this rage in me. I have to do something, anything, to get even." She spoke through clenched teeth. "I don't even know what I could do." She sighed, defeated. "And then I collapse and hate myself for my vindictiveness."

"Strong feelings like anger can be helpful if they are utilized to move you forward to personal action." Soulara paused, then continued, "What do you believe you can learn from this lesson?"

Stopping and facing to the west, Sallie absorbed the soothing scene of dazzling turquoise water rushing into nooks and crannies of rocky points, constant in the sound of life. Taking a deep breath, she answered hesitantly, "I don't know. I have exhausted myself in analysis."

Soulara reached through to touch Sallie with her voice. "It is in your remembering that you will gain the power to make the required change. Look into your heart and hear its message. Let it heal you of this difficulty."

Sitting down awkwardly and putting her head in her hands, Sallie responded, "I am uncertain. I think there is something wrong with me." She looked up at Soulara. "I had the perfect life. I thought it would last forever. What happened?"

"It was a perfect job for what you needed at that time. You also have a beating heart. As long as you do, there will be new challenges and new traits to master." Her compassion was clear, though the message was firm. "Time to move on."

"I just think I am useless right now."

"Do you remember anything from our soul discussions before you joined with the body of Sallie?"

Sallie focused, struggling to recall their conversations. Finally she answered, "No, I guess I don't."

"Before you were born, we worked together to determine your personal mission—your strengths, your challenges, and all the lessons that would come your way."

"It all sounds so ominous, as if my life has a purpose."

Soulara nodded. "Exactly. You are always on your purpose. Everything is always on purpose."

"Everything is always on purpose? Sometimes there are accidents. Aren't there?"

"To be on your purpose means that everything happening to you, even accidents, are on purpose. Your purpose."

"Why would I want this betrayal from Mike?"

"All the experiences you encounter lead you toward your greater destiny."

"I thought if I did a good job, everything would work out."

"There's more to this than you now realize. There's also the aim of fulfilling contracts with others, learning from past mistakes, and growing in the process. You chose the body of Sallie, your family, and the outer circumstances of your life so that you would also meet your intentions in this life."

Sallie gave a brittle laugh. "I chose this family?" She turned away, not wanting this to be true. "I don't think I belong with them. I came from another planet, or perhaps they did."

"Note that you keep saying how you think, rather than how you feel."

"Yes, I think about things a lot."

"So you do. However, it is through experiencing your feelings that you will find the answer to your current dilemma."

"I like to be analytical and not rely on feelings. They lead to disaster," said Sallie, defending her position. "Besides, I want to be reasonable. And there's perfection in being logical."

"There are many definitions of 'perfect' for you to explore, and many ways to reach your goals. Having a sense of belonging depends upon your ability to live with yourself as you are, while allowing others to be themselves."

Sallie sat down on the bench that circled the enclosure, looking over the railing at the peaceful sight before her.

"At various stages of your life, you have ignored some of the signals we had agreed would activate your soul memories. You have deeply ingrained patterns that at the outset you professed a desire to break."

Sallie whipped around. "I've missed some opportunities? I spent my early life planning and working hard to be the perfect daughter. I thought that was what I was supposed to be doing."

"Your mission is to break old patterns from your past in which you believed your worth was less than others in your family."

"I'm not really interested in doing anything with my family. They rejected me."

"Are you so sure?"

"Of course I'm sure."

"You must learn to feel, to listen to your emotions, for they will be the key to your healing. You use your mind to justify your actions when your emotions are uncomfortable."

"What's wrong with that?"

"Your mind's job is to strategize the course of action called for by your heart. Your challenge is to first let your heart decide the destination and the path."

"That's how I've gotten hurt before."

"Yet, it is in the balance between the mind and the emotions where you serve your highest desires."

Sallie collapsed on the bench, curling into a ball. "It hurts to feel. I am uncomfortable using my emotions to make my decisions for me."

Soulara moved protectively toward Sallie, soothing her charge with her gentle presence.

"It has just not worked out in the past." Sallie's voice was nearly a whisper.

"I know. That is why I am here. The simplest way for you to find what is in your heart is to maintain a focus on who you actually are— pure, timeless, Oneness. You are not your life, nor your circumstances. You are your soul essence. Maintain an awareness of your soul at the center of all you know and perceive."

Sallie sat up and looked intently at Soulara. "What exactly does that mean?"

"To be aware means to observe the self as separate from your life and your actions. You must be a witness to that self. Awareness is standing outside your body and observing what you do and say just like a stranger would." Soulara paused to let the words settle. "If, in that separate space, what you do and say arises from the core of who you are, your words and actions will reflect your essence."

"You mean to see myself just like others do?"

"Similar, yet not the same. Being mindful is to see yourself as you truly are—a soul essence. Once you begin to develop this new consciousness, you can also begin to observe what is around you and respond from your personal truth."

"Sort of like a soul reality check."

"When you can take this awareness into the flow of your life, you will be more alert to the messages I send you through people, books, and other insights. Listen to your intuition, as it is often a truth from within, another message from your guides. You and I are a partnership. Just as you desire to fulfill your mission, I also desire to fulfill mine of assisting you and being the emissary between you and Spirit."

Her voice beginning to exude confidence, Sallie nodded. "I would like to do that." She smiled and breathed a deep sigh, relaxing into the message. "I appreciate your help."

"Remember, every disappointment has a gift. Watch for synchronicities to find the reason for this trauma. I will wrap my love around you as you explore this new territory."

"I will look for you," Sallie replied, a touch of hope in her voice.

"Before we last parted, we discussed using sounds as a trigger that I was near to point something out to you. A couple of times recently your conscious mind was close to noticing my call."

"That was you at the bookstore!" Sallie jumped up, excited to find a connection to her guide. "And on my front porch when I came back from my walk." She spun around with joy. "I wondered why the bells chimed when the air was so still."

"Pay attention to the words of others. Keep a journal of your life and dreams. Look for books and words that might provide a message with the love, support, and guidance that I send to you. That is all for now."

Sensing Soulara's imminent departure, Sallie asked, "Will I recall our conversation?"

"The answer to that question is both yes and no. You will have a sense of wonder and contentment, a new hopefulness as you put into practice that which you have learned here. In the future, you will have more messages from your other guides. As you begin to evoke them, you will have a sense of déjà vu when you hear or see something we have discussed.

"Over time, as you recollect more, you will become alert to your surroundings and will begin to hear our message of love and support more easily in your waking hours, not just in your dreams. For now, just feel all your emotions."

With that, Soulara gave her a soft touch upon her shoulders and Sallie was back in her bedroom, peacefully sheltered in her sleep.

PART II
Soul Loss

Of all the souls that stand create
I have elected one.
When sense from spirit flies away,
and subterfuge is done;
When that which is and that which was
Apart, intrinsic, stand,
And this brief tragedy of flesh
is shifted like a sand;
When figures show their royal front
and mists are carved away, --
Behold the atom I preferred
to all the lists of clay!

Emily Dickinson

CHAPTER THREE

Memories of Childhood

Awakening from a deep sleep, her body still heavy from its nightly wanderings, Sallie's consciousness began its appraisal of her mourning. As she arose from the depths of her dream world, she sensed a physical change and found herself listening to the sounds of her neighborhood for the first time in a long while.

Through the open window, the dawn flooded her bedroom with an aura of golden light. She heard the song of birds, the automatic sprinkler system as it started its persistent buzz, and the noxious energy of a passing garbage truck.

Sensing that she had been far away, Sallie closed her eyes and strained to remember her dream. Her mind blank, she relaxed. Gradually a buoyant sensation streamed through her, providing a release from the recent drama in her life. She breathed deeply with a newfound freedom, an awareness of a return to life, although perhaps not the one she had once been leading.

As she opened her eyes, she acknowledged the hurt, anger, and sadness of the last chapter of her life. Yet, for the first time, a perception of a greater plan surged from her heart, along with a sense that there might be a gift hidden in her disappointment. *Perhaps there is a new beginning in store for me after all.* The thought lifted her spirits.

Truly awake to her surroundings for the first time in several weeks, Sallie attacked the disorder around her with a new fervor. A rush of pleasure accelerated through her body as each room sparkled from her attention.

As she finished her work, the doorbell chimed. Sallie opened the door to find Jean, her neighbor, holding a platter covered with a tea towel.

"You've been a hermit for a while," the older woman clucked with a motherly smile. "I thought I'd drop off one of my favorites to lighten your day."

"Oh, Jean, what a dear you are. I'm so lucky to know you. Come on in."

Sallie peeked beneath the towel. "Your famous cinnamon rolls." She sniffed. "And just warm from the oven, too." She gave Jean a smile. "Let's have a tea party."

Jean had been Sallie's first client. When Jean was widowed, Sallie had helped her sell her big house of thirty-four years and move into a smaller one close to downtown. When Sallie became Jean's neighbor two years later, it became an unspoken agreement that they looked out for each other.

As they walked into the kitchen, Sallie slipped her arm companionably into Jean's. "How's Tom and his family?"

"My granddaughter is thinking of applying to college out here. I would be so thrilled to have her close."

Sallie motioned Jean to the table. "Sit, sit," said Sallie, going toward the cupboard. "Tea or Coffee?"

"Tea."

With practiced ease, Sallie prepared tea and slipped into a seat opposite her neighbor.

"What college?"

"I'm not certain."

"You know I could help her get into my college. Then she would definitely be nearby."

"That's kind of you. However, it's early. She's only a junior. We'll worry about it next year."

Sallie separated the rolls, putting one on a plate and handing it to Jean. "A good friend and a cinnamon roll. The perfect antidote for everything wrong with the world." Sallie sighed as she felt a small glimmer of her old self rising from the ashes.

Jean patted Sallie's hand with motherly affection. "Oh, honey, you don't have to put up a façade with me. I know what it means to be disappointed." Sallie took a sharp breath, willing away her feelings as Jean continued, "I just want you to know you're still my favorite person in town."

With a crooked grin, Sallie gained control of herself. "You're amazing."

"Anyway, there's always something new going on around here. This week, the big news is the engagement of Jeff Owens and Connie Sanders. Wasn't he the one who was always after you to go out with him?"

Sallie shrugged. "Something like that. Anyway, not to change the subject, but I've been thinking. Perhaps I need a change of direction. You know, keep moving forward."

Jean gave her a close look. "I hope there are no major changes coming. I like having you for a neighbor."

"No answers yet."

"Well, just remember, you'll still meet yourself, whether you're coming or going." Jean got up and brushed off her skirt. "I must be going. Lots of errands today."

"Of course." Sallie laughed. "You are the busiest retired person I know!"

Surveying her garden, Sallie's practiced eye took in the multitude of weeds needing attention. As she worked to clear the path, Sallie spied some volunteer plants, always sprouting up in unexpected places. Looking closely, she discovered a tiny alyssum seedling and a viola just beginning to emerge from the soil between the flagstones on the walkway.

In the past, Sallie would have yanked them out to maintain the pristine look of her path. Today, she stopped to observe their minute completeness, squatting down to focus on them with a changed perspective. *They are quite lovely.* Giving them a nod of approval, she sank placidly to the ground. Time passed and the peacefulness of the garden suffused her.

Rising at last, Sallie surveyed what she had accomplished. *More questions than answers.* Somehow, though, a new sense of hope rejuvenated her as she headed back inside.

There were nineteen messages on her answering machine. She knew that most were from Anne, who had called frequently to let her know she was missed. She supposed that one was from her brother. Reaching toward the machine to listen to the messages, she cringed. *Later. Maybe later.*

Rather than think about her family, she turned to her closet and began to de-clutter the back area where she put items that she was considering for donation. If she didn't think about an item for a year after it went into the closet, she knew it was time to let someone else use it.

Sallie was ruthless as she determined the fate of her old clothes and shoes, sorting them into piles until she pulled something long-forgotten from the back of the top shelf. Her heart jumped as she looked at the colorful box. Taking it down, she held it in her hands for a beat, unwilling to open it. *Some things are just better left in the past.*

She took a deep breath and threw the entire box into the waste can with a flourish. *That old childish stuff. I don't need any of it.* She turned and took the can and put it next to the front door, ready for the garbage bin, then walked determinedly toward the kitchen to prepare a late lunch.

Surveying her refrigerator contents with a distracted air, she grabbed a bottle of wine and the carton of eggs. Cracking two for an omelet, Sallie opened the wine and poured herself a glass. *Time to move on. My family is here. Those old things, time to throw them away.* She took a gulp of wine, turned the burner on, and slapped a pat of butter in a skillet. Her eyes glazed as she remembered the responsibilities she'd had after her mother died that were beyond her youth. Looking down, she discovered the butter had burnt. In a quick motion, she turned off the burner and threw the pan in the sink. *Just one go-through, then they're history. Get it out of my system forever.*

Grabbing her wine, Sallie returned to the living room and pulled the box from the trash. Sitting down on the floor, she brushed her hand over the collaged covering that she had created from magazine clippings through her school years. *A lifetime ago.* Opening the Pandora's box of photographs and memorabilia, Sallie's eyes blurred as memories began to assail her. *Just a quick sort and maybe I won't throw them out. I can just file them away again in the back of the closet.*

She picked up a picture of her with her freshman roommates. After graduation from high school, she had wanted to get as far away as she could from her Southern California childhood home while staying within the state, so she had enrolled at a small private college in Marin County. She had loved the freedom to make her own choices, the camaraderie of like-minded women, and the chance to earn a degree. For the first time, she felt in charge of her own destiny. She vowed to never let another have control of her life.

The next photo in the stack showed her brother, Mark, standing straight in a new police uniform upon his graduation from the Police Academy. A tug of love nestled in her heart. She had always been proud of him; so straight and tall, as if he would singlehandedly maintain the peace in town. He stayed home after she left. *How long has it been since we last spoke? And now he wants to talk.*

All of Sallie's old fears about her family arose as an ache in her body and she shrank from the idea of contact. Always sensing she did not fit in with them, she had taken on the mantle of outsider, the black sheep of the family. She looked down at the rest of the contents of the box. *Just a few more minutes on this project and then on with other things.*

A blurry black and white picture caught her attention. *Just like my memories of childhood.* Looking closely at the five-year-old child and tiny woman dressed all in black, a half-smile crossed her face as she recognized her father's mother. She was standing on the wide porch in front of a house made of rocks, a placid look on her face. There were several other children in the picture. Sallie couldn't remember who they were, yet she remembered playing in the basement of that house.

Another picture taken that same year showed her bundled up in a thick down jacket, pulling a sled through fluffy white snowdrifts. She remembered her screams of joy as she sledded down those snowy hills in the middle of winter. *My first taste of snow, the cold wind on my nose, that was a great day.*

In the next, her seven-year-old self was standing next to her new Christmas present, a two-wheeler bike. She remembered her pride in riding with her father's hand behind her, guiding her and helping her take off on her first solo ride. She had longed to have his hands touch her again with such affection.

That spring, in her first experiment with gardening, Sallie had planted snapdragon seeds in an old coffee can. She had so delighted in those talking flowers. She found a photograph of her standing on a small front porch proudly showing the can with her small sprouts just beginning to emerge. The seedlings were so tiny, only an inch high, yet so green and complete. She remembered her eager anticipation of the beautiful flowers they would become.

It was a triumph Sallie would never see. A short time later, her father had announced another move, the bi-yearly transfer to a new base for his job in the Army. On moving day, Sallie appeared with the coffee can in her tiny hands, her only possession. Her father had ordered her to "leave that dirt behind." Remembering his exact words as she held the picture to her heart, she re-experienced the loss of slowly putting them down on the front porch and turning away, not wanting to look at them again. She put the photograph aside and picked up the next.

There she was as a smiling little girl, sitting on the grass with her brother cuddled in front of her. *I must have been about five and he's almost two,* she thought, the love rising unbidden in her chest. Her lip quivered as she wondered what she had been thinking when the picture was taken.

A stack of report cards from her school years caught her eye, each year with the name of a different school. There had been countless schools where she had started in the middle of the year, finding herself an outsider with the other girls already paired up. She became proficient at jacks, hop scotch, and jumping rope so she would be included in their play. *Oh, how I could double-dutch.* Her skill in sports got her chosen early in any games of Red Rover.

Rummaging through the stack of report cards, she looked for her fourth grade marks. Mr. Fitzgerald, her first male teacher, had opened her mind to the intricacies of math and it had quickly become her favorite subject. She could beat any boy on any day, a fact that made her smile. She'd known she was a whiz just by the way Mr. Fitzgerald had praised her.

Later, in junior high, Mr. Booker explained algebra with the example, "How do you know Paris exists if you've never been there? That's how algebra is. Some things are givens in life." Sallie remembered that knowingness of which he spoke, truth that came from within. When she knew something, she knew that she knew it.

As she sorted through the pictures, Sallie's eyes began to mist. A frozen part of her did not want to feel her childhood. Now, she put her hand over her heart as if to keep her childhood safely locked inside. She took a gulp of wine and closed her eyes, feeling forces beyond her control calling out to be heard. *If I resist, I shall die some more*, she thought.

Sallie jumped up from the floor and turned on her heel, willing herself to leave the mess behind. She went into the kitchen to pour herself another glass of wine. Glancing at the incessant blinking of the answering machine, Sallie took a deep breath and pressed play. She listened to a couple of words from each message and deleted them until she came to another one from her brother. She let it play through, listening with detachment as Mark firmly repeated his request for a call. Shaking her head, she hit the delete button. *I don't need their judgment of me and I don't want to have to explain my current situation to them.*

Most of the rest were from Anne, and Sallie felt a pang of guilt at ignoring her best friend. She pledged to get cleaned up and walk to Anne's bookstore to pay her friend a surprise visit. The idea of starting a journal had also begun to simmer at the back of her mind. *Perhaps if I go back through my childhood, I can find a thread that explains why I feel so betrayed by the men in my life.*

A quick shower and a comb through her hair and Sallie was ready to go. As she pulled open her front door, a feeling of panic assailed her and she closed it quickly, leaning back against its sturdy surface, as if it could shield her from the harsh realities of the outside world. What ifs chased each other through her mind and she took a deep breath to calm her racing thoughts. *I don't need to be ashamed of anything I've done. Eventually, my innocence will be clear for all to see.* With that thought, she opened the door and resolutely walked to town.

In front of the bookstore, she peered in the window to see Anne finalizing a sale with a customer she did not recognize. Sallie walked in with a nonchalant wave at Anne and quickly moved to one of the stacks. When the customer left, Anne was quick to catch up to her and give her a hug.

"Am I ever glad to see you!"

Sallie pulled back and looked at the love in Anne's eyes. "I didn't mean to push you away."

"You didn't. I just missed you."

Sallie's carefully maintained composure cracked in the face of her friend's caring words. She turned away as her eyes began to tear.

Anne put a gentle arm around her and pulled her deeper into the stacks, chatting lightly to catch her up on the news of the town. She shied away from any mention of Mike or the loss of her job. Sallie would talk when she was ready.

"Matt's team won the championship," Anne announced, choosing an upbeat topic.

"Really? That's great. He must be really pleased."

"He got Most Valuable Player for the year," Anne said, pride of parenthood in her voice. "And, believe it or not, he has a girlfriend."

"What, at his age?"

"Yeah. They're just friends, he says. After all, this is junior high. Anyway, change of subject, the G-men are hosting the Dodgers and we have tickets for Sunday. There's an extra one for you if you'd like to come along. Matt and Joe would love to see you."

Sallie and Anne shared a passion for the San Francisco Giants. Anne's family had season tickets, often inviting Sallie to make a fourth.

"Oh, I don't know, Anne. I'm not certain I'd be very good company."

"Just let us know by Sunday morning. We'll save the ticket, just in case. We usually leave around ten. Get there a little early. Get the feel of the ballpark. You know, smell the peanuts, taste the popcorn, hear the buzz of the crowd."

"Thanks," Sallie paused. "Have I told you lately what a great friend you are?"

"You have," said Anne, giving her a quick hug.

Glancing toward the shelves, Sallie changed the subject. "I think I'm looking for a book."

"Anything special in mind?"

"No, I'm just going to let it jump out at me."

"Well," Anne laughed, "there are definitely books here. Take your time and look around. I'm getting an order ready. Let me know if you need any help."

"Thanks."

Sallie wandered aimlessly among the shelves, as if actually waiting for a book to hit her on the head. Her thoughts rambled as she reminisced about the libraries of her childhood and how she had always loved to read, often choosing books that were thick just because she read so fast and wanted the pleasure to last a little longer.

Running her finger along a row of books, she edged down the aisle.

There are so many interesting books in the world right now. Which one do I want to read today? Her finger paused on a spine labeled *The Inner Child.* The book seemed to leap into her hands.

She read the back cover and scanned the table of contents, then opened to a page at random and began to read a section called "Breaking the Perfect Daughter Syndrome." *How appropriate. And a little eerie. Guess this is what I need right now.*

Returning to the front counter, Sallie showed her choice to Anne. "Have you read this?"

"I've perused it," said Anne. "Liked what I saw." Anne took the book and turned toward the cash register.

Sallie took a deep breath and sputtered, "My brother called and wants me to come home."

Anne placed a calming hand on Sallie's shoulder. "Let's have a cup of tea in my office." She flipped the sign on the door to the side indicating "Back in 10 minutes" and led Sallie to a small space at the back of the store.

Sitting with their cups, Anne waited for Sallie to begin. After a few moments of silence, she gave her friend a gentle nudge. "You've never talked much about your family."

"There's really not much to say. I've always felt as if I didn't belong. You know, like the childhood feeling that these aren't your real parents? When my mother died, I felt my only function was to be a housekeeper. The happiest day of my life was my first day of college." As she finished, Sallie's shoulders drooped. She looked up at Anne and what was truly weighing on her tumbled from her lips. "Do *you* think I'm guilty?"

Anne's gaze held compassion. "No, Sallie. If you're guilty of anything, it's of being a good friend, of believing in people, in their innate goodness. You don't consider that any of your friends can do wrong."

Sallie frowned. "I think we need to give others the benefit of the doubt. That we need to do our best, that we need to…" Her breath caught in her throat as she struggled not to break down. "Oh, Anne, I don't know what I think anymore."

"Oh, Sallie, see if you can find what you feel in all of this."

"Feel?" Sallie voice was harsh. "I don't want to feel. Feeling gets me in trouble. No," she shook her head, "I definitely don't want to feel right now. I might go crazy if I feel."

Anne reached across and squeezed her hand. "Have you ever considered writing a journal? My experience is that they're helpful in processing old stuff."

Sallie shot straight up. "How funny! I was just considering starting one. Helpful how?"

"To clarify your thinking, to ask important questions, to reflect on the bigger picture that is life," Anne's arms swept up as if to clear the air. "Most of all, it helps you notice your feelings. And, my friend, that might just be what you need."

Anne rose from her chair and headed toward the front of the bookstore. "Come. Let me show you some beautiful choices. You'll feel as if you're writing a book." She smiled at Sallie. "Not that anyone except you would be reading it."

Later that evening, opening her pristine leather bound blank book, she found a pencil and poised her hand above the first page. Anxious thoughts raced through her mind. *Where do I start? Anything I write will be permanent and must be perfect.*

She took a deep breath and laughed at herself. *There's that perfect again. Perhaps I can consider that just starting the journal has its own perfection. After all, no one is going to see it except me. Yet, the first page. What do I do with the first page? Well, just give the book a title.*

65

What kind of a title? Sallie's Journal sounds too trite. Then what is it? She sat with her pencil in her mouth, her eyes unfocused. *I know what… I'll call it "The Sound of My Soul."*

Spurring herself into action, Sallie put pencil to paper and wrote the title page. She left the next page blank, then hesitated, her hand poised above the third page for a long moment. Finally, she began to write.

Sallie's Journal—May 12th

A blank book. Perfect in every way. I hesitate. As if to put word to page will… Will what? Make them… Make them what? The first mark will… What? Where to start? If I use pencil, I can erase, yet the marks will still remain to spoil the page. I hesitate.

Anne says to just keep writing and not stop for what… 15 minutes… that's too much. La La La. Never take the pencil off the page, she said. LaLaLa. I couldn't decide whether to use pen or pencil. Now what… Who really cares? Someone has to care. LaLaLa. I must prove my innocence. Anne says not to re-read anything. At least, not at first.

LaLaLa. I don't know what to write. I feel like I'm seven again— seven again—LaLaLa—seven again, second grade. What happened? LaLaLa. I broke my arm. We moved… again… LaLa… My chest hurts just thinking about that time. The small bedroom…the streetlight shining through the old-fashioned blinds… the hurt… La

How many minutes have I been writing? This is silly. My mother told me stories. About Germany. She missed Germany. What did she miss? I can't—can't. What is this word? I hate the word "can't." I CAN remember… Just must concentrate… really concentrate.

Angel wings, she called them. Crispy, sugary, melt in your mouth… pastries? No… then what were they called? Ah, palmiers… that's what they're called, as big as a baseball glove. Baseball glove… What is it about baseball? Strategy… What can I do to prove my innocence?

66

Maybe if I go through all the records. That was so stupid of me. Trust. I trusted Mike. That's what I get for… what?… my naiveté. I must pull myself up… by my own bootstraps. Now why did I think of that? That's what Dad would have said. I'm not like him at all.

A quick look at the clock confirmed her fifteen minute goal had been reached. Her task complete, she turned off the light and fell into a deep sleep.

CHAPTER FOUR

Rose: The Angel of Childhood

The day was cool upon her face as the brisk breeze ushered the golden clouds across the sky. Seven-year-old Sallie, surrounded by the fairy tale world of picture books, heard the rich, fluty warble of a blackbird. She looked up to find the source of the song, shading her eyes against the bright sunshine. The blackbird appeared to beckon her, and she followed him along a path that wound around the edge of a forest and over a hill, ending outside a stone castle wall.

Sallie looked up at the high arched opening supported on either side by tall watchtowers. The bird sat there looking down at her as if to say, "Here is your destination."

The doorway enticed her, and she advanced shyly through the gate along a walkway that led straight to a palace. The building was made of large, irregular-shaped limestone and loomed several stories high, its rough walls punctuated by small windows covered with lattice edgings.

Just inside the entrance was a fountain, its water tinkling like the musical notes of a melody sung by her mother. Sallie walked over to peer inside its base, looking for fish swimming in the pool. Nearby, a small bench welcomed her to sit.

There was a mystery about this garden before her, yet a sense of familiarity at the same time, as if she had visited it many times. Sallie looked around at the twenty-foot-high walls of the castle, with tall, graceful sycamore trees providing much needed shade to the garden. Below the leafy canopy was grass of the deepest green she had ever seen, so green it appeared almost blue.

She sensed this was a paradise for the amusement of children, with dark nooks and spacious areas offering trees for climbing, walled shade gardens for hide-and-seek, and the rich smell of jasmine at the end of a warm summer day spent in the unabashed joy of childhood play. Suddenly, Sallie jumped up. "I know this place! Rose lives here."

She raced around the house, following the sun to where she knew the rose garden to be, with its heady smell of robust grandifloras and floribundas sporting riotous colors of pink, magenta, salmon, deepest yellow, blood red, and lavender.

As she sprinted through the rows of blooming flowers, her excitement bubbled up. It had been a long time since she and Rose had played together. Rounding the back of the house, she saw Rose and gave a cry of joy. There she was, sitting on a terraced patio under the shade of a large haoma—the mystical tree of ancient Persia symbolizing life and the joining of Heaven and Earth. Rose waved to welcome her friend. Sallie beamed.

"Rose, where have you been? I thought you had gone away." She smiled at the petite, brown skinned woman with long black hair to her waist and dark, almond eyes that seemed to carry all the sadness of the world. Barely taller than Sallie's youthful stature, Rose was dressed in a velvet gown of the deepest purple with a light silk scarf of palest pink around her shoulders and tiny slippers encrusted with sparkling jewels. She welcomed Sallie with a warm embrace.

Rose, a spirit guide who had spent time on Earth, had graduated to the role of assisting other souls on their path, those having similar experiences and soul patterns. As the angel of Sallie's childhood, she had watched over her charge since infancy, holding her youthful energy. When she was a child, Sallie had imagined a playmate, a confidant to her stories. She had called her playmate, "Rose," and had pictured her as a Persian princess from the stories her mother had told her about Scheherazade and the Arabian Nights.

Holding the memories of Sallie's unrealized lives and dreams yet to be fulfilled, Rose's charge was to guide Sallie to live her yearnings. Rose carried the fragments of Sallie's childhood, the pieces of her left unexpressed or discarded and were now seeking to be reunited with her soul. She sought to encourage Sallie's strengths, including the courage to learn the lesson of alliance with her soul. From that point of view, all is possible and there is no separation from one's highest good.

"Sallie, my friend, I never went away," she said, inviting the child to sit beside her.

"I remember you so well. I've thought about you and wondered why I didn't hear from you anymore."

"I never left you, little one. You grew up and no longer sought my friendship. Just open your imagination and I shall be there always."

Sallie smiled. "I'm just so glad to see you now." She put her arms out and Rose encircled her with a hug. They sat there quietly for a while.

Eventually, Sallie sighed and gazed at her guide with longing. "I'm so sad most of the time. Yet when I'm with you, I always feel happy."

"Tell me about your sadness, little one."

"I feel like the princess locked in the tower. And then something bad happens and the tower crumbles." Sallie buried her face in Rose's lap.

"What happens then?"

"I'm lying on the rocks and I think I'm dead. But I don't feel dead. I get scared." She looked up at Rose for guidance.

"What else?

"I feel sad, like it's all my fault and I don't know what I did."

"Tell me about your feelings of being sad."

Sallie scrunched her eyes. "I just don't want to feel sad. I just don't want to feel at all."

"Hmmm," said Rose. "That's not good, is it?"

Sallie shook her head.

"Feelings are important and you should always want to feel them."

"Why?"

"Because it's the way your soul has of telling you what is important for you to experience."

"What if I don't want to feel?"

"How can you stop feeling?"

"I just tell myself it doesn't matter."

"Ah, that's your mind talking."

Sallie looked quizzically at her guide. "My mind?" She stared off in space to grasp the concept. "Yes, my mind. I like my mind to take care of me."

"Yes, I know. Do you want to know what happens when you listen all the time to your mind and not to your feelings?"

Sallie nodded.

"Feelings are when your soul wants to tell you something is important. Good feelings tell you that you're on the path your soul chose. Uncomfortable feelings tell you to pay attention to past hurts you have been ignoring."

"What do you mean, ignoring?"

"When you get upset and feel sad, it's for you to see things in a different way."

"I just want to make the sadness go away."

Rose reached out to hug her charge. "That's when we, your spirit guides, usually can get your attention."

"Get my attention?" Sallie asked as she pulled away, her eyes wide. "What do you mean?"

"You are a soul in a physical body, one with its own needs. Feelings come from your soul, telling you something needs to be healed."

Sallie shook her head, "No, no I don't want to feel."

"Yes, I know. You like to use your mind and you believe everything it tells you."

"Yes, I'm smart and I like using my mind."

"Your mind often tells you things that are not true. We call it 'mind chatter.' It's your mind making things up that may not be true."

"My mind wouldn't lie to me."

"Not exactly lie. Your mind can only tell you things it knows from what it sees. And sometimes your mind, because you are so smart, decides something is true that may not be true."

Rose stopped and began to tickle Sallie, who struggled to get away. "We just want you to feel all of your feelings. That way, you like yourself, and when you meet people, you don't have to change just to have them like you in return." Rose pulled Sallie into her arms as she spoke, this time holding her tight. "Does that make sense to you?"

"I'm not sure I want other people in my life." Sallie sat up straight and pulled away. "I can take care of myself. Anyway, when I ask others, they don't want to help me."

"Who do you ask?"

"Well, my father," Sallie said hesitantly, searching Rose's face for signs of approval.

Rose reached out and touched her arm gently, sending shivers of love through her body. "There are connective threads binding you to your family."

"What do you mean?"

"You know how much you like the game of baseball?" Rose asked. Sallie nodded.

"Just think of your life like a baseball game. You must do your part separately, while still remembering that life is a team sport. When you're up to bat, you're all by yourself and you need to help the team." She looked at the little girl to make certain she understood.

Sallie jumped up and down, clapping her hands. "I know how to hit a ball! I can do it all by myself!"

"Yes, I know. And once you're on base, you need someone else to hit it to get you home." Sallie nodded and Rose put her arms around her. "You need them to make their play, just as they depend on you to make yours."

"I'm sad when I have to rely on others." Her conviction came through in a plaintive tone.

"Yet you like to win the game."

"Yes, I get all excited and we all jump and hug each other."

"See, that's what I mean. It is when you play with others that you are the happiest. You feel like a winner. They are part of your life and you've all agreed to work together. Every time you meet them, you must choose again to play without knowing what will happen. Sometimes the outcome is fun and sometimes it isn't."

Sallie looked at her with unanswered questions swirling through her mind. Rose continued, "Sometimes, when things don't work out, and you feel bad and don't listen to your feelings, pieces of you shut down and leave dark corners. It's like losing little pieces of your soul."

"What is a soul?"

"It's the part of you deep inside that knows who you truly are." She put her hand flat on Sallie's heart. "Take a deep breath." Sallie's chest rose as she slowly filled her lungs. "Now, feel inside your body for that part."

Sallie closed her eyes and felt a soft spot inside her begin to sparkle. "It's like happy little bubbles breaking out all over my body and jumping into the air," she said as she opened her eyes, a triumphant look on her face.

"That's a good way to say it," Rose said, smiling at the imagery.

"Whenever something happens to you that takes away those bubbles, parts of your soul break away from your body. These pieces get buried deeper and deeper as you grow up."

"I don't understand."

"Some of those bubbles get trapped, like in a glass where they can't escape, and they stay in the past. Then, when something happens to you that makes you feel sad or angry, you get sucked into that jar and are unable to be your spontaneous self. Do you know what I mean by spontaneous?"

The small girl shook her head.

"It's like when you just do something that comes into your head because it sounds like fun. You don't have to think about it or hold back," Rose explained.

"You mean like when we have a water fight at the pool?"

Rose nodded and tousled her hair. Sallie pushed her hand away and came closer to be held.

"Soul loss, like being trapped in that jar, occurs when things happen to you that hurt your heart. This keeps you from being here in this moment."

Sallie put her hands on her heart. "I've been trapped in that jar, haven't I?"

"Yes, dear one. With children, small events that the adults in your life often don't even notice may be very big for you. You think whatever happened is your fault and you blame yourself."

"Daddy gets cross with me sometimes and I think I did something wrong. Mostly, I don't know what it is."

"Sometimes you can get the wrong idea about what others are thinking."

"What do you mean?"

"Because you don't know what your dad is thinking, you think it's your fault. It may be that he's just busy or worried about something else."

"I think he's cross with me and doesn't love me," Sallie said.

"Exactly. And then a part of your soul-self breaks away and stays stuck in the past because you believed you did something wrong and don't deserve to be loved."

"Exactly," Sallie repeated the word, relishing the sound on her lips. Her voice was quiet. "I always tried to remember what I did that he didn't love me."

Rose took her hand and nodded. "You did nothing, little one. You lived through the experience, yet you were no longer your whole self."

"I remember my snapdragon plants. I had to leave them behind when we moved. My father was loading the truck and he yelled at me. I felt bad all over. Is that what you mean?"

Rose nodded. "Because you're a little girl, you thought taking them was wrong and so that meant something was wrong with you. So pieces of your soul became lost as you tried to forget the pain you felt."

"I don't want to feel that pain."

"Yes, I know," said Rose. "When you get older, if you don't feel that childhood pain, the disappointments of life will cause even more pain. And because it makes you even sadder, you'll push down those feelings until you won't feel anything anymore. Over many years, as more and more pieces of your soul get left behind, it will be harder to face even minor disappointments. You will continue to feel like you're in a jar, unable to let others into your life, and to give and receive love, despite how much you want it."

Sallie laid her head on Rose's lap. "I don't want to lose those pieces."

"No one does." She pulled Sallie onto her lap and leaned back. "Close your eyes," Rose said, putting her hand over Sallie's eyes, allowing her to drift into a reverie. "The part of you that is grown up lived through the losses you ignored: the death of your mother, the feelings of rejection by your father, the loneliness of constantly moving, among others. As an adult, you continued this same response to abandonment when you divorced your husband, had misunderstandings with friends who left your life, and now your sense of betrayal by Mike. With each encounter, you left pieces of yourself on the doorstep of your soul. Some of these people who tried to control you still have power over you today, even if you haven't seen them in years. Others have simply drained your soul."

"Can I change this?" she whispered, looking up at Rose with hope in her voice.

"You are a helpful person and like things to be perfect. You want to help others be the best they can be. Yet, sometimes they don't want help and you don't take care of yourself."

Sallie looked down, knowing the truth of what Rose said.

"In order to help others, you must take care of yourself first. If you don't, you will become tired, making you helpless to do what your soul wants to do."

"What must I do?"

Rose took Sallie's chin in her hand, looking at her with love. "Live in the moment. You cannot find wholeness with another unless you are whole within yourself. Community with others comes when you are in communion with yourself. Look at your dreams that remain unfulfilled to determine your path. Discover a way to be in the present by finding your deepest longings from your youth, and use these childhood dreams as stepping-stones to discover a path to your future. For it is a truth that all the wishes in your heart are unique to you and must come to pass in the living of your destiny."

Sallie looked at Rose and nodded her understanding. Rose gave her a kiss on her forehead and they sat together quietly, both lost in a communion of their souls. Then Rose sent her back to her dreamtime, knowing Sallie would remember in her heart.

PART III
The Nature of Time

Men's curiosity searches past and future
And clings to that dimension. But to apprehend
The point of intersection of the timeless
With time, is an occupation for the saint—
No occupation either, but something given
And taken, in a lifetime's death in love,
Ardour and selflessness and self-surrender.
For most of us, there is only the unattended
Moment, the moment in and out of time,
The distraction fit, lost in a shaft of sunlight,
The wild thyme unseen, or the winter lightning
Or the waterfall, or music heard so deeply
That it is not heard at all, but you are the music
While the music lasts. These are only hints and guesses,
Hints followed by guesses; and the rest
is prayer, observance, discipline, thought and action.
The hint half guessed, the gift half understood, is incarnation.

T.S. Eliot
Four Quartets 3: The Dry Salvages

CHAPTER FIVE

Past into Future

A shrill ring woke Sallie from a deep sleep. Automatically, she reached over to the table beside her bed and picked up the phone. "Hello?" she croaked, sleep heavy in her voice.

A woman tentatively answered, "Dick? Is Dick there?"

"You must have the wrong number," Sallie mumbled politely.

"Listen, I know he's there! Just put him on the line!"

Sallie held the phone away from her ear to dull the increasing volume of the shrieks on the other end of the line. When they had ceased, she cautiously asked, "What number are you dialing?"

The woman sputtered her intended destination and Sallie calmly replied, "You've reversed the last two digits. Really, there's no one here except me." She placed the phone back in its cradle and glanced at the clock. 6:32 AM. With a sigh, she turned over, willing herself to settle back into sleep.

As her consciousness drifted, snatches of memory floated just out of her reach. *There was a dream. What was it? I was a little girl. Who else was there?* Letting her mind relax, she recalled another day when she had been awakened with a harsh shake.

"Game day. Time's a'wasting. Up and at 'em." Her father's voice, drill sergeant shrill, penetrated her mind with its razor sharp tenor. Sallie had turned over for just a few more minutes of sleep, wanting to bring her consciousness into focus. As a child, she liked to awaken slowly, and her father's calls had intruded upon her remembrance of a dream, one that seemed to presage some dilemma just ahead.

It was just the three of them now. Already Sallie was unable to recall much of her mother, other than the last few years of her illness. Her own role as caretaker to her father and brother dominated much of her time and awareness. Sallie wondered how she could possibly manage high school and keep a house too. *I'm too young for all this.*

Not waiting for her to rise, her father came into her bedroom and stripped the bedcovers off her body. "Get up. Now." His commands left no room for argument. "Your turn in the bathroom."

Slender, almost delicate in his appearance, David Henry Whitaker stood so straight that he appeared taller than his five foot ten. His strength was in his voice and in his hands, and Sallie spent much of her childhood staying out of his way. When he was not getting the respect he thought he deserved, or the response to his request was slower than desired, those hands could reach quickly across the space separating them to grab her. This time, she immediately jumped out of bed and headed for the bathroom.

Yes, it was game day. Her brother played shortstop for one of the local Little League teams, the Police Panthers. The day started with a practice session between her father and brother on the front lawn under the two large jacaranda trees that stood sentry like parents watching out for their children.

While Sallie prepared breakfast, she could hear her father's voice as he ran Mark through a series of drills to get ready for the game. They always started with an infield practice exercise in which her father threw grounders to Mark, one after the other, with no let up. Mark had to catch the first and look up for the second, already on its way, with her father shouting at him to pick up the pace all the while.

Next was a back-peddling drill, followed by the bucket drill, in which Mark had three seconds to catch a ball and flip it into a bucket, warming up his arm and shoulders. Sallie knew where they were in the routine by her father calling out the three seconds in a staccato rhythm.

Her job was to make breakfast, prepare some lunch, and be ready when the car left the driveway. She was still learning to cook, so for now her attempts were very simple: cereal with bananas and milk for breakfast, bologna sandwiches and fruit for lunch, Kool-Aid to drink. As she mechanically prepared their food for the day, her mind wandered to what made him so strict.

At the game, her father continued cheering and coaching Mark, focusing on every play with an intensity that made Sallie shrink away and sit alone at the end of the bench. Afterward, her father excitedly ran out onto the field to congratulate Mark for his winning catch. Leaving the field, he had asked the coach to take a picture of the three of them— a picture Sallie kept to remind her of why she left home.

She knew some details of her parents' lives through snippets of overheard conversation between them in her childhood years. Emigrating from England, her grandfather had developed a harsh temperament from his inability to find work during the Great Depression, leaving David to scramble for odd jobs during his childhood. When David's father died at the beginning of World War II, he entered the military.

The Army was his salvation. He began to send money home to his mother and gained a new self-respect that he had lacked growing up.

While serving in Germany after the war, he met Sallie's mother, Hannah. She was young and spoke only her native German when they first met.

Both of Hannah's parents had died in the war, and the story Sallie had heard was that she became enamored with this young American G.I. and her dreams were filled with wanderlust. They married and the children were born. His life was the military, while hers was the home and kitchen. These were the facts she knew, yet Sallie had a feeling there was more. A lot more.

The kitchen was Sallie's domain now, except for the occasional Sunday when her father would make his famous dollar-sized pancakes, a rare treat. Sallie felt a tenuous camaraderie during these times, though it quickly dissipated as the week left her strapped with schoolwork and her chores at home. She wanted to go to college, and she knew that to do so she would need to make good grades. The daily demands at home conflicted with her schoolwork, leaving her little time for sleep.

In the spring of eighth grade, Sallie came home with her list of classes for high school, excited at the prospect of all college prep classes. She bubbled with enthusiasm as she showed her father the schedule.

"Look, Dad, here's my freshman classes. I've got Algebra, World History, English, Biology, Spanish and P.E."

"Let me see that list," he said, snatching it out of her hand. His eyes narrowed and he scoffed as he inspected the sheet.

"My counselor said these are the classes I need for college," she explained weakly, her tone deflated.

"She doesn't decide your future. I do." He looked at Sallie harshly.

Sallie stared back at him, puzzled. "Well, I'm smart, and I guess she just assumed I'd go to college. Anyway, I really want to. It would be exciting."

"Well, you'll learn when you grow up that life isn't about exciting," he replied. "It's about discipline. Realistic goals. Good old hard work."

Sallie became very quiet and shrank inside herself, murmuring, "Why shouldn't I go to college?"

"Well, for one thing, there isn't enough college money for both you and your brother. You need to learn to be a good homemaker. Girls just get married and have children. Girls don't need college." He looked at her quiet, ashen face, bereft of its earlier jubilation. "If you need a career until you get married, you can be a secretary. I'll pay for secretarial school."

Sallie had kept her eyes downcast, not knowing how to respond. Her father made it clear there was nothing left to discuss with a curt, "And that's final."

The next day at school, Sallie quietly added typing to her schedule without changing the rest. Her father's words only fueled her determination to find a way to pay for college on her own.

Sallie's eyes fluttered open and she awoke back in the present. She noted with surprise that the clock now read 8:31 AM. *I must've fallen back asleep.* Though the sun shone bright, beckoning her to a new day, she couldn't quite shake her unease about the painful memories from her childhood surfacing at this crucial juncture in her life.

There was nothing left to be done around the house. With the easy stuff out of the way, it was time to tackle some bigger fish. Sallie's mind flitted from thought to thought, trying to get a handle on her present predicament. *Doesn't Anne always tell me to just live in the moment and relax and let life speak to me? I know I've heard this from someone. I am living in the moment. I just don't like this moment. I want another moment in time. I don't want to keep reliving my childhood. Nothing can be changed.*

Picking up the remote control, Sallie turned on the television and flicked through the channels, listening to each just long enough to know it wasn't of interest. She paused on a talk show where the host was discussing a popular new book, catching the last snippets of conversation before a commercial break. The woman being interviewed was the author of the book she had just bought at Anne's store.

Interest piqued, she made herself a cup of tea and sat down to listen. As the author talked about her research and how she came to write the book, Sallie again felt a sense of déjà vu as if she had heard these words before. "Look to your daydreams," the author said. "Use these dreams to discover your future." *It's been years since I've had any daydreams,* Sallie mused. *I've been too busy living my life.*

Turning off the television and tossing the remote aside, Sallie curled under a knit throw and let herself be guided by her unconscious yearnings. The image of her mother arose unbidden into her mind. She allowed her body to relax, remembering the comfort of Hannah sitting on her childhood bed, reading her a story.

"This is a story of a time long ago in a kingdom far away, and a princess who was very beautiful." Her mother always began with the same words, each time retelling the old tale with different adventures for the young maiden. The ending was always the same, though. Sallie could rely on that. The princess always lived happily ever after.

They were imaginative stories in which the natural order of the world was suspended. Animals, plants, and people all talked in a strange and wondrous language, and magical helpers offered helpful hints to those whose hearts were pure and loving. Often she spoke of princesses who married the handsome prince. Sometimes, though, she spoke of maidens who rescued themselves, had their own adventures, and solved their own problems all by themselves, ending with a happily-ever-after contentment from having accomplished great feats by their own efforts. This was the memory of her mother that Sallie had kept buried deep inside.

There were also her own daydreams, carefully concealed beneath a layer of bravado, that she often considered beyond her wildest thinking. Mere pipe dreams, as her mother would have said. They were not shared with anyone, just kept silent within her soul. To open them to others meant they would be ridiculed and then they would not come true.

There was her dream of being an engineer, fostered by her love of math. Or her fantasy of writing an interesting book, one that pulled the reader into the life and times of the heroine, just as she had been enamored of the real-life women of the historical fiction books she had read as a child. And, of course, there was her dream of living in a loving family. *Ah, if dreams came true, they would bring me all I desire.*

In this mood, Sallie let her consciousness drift into the timeless space between worlds. When she awoke, she looked around, disoriented by the feeling that her mother was just in the next room and would come in, sit down next to her, and ask her about her dreams. *I wonder about my mother's life. She never said much. Perhaps she had dreams that weren't realized either. I wish I knew more about her and my grandmother.*

Sallie's thoughts were interrupted by the phone ringing. She let it ring until she heard Gail's voice begging her to answer. Diving for the phone, she grabbed the receiver. "Gail, I apologize for not returning…"

Before she could finish her sentence, Gail interrupted, "Oh Sallie, don't give it a second thought. I was just checking to see if you were ready to talk about the office."

"Just for you." She was anxious to know what had changed in her absence.

"May I come by? I have those boxes of records you wanted."

"Give me a half hour and then come by. I don't have anything in the house to offer you."

"Hey, not to worry. I'll bring something."

Almost an hour later, the doorbell rang. Sallie looked with appraising eyes at the living room as she opened the door to Gail, who was laden with offerings. Within a few minutes, they were comfortably perched around the coffee table, which was now covered with documents, hot tea, and profiteroles.

"What's with the profiteroles?" A smile reached Sallie's eyes, the first in weeks.

Gail's eyes twinkled. "I know your faves. You know the old adage about eating dessert first."

"Why not, indeed." Sallie picked up one of the chocolate covered morsels and popped it in her mouth. "From Nick's Bakery," she mumbled with a hand near her mouth, ready to catch any errant crumbs. "The best in town. Did I ever tell you the time I…"

"…had them in Paris stacked in a pyramid?" Gail laughed as she finished Sallie's sentence.

"Oh, I guess I have." Sallie grabbed another. "One of the best memories of my marriage." Her eyes closed in delight as she took a dainty bite, then her face turned serious as she surveyed the table full of files. "What've you got for me?"

"Well, I've gone through all the files for the past seven years, every transfer in and out of the escrow account, and marked those I think you should see." Gail riffled through the files, showing Sallie the system she had organized. "There's really only the three that Phillips found that are relevant. See, I've put a colored clip on each of them."

Sallie started to reach for one of the files, but Gail stopped her. "Wait, that's just the back up. Here's a summary." Handing her a spreadsheet, she moved to sit beside Sallie on the couch. "Here's a listing of all the transactions. I also went back the seven years. Dollars

86

in and dollars out. It's organized by escrow."

"The highlighted transactions are the ones that will probably be questioned." Gail paused, the silence heavy.

Sallie looked at her expectantly. "Go on."

"It doesn't look good." Gail handed her another spreadsheet. "Carol gave me access to their bank statements. Mike made a house payment with this deposit."

Sallie perused the records with a practiced eye. "Looks as if there's another house payment here, and Lisa's school on this one." Sallie watched as Gail pointed to several places on the forms.

Gail handed her additional files. "There are also another three in the records going back seven years. These were before you began signing the forms, back when Stephanie worked for him. Remember her? She was licensed, yet was only his assistant."

"She left abruptly, didn't she?"

Gail nodded. "Something went south with their relationship." She brought Sallie's attention back to the three recent transactions. "The evidence is pretty incriminating. What are you going to do?"

"I think the biggest part for me is how it looks."

"What do you mean?"

"Well, I'm either a fool for signing a form without an account number, or I'm complicit in breaking the law. Either way, I don't look good."

"How could you know there were two accounts?" Gail hesitated. "Those who know you…"

Sallie interrupted, "Those who know me will believe what they want. And they should." She shrugged. "Give me a couple of days to review the files. Get a copy of everything to Fred. We'll see what he says. Anyway, enough of this." She put the pages down and looked at Gail. "Update me. Please. On Carol."

"Carol doesn't want to sell to Samson, so we've created a

temporary plan until you can get your license straightened out."

"Oh?"

"Carol's going to run the business."

"How can she do that?"

"Eric said we could use his senior broker's license and he will act as manager of the licensed staff. I'm to be her assistant, and together we will supervise the support staff. The state has a special program to help widows get their license and maintain a sole proprietorship business."

"That's good." Sallie picked up her cup of tea to hide her shaking hands.

"We see this as temporary until you come back."

"Yes, I know." Sallie saw Gail as far away. *Perhaps. Perhaps.*

"You do see it as temporary, don't you, Sallie?"

She looked at Gail as if she didn't understand the words, then shrugged. "I don't know. I just don't know."

"Listen to me. You're a friend. You're important to me. To us. Please keep the faith. This or better, Sallie. Keep the faith, this or better. There's something better coming. There has to be."

Sallie nodded. Perhaps Gail was right. "I'll do my best." She tried to adopt an upbeat tone, but the words sounded hollow even to her.

Gail hugged her. "Let me know if there's anything we can do."

"Just get these copies to Fred. If anyone can represent me, it would be him."

"Done," said Gail.

After Gail left, Sallie collapsed onto the couch. She pulled her throw over her head and sobbed.

Without thinking, she grabbed her journal from the coffee table and opened the cover, caressing its edges.

Sallie's Journal—May 25th

Dreams are mysterious things. They seem so clear, yet when I awake it's as if there's another person doing… what? Doing something and yet nothing surfaces. Maybe I don't want to remember my dreams.

Yesterday I found an old box of photographs—all black and white and grainy. There was one of my father and me as a toddler. He holds me in his arms. I cannot make out our expressions.

All those photographs in shades of gray. Like my childhood.

I shared a bedroom with my baby brother and can almost hear his breathing, quiet and innocent.

I am not innocent.

What have I done that I could not be forgiven?

If I could just remember.

I pleaded as that little girl's body tensed. And the despair… Why am I remembering this now?

I met my father's mother once at the candy store where she worked. She was Italian and dressed all in black as a widow. She seemed tall to me, yet my father towered over her. She was soft and loving and gentle. She gave me candy.

What is this yearning? This lacking? What am I doing here writing in the middle of the day? Yet what can I do? I must think. Something will come to mind.

Drained, she lapsed into a fitful slumber.

CHAPTER SIX

Sedorah: Grandmother Angel

The drums beat incessantly with a persistence that demanded attention. Sallie felt their rhythm pounding in her chest even though she did not see them. Looking around to get her bearings, she began to walk in the direction of the deepening sound. Her route was slow and halting as there was no path to follow. The foliage hid her way and tall trees blocked the sky. As she persevered and the sound came closer, Sallie's breathing began to match its resonance, as if her name were being chanted by a thousand voices.

Through the trees, Sallie saw the bright red-orange light of a fire ahead. She quickened her pace, emerging on the edge of a clearing before a circle of women. Here, in the Grove of the Ancient Trees, her ancestors met in ceremony. These women were ancient and wise, and they knew the world in a way that was unknown to Sallie or her contemporaries. They exuded a sense of quiet authority; they knew who they were and were comfortable with themselves. They were Sallie's bloodline, going back to the beginning—to the Mother of All.

They were each unique, these grandmothers, and they carried essential energies that pulsed like hearts beating to the same primal tune. It was a song few heard, yet was hauntingly familiar to all; the first song of the universe from which all other songs flowed. The sound of it soothed Sallie's heart, and, for that moment, let her know all she needed to know to be who she truly was.

Arms outstretched, one of the ancient ones approached her. "I am the Angel of the Ancestors. I am Sedorah. When you think of your family and its history, you are thinking of me. For I am your great-grandmother, Isabella Signorelli, and I have given you my blood as I now give you my spirit."

Sedorah took Sallie's hand and led her toward the circle. "The Grandmother Angels carry the story of life on Earth from the beginning. We meet here in ceremony to oversee the unfolding of the ancient knowledge that nourishes all." She looked at Sallie as she nodded toward the others. "Your life moves in a cycle of beginning, middle, and end. Each cycle spirals from the roots of the past, unfolding and providing new information as it becomes necessary for your growth.

"Come and join our circle as we celebrate our lives. This is a commemoration of joy and sorrow, triumph and tragedy, as we honor all aspects of the human experience as equal."

Drawing Sallie into the heart of the circle of grandmothers, the rumble of drums slowed to a soft vibration, carrying the resonance and rhythm of a beating heart. As the reverberation reached her, a soft echo of voices hummed a wordless tune that danced between the notes. A harmony she had never heard before drew her into deeper union with these women. The connection was like a microscopic thread spun of the finest metal, even finer than gold, with a gossamer glow emanating from Sallie's heart, encircling the group and passing through each of the grandmothers.

Sallie's whole being began to soar in remembrance of her dreams of flying; dreams that felt so real and always ended with the knowingness that she could take off when awake and fly out of her confines. It was just a matter of letting her soul be in charge of her body. It knew how to soar. If only she knew how to get out of its way. Suddenly, the sound was hushed. Silence uplifted the space. Alert to her surroundings, Sallie awaited the beginning of her initiation.

As each woman began her part in the ceremony, she took Sallie into her soul to recite her ancient story. Sallie resonated with a sense of commonality, the connection of her life to all those who had gone before her, and its extension into the future and beyond.

Leading the ceremony was Grandmother Bella, her father's mother. Merging with her, Sallie recalled her presence from the candy store and recognized her zest for life. Her gift was simply herself, her love expressed in the food she cooked and all that she created with joy. Embracing Sallie, she presented her with a cookbook, handwritten in her tiny script.

Opening its pages, Bella pointed out her favorite recipes and the pleasure that was hers as she created food for the table of her family. Her pleasure in cooking helped her to cope with her alcoholic husband, who had difficulty keeping a job and providing for his family.

Next was Sallie's mother, Hannah, who gave Sallie a picture of the two of them curled up in bed, reminding Sallie of the nightly fairy tales her mother would recite in both English and German. In the photo, her mother was laughing and pointing to the camera, to David taking the picture. Sallie could see her father through her childhood eyes, smiling with love for his two beautiful girls.

Sallie reached out and took her mother's hand as Hannah spoke of her unrealized hopes, her compromises, and her loneliness in the end. Her greatest joy was Sallie. She was in awe of her daughter's tiny perfection, yet became lost in an unfamiliar world when she left her native Germany and assumed the overwhelming role of a military wife.

Sallie was next introduced to another grandmother who humbly served all those with whom she came in contact. Her life was devoted to her family. She gave Sallie a piece of hand-embroidered linen that was stiffly starched and pressed. She told of the timidity that kept her from experiencing all of the wishes of her own heart. Her father had married her off to the first man who had come calling, one who was much older than the youth whom she had fancied.

Another grandmother showed selflessness and devotion to her children. Even though she had been abandoned by her husband, her love shone through their poverty. Disgraced by his desertion in their small community, she spoke to Sallie of happy family times spent with her children and grandchildren, presenting her with a small medallion that had been a treasured keepsake.

Her next grandmother, a servant in a household of the bourgeoisie, had lovingly cared for the possessions and children of others until rape and betrayal by her employer had shamed her and driven her to prostitution on the streets. She gave Sallie a small ring with a heart-shaped stone that had been her only possession. Battered in life, her spirit had never been crushed.

Another grandmother presented Sallie with a flowing cape the color of the midnight sky, woven from yarn she had gathered and spun. She lovingly placed it on Sallie's shoulders and Sallie felt the spirit that permeated each thread of the mantle. This grandmother's life ended as a martyr for her faith during a time of persecution by the Church, when small outcast sects were perceived as a threat and obliterated.

A grandmother who was sensitive to nature energies and gifted with wisdom about plants and their healing properties showed her wounds from being burned at the stake. She presented Sallie with a bundle of carefully wrapped herbs and told her of their virtues, including the healing of her own soul through the energy that Mother Earth and the Nature Spirits injected into every living thing.

Another grandmother, a member of a nunnery all of her life,

presented Sallie with an exquisite piece of lace she had made. The fineness and beauty of her work helped to keep her convent in basic goods, though much was sold or bartered for far less than its value. Her productive years had been cut short, her eyesight ravaged by poor lighting conditions.

As she passed from one grandmother to the next, Sallie was buoyed by the resilience of these women. Their diverse skills reflected a harmony of soul and beauty with a timelessness that she revered. Returning to the center of the circle, Sallie trembled in the presence of her ancestors, all of whom had made a contribution, and each of them wounded in some way.

"Who am I? What must I do to follow in your footsteps?" she asked of this family of hers.

They responded to her as a Greek chorus, their minds joined in a unison that belied their individuality. "There are two things we request of you. The first is to do a ceremony of remembrance to all who have gone before you; an acknowledgement and prayer on our behalf. The second is to find your contribution to the circle by healing your wounds, for it is in your healing that all are healed in the unlimited circle that is life, where there is no time and all is occurring simultaneously."

Sallie was astonished. "You say my healing can heal you? How?"

Sedorah gently drew her into conversation. "In the evolution of the world today, one of the missions of humankind is to bring peace to Earth. This is accomplished through the healing of your wounds as individuals, which radiates out and affects even larger groups, until eventually all the wounds of the ancestors are also healed. This, in turn, will cause the planet to be healed."

"What can I do?"

"Your intention to pursue the healing will direct your path. There are some things to know, however. The time when the wounds were inflicted no longer exists. It is still alive in you as a dark energy that perpetuates judgments about yourself and others. Some of the conclusions you've drawn were based on a child's perception that may have been inaccurate."

"What do you mean?"

"When you were very young, you developed the idea that you must've done something wrong that could not be forgiven," said Sedorah. "It was based on a childish perception that your father did not love you."

"It was true," Sallie started to remonstrate. "At least, at the time, it felt true," she finished quietly.

"Exactly," said Sedorah, with a smile. "It is a wound you carry that may have little foundation. These mistaken conclusions you made as a child still influence your relationships. It is up to you to discover and correct these wounds."

"You're saying that I need to give my family another chance and be open to who they are now," Sallie said, looking pleased at her insight.

Sedorah smiled and Sallie felt a surge of energy between them.

"If I do this, how does this heal all the wounds of my grandmothers?" asked Sallie.

"You have to look at time a little differently than you have been taught and consider a new type of time, imaginary time."

Sallie gave Sedorah a quizzical look. "Imaginary time?"

"In my realm, we do not measure time as you do. You deal in linear time, which only exists in your dimension. You do something now, then you do something else now; the only time you can experience is that which happens right now in the present. This now time is tied to the past by your memories and linked to the future by your dreams. Yet, time does not exist except as a subjective perception."

"Wait a minute. You're saying there's no such thing as time, yet that is the basis of my reality."

"The universe of Spirit vibrates at a different intensity than your world of form, causing the dimensions to expand beyond those of space and time that you know. When you put a structure to time, you create barriers to your total experience of All That Is. You become limited. The universe was not created in time; it was created *with* time," responded Sedorah, waiting patiently for Sallie to consider this new information.

"What else is there if there is no time? How can this be?"

"Consider this time out of time—no time or timeless time—for it is imaginary time. Imaginary time moves in curves and thus has no beginning and no end."

"Time is part of reality. I know the earth is real because I experience it through time," challenged Sallie.

"You recognize linear time, as it has a past that looks like it is behind you, it has a present, the moment by moment in which you live your life, and it has a future, that time spreading out in front of you. Imaginary time is like making a left or a right turn and curving through the universe. That is how you meet your ancestors in your dreamtime and how the energy of transformation moves from you to them as your heal your wounds."

Sallie nodded, as she considered this new concept. "I'm not certain what to do to cure my wounds."

"You must reconnect with your family on Earth. They carry the same issues you do. In order to heal yourself, your family must be part of your process. They are also wounded and must be healed."

Sallie looked at her and nodded. She wasn't certain she liked this advice. Sedorah went on, "Listen to the messages that come your way in your reading. Pay attention to what others, even strangers, tell you. This information will provide an electrical current that will resonate with your body. Just follow your heart and your intuition. It can be very simple. You will know, so trust yourself."

With that, the grove slowly dissolved, leaving Sallie in a deep, dreamless sleep.

PART IV
The Nature of Life

All are architects of Fate,
Working in these walls of Time;
Some with massive deeds and great,
Some with ornaments of rhyme.

Nothing useless is, or low;
Each thing in its place is best;
And what seems but idle show
Strengthens and supports the rest.

Henry Wadsworth Longfellow
The Builders

CHAPTER SEVEN

Butterfly Effect

Off the shores of a small island in the Japanese Sea, a butterfly awoke for the day. Poised on the verge of flight, with the wind off the ocean shrieking around it, this winged insect anticipated a single second, an exact moment when the air signaled it to take flight. Perhaps it waited for the perfect condition to show itself, a sense that destiny was in motion and the time had arrived to initiate its mission.

When conditions appeared optimal for its venture, its wings unfolded and the butterfly gently rose, sure of its role in the bigger picture of life. As its gossamer wings fluttered and picked up speed, the delicate creature generated a slight change in the air current. Around its fragile body, the air began to swirl. Wind that had been incoming started to mix with the air that was outgoing. When the air currents collided with each other, their overall structure changed. New clouds began to form offshore and a gentle breeze carried them outward until they mixed with the currents of the Pacific Ocean.

By the time the gale force winds hit the west coast of California, the unusual storm had driven fishermen to their homes; a couple whose paths only crossed because of the storm took comfort in each other's arms; a daughter reunited with her mother out of concern for her safety; and a teacher took a struggling student home, giving him encouragement that would ultimately help him become a fledgling author. All this occurred because a butterfly flapped its wings earlier in fulfillment of its destiny.

Sallie awoke abruptly from her deep sleep to the sound of the incessant wind and rain beating upon her French doors. The clock by the side of her bed read 3:18 AM. Never since its invention had the measurement of time been so precise. A cursory glance at an analog clock would have told her it was approximately 3:15. Time was told in generalities: almost 3:30, about 10:00. Now, in the digital age, a land of ones and zeros, precision lets you know it is exactly 3:18 AM. *Do we really need such precision?* She thought of ancient peoples who used the rising and setting sun to gauge time, its position crossing the horizon and the movement of the stars across the sky telling them of the seasons and the ages.

Her body, still tinged with adrenaline, was burning up, as if with the heat of a summer's night. Even though the night was cool, she threw off her covers, letting the dampness permeate her. As she waited for her body to relax, she could feel every one of its functions disjointedly. Just as the storm raged against her house, so her body took part in the chaotic melody.

Her joints crackled like the nearby thunderclap; her muscles tightened as the echo of the wind curled against her windows; the stiffness of her neck resonated to the storm's pounding fury; and her heart beat in time to the branch lashing against the roof. Each body part spoke to her as a distinct entity, and she discerned the separateness of the parts as well as the totality of the functioning whole.

The events of the past few weeks came back to her with their own insistent cry. She began to review each event that had occurred to see if she could find the flaw, the one thing she could have done differently to create another outcome, one in which she would be working with Carol as a partner in their joint business.

Her musings took her to the phone calls from her brother. *What can I do about my father? How long has it been since I've seen Mark and Nancy? Brian was only a toddler. He must be a teenager now.*

She thought back to the last time they had spoken and the vicious argument that had arisen when she'd announced her intention to divorce her husband. The memory was still clear in her mind's eye— standing in the living room of her childhood home as her brother leaned against the fireplace and her father commanded the room from his easy chair. Their questions had made her feel as if it were two against one, and she was being judged for her failure. She could no longer remember the exact words of their dispute. What lingered was her sense of being an outsider. *I'm not like them. I don't want anyone to tell me how to live my life.*

Sallie considered the pros and cons of returning to Los Madre. To see her father and brother again would be welcome, yet what if they were as intolerant of her as in the past? What if they tried to tell her how to deal with her situation here, or get her to assume an unwanted responsibility there?

As the minutes ticked toward dawn, she continued to dissect all of her recent actions, ending with her visit with Anne at the bookstore a couple of days before. *She's such a dear friend.* Anne's advice resonated in Sallie's head. *What others think of you is not your concern. And don't take everything so personally.* Yet, even with all the good advice, Sallie was still dejected, in a deep melancholy thinking she had lost her way. Vacillating as to what course to take, she drifted into a fitful sleep.

With a gasp, Sallie came wide awake, conscious of prickles across her torso as her heart pounded acutely. *My dream. It felt so real. What does it mean?* Fear sank into her body, filling all the spaces of her cells. She grabbed her journal.

Sallie's Journal—June 2nd

Dream: I am in a room with Mike and he is dead and I killed him. A stranger comes in the room and says he will take care of burying him, although he will not tell me where, thinking that will erase my guilt.

I have some papers from Mike saying he wants to sell me the business. Time goes by and I am not caught for his murder. The business is successful and I am confident. Eventually, I cease to feel any guilt.

Later, I am at a party with the entire staff of our office. I can see in their eyes that they know I am responsible for Mike's death, yet they can find nothing to tie me to it.

I find some papers he gave me and know they connect me to him. I must destroy them, and thus eliminate any connection to my crime. Gail comes in the room and innocently reads one of the papers. I know she will eventually figure it out. I am frantic to destroy the evidence.

I put the papers with some other trash and take it out to the garbage. Gail follows me, looking at me like she knows I'm guilty. I find the stranger who helped me dispose of the body and ask him to meet me later. He tells me he is too busy, and I start to give him the papers to hide and burn later. Someone comes up to us and asks him for the documents.

This dream has hit me hard. I am in a state of horror, as if it really happened. How could my subconscious even consider murdering Mike? The guilt feels so real and intense. What does this dream mean?

Sallie closed her journal and relived the terror of her dream, letting it take its course, twisting like a Grand Prix race car as it wound and curved its way through the circuits of her body. As she started to breathe into her revulsion, she wondered whether it was an omen and vowed to pay attention to what might show up in her life. *There must be something crucial I need to know. Am I so angry that I would resort to murder over past injuries rather than find a new life, even if it were only in my mind?*

Rising from her bed and putting on a robe, Sallie moved slowly and consciously through her morning routine. Reading the news after a several week absence gave her a renewed connection to the world outside her boundaries.

One article in particular commanded her attention. Steve Martin, one of her favorite actors, was interviewed regarding how he had handled disappointment. She gave his words her full attention.

"I now understand that you have to recreate your life… There are some who can transform themselves and become new creatures. When you couple that kind of transformation with a wisdom about what life is and the way it works, then you don't depend on others to make you desirable."

Quietly reading those words, Sallie's eyes glazed over, as if looking into another dimension of time. Her body shuddered as a sliver of truth ran through it, as though she were sharing words of wisdom with an old friend in a language that resonated in her soul. *I want to transform myself. I want to become a totally new creature. I want to know people who embrace change as a structure of their life.*

A current of electricity coursed through her and she felt alive for the first time in several weeks. *If my dreams are always only about me, perhaps there is a side of me that needs to die in order to find my way.*

Glancing at the clock, she saw that she still had just enough time to make the baseball game.

By the time Anne, Joe, and Matt showed up at her door, Sallie was decked out in orange and black and ready to rally her team to victory.

Anne laughed as she took in Sallie's outfit. "We look like twins!"

"That we do. And proud of it!" Sallie responded with a high five, feeling her heart lighten as she took the first step in a new direction. Conversation was lively on the trip across the Golden Gate Bridge to the ballpark. The Giants were on a four game skid, and they all hoped their team would turn things around today.

It was a windy, bright San Francisco day as they settled into their seats on the third base line just twelve rows up from the playing field. The game started fast as the Giants pounced on the Rockies' starting pitcher with three first-inning runs.

"That's my team!" Joe shouted at the end of the inning. Standing up, he looked at Sallie and Anne. "How's about something to eat? Matt and I are at your service today," he said with a bow. "What about some crab sandwiches?" Moments later, orders in hand, the two guys climbed the concrete stairs and headed to the concession stands.

Anne smiled gently at her friend. "What made you change your mind?"

"Well," Sallie hesitated, "I had a little revelation this morning. Decided it was time to move on."

"And what better place to start than the ole ballpark?" Anne playfully nudged Sallie's shoulder.

"Yeah, something like that." Sallie smiled. Her friend's grin was infectious.

"So," Anne pressed, "what do you want to do next?"

"I've been mulling over my options. I could stay here and put all my energy into getting my license back... Just the way things fell out with Mike and all the gossip makes me feel like I need a break. Get away for a while, let things settle."

"Well, at least you're feeling. I was worried about you for a while there."

Sallie made a noise in her throat like a frog, and then spoke in a quiet voice. "I could go back to Los Madre and see what's going on with my dad." She paused, searching for a way to explain the worries gnawing at the edge of her mind. "I don't know what to expect. I've been away so long."

"Well, what's the best and worst that can happen?" Anne countered.

"The worst is that I could get rejected again."

"And the best?"

"Good point."

Joe and Matt arrived with the crab sandwiches, peanuts, and beer, and all attention returned to the game. With their pitcher keeping the Rockies off the bases, the Giants continued their scoring, one in the third, another in the fourth, and a two-run rally off a single in the fifth, sending the win-starved fans into ecstasy.

In the bottom of the seventh, a foul ball was hit high in the air toward the third base line. As it drifted their way, the fans in the area jumped up. The ball appeared to move in slow motion. Sallie watched its arc and unconsciously raised her hands. Joe jumped up, stretching his tall frame over them, and came down with the ball in his glove. A big smile on his face, he held it in the air as a roar erupted from the crowd.

In a spontaneous display of generosity, Joe handed the ball to Sallie. She was surprised and pleased at this unexpected delight. As the fans directed their attention back to the game, Sallie stared at the ball in her hand, lost in memory.

The sounds of another ball game echoed in her ears—young boys screaming and parents yelling their support. The action before her dissolved into a Little League game buried deep within her memory. She heard her father's voice urging her brother to make another hit. "That was your pitch. What're you waiting for? Keep the bat high. Late swing. Keep the focus." All the noise drowned out a young girl, sitting while others stood.

Her attention returned to the present game as a home run was pounded out of the park. Fans in the stands jumped up and high-fived each other all around. Sallie decided she had picked a good day to get back in the game.

Strolling from the ballpark after the game, Anne took Sallie's arm in hers. "You're going quiet on me again."

Sallie gave her a weak smile. "I was just reminiscing about how my father was so strict with us, and how he would train my brother to perfection for his baseball games."

"Hmm. And?"

"And I always felt left out."

"So, what did you do?"

"Guess I went on the offensive," said Sallie. "Thought if I got straight A's, he'd notice me. Then, if I got elected to the Student Council and became Council President. Then, if I wrote for the local newspaper. Then, if I went to college. Never enough." She shook her head.

"Perhaps so; perhaps not," Anne said quietly.

"After Mom died, nothing I did was good enough. It was like I didn't count except to do chores around the house."

"Perhaps it's not entirely as you recall."

"If I return to Los Madre to see Mark and Dad…" Sallie's voice drifted off into silence.

"Mmm hmm?" Anne waited patiently for Sallie to collect her thoughts.

"I'm not certain how I'd be received."

"Hmm, I can understand that," said Anne, companionably placing her hand around Sallie's waist. "Well, you're not defined by what others think of you, even family. Just remember, if you're running away, you'll meet the same people, just in different guises." Sallie nodded in agreement. "Also, you'll be missed. You're part of our family here, and I just hope that, if you go, it'll be temporary."

"I'm not running away, Anne. I promise."

"What about Carol and your license?"

"That's on my agenda for tomorrow."

With that, they caught up with Joe and Matt at the car and the conversation turned to the brilliance of their team's performance that day.

Back home from the game, Sallie checked her phone and found another message from her brother, imploring her to call. This time she picked up the phone and dialed his number without hesitation.

Nancy answered the phone and when she heard Sallie on the other end of the line, she shrieked, "Oh, it's so good to hear your voice! We were beginning to get worried."

Her brother sounded warm and inviting. When she told him she would be driving down within the week, he sounded genuinely excited. Her misgivings were allayed and she smiled, remembering the days in their youth when he had followed her around, always wanting her attention.

That night she had another dream.

Sallie's Journal—June 3rd

Dream: I am in a meadow and I see a gnarled oak tree in the distance that beckons to me. It is the senior statesman of trees and my impulse is to fold myself in its embrace. As I touch its rough surface, I see a wide shaft descending into the center of the earth like a waterfall, except there is no water.

Pulled into the interior of the tree, I plummet down, down through the depths of the earth, like riding a slippery slide, as I move quickly into another realm.

Deposited gently onto the ground, I am surrounded by a dun-colored landscape, reminding me of a velvet blanket. Directly in front of me is a Native American elder in full regal dress. He is Grandfather Sitting Eagle, here to take me on a tour of my world.

I ask him about his name, as I don't think of eagles as sitting, but rather as soaring. "Ah," he answers, "good question!" Then, he changes the subject, pointing to a clear crystal globe suspended just slightly above his outstretched hand.

This is your own personal Earth, he explains. As it spins slowly, I note it has the same landscape as the one in which we are sitting, with two miniature people in the middle. Why, they are replicas of us, I think, as we are instantly transported into the globe and deposited in the middle of my world.

Standing on the equator line, I follow Grandfather to the edge, where the orb begins to bend upward toward the northernmost point of the circle like a geodesic dome roof. Grandfather tells me to walk up the edge of my world. I look at him astonished. "How can I walk up the edge? It bends backward."

He tells me to just do it. Hesitantly, I start walking up the edge of the wall. I find myself walking upside down and backwards and am unexpectedly gleeful. I am doing something I believe impossible. How can this be?

Suddenly the walls of my world expand and the part on which I stand flattens and I am again on flat ground, except the size of my world has expanded. Grandfather tells me that as I change and progress and do things that put me off balance, my world will expand. And not just where I am standing; it increases equally in all directions, making a bigger globe.

Then, he points to a door at the edge of my world, colored a Provençal blue that sparkles with the depth of the deep blue ocean. He tells me to open it. As I stand in the doorway, I look at what appears to be several movies all unfolding at the same time, with me in the middle of each of them, interacting with a host of other people.

He tells me I am watching all the activities that are going to happen in my upcoming journey. I will meet many people and have many experiences. There will be times when I need to initiate action, and other times when I need to wait and let things come to me. The balance between these two ways of being, taking action and learning to be receptive, is my destiny, he says. It's the difference between sitting and soaring, and I understand how he got his name.

"It is time to return," he tells me, and in the flash of a light, I find myself leaning against the oak tree.

After recording her dream, Sallie was certain she had made the right decision to return home. She made a peaceful affirmation about her upcoming journey back to Los Madre and began the task of preparing herself for the drive through Los Angeles. As tempting as it was to shift her complete focus to the trip ahead, the unfinished business with her license would not be ignored. After analyzing the files Gail had provided and doing an online search on the use of trust fund accounts in California real estate law, Sallie had an idea. She called Fred, getting right to the point when he came on the line.

"Fred, I've looked into the history of these accounts. Gail went back the seven additional years, plus the one Phillips audited. The first account was set up as a personal account very early in his business. That one had Stephanie and Mike as cosigners. Then, when Stephanie left and I came on, we started the new account as a business account." Sallie paused, not wanting to acknowledge any complicity in Mike's supposed wrongdoing.

"Keep going, I'm following you."

"Okay, then, can't we just say it was a bank error on the last three, the ones I signed?"

"Were both with the same bank?"

"Yes."

"Hmm. Give me a minute here." Fred went silent as Sallie held her breath.

"I don't think so, Sallie. At least not from Mike's point of view. He did make a second deposit within the three days, transferring funds from the one account to the other. And your signature is on both documents."

"It could still have been a bank error."

"It could have. Do you believe that? Better yet, do you think the State will believe it?"

"Can you ask?"

"Probably not. Let's just wait and see what they say and then create a plan."

"What's your thinking?"

"My initial thoughts are more along the lines of damages. The fact that there was no harm to clients may be our best argument. Also, you might have to say you didn't know."

"That's like saying I didn't perform my duties. That I'm not very bright, or at least not very responsible. In other words, a failure."

"Not really. It could also show that you're trusting."

"Right," her voice was sarcastic. She sighed. "What's the worst that can happen to me if they believe I knew?"

"You could lose your license, have a large fine..." He hesitated. "Let's just wait and see. Trust, Sallie. Let's just trust that we can find a solution."

Sallie hung up the phone, her stomach still in a crunch.

Trust. There's that word again. Trust. Stop! I have to stop this. Not much I can do except move on. She straightened as if to summon her efficient self and called Carol, setting an appointment for later that day.

Sallie arrived at Carol's house laden with printouts from her research. As Carol opened the door, they each gave the other a once over.

"You look like you're doing well." Carol's voice was strong.

"You look good, too." Sallie responded with a smile.

"It's still day-to-day."

109

Sallie nodded. "Same here."

"C'mon into my office," Carol said as she headed toward the kitchen. "The dining room table is my desk. Haven't been able to face Mike's office yet." She nodded toward the hallway where the door to Mike's domain was closed.

"That's understandable." Sallie followed her to where stacks of files occupied most of the table and two of the chairs.

"You've really gotten involved, haven't you?"

Carol nodded. "Keeps me busy. And, as you know, it's my livelihood. There's not much else if it goes under. Sit, I'll get some tea. Chamomile okay with you?"

Sallie nodded and sat, arranging her materials in front of her.

Carol returned with a tray. Placing it on the table, she handed Sallie a steaming cup of tea and a small plate with two dainty madeleines. "Made especially for you."

"You do know my propensity for sweets. You didn't have to, you know?"

"It's no trouble. Baking has always been a passion of mine." Carol pointed toward the tray. "There's sugar and lemon for the tea, if you want."

"Thank you." Sallie smiled. "You do know how to take care of others, don't you?"

Carol returned her smile and plopped down opposite Sallie, pushing aside a stack of papers to make space to review the new files. "I haven't worked so hard since I was just out of college."

"How is the office? And how are you really doing?"

"Well, there's just so much to do. I really rely on Eric and Gail. It's mostly them. This month looks good, though. We finally sold the Princeton house at almost full price. I was able to pay up the mortgage here, so the foreclosure is a thing of the past."

Sallie's eyes lit up. "That's great!"

"That was Eric. He loaned me his commission on one of his sales."

She shrugged and offered a rueful smile. "I'm not certain I have what it takes to do what they do."

"You'll get the hang of it. You're as smart as the next." Sallie patted her hand.

"I'll take your word for it, at this point. Now, it's your turn."

Sallie turned her attention to the papers in front of her. "I've hired Fred as my attorney, and we've gone over all the records. There are only six suspicious items." She gave Carol several stapled pages. "For your records. I've highlighted what's important. Three are when Stephanie was his assistant. Those don't have any bearing on me. It's the three from last year that are my responsibility."

Sallie sipped her tea and took a bite of a madeleine to give Carol time to review the information, then went on, "The main issue seems to be whether there were any damages to clients. As Mike paid the funds back within a few days on each item and nothing was held up, there's no need for restitution."

Carol breathed a sigh of relief. "It's just a matter of paperwork then."

"There's more. This one." Sallie handed her another paper. "This one is over $10,000, which automatically caused my license to be suspended pending a formal hearing."

Carol frowned. "Explain."

Sallies' voice was low, as if to soften the blow. "What Mike did was basically embezzlement. Whether he merely 'borrowed' the funds intending to return them is of no import. However, the return is a mitigating factor determining the broker's sentence."

"Then you should be able to get your license back."

Sallie shrugged. Not wanting to tell the whole story, she put a positive spin on the situation. "Fred thinks there's a good chance. However, there could be a suspension and fine. And it will still take some time to sort." Sallie stopped, giving Carol a chance to ask questions.

"What are you going to do in the meantime?" She gestured to the piles on the table. "I could really use your help right now."

Sallie reached across the table to touch Carol's hand, her voice quiet. "I understand, but I don't want to get you in trouble. We should just wait and see how this shakes out."

Carol sighed. "I understand. How are you dealing with everything?"

"I'm alright. I'll be going back home to Los Madre for a few days, maybe a week. Hopefully, it won't be any longer. I'll keep in touch."

Carol nodded. "I'm glad Fred is helping you. Going home? Is everything okay?"

"I think so. I just want to make certain my dad is alright. My brother says we need to make some decisions about the future."

"Well, don't stay away too long. I really want you back at work with me."

"Me too." Sallie rose from the table and gave Carol a hug of support. "More than I can say."

It took Sallie only a few days more to organize her life and pack up what she needed for a short visit. "I will be back," she told everyone. Gail agreed to take care of her house and garden. Jean said she would keep an eye on Gail so that everything was maintained in its pristine condition. They'd all had a good laugh. Just one last dinner with Anne and Joe and she would be off in the morning.

Before she left for Anne's, Sallie wandered through her home, touching the walls and looking at the changes she had made over the years. *My home has been such a sanctuary for me. I don't want to leave it for long.*

Rummaging through her photo drawer, Sallie retrieved more images from her past, ancestral records that had long escaped her memory. Now, sitting on the floor of her home looking through the pictures, she wondered about these people whose images peered out from a moment of time.

Many she did not know. She began to speculate about their lives, their joys and disappointments, paths taken and moments lost in their brief tenure on Earth. *All that I am is the result of the genetic path that came from my ancestors.*

She walked through her garden, taking in the scene to imprint it in her memory, continuing to venerate her past, and, at the same time, asking for guidance for the future. It was a ceremony of her life to date and all she had accomplished while living in Las Rosas. Her ritual complete, she left for Anne's house.

After a quiet dinner conversation spent recalling fun times together, Anne and Sallie began clearing the table and cleaning the kitchen. Only then did Anne broach the subject. "How do you feel about leaving your home and garden?"

"As you can guess, it tugs on my heart somewhat. You know how much I love my home."

"We will certainly miss you."

"And I will miss you, too. Your sound advice is always such a comfort." She hesitated. "Old memories from my childhood keep coming back to me. Perhaps there's unfinished business."

Anne's voice was soft as she reached over and touched Sallie's hand. "Just know that sometimes the way you see things isn't the same as how others do. Memory can deceive. Joe tells me I was wearing a pink dress when we met. Well, I know for certain that I do not do pink," Anne said emphatically and laughed. "It was green. Of course I remember. And then he showed me a photo. I'll be damned. Pink. Can you believe?"

Sallie smiled. "I'll keep that in mind. Thanks."

"I had a thought. How about calling me this Sunday night with an update?"

Sallie's eyes lit up. "Hey, that's a good idea. Hopefully, I'll only be gone for a short time."

"Well, let's reserve Sunday nights for however long you are gone."

"Sunday nights it is. An official girls' conversation night. And, a tie to home." Sallie's eyes became dreamy. "I'm already looking forward to it. You are a love." Sallie reached out and hugged her friend. They clung to each other, as if to imprint the warmth of their friendship for the lonelier days ahead.

"Are you ready to go?"

"Yup, car's all packed. I'll wave as I pass through downtown."

Sallie's smile was soft and her eyes tinged with love as she said goodnight to her good friend and headed home to sleep and dream of her trip south.

Sallie's Journal—June 7th

Recently I felt a resonance with words that set me in flight from my fears. The message penetrated my spirit with a desire to discover who I am at the depth of my soul.

I've been told over the years that I can be loud, emotional, awkward, overbearing, etc. It has taken some time to find my expression. My escape has been in reading and the written word, taking me places where no one can follow. When I return, it is always with new wisdom and new tools to expand my life. In high school, it was historical fiction—stories about real people from the past and the lives they lived inspired me.

There have been times in my life when I have been struck out of the blue by a sense of clarity about life, one that is beyond surface understanding. These power moments—my first day of college, my college graduation, starting work with Mike, buying my first house—times of achievement presaged the knowingness that I could be, do, and have all that I desire, and all it takes is dedication, perseverance, and time. These events helped me transcend my history and transported me to living dreams beyond who I think I am.

The loss of my work has left me angry, hurt, and sad. I was betrayed. As well, I've had to look at my responsibility. Yet beyond the disappointment, at the core of my soul, inside is a small stirring of exhilaration because a whole world may be opening for me. I realize again that I can do anything I want with the rest of my life.

I desire to discover my highest destiny and become it. I want to be more expansive and to live a larger dream than my everyday life today. I have made the decision to return home to reconnect with my family as the first step. I am anxious yet excited.

CHAPTER EIGHT

Eudarge: The Angel of Destiny

The theatre was small, built with seats for only two, yet the screen was large, larger than any Sallie had ever seen. It seemed to spread to the end of time with the backdrop unfolding beyond the far reaches of the universe. Music from an unseen organ swelled through the high-ceilinged room, its melodramatic tone an accompaniment to the silent movie she was watching.

Playing on the screen was the chronicle of her existence to date, and Sallie patiently watched images of her story projected through her eyes; all of the high and low drama, the best times and some incidents she would just as soon forget.

Seated next to her was Eudarge, the Angel of Destiny, whose love and acceptance pervaded her consciousness. *Why,* she mused, *he has no judgment of my soul, only love and compassion for me.*

His thoughts poured directly into her mind, soothing as a cup of chamomile tea. "Life is a choice," he said. "We, in the dimension of

Spirit, admire you for your decision to experience Earth and its lesson of duality." He waited as she continued to watch the scenes unfold on the screen.

Her voice had a faraway sound. "That's my life." She turned to look at him. "It's strange to see it on the screen as if I'm in a movie."

He nodded. "It can be surprising."

"Especially if I don't want to remember some of the things I've done."

"Ah," he said, "that's why we're here." He patted the leather-bound manuscript in his hands.

She peeked over his shoulder to get a better look at the tome. Her name was written on the cover in a beautiful script, illuminated with a pearlescent glow.

"I carry the Book of Destiny in which all is written for you and your world. You are at a crossroads, and thus, we are meeting to review where you've been and what you have chosen as your destiny."

Curious, Sallie touched the book, outlining the letters of her name.

Eudarge continued, "Every soul has a unique purpose for its life, and everyone on Earth at this time is part of a universal lesson in which all souls have agreed to participate. I'm here to help you remember the plan your soul put in motion prior to this incarnation."

He stopped and looked at her, anticipating her unasked questions. Her thoughts spiraled outward into space as she contemplated this task. *What is my purpose? Have I been fulfilling it? How does one know?* Eudarge was quiet.

She looked at him with a frown. "If I have a plan, why don't I just know it? Wouldn't it be easier? Then I could just get on with it."

"That would obviate your free will as Sallie," he said as he glanced at the screen, causing Sallie to look up. She watched as the scene shifted to the last time she had seen her family. She was sitting on the couch, with Mark leaning against the mantle and David in his chair.

Before she had the chance to tell them the details of her marriage, how her husband had changed over time, judging her behavior and belittling her in front of their friends, her father leaned toward her, his finger outstretched, admonishing her. He had told her that divorce was wrong and women were responsible for holding the family together. Then he had uttered the words, "You made your bed; now you have to sleep in it."

Those words had cut her to the core. Without responding, she'd turned away and walked out the front door, leaving her family for good. *He didn't even want to listen to my point of view.* Even her beloved younger brother wasn't able to comfort her, having absorbed the same old-fashioned values about women. She had returned to Northern California and had gone through the divorce by herself.

Sallie turned away from Eudarge. "I don't want to relive those awful memories. They're gone. They are what they are."

"Would you like to see if there's a chance for a different outcome?"

She turned back to him, pain and confusion clouding her expression. "How can there be another outcome? It's what happened."

"There are always choices. That is why you have free will."

She stared at the screen.

The scene rewound and her father once again said those fateful last words to her, yet this time she watched a different Sallie walk over toward her father and say, "Dad, I understand your point of view. Would you consider listening to mine?"

He nodded, and she sat down opposite him and explained that her husband was emotionally abusive to her and would not even consider going to therapy. Once her father understood her reasons, he told her he would support her in any way he could.

Watching the events unfold along a new path, Sallie began to weep. "You mean, all these years it could have been different?"

"You have another chance coming up," Eudarge said in a quiet voice. He soothed her restlessness by gently surrounding her with the white light of consciousness. "Sallie, you and everyone on Earth are charged to fulfill your destiny so that future generations can fulfill theirs."

Sallie looked down at her hands as her thoughts quickly spiraled with new questions. *Who decides my destiny? Why am I so small in this vast universe? What does it mean to have a free will?* Her thoughts tumbled out faster than he could answer.

Sallie looked back at him and focused on the one question that could answer all the others. "How do I fulfill my destiny?"

"A destiny may be very simple or very complex. It could be a job as a gardener or farm worker or dishwasher—acts of service well done means that others can do theirs. All work is equal, as each is necessary for all others to perform at their highest level."

"I've never thought of it like that. I always wondered why each of us has such a different experience. Life just seems unfair."

Eudarge went on. "No one who is president of a country, a leader of a major corporation, a writer, or any other job that appears to be important, can do their job unless the hidden jobs are done."

"Why would I choose one life over another?"

"The choice is always made based on what the soul wishes to experience."

"It's like an enormous game of chess then?"

He nodded. "Each of you on Earth takes on a piece of the collective lesson of the consciousness of all of you. For example, someone experiencing homelessness might take on that role so that all who encounter him or her can experience the totality of all there is in the practice of being human. It is the same with other differences that you see, including handicapped people, mental retardation, and all statuses, cultures, and races."

"It's not always easy looking at people who are marginalized."

"When you turn away from truly seeing another person, you turn away from the knowledge that allows you access to the totality of your soul."

"I've reached out to women who are homeless. Yet, when I give them information on organizations that can help them, they seem to ignore me and stay as they are. I don't understand why they wouldn't want a different life."

"Even as you look at them and think they are useless to this world and could contribute if they would only do something, they are necessary just as they are for your experience to be complete."

"So they chose that life to help me learn my lessons."

"There are many reasons for it, yet that is one of the effects," he said.

"Then I should be thankful to them that they're willing to contribute to our destiny."

"Earth has a destiny, just as humankind as a species has a mission that is a part of that destiny. No one is wasted. All are necessary for the great experiment to work."

Sallie thought about what he had said. "I want to believe you. It's just that my reality says differently."

"Above and beyond all that you think and believe about your life and the meanings you attach to events, there is a greater truth to your existence."

"Whenever I try to figure out the real truth of this world and who I am and why I have this body and this life, I get disoriented. The images seem to spiral out beyond my ability to imagine, leaving me confused, alone and uncertain. It's as if the answer to our purpose is beyond my imagination."

"Not beyond it. To achieve that understanding is to take baby steps. Each one leads to a new insight that leads to more insights."

"What a nice thought."

"One of the steps is to maintain a balance between the destiny you have chosen and your personal will. This will cause you to grow and to change your circumstances."

"What is that balance?" she asked.

"Everyone must do what they do believing that their job is the most important one on the planet, because it is."

Sallie sniffed. "Why, you make it sound like it is all predestined. You told me I had free will to do whatever I want."

"In one sense, you do. Your will is influenced by cultural factors. Some cultures place a higher value on destiny, or your soul's plan. Your culture places greater emphasis on will. It's called 'free will' as if there were something freeing about it."

"Well, it's better than thinking someone is pulling strings as if I were a puppet."

"Perhaps it would be more appropriate to call it personal will, as your will is individual to you in your world. It can be a blessing and a curse, creating chaos, yet also cutting a path through the harshness you sometimes make of your life."

"I am not certain I understand." Sallie's face wrinkled into a frown.

"Your destiny can override your will through passivity, and your will can override your soul's destiny through your attempts to control the events of your life. Remember earlier the choice with your father? You made the decision to walk out the door without responding to him. There are always other choices to make."

"I'd like to think the choice I made was right in that moment."

"Right presumes wrong. Life is not so black and white. Rather consider using the words 'appropriate' or 'inappropriate' to the moment in consideration of your destiny."

"So, it was inappropriate?"

"In a way, it was. You must remember that your words are like a sword that has two edges. One edge of the sword is your weapon of personal responsibility. The other side can be sharp and penetrating if used to dominate others to achieve personal desires. Walking out on your father was your effort to control him rather than let him have power over you."

Sallie took a deep breath and looked down, acknowledging her actions.

"When will is used for your personal desires, you may cut through a jungle of obstacles; however, you run the risk of damaging the lives of others. There is an honorable way to assert your will and there is a distortion."

Sallie glanced at the screen. "That's what I've done, isn't it? I've dominated others to my own aims." She hesitated, considering her life in a new light, then sighed. "That's not what I want to do."

Gently, Eudarge responded. "Sallie, you emphasized your will to maintain a false order in your life. You had the idea that it would erase your fears and keep you safe. Perhaps your destiny is greater than the life you have created by controlling your day-to-day activities and the other people in your life."

Sallie was silent for a minute, thinking over what Eudarge had said. "There is so much danger in the world. I've been disenchanted by certain things that have happened in my life, and it has caused me to pull back and create a structure to protect myself. It helps me maintain an order that keeps my life like I want it to be."

"That is just your fears encroaching upon your awareness of your choices. Fear arises out of a need to make sense of the world."

"The world is perilous. I just want to build a life around me to protect myself."

"Perhaps you have forgotten who you truly are. When you forget who you are, you disregard your plan. You are a soul having a physical experience. Your plan in this life might simply be making contact with your soul in your quiet time."

"You make it sound so easy to make that soul contact. Yet all I hear is my mind giving me its logical point of view."

"It is in quieting the mind that you will hear the message of the soul. What if there is no karma, no evil, and all is the Oneness, including you? What if you are not separated and what you are experiencing is a figment of your soul's imagination?"

"That is not what I've been taught to believe."

"Your world is an illusion generated by you so that you can have an experience. Those imaginings are a pale substitute for the true reality."

This was a startling revelation to Sallie. She paused to absorb his words. This idea went against all she had been taught to believe, yet in this space somehow she knew it to be true. "How could I open up to a greater truth?"

"Live your life looking for the Oneness within you and all others. All of you are sparks separated from the Oneness by a thought of what being apart might be like. The reality is that all is one."

"You mean, all of us on Earth are linked?"

"Yes, you are beginning to understand," responded Eudarge. "The world is in the developmental stage of a new paradigm that will make it easier to be in the flow and to follow the will of the One. The new model will appear as each individual discovers their own internal truths that resonate with the One."

"Sometimes I feel disconnected from others and the universe as if my struggles don't count for much."

"If everything is part of the whole, then are you not always following your will? When life flows and it is easy, then you feel safer, and when there is effort, you resist. Just look at the struggle as a way of learning."

"It sounds easy when you say it, yet I know the panic that arises when I am frightened."

"There are things you can do to allay that fear and to continue your walk upon the path of Light, while still remembering that all is always the One. You are always on purpose. It is just your reaction that is being tested and honed."

"What must I do?"

"Be alert to the environment around you. Send your love ahead of you to those whom you will meet upon your path."

"What does that look like in the real world?"

"Would you like to practice?" Eudarge asked.

Sallie nodded, eager for the training.

"Tell me about your day tomorrow."

"I'll be leaving my home of the last decade and driving back to the town where I spent most of my teenage years to reunite with my family."

"Now, think about the intentions you want to manifest."

"Well, I'd like a safe and easy journey while I drive." Sallie was quiet, thinking through the following day. "And then when I get to Los Madre, I'd like to drive through town and see all the places I remember."

"You've been gone a long time. Do you think it has changed much?"

"I don't know. Perhaps."

"Now, think about the people you will meet that are part of your destiny, some of whom you know and some of whom you are yet to meet."

"There's my father, and my brother and his family. I haven't seen my nephew since he was a toddler."

"What would you like to happen when you see them?"

"My dream is..." Sallie trailed off as old hurt feelings came up. "I'm so conflicted. I love them, yet feel judged by them."

"Then send your love in advance to them and to all those who you will see tomorrow, regardless of whether you know them or not. Let them know that you desire to be of service to them, not control them, as you know they will be of service to you."

Sallie's eyes widened with the new insight she was receiving. "That sounds so simple and so caring. How do I put it into practice?"

"Stay open to synchronicity and allow others to be who they are without personalizing their behavior. Those whom you meet also have lessons to learn and a destiny to fulfill—one they are unable to complete without you."

"I've never thought of it that way," Sallie said, realization dawning. "They need me as much as I need them."

"Exactly. Also, how they act says more about them than it does about you, so do not personalize their actions as them being in judgment of your life. Be selective and take on only that which is yours."

"How will I know the difference?"

"You will always feel a resonance to that which is yours if you are open to your feelings."

"Ah, those feelings again."

He smiled inside at Sallie's growing recognition of her feelings. "Your feelings are your soul speaking to you. As you move forward, you will be tested until you learn the lessons that are yours."

"Your message is so loving and kind."

"Would you like a glance at the plan you put into place before coming here?"

Sallie nodded eagerly as the screen lit up with the energy of the souls of Sallie, David, and Mark. The remembrance of their soul group and the decision they had made to work together as a family infused her, and she felt the love the three of them had for each other.

Eudarge gave her one final message. "You can do anything you believe you can do. As well, you must do that which fills your dreams so that your destiny is fulfilled and the planet is enriched. You can only will what you will."

With that, he gently withdrew, leaving Sallie fast asleep.

PART V
The Illusion of Duality

Lives of great men all remind us
We can make our lives sublime,
And, departing, leave behind us
Footprints on the sands of time;

Footprints, that perhaps another,
Sailing o'er life's solemn main,
A forlorn and shipwrecked brother,
Seeing, shall take heart again.

Let us, then, be up and doing,
With a heart for any fate;
Still achieving, still pursuing,
Learn to labor and to wait.

Henry Wadsworth Longfellow
A Psalm of Life

CHAPTER NINE

Return to Los Madre

The crack of the bat and the cacophony of boys' voices drifted through the open window of her car as Sallie slowly passed the Little League field in Los Madre. Pulling to a stop next to the park, she listened to the familiar sounds of a game in progress. Parents cheered their support and coaches yelled commands as the boys played ball and shrieked their own form of banter.

From the street, she could see through the fence to the field. There were upgrades, she noted, from when she had last watched a game here. A new backstop, improved aluminum stands, and some additional sponsor logos graced the wall in left field. Some of the old teams were still there as well. The Benny's Bruins had clearly continued their long-standing rivalry with the Police Panthers, her brother's team, which he now coached.

Pangs of nostalgia flooded her body, reminding her of the heady highs and gut-twisting angst of her life there as a teenager. Yet, no matter what turmoil was going on in her life, she had never missed one of her brother's games. Her eyes wandered to the stands and for a moment she considered taking a seat amongst the cheering crowd. *Perhaps later. For now, I need to find a place to stay.*

She had not been specific with her family about when she would arrive. Slipping into town unannounced gave her some much needed time to get reacquainted with her childhood haunts before facing the daunting task ahead.

Turning onto the main road leading to the center of town, she passed her old high school. Though freshened up with a new paint job and modernized computerized sign with rolling messages spelling out upcoming events, she was glad to see the old majestic trees remained, giving stateliness to the post World War II buildings. There was the football field, with its memories of her first kiss. *I wonder what ever happened to Hank. He was so good to me.*

Continuing on, Sallie felt a lump in her throat as she saw the familiar town hall rise up at the end of the road. Centered in a large green park reminiscent of its Colonial Mexican heritage, the town square still retained its original charm with hundred-year-old restored adobe buildings across the surrounding streets, now jammed with restaurants, wine tasting rooms, and retail shops. Sallie noted the old standards still in business: the hardware store, still owned by the Carlstrom family; the local diner in the same building but sporting a new name, "Ida's Eatery;" and the small town newspaper building, looking exactly the same as in her youth. Most of the antique stores were gone, yet Antique Heaven still stood across the corner of the square with the same weathered façade she remembered.

Yet the town was not untouched by the vagaries of progress. Trendy new coffee houses, restaurants, and clothing shops peppered the block, along with a paper store and an upscale kitchen and china retailer. The old theatre, which had been her Saturday retreat, was now reborn as a dinner playhouse. The town looked the same, yet different. She liked the blending of colors on the well-maintained buildings. The trees in the park, now larger, gave continuity and a settled air of prosperity.

Sallie parked the car and approached the old building that had housed the local newspaper for more than forty years. She recalled when she'd first met the publisher, Frank, as a teenager. Her high school English teacher had told her of his interest in running a column of high school events, and she had been thrilled yet nervous at their first meeting.

As she walked toward the building, she began to reminisce. *He gave me my first real job and it was something I loved and did well. I guess I've forgotten that. He taught me so much about writing for a newspaper.*

Entering the building, she took a deep breath, smiling at the familiar tinge to the air. *The smell of a newspaper office never changes.* At the front counter was a young woman barely out of high school. Sallie smiled and asked if Frank still ran the paper. The woman gave an inquisitive look until Sallie added, "I'm an old friend."

"He's out back," she said. "I'll go get him."

As she waited, Sallie turned and surveyed the lobby, still with its mid-century modern style furniture. She absently picked up a copy of *Los Madre Living* and began to flip through the pages, quickly glancing at the titles of the articles.

Looks as if the town has retained its character, even as new businesses have opened. She turned the magazine over to the back cover to see a meandering circle of rocks with a path moving toward its center.

Before she had a chance to read the advertisement, a voice barked behind her. "Well, as I live and breathe, if it isn't Sallie Whitaker."

Turning, she was welcomed by a slender, slightly stooped older man who still had the commanding voice of his youth. He was fast on his feet, and before she could reply, Frank had embraced her. "It's been a long time." Frank stepped back, looking her over. "You certainly look good. Where've you been all these years?"

Sallie was speechless, not knowing where to start. "I went to college up north and just stayed on," she finally managed to say.

"Well, it's good to have you back. We could use a good cub reporter right now." His tone was jovial and she smiled at the teasing, as if they had picked up right where they had left off so many years ago.

Holding up the magazine, Sallie regained her composure. "I noticed you have a new publication. Very impressive."

He nodded. "That's my son's idea. I wasn't ready to retire and he wanted to join the business. Had to keep him out of my hair." His tone registered pride in having his son as a partner. "It's had a good reception."

"I like it so much I want to subscribe."

"I'll tell Kent. He'll be pleased," said Frank. "How about a tour?" He swept his hand toward the back of the building. "Things have changed a lot since you were here. We've become quite computerized."

Walking through the building, they shared memories of the past and reflected upon the changes that had happened to the world and to the newspaper business since they had last spoken. She told him of her real estate background and he told her of their need for experienced writers for the fledgling magazine, hinting that her writing experience could be useful.

As they walked, Sallie smiled, recalling happy moments from the past. "There's something I've always wondered," Sallie said, a hesitation to her voice. "I thought perhaps you might know the answer."

Frank raised an eyebrow. "Well, spit it out." He chuckled.

"I've always wondered about the town name, you know, 'Los Madre.' From my high school Spanish, I remember that 'los' is a masculine plural article and it's paired with 'madre,' which means mother." Sallie looked at him with a serious expression. "It's just jarring. Do you know how the town got its name?"

Frank put his hand to his chin and knit his brow. "Never thought about it before. That was way before my time." He winked at her. "Perhaps you should look into it—might be a bit of hidden history you could explore in an article. Speaking of which, how about a sample column? We could use something creative in the real estate section and your expertise would be valuable. I can talk to Kent."

Sallie smiled demurely and offered a noncommittal shrug. "Let me get settled in and I'll see what I can do."

After a bit more chit chat, she left with the magazine and a copy of the paper. She sat in her car and looked through the classifieds until a small ad for a cottage caught her eye. As she drew up to the curb in front of the main house, she could see the cottage down the driveway. *Looks like it might be perfect.*

Several hours later, after talking at length with Candace, the woman who owned the property and lived in the main house, Sallie was ensconced in the studio apartment. Repurposed from a garage, it had good light from large windows, simple elegant furnishings, a small functional kitchen area, and a bathroom.

As she put away her belongings, a feeling of happiness permeated her body, like a bud beginning to flower. *I can get what I want,* she thought, hoping she could also do the same with her family. *I'll just take a couple of days to get organized, then go see my father. Yet, why procrastinate?* It was as if she were two people having a conversation. *I just need to get my feet on the ground.*

She went back and forth in a senseless conversation until she picked up her cell phone and dialed her brother. There was no point in delaying it; the time had come to announce her arrival in town.

Sallie stopped her car a house-length away from her father's home and peered out the window, observing it anew. Something looked out of place. Gone was the meticulous symmetry that had reflected her father's high expectations for the maintenance of his domain. The grass was a little longer, shrubs needed pruning, and the colorful bedding plants were missing. No longer did it have the pristine appearance she remembered.

Her eyes followed the straight, narrow walkway that bisected the yard and led up to the generous covered porch across the frontage of the house. Suddenly she recognized the source of the imbalance: only half the lawn was covered in the spray of iridescent purple flowers from the jacaranda tree. The other tree was missing, giving the house a lopsided appearance with the sun shining harshly on the grass.

Sallie parked her car and gave herself one last quick look in the rearview mirror, willing herself to project an air of confidence that belied the twist of the butterflies in her belly. Spurring herself forward, she slammed the car door behind her, straightened her blouse, and marched up the walkway. As the house loomed, she wondered how so few steps could cover such a long distance.

Before she could reach the porch, the front door sprang open, and her family hurried out to welcome her, all clamoring to say hello. Her father, David, leaned on his cane as he reached a trembling hand toward her. Mark gave her an awkward hug, and Nancy started gushing about how excited they were to see her. Even her nephew, Brian, smiled and reached out to touch her arm. "Come in, come in!" Nancy insisted, and they all started talking at once.

"Did you have a good trip?"

"Where are you staying?"

"We're so glad you're finally here."

"Will you come to one of my games?"

As they walked inside, Sallie answered one question after another, the bustle of conversation overcoming her anxiety.

The house and its furnishings looked as if it existed in a time warp. Built in the 1920s, it was a pre-milled, middle-class interpretation of the Arts and Crafts movement, one of the first tract housing projects in Southern California. Inside, the furniture was the same as she remembered and arranged in the same manner. The only semblance of change was the magazines and newspapers strewn around the room.

"Wow! Everything looks the same. You haven't changed a thing!" she exclaimed, relaxing into the home's well-worn atmosphere.

She walked to the fireplace. "Here's that old ceramic trivet I made when I was eight! And Mark's Little League trophy for Most Valuable Player." She lovingly touched each item on the mantle, overwhelmed with nostalgia for the happy moments they had once shared.

She turned as her father cautiously worked his way over to his favorite chair, supported by Mark on one side and his cane in the other hand. His transformation was shocking. He still had dignity in his measured movements, yet the intensity of his former personage was stilled. *My father is not the man he was.*

Her childhood image of him was shattered by the sight of this elderly, slightly stooped man moving hesitantly across the room. He was thinner and shorter than she recalled, and his skin was draped over his frame like a velour throw over a sofa. He sat down, glancing up at her with a welcoming smile. Smiling back, she looked at his face, and in those eyes she recognized her father. *There is the man I knew.*

Turning her attention to her brother, Sallie took a step back to see more of him. *Why, he is the image of my father.* Not in his appearance, though. Mark was taller than their father, with the same brown hair starting to recede, and a muscular frame just beginning to expand. He resembled their father in the way he carried himself, the direct gaze he gave her. Sallie felt her old sense of intimidation, as if Mark had taken her father's place in the hierarchy of domination, that unspoken entitlement only a generation of men can unconsciously pass to the next.

Sallie replaced the trophy on the mantle. She heard her brother's voice without hearing the words and she had to focus to call her thoughts back to the present. His voice was soft spoken, as if on purpose, forcing all conversation to halt so that he could be heard.

"Say again?" Sallie said, turning back.

"Oh, it's just Dad. He doesn't want us to change anything. He likes things the way they are."

She glanced at her father and gave him an appreciative smile. "Good to know some things stay the same."

"Come in, sit down," said Nancy. "Let me get drinks for everyone." She turned to Sallie. "What would you like?"

"Whatever you're having."

"Does red wine work for you?" Sallie nodded, and Nancy turned and headed toward the kitchen, her heavy steps making the floorboards squeak. "I'll be right back."

Brian, on the edge of puberty, reminded Sallie of her brother at that same age. She watched as he stood awkwardly on the edge of the sitting area, waiting to get his father's attention. "May I please be excused, sir?" Mark nodded and Brian left the room.

"Sit down," said Mark. "Make yourself at home. Where did you say you were staying?"

"I found a small cottage behind a house over on Springer Drive. It's on the 500 block."

"Oh, that's really close," said Mark, looking from their father to Sallie.

"You could've stayed here," David said, barely audible.

Sallie ignored the plaintive note in his voice. "Oh, Dad, I just didn't want to disturb you." She backpedalled. "I wouldn't want to impose."

David shook his head. "It wouldn't be an imposition."

Nancy returned to the room with a tray of drinks. "Dinner's almost ready. I'll call as soon as it's on the table." She turned to Sallie. "I always give a little warning. I like to serve when the food is hot."

The room was quiet with Nancy gone, and Sallie looked down at the coffee table covered with everyday items from her father's life. A week's worth of newspapers were piled on one end, with a stack of news magazines on the other. In between, there was a laminated folder with a picture of a squat modern stucco building in front of a perfectly manicured yard. The words "Shady Acres Retirement Home" were printed across the top in elegant script. Sallie reached to pick it up and then pulled back, glancing first at her father and then her brother.

David glared reproachfully at Mark, then turned to Sallie. "It's his idea," he said, with a nod toward his son. Sallie frowned, feeling like she had entered in the middle of a conversation.

"He might've spared me from the end of the road," said David.

Sallie frowned. "What do you mean?"

"He means the retirement home," said Mark. "He calls it 'the end of the road.'"

"I'm not ready for that. I do just fine here." David's voice raised a notch.

Mark started to placate him when they heard a cheerful voice ring out from the kitchen. "Dinner's ready!"

Mark gave Sallie a look. "We'll continue this later."

The rectangular table was set formally. Nancy carried steaming bowls laden with traditional, down-home comfort food to the table as they filed into the room. She placed a large bowl of mashed potatoes on a trivet as she pointed to a seat across the table. "Sallie, you sit here." Mark helped their father to his place at the head of the table and took his place at the opposite end. Nancy and Brian faced Sallie.

As they all sat down, Mark reached a hand out to Sallie at the same time David offered his. She gave her father a heartfelt smile as she took his hand, and they all bowed their heads while Mark said a blessing.

Nancy's voice was first to end the silence. "Mark, would you please slice the roast? Sallie, start those potatoes around. Brian, serve yourself some salad." Brian made a face as his mother continued, "Yes, young man, you must have some salad."

They ate in silence for a while and Sallie wondered whether it was because of her presence. Between bites, Mark turned to Brian. "Have you been working on your fundamentals? Do we need some extra practice?"

Brian said, "Yes, sir. Every day. And, no, sir. I think I'm doing okay."

"The game's coming up with Benny's Bruins. They're one of the best."

"Yes, sir."

Again, a quiet descended, pierced only by the sound of cutlery scraping plates. David and Mark both started talking at the same time.

"What about your work?" Mark asked.

"How long will you be here?" David queried.

Sallie looked at Mark. "My work's okay right now. Not much is going on. I'm on sort of a hiatus." She didn't want to outright deceive them, but she wasn't ready to share the whole story. She turned to her father. "Just as long as I'm needed."

David put a hand out and patted her arm. "Well, honey, it's good to have you home. I'd like it if you stayed permanently."

She looked at her father, holding her body tight with her smile still on her face, masking the panic coursing through her at the implication of his words.

The meal continued in awkward silence until Brian looked at his father. "May I be excused, sir?"

Mark inspected his clean plate and nodded his approval. The sign that dinner was over, Nancy stood up and said, "Why don't you men watch the game while Sallie and I clean up? I'll serve dessert in there."

"Just in time. The game's about ready to start," David said, a pleased tone to his voice.

Nancy stacked the dinner plates and left, leaving Sallie alone in the dining room. She glanced toward the living room and picked up a couple of serving bowls, following Nancy into the kitchen.

"Where would you like me to put these?" Nancy was bustling around the kitchen as if it were her own. Sallie stood awkwardly at the door. This wasn't how she remembered it.

Nancy glanced at the dishes in her hand and pointed toward a counter. "Put the food there, next to the refrigerator. If you want, you can get some plastic containers out of that cabinet to put away the leftovers." Sallie did as instructed and they silently finished clearing the table.

Nancy began hand washing the dishes. Sallie pulled a dishtowel out of their same old drawer and accepted the dishes Nancy handed off to her. "Dad still doesn't have a dishwasher?"

"No, he says he likes things the way they were when the family was together."

Sallie quietly dried the dishes as she contemplated this insight about her father.

Nancy chatted lightly to fill the silence. "Brian is really doing well with his game. Each year he seems to improve. I think Mark's year-round coaching is seeing results. We're hoping for a baseball scholarship for him for college." She stopped for a minute, realizing she was rambling, then changed the subject. "How are you getting settled in town? It's been a while since you've been here. Ten, eleven years, if I remember correctly."

"Almost ten. And much of it looks the same."

"Yes, it's one of the things I like about our town. It stays the same, at least in the important ways." They continued to work in an amicable silence until Sallie confronted the elephant in the room.

"What's with Dad?"

Nancy responded, "Oh, he's getting forgetful. And the house is a lot for him to keep up alone. Mark just thought it would be easier for him and he'd have more of a social life at Shady Acres. It's a great place with nice rooms, good food, social events, that kind of thing."

"He doesn't seem to want to go."

"Mark thinks he'll like it once he's there. So much for him to do. Not like here with so little companionship. I try to come over a couple of days a week, cook for him most nights."

137

"Why not let him stay, if he's happy here?"

Nancy unconsciously pulled back. "Oh, it's Mark's decision. I wouldn't interfere."

Sallie frowned, but let the topic drop for the time being. They reminisced about their teenage years when Nancy first met Mark while in high school. Even though they had been four years behind Sallie in school, their memories of teachers and events were fairly consistent.

Nancy was boisterous, her stories filling the kitchen and making Sallie want to shrink from her or ask her to talk more quietly, yet her easy laugh was infectious and drew Sallie closer to her. She recognized a woman at ease with herself; Nancy knew and accepted her place in the world. *I wonder what that's like.*

After they finished cleaning the kitchen, Sallie walked through the house to her old bedroom. She was surprised to find that many of her childhood things were still there—pictures of her growing up, her red portable typewriter, and her last doll, a plastic Terri Lee still in its original prom dress. Her old yearbooks and a complete Nancy Drew series lined the built-in bookcase.

The small den, which had been her brother's bedroom, was the only room that had changed, now with a 1940s oak roll top desk, a matching file cabinet, and bookcase. The desk had several piles of papers and an older issue of *Los Madre Living*. She flipped the magazine over to the back cover and was greeted by the image of the twisting path she had seen earlier. *What's this? A labyrinth! I didn't know we had one of those around here. I should go check it out.*

On the bookcase, there were some old pictures in frames—one of her and her mother laughing and another of the four of them before her mother got sick. Next to them was a baseball signed by the Dodgers World Series team. She picked it up as a distant memory tugged at her consciousness with an ache long denied. *Don't think of it. It didn't mean that much.* She put the baseball down and turned to leave. *I'll go check on the game.*

Later, after she had said goodbye to David and Nancy, Mark walked her out to the car.

"I've decided what we need to do about Dad," he said.

Sallie stiffened. "I thought you wanted my advice."

"I'm asking for your support."

"Look, I just got here. I'd like to do my own research."

"I've looked at it from all possible angles. You're not going to learn anything new." He pulled the brochure out from under his arm. "This is the best solution." He shoved it toward her.

Sallie looked at him for a long moment, then accepted the brochure. "I'll read it," she agreed, though her tone made it clear that she would make her own decision. "I've enjoyed this evening. Let's continue this conversation later."

He nodded. "I think you'll come to the same conclusion when you know all the facts."

As she got in her car and drove home, Sallie's mind whirled. *Here we go again. As if I didn't have enough on my plate. Just like with Mike. He always said he wanted us to be scrupulous in our work. That's the word he used. All the time. Scrupulous. Also known as meticulous, careful, thorough, honorable. All the things he wasn't. But he was! He was! And so am I! And now my brother wants me to just accept his decision. He knows best and I'm supposed to just follow along and trust him. Never question, never check. Not fair. It's just not fair.*

Parking in front of her cottage, Sallie slammed the car door a little harder than she intended. Casting a guilty glance toward her landlord's darkened windows, she walked to her cottage, quietly let herself in and leaned back against the door. *How can I challenge my brother if I never challenged Mike? Who am I? What am I doing here?*

Has it really only been a week? As Sallie settled into the corner of the couch and picked up the phone for her first weekly phone session, she reflected on the great shift in her life in such a short time. She felt as if she were in a completely different world than the one she had left behind just days before, for better or for worse. Hearing Anne's familiar lilt on the other end of the line, a flood of love enveloped her and she relaxed with a renewed belief in herself and her decisions.

"Hey, Anne, it's Sunday." Sallie's voice was light and vibrant.

"Oh, Sallie, I've been waiting for your call. How's it been?" replied Anne.

"Well, quite a week, I'd say," Sallie said with a slight chuckle. "Seems more like a month."

"I want to hear everything, starting from the beginning."

Sallie recounted her trip, her first view of her hometown, and the visit with Frank.

"Did you find a cute place?"

"Well, driving down, I was daydreaming about finding a little house similar in style to what I like, perhaps with a nice little garden. Would you believe, I found a charming furnished bungalow adjacent to a craftsman house, a few blocks from my father?" Sallie gushed. "It's absolutely perfect and the woman, Candace, who owns and lives on the property loves to garden too."

"I had a feeling you would find the perfect place," responded Anne warmly. "What else?"

"Then I called my father and was invited to dinner, and it was so… different, yet the same."

"Oh, come on now, Sal. This is me you're talking to. What about your brother?"

"He's just like my father," Sallie admitted. "He talked as if I have no say and he's already made the decision to put Dad in a retirement home."

"That sounds a little narrow. Didn't he want to hear your opinions?"

"Not exactly. I think he's made up his mind, and I need to fit into his scheme of things."

"Oh, Sal, I'm sure there must be more. Give it time. Remember the talks we had about always being in the right place at the right time?"

"Yeah, right. I'm exactly where I should be," Sallie said with a sarcastic edge.

"Everything is always perfect and appropriate just the way it is. Just keep an open mind."

Sallie hesitated a moment, wondering if what was on her mind was too silly to discuss. Yet, Anne was never one to mock unusual ideas. Trusting her instincts, she blurted out, "Anne, do you think we have a guardian angel?"

"Of course I do."

"How do you know?"

"Sometimes I feel as if I am guided to do something and I don't know why."

"What happens if you don't do what you're guided to do?"

"I guess I've learned over the years that things just work out better when I do. Why do you ask?"

"Oh, it's as if I travel a long way in my dreams and there's something I need to remember when I wake up."

"What I do in the morning when I start to regain consciousness is to spend some time just listening to my feelings and seeing if I can resurrect the message behind my dreams. I try to focus on the meaning, not necessarily the literal things that happened in the dream."

"I'll try that."

As they continued their conversation, Anne brought her up to date on the happenings at home, and they chatted until Sallie began to know she had made the right decision. Hanging up, she sighed and settled into bed, appreciating the warmth of her cottage.

I always felt I had to be the perfect daughter. Yet, what does "perfect" mean? And how could I determine I had succeeded? My father's feedback was inconsistent. Looking to the outside world to define my behavior yielded imperfect results. Yet, here I am at this time in my life, still uncertain as to who I am.

I worked to mold myself to the concept I had of what a woman should do. I became an acceptable cook as a teenager, and then later, an excellent one. I kept a neat house, beginning when my mother got sick when I was only ten. Even when conforming to what I considered my father's values, I lacked a sense of my place in the world separate from his perception.

Yet, for all the praise I saw him give my brother, my efforts went unacknowledged. My conformity to his expectations was presumed, and praise was not deemed necessary. The rule of the times that children, especially girls, should be seen and not heard translated to my life as an adult as a constant worry about my effect on others.

I accommodated by getting along. Being reliable and faithful. Looking to do the right thing. Always watching that I did not step on a crack. I observed the signs so that I blended into my environment. Always chafing against these restrictions at home, I looked to shine in my exterior world.

Taking my perfectionist tendencies to school, I excelled as a way to get attention and prove my worth. My high school years, spent conflicted between the demands of home and school, left me constricted.

I learned my part thoroughly. I came on stage in response to my cues and my lines were correct in every detail. Still, I did not hear the applause of recognition from my father. I was the odd "person" out, the third note, which is one of the intervals of music that is called "imperfect." Reaching the highest degree of proficiency only registered in the outside world, not at home. Not where it mattered.

Sallie stopped and put her pencil to her mouth. *Oh, whatever. Who really cares what I think?* She threw the book on the floor, turned out the light, and tossed with restless abandon to find a comfortable position until sleep took her.

CHAPTER TEN

Archangel Sandalphon: The Angel of Harmony

Sallie stood in front of an old-fashioned theatre with lavishly decorated turquoise columns that looked as if it had been designed during the Belle Époque era. At the top of the pillars, multiple curving copper arms extended upward to a marquee that read: "Merlin the Magician! One Day Only!"

Curious, she entered a walkway and strode through wide double doors that opened automatically for her. Inside was a spacious lobby with another sign of a finger pointing toward an opening.

Inside was a large auditorium that could hold five hundred people or more. Its sloping aisle ended at a large stage that appeared to be hundreds of years old, with a bowed front and wooden slats. The folds of the dark green velvet curtain looked like tall trees in an enchanted forest, promising wonder in the space beyond.

When the curtains opened, the wooden slats of the stage stretched endlessly back into the shadows. Sallie got the impression she could start walking from the front and never reach the back.

Almost supernatural in its façade, the wings of the stage exuded dark clouds that billowed ominously on the periphery of her vision. She walked slowly down the aisle of the silent cavern, hearing only the soft squish of her steps on the plush carpet. Glancing first at her ticket, she looked for the row number that would lead to her seat.

An usher strolled toward her in slow motion, flashlight in hand. He looked like a puppet with limbs moving in an exaggerated syncopation. A measured voice to match the mood, his fingers pointed toward center stage. "Here is your seat, front row center; come, enjoy the show."

Instantly, she was sitting in her seat, watching as a flamboyant magician stepped to the front of the stage and gazed directly into her eyes. With a swish of his cape and a bow toward her, his deep voice intoned, "Welcome. I am Merlin the Magician."

Sallie glanced around the theatre. She was the only person in the audience. *I'm in a dream, yet this is as real as my everyday life. I'm awake and dreaming at the same time.* Before she had time to think further, the show began.

"For my first trick today, I will show you the Magic Chopper."

He turned to the gold-painted wooden box situated on the table in front of him. Taking a carrot from his vest pocket, he put it through a round hole in the guillotine-like container and slammed down the handle with a loud bang. Sallie's eyes widened as half the carrot bounced off the stage and landed at her feet.

"Now," the magician spoke slowly in an inflated voice, "I need a volunteer from the audience."

He looked directly at Sallie, and instantly she was standing by his side on the stage. The magician moved toward her, taking her hands in his.

"Put your hands through here," he instructed her, pointing toward the round openings on the box. "There's nothing to worry about," he clucked as she shrank back from the apparatus, pulling away from him and winding her wrists behind her back.

Despite her resistance, she suddenly found her hands magically ensconced in the two holes in the wooden box. She struggled to pull them free to no avail. As the magician began his movement to push down the lever, Sallie screamed and found herself back in her seat. She gasped as the stage and the walls fell away and in their wake stood the tallest angel imaginable, his aura stretching several stories into the air. Sweeping her gaze back toward the box on stage, Sallie saw herself place her wrists in the same opening and the blade pass through them without harm.

"It is an illusion," the Archangel Sandalphon's voice soothed her fears, "as is everything you see in your world. Come and let me take you on a tour of your universe."

Suddenly she was aloft, soaring through space at the speed of light. As they flew, Sallie's body fell away and her soul began to align with the expanding universe, until she was here, then there, and then everywhere at once.

She became all the bodies of all the souls that ever existed, and then of all the plants, animals, rocks, mountains, and even the alive and breathing Earth itself, and then she was all of the stars and planets, and all of the primordial explosions of stars forming and disintegrating.

As they passed, the sky was ablaze with the fiery colors of red ochre, brilliant orange, cadmium yellow, and iridescent blue, all blended in swirls like a Van Gogh painting. The cosmos grew beyond the scope of her imaginings as she began expanding in concert with the universe, stretching into the darkness and spreading light as she went.

Sandalphon's voice infused her as he spoke. "You are looking at the ancient sky of the past. At the outer reaches of its borders, the universe is expanding into the future at a massive rate. In the night sky, you can see the past, present, and future fused together in one. This is the real world in which there is no time and no separation."

Sallie allowed the experience to permeate her being, feeling a sense of peace and unity as her consciousness merged with the cosmos. "This feels amazing," she said, a laugh rising from deep within her. "I'm everywhere and a part of everything, all at the same time."

"You are experiencing your true unlimited nature. Similar to the ocean, you are everywhere—boundless and eternal."

"I want to feel like this every day," she said, giddy from the sensation.

"Your evolution toward this point has taken place over many ages, yet the final merger can happen in an instant of your time when you create a link of consciousness to us in the spirit world, something you have started to do."

"You're saying that this feeling is my true nature and everything in my everyday world doesn't matter?"

"Exactly."

"Then, what is the purpose of having a life anyway?"

"At one time you were in perfect harmony with Spirit. The word, atonement, at-one-ment, recalls the original unity you had with the All. Then, you had the thought of what it might be like to live outside of that harmony. In that instant, the dualistic universe in which you live was created."

Sallie stared at the wondrous sights around her. "It seems so different from my everyday world," she said wistfully. She closed her eyes, attempting to capture the ecstatic unified feeling and imprint it upon every cell of her being.

"You hold yourself back from this experience with your belief that everything happening to you in life matters and that everything and everyone is separate."

"It does to me in the moment."

"You create the world in which you live out of your thoughts and intentions. You believe you are a certain person because you know yourself in reference to others around you. You have created a story about yourself and then believed it."

"If I'm not who I think I am, then how do I find out who I really am?"

"Search for the cosmic harmony in life. The order that came from chaos in the beginning arose through sound before it congealed into matter. Harmony is a systematic and pleasing joining of opposites. It can be seen through music, architecture, or the design of a garden. You can also apply it to your everyday life through seeking harmonious relationships."

"Wouldn't that mean having to give up who I truly am to please others?" Sallie questioned him closely. "I don't know how I could get along with everyone all the time."

"The concept of order maintains your individuality yet also allows others to preserve theirs. You each have your own point of view so that you can follow your own purpose."

"Well, how does this cosmic harmony work? When I'm in my garden, I'm in complete control of what to put where."

"Let's step back a minute to consider your question. Life is made up of opposites. You live in a dualistic world. In the beginning was chaos. Emerging from that was its mirror image, order. Where before you had known only love, you now began the descent into its opposite: fear. This was the beginning of the lesson of duality in your world."

"You're saying the lesson then must come through conflict," Sallie said, wanting to understand. "And harmony comes from resolving those conflicts."

"You have made the descent. You have experienced duality and are now on the path to unity. The act of atonement is the act of reconciliation, all souls with each other, and all with Spirit."

"Yet, in my everyday life, it's like looking into a cloudy nighttime sky. I can't see the stars anymore."

"Look within. You are the universe. Everything you observe is located directly within you. As above, so below."

"What exactly does that mean?" Sallie asked.

"Everything has its birth from the One. The universe is a living system; an inter-connectivity of all sentient beings that looks like a great thought, not a machine. Within your deeper self is everything that is also in the entire cosmos. Your soul's original intent was to form a dualistic world to let you experience opposites."

"If below reflects above, why isn't my world below like this wondrous one above that you've shown me?"

"In a dualistic world, you cannot know the good unless you see its opposite, error, like seeing a reflection in a mirror. Just as the dark is the absence of light, so error is the absence of grace. Error uncorrected becomes evil. In a world of opposites, it is a reflection so you can create a model for your life."

Sallie was quiet for a moment, piecing together what she had just learned. "If I created my world, then why isn't it the way I want it to be?"

"Duality is based on limitations. One of the limitations is seeing what is real. Remember the magic act and your fear at having your hands chopped off?"

She nodded.

"In the magic act, there are two worlds—the materialistic world that runs on the idea that actions have consequences, and the magical world of illusion. The magician does something in the material world, like appearing to cut off your hands, and you believe it. Yet, without you seeing the transition, he opens the magical world and your hands are still part of you."

"It seemed so real."

"Just as your world seems real. Yet behind the visible world there is an invisible one, a world that is temporarily concealed from your senses. By connecting to your soul and the capacities lying dormant within you, you can enter this hidden world."

"How do I do that?"

"By looking within, you can find all the secrets behind what is seen without. For example, look at your relationship in the past with your father, and now with your brother. Even though you are no longer under either one's control, you remain controlled by their ideas of who you are."

"My father wanted me to be just like him. I'm not, and I want to be acknowledged as a separate person," Sallie argued fiercely.

Sandalphon's answer was tinged with irony. "Are you so sure? Sometimes conflict arises because you are so alike. It's the part of you that you do not like reflected back. It must be honored and accepted so you can be all of who you truly are."

"I'm not like him," Sallie spat. "He was dictatorial and wanted to control me. Now my brother is doing the same thing."

"Remember what I said earlier about the people that show up in your life being a mirror to your lessons? What if that's their mission?" responded Sandalphon. "Notice repeated issues arising with more than one person. These are signs you must heed."

"They don't see me—who I really am," argued Sallie. As his words sunk in, she asked, "What do you mean their mission and issues that show up several times?"

Sandalphon's answer resonated. "It's important to pay attention to issues that repeat themselves in your life. Like I said, what if that's their purpose? You have taken on that same characteristic of control to make sense of your life. Perhaps, you are more upset with your own control issues than with your father and brother."

Sallie was taken aback. "What do you mean?"

"Let's go back again to the magic act in which you feared your hands would be cut off. The loss of your hands represents the loss of your capacity for feeling, with the concurrent loneliness and suffering it brings to your life. Feelings allow us to create real values for ourselves. A woman with no hands cannot do anything for herself and thus does not live out the feminine purpose. This symbol is seen in a culture that has so many material goods that the true meaning of life has been lost."

Sallie nodded meekly.

"Perhaps you are confusing control with order," Sandalphon went on. "It isn't control you want, it's connectedness. You do not exist independently of your personal relationships with others, and duality is the medium through which you perceive them."

"Are you saying I have to take the good and the bad in everyone?"

"Relationships are absolutely necessary for your lesson of duality to be complete. When you are in conflict with another, if your dominance arises out of your own weakness, there will be a power struggle. If your power arises out of strength, then a solution will evolve from your true response. Being yourself and respecting the other will bring empowerment."

"How will I know what to do when I get in a situation that upsets me?"

"Your goal is to live in harmony with all creation. However, your mind is limited by seeing opposites and conflicts. Open up and listen to your heart. It contains the answers your mind cannot discern."

"How can I do that? It all sounds so impossible."

"To find your way out of your internal turmoil and to change yourself, you must change your point of view. Live with your father in the tension that does not allow either of you to dominate the other. That tension arises when you have a physical response to what happens in the interactions with your father and brother. Note that physicality and respond to it, not to the words that someone else is saying. Look at the feelings that arise from the love that is in your heart for these people.

"You make up the world to ease your fears. You can make it up any way you want. That for which you wish in the secret reaches of your heart is part of your life plan and must be pursued, as those desires are linked to your destiny.

"There is a progression to your thoughts and feelings that can eventually move you toward wisdom and a reunification with the spirit world. First, you must leave the past behind. You have taken the first step by going back to Los Madre. Now, you must also do the same in your emotional body. It will seem like a new world, as though you are adrift on the ocean. You are beginning to experience this. Next, some sort of trouble usually arises; a storm at sea. Once you have gained some clarity, you will begin to rise toward the light. This is your journey. Relish it and live fully in its manifestation.

"Listen to the call of your heart and follow its wisdom. Know that I am a part of you and also reside in your heart, waiting upon your request."

PART VI
Surrender

Take me out to the ballgame,
Take me out with the crowd
Buy me some peanuts and Cracker Jack.
I don't care if I never get back.
Let me root, root, root for the home team.
If they don't win, it's a shame.
For it's one, two, three strikes, you're out
At the old ball game.

Lyrics by Jack Norworth, 1908
Music composed by Albert Von Tilzer
Published by the York Music Co.

CHAPTER ELEVEN

Meeting the Parkers

The scoreboard showed a tie in the middle of the fourth. There were two outs and a runner on first. Speed was not that player's strong point, but with Brian at the plate for the Panthers, it might not matter. Mark's voice, like a staccato drumbeat, yelled support, backed up by Brian's teammates screaming from the first base dugout.

From the opposing dugout, voices cheered the team on the field, encouraging the pitcher. He was a good pitcher, one of the top three in the league. The Police Panthers and Benny's Bruins were always at the top at the end of the season, and this was their first showdown.

Strike one came and went. The next pitch was high and outside, and then another went flying past the plate into the glove of the catcher. Strike two. The suspense mounted as Brian hit a high fly ball that went foul. Then, at last, his bat connected with the ball with a satisfying thunk that meant business. There was a collective intake of breath from the spectators, but it ended in a sigh as the ball headed straight toward the shortstop.

"Can of corn!" a voice near Sallie's ear shrieked as the shortstop pushed the ball to the second baseman. Out. Inning over. The groans from the first base line were matched by the cheers from the third base dugout.

"That's my boy! That's my star!" Turning to seek out the source of the ruckus, Sallie was surprised to match the voice to a petite white-haired woman. "That's my grandson," she said, leaning over to Sallie, her voice becoming very soft with a slight Italian trill that accentuated her measured pride.

Sallie smiled at the delight on the woman's face. "My nephew was at bat," she said, aware of her brother as he yelled his displeasure at the play.

"My Tim's the shortstop," the woman replied. She looked more closely at Sallie. "I haven't seen you here before."

"I've just returned to town. I went to high school here. My father and brother and his family are still here. That's Mark, my brother," Sallie said, pointing toward him. "He's the coach of the Panthers."

"Oh, I see. Well, welcome back." The woman reached out and touched her arm. "I'm Nonna."

Sallie was warmed by her familiarity. There was a gentleness in her, reminiscent of a grandmother who enveloped all who came across her path with the receptive arms of family. As she introduced herself, Sallie leaned toward Nonna, drawn to this tender woman's persona.

Nonna raised her hand to wave and Sallie looked up to see a man with sparkling green eyes approaching them carrying two bags of popcorn. He leaned over to give Nonna a kiss on the cheek, spilling the popcorn all over Sallie, who jumped up in shock.

"Looks as if I'm exuberantly pleased to meet you," he quipped.

"Oh, Robert, look what you've done." Nonna fretted as she grabbed a napkin and helped Sallie wipe away the remnants.

Sallie looked at her dress. "No harm, no foul, I guess." She couldn't be angry at his flirtatious smile.

"This is Robert. He's my favorite son."

"Your only son, unless I'm mistaken." He took off his baseball cap and saluted Sallie. "Nonna always says that."

As the game progressed, their conversation was lively and a warm flow of the energy from their connection began bubbling inside Sallie, like a tiny sun peeking out from behind dim storm clouds to shine brightly upon her life. Toward the end of the game, a woman waved at Nonna and joined them.

"Oh, Iris, I want you to meet someone. This is Sallie." Nonna turned toward Sallie. "This is my daughter, Iris Stevenson. She's Tim's mother."

"Sorry I was late, today of all days," Iris said with a wry smile, her dark eyes bright behind thin-wired glasses. She pushed her long dark hair from her face and nodded to Sallie. "We're very proud of him."

"My daughter teaches English at the high school and just started a summer workshop," Nonna explained as she turned to Iris. "How was class?"

"Interesting." She smiled at Nonna, and then included Sallie in the conversation. "I'm taking a creative writing class at UCLA about writing descriptions in fiction using the five senses. Today was great. I learned a lot."

"Are you a writer?" Sallie asked.

"A would-be writer." Iris gave a shrug. "I've been taking classes for several years now to better teach creative writing to my students. This is the first time I've taken a class just for me."

"Tell her what you want to do." Nonna's eyes shone with pride.

"I've been working on a short story. I have this idea and a friend who edits a quarterly journal has asked me to submit to their editorial committee for possible publication. I thought this class might give me more confidence."

"Sounds great," said Sallie, a tinge of envy in her voice. "That would be exciting. I just started writing a journal." Sallie pulled back. *Now, why did I say that? I've only just met them.*

Iris responded with the natural authenticity of someone who could easily share intimate secrets with a friend. "That's a good place to start. I've been journaling for many years now. It's great after some time goes by to re-read them and see what's changed and what's the same."

"Ah, that does sound tantalizing. Right now, I'm just starting. Not much to review." *She seems like someone I'd like to get to know. Perhaps we can become friends.*

"That comes with time." Iris smiled her encouragement.

The game was over too soon and Sallie felt a tinge of regret as she stood to take her leave.

"You're not leaving us already, are you?" Robert protested with a flirtatious smile.

Nonna touched her arm gently. "What are you doing tomorrow night? You should come for dinner."

"I wouldn't want to put you out."

Robert instantly dismissed her objection with a wave of his hand. "A crowd definitely does not put Nonna out."

"Oh, no, child. I love having company. Come, I'll have Robert make my famous Ragu alla Bolognese."

Iris jumped in. "It would be nice to get to know you better."

Sallie became flustered. "I'm not sure. I need to check in with my father." She looked around to see if Mark and Brian were ready to go and spotted them gesturing to her from beside the dugout. She waved back. "Thanks for the invitation. I need to go. Mark and Brian are waiting for me."

"You are always welcome. Just let us know," Nonna said.

Upbraiding herself for her indecisiveness, Sallie called Nonna early the next day and accepted her dinner invitation. She stopped at the local florist for a bouquet and made her way to their Spanish-style bungalow. As she parked, she admired the garden, lavish with tightly nestled Mediterranean plants.

The house was definitely a family home. Wicker chairs on the porch were covered in colorful cushions reflecting the garden flowers, worn indentations showing their regular use. There was a happy energy to this house. Sallie embraced her surroundings as she rang the doorbell.

She could hear the sounds of many approaching steps as the front door was flung open. Nonna reached out with welcoming arms to give her a hug. "Oh, my dear, there you are." Sallie handed her the flowers. "Oh, how beautiful. And so thoughtful of you! Come in. Come in."

Nonna turned toward her family. "Come everyone, this is Sallie." She took Sallie's arm and ushered her into the house. "You remember Iris. Here's Tim." Nonna pointed out their familiar faces. Sallie smiled and nodded at them as Nonna continued, "Here's Maria, my youngest daughter, and her husband, Sam, and their baby, Tina. And here comes their son, little Buddy."

Sallie looked down as a toddler grabbed for her legs. She stooped to his level to welcome his embrace. "Hey there, little man. You want a hug?" Sallie cuddled him as Nonna watched with approval.

"You seem to have made a new friend already!" Nonna laughed as she led the way into the kitchen, where a young woman sat at the counter with her finger in a book. "This is Tara, whom we've adopted into our hearts. She's working with Robert to pass her SATs so she can start college this fall." Even Tara rose to give Sallie a hug.

Flushed from her welcome, Sallie arrived in the middle of the kitchen as Nonna made her final announcement. "And, of course, Robert, our cook tonight."

Robert turned from the large range with steam rising over an array of bubbling pans and waved in her direction. Turning to Nonna, he dipped into the pot and presented a large spoonful of sauce for her to sample. "How's it taste tonight?"

Nonna took the spoon and sampled the sauce. "Ah, it's wonderful. Just like Grandma Patrizia used to make," she said with a wide smile that made her eyes crinkle.

Robert laughed. With an exaggerated cowboy drawl and a wink toward Sallie, he said, "It's an Eye-talian specialty Ah learned at my mama's knee."

He returned to the stove and immersed the long spaghetti strands into boiling water, holding them until they began to soften in the pot. His movements were smooth; he seemed comfortable in his body. His wavy brown hair framed a warm, open face and his eyes sparkled, showing gold flecks in the center that matched the frames of his glasses.

"Do you like to cook?" Sallie asked politely.

"Well," he said in the same sardonic drawl as the steam wound tendrils around his head, "it's like this, ma'am, Ah can honestly say Ah only do it under the expert tutelage of my mama." Sallie smiled at him as he glanced at Nonna and gave her a wink.

"Pay no attention to him," laughed Iris.

"To be serious," Robert said in his everyday tone, "most of what I cook I've learned from Nonna. I enjoy it most when I'm cooking for my family."

Sam handed Sallie a glass of Chianti and pointed toward a bar stool where she could watch the preparations.

"Tara?" Sallie hesitated, as she picked up a knitting project from the bar stool and sat down.

"That's right," she said. "It gets real hectic around here about dinner time. I suggest you just sit back and enjoy the view."

"I see what you mean," Sallie said. "Doesn't seem like there's much need for our help."

"Nope. It might look unorganized, but believe me, everything gets done right on time."

Sallie glanced at the book on the counter. "You're being tutored?"

"I fell behind my last year of high school. And I want to go to a good college. I met Robert through an outreach program that helps people like me."

"How're things going?"

"I'm taking some classes at the community college. If I do well on my SATs, I can transfer to UCLA next spring."

"That's great," said Sallie. "UCLA's a great college. That degree will jumpstart your career." Tara nodded.

Sallie looked at the knitting project in her hands. "Is this yours?" she asked Tara.

"Oh, no, that's Nonna's. She's always got a project or two going."

Nonna turned. "It's a sweater for the baby."

"The colors are beautiful," said Sallie, caressing the yarn.

"Would you like to learn to knit?"

"It looks difficult."

"It's really not. If you're interested, we could go to the yarn store," Nonna offered.

Before Sallie had a chance to respond, Robert called to the group, "Believe it or not, soup's on. Let's *mangia*!"

A riotous dinner ensued. Sometimes several people talked at once, a lively conversation about the ups and downs of their lives, their dreams and hopes, with everyone supportive of whomever was talking. They asked Sallie all kinds of questions, and compared their lives in Los Madre with hers.

"Nonna said you went to high school here," Iris said, hoping to find a connection to their joint past.

"I went during the glory days when the football team won the regional championship three years running."

"We arrived in the last year of that era," said Iris. "Sounds like you were a couple of years ahead of Robert."

"What teachers did you have?" asked Robert.

"Well," said Sallie, thinking for a moment. "There was Sharpley for

Civics, Ferguson for Math, Thompson for Chemistry. Let me see. Oh, my favorite class was Mrs. Lindsey's Senior English. She sure made us work, and I learned a lot."

"She was my favorite, too," said Iris. "She made literature come alive."

"I think she was everyone's favorite. She made you think," said Robert.

"Where is she now?" asked Sallie.

"She retired about ten years ago and, as far as I know, moved out to the Mojave Desert with her husband," said Robert.

Sallie leaned back in her chair and smiled. "Great memories."

"What brought you back to town?" Robert asked.

"Oh, Dad is getting older and my brother asked me to help sort things out." Sallie hesitated, unsure what else to say on the matter, and the table became quiet.

Nonna broke the silence. "We know Mark and Nancy through Little League. We've seen Brian play. He's pretty good. We know who the real champ is, though." She winked at Tim.

"Oh, Nonna," Tim groaned, embarrassed by the attention.

"Well, the championship game is coming up soon," Iris said.

Nonna looked around the table, catching everyone's eyes. "And we know who the best team is, don't we?" She raised her hand to get everyone in unison and they all chimed in, "The Bruins!"

Tim's blush deepened until Robert came to his rescue. "Well, we'll definitely know by the end of the season, won't we?" He hesitated a moment and then in a plaintive tone said, "Well, no one has said anything about my dinner." Immediately, everyone began to speak at once, raucously praising his cooking.

"I hope you've all saved room for dessert," said Robert, lifting his eyebrows and looking around at everyone, all with expectant smiles. "Can anyone guess what we're having?" Groans went up from around the table and Sallie looked at them with a questioning smile.

"Oh, no, not your favorite *again*." Iris shook her head in mock disapproval and leaned over to clue Sallie. "Ever since we were kids, Robert has loved éclairs. He seems to have a passion for them."

"No one can beat Wilson's Bakery for their éclairs. You've got to admit it now, Iris." Robert stood up and went into the kitchen. "Don't forget," he yelled back, "the cook doesn't clean." There were dramatic moans as Sam and Iris began to clear the table.

As the evening wound down, Sallie prepared to take her leave.

"Oh, so soon? We're just getting started," Nonna objected.

"I've enjoyed myself very much. I have laughed more tonight than I have in a long time. It's been wonderful. Thank you for inviting me."

"Let's get together soon. We have a lot in common," Iris said with an eager nod. "I'd like to get to know you better."

"I look forward to it," Sallie agreed.

Nonna took Sallie's arm to walk her to the door. "Listen, my dear, please come by anytime. You are always welcome here and I want to see you again. Oh, and…" she paused for effect, "go Bruins."

"And, go Panthers," Sallie countered. They both laughed.

Robert joined them at the door. "How about I walk you to your car?"

Sallie nodded shyly as Nonna gave her a hug.

"That's a good idea," Nonna agreed. "Goodnight, my dear. See you again soon, I hope."

"Yes, I would like that. See you soon."

"Well," said Robert as he walked out the door and linked his arm with Sallie's. "What do you think of the gang?"

"Oh, my," she said, cheeks flushed. "You see, I'm not used to so much, well… commotion. I enjoyed it. If this is just any day, what happens when there are family birthdays or other celebrations?"

"Oh, that's when she really gets things going. Most of our life revolves around food and Nonna is a great Italian mother. As I hope you'll find out." He grinned flirtatiously.

162

Sallie felt an unfamiliar warmth rising in her cheeks and quickly changed the subject. "Tell me about Tara. You're mentoring her?"

"Yes, I'm a volunteer for Children's Action Group. We work primarily with at-risk youth."

"I'd like to know more." Sallie found herself suddenly shy and uncertain as to her motivation.

"How about coming by my office tomorrow? We can talk some more."

Sallie hesitated, not sure whether she really wanted his attention. "May I let you know?"

"That'll work."

Sallie opened her car door and gave a small wave as she slid into the driver's seat. *I'll just call later and cancel.* She watched through the windshield as he walked back up to the front porch where Nonna was waiting. Nonna waved to her as Robert took her arm and tucked it under his with his free hand on top of hers.

Sallie gave a wistful sigh. *Oh, to have a family like that. Oh well. I must make do with what I have.*

An invitation to Mark's house had Sallie somewhat apprehensive. Their last conversation had left her full of anxiety, and she had practiced over and over in her mind what she wanted to say to him.

She pulled up to their bungalow, which still sported its mid-century modern symmetrical façade. Originally a small square building, Mark and Nancy had opened up the interior and expanded the back. The entrance now led into a light-filled living, dining, and kitchen area that was open and hospitable.

"Wow," she said as Nancy let her in. "You've done a lot to the house. It's really open and casual."

Nancy nodded, pleased by Sallie's praise. "We like it."

At the other end of the large area, Mark sat at the dining table.

"Come on in," he said, rising from his chair and walking over to give her a quick hug.

"Would you like some coffee or tea?" asked Nancy.

"Tea would be nice."

Nancy put some water on the stove and Mark pointed to a chair opposite his. He got quickly to the point. "Have you done your research?"

"I'm just not convinced he needs to move right now. He certainly doesn't want to."

"You haven't seen him deteriorate over the last few years."

Sallie sensed she had to be careful what she said and considered the response she had been reciting in her head. "I know you have more experience with the situation. I just don't think we should rush things."

"What if something happened to him? How would you feel then?"

"What if he moves and deteriorates worse? What if he dies because he's so unhappy in a home?" she asked.

Nancy returned with tea for her and Sallie and coffee for Mark. "Here's some brownies I made this morning. I know how much you like chocolate." Nancy had clearly picked up on the shift in the mood at the table and was doing her best to provide some nurturing. She sat down next to Mark, her arm resting next to his, and Sallie sensed their solidarity in the matter.

"Thanks so much, Sallie, for offering to fix some meals for him," said Nancy. "It certainly takes pressure off us. We both appreciate it." She affectionately rubbed Mark's arm.

Mark's face was restrained as he stared at the papers in front of him. Nancy's words did little to lessen the cold feeling creeping through Sallie's body and causing her hands to shake. She placed them both around the steaming mug to warm them up. *I need to get out of here.*

Sallie's desire to know more about Robert's volunteer group

eventually overrode her reticence at his possible interest in her. She arrived at his building a few minutes early for their meeting, admiring how the old courthouse had been artfully converted into boutique office space. The perky receptionist had directed her back toward Robert's office, formerly one of the old courtrooms.

Large and airy in a corner of the building with long windows on two adjacent walls, it had the original narrow oak floors and the low wall that had separated the space for the legal staff from the gallery. The judge's bench, the jury box, and the gallery seating were gone. In their place were three neat desks arranged in a triangular pattern.

Hearing her approach, Robert looked up from his stack of papers and met her with a warm smile. He jumped up from his desk and bounded over to her, opening the short swinging panel to let her into the main part of the office.

"Welcome to my humble domain." He swept his hand in a wide gesture to acknowledge the entire room. "Come on in. You just missed the rest of the staff. They're at lunch."

Sallie walked over to the one solid wall peppered with a great many plaques and framed posters showing past ad campaigns. She scrutinized a picture labeled "Ridge Valley Winery" with several award ribbons posted next to it. Turning back to him, she asked, "You do the ads for Ridge Valley? They're good wines."

"It's the family business," he said. "Actually, my cousins run it now."

"Your family makes Ridge Valley?" She raised an eyebrow, impressed. "Their Pinot is one of my favorites."

"I'll remember that."

Sallie turned away to hide her blush, walking down the wall and coming to a plaque proclaiming "Los Madre Man of the Year" for the previous year. Robert, totally at ease in his environment, let her wander in silence.

She turned to look at him. "I'd like to get involved with the volunteer program."

"Are you planning on staying here a while?"

"I don't know. Does it matter?" She avoided his eyes.

"It might." He shrugged, and then asked, "What made you move away?"

Sallie looked out the window, matched his shrug, and then turned back to him. "I went to college up north. I liked it there so I stayed. What about you? What made you stay here?"

"I went to UCLA, got married, took over this business from my dad, and things just moved along from there."

"It's no wonder," Sallie said, remembering her dinner with the Parkers.

"What makes you say that?"

"Oh, just observing your family. I'd probably stay too." She hesitated and then asked, "What happened to your marriage?"

"She was in medical school. Just too little time together."

Sallie nodded. Turning away from him to focus on a framed poster, Sallie changed the subject. "Would you mind if I got involved with your group?"

"No. It would be great. I've already put a call in to Doris, the volunteer coordinator."

"You don't seem to waste any time."

"Not when it's important. So, how about lunch? There's a great little bistro nearby."

Sallie put her hand to her throat. *Oh my, this is moving too fast.* "I do need to get back."

Robert nodded, keeping his face noncommittal. He opened the swinging gate. "Is any day better than another to see Doris?"

"No, make it at her convenience."

Leaving Robert's office so abruptly, Sallie frowned, wondering why she had reacted as she did. *Not really like me. It's not as if I have an attraction to him. All I really want is just to make some friends.*

Volunteer work always found me friends in the past. She hurried down the street toward the *Courier* office to see if Frank had meant what he said about writing a column.

Sallie made it her mission to bring her father's garden back to life. Remnants of roses, an old orange tree, and sprawling salvia had all responded to her severe pruning.

"The orange tree will come back stronger and more prolific than ever," she had replied to her father's remonstrations. The garden was showing signs of order—not the straight order of soldiers on parade, more of a pleasant curving, like a garden party filled with groups of partygoers.

"That's the ticket," her father said, sitting on his redwood chair on the concrete patio next to the garden where Sallie knelt nearby. "You certainly have a way with plants."

"I enjoy it," Sallie said, standing up and tossing aside the weeds she had just finished plucking from the bed. "How about some lemonade?"

"Sure. Can I help?" He started to rise slightly from his seat.

"Oh, no, sit. I can get it," Sallie said, gently touching his shoulder.

Sallie entered the kitchen and began juicing lemons just picked from his tree, adding honey syrup and water. She brought it out to the porch and sat across from her father.

"I sure do enjoy your dinners," her father said.

"I enjoy cooking for you."

"Are you staying tonight?" His voice was expectant.

"No, I've got a meeting. I'm thinking about doing some volunteer work."

"Oh, you could volunteer here."

A quick laugh escaped Sallie's lips. "I thought I was."

"I'd like to see more of you."

She reached over and curled her fingers around his hand with a soft smile. "I know," she said quietly.

"Your room is still open."

"Do you want me to pick you up tomorrow for Brian's game?"

"Of course."

"I can stay for dinner afterward."

"Oh, that'd be great." He leaned toward her as she got up to take the glasses to the kitchen. His hand reached out to hers and she leaned over to embrace him, giving him a hug as he patted her arm.

"I don't want to leave my home. I'll know when the time comes. I'm fine right now."

"I know." Her voice was soft. "I wouldn't want you to have to leave it. Not until you're ready."

His voice was so low she barely heard it. "Thank you."

Doris' plump body was squeezed into her office much like it was pinched into her brightly colored dress. There was barely enough room for the three of them to sit around her small metal desk, which was piled high with books and various documents. She pushed some papers aside and dropped a stack of files on the floor as she apologized for the mess.

Despite the apparent disorganization, Doris' quick laugh, easy smile, and chattiness made Sallie immediately at ease. She seemed a natural for the job of supervising volunteers at the Children's Action Group.

Chatting with Robert about his progress with Tara, Doris nodded her approval, then turned to Sallie and asked about her background. Sallie talked about herself more openly than usual with a stranger. At one point, she caught herself glancing shyly at Robert, wondering what he was thinking.

Her mind wandered, and she had to quickly turn her attention to hear Doris' words. "…tells me you have some experience in the nonprofit world."

She looked at Robert quizzically, wondering what he had told Doris about her.

"I told her you did some volunteer work at your local real estate board," he said, reading her mind.

Sallie nodded and turned back to Doris. "Yes, I was involved for several years. I also served on a Chamber of Commerce committee."

"Well, isn't that just serendipity!" Doris shuffled papers on her desk until she came to the one she wanted. "We've just been given a grant to bring the arts to junior high schools. We're initiating a new task force and we need a solid plan."

She turned to Robert. "I was hoping to get you involved too." Looking back at Sallie, Doris asked, "What do you think? I've got a couple of teachers, a principal, and a staff member from the County Art Commission."

Sallie looked from Doris to Robert, her mind rapidly considering the consequences of joining this committee. *Is this what I want? I was only going to stay a week. Why am I doing this?*

With a calm voice, she gave Doris a direct gaze. "How long do you envision this work will take?"

Doris looked at Robert. "What do you think? I was hoping maybe one or two meetings. Maybe a couple of weeks at the most."

Robert nodded and looked at Sallie. "I know the people involved. I don't think anyone wants this to go on indefinitely."

"Well, tell me more about the project."

As she listened to Doris, Sallie began to believe in the project. *If I do this, it will take my mind off all the other issues in my life right now.* Having reached her decision, Sallie had just opened her mouth to voice her agreement to join the task force when Doris added, "I am really hoping you will chair the group. Everyone else is so busy."

Sallie's mouth remained agape as her mind raced to process this new request. "Me?" Sallie finally sputtered. "I don't really think I should. After all, I'm new here." She turned to Robert. "What about you? You already know everyone."

"I guess I could, but you have the experience and I'm a little overbooked right now."

Sallie's mind reeled. *What am I doing? Is this the right thing for me to do?* She put her hand to her heart. *Something tells me to just do it.* She looked pointedly at Robert. "You have to be the Vice-Chair, then, and assist the Chair when needed."

He laughed. "A pleasure."

Leaving the meeting, Robert's enthusiasm rubbed off on Sallie and they spent the walk back to the parking lot brainstorming possible ideas to bring the arts to the disadvantaged youth of the county.

Sallie watched from the front porch as her brother took Brian through his pre-game drills, smiling at her déjà vu. It was like an instant replay of those scenes from so many years ago. Mark's intensity never wavered.

"That's enough now. Go inside and help your mother." He tossed the ball to Brian, who bounded up the stairs, slamming the screen door as he entered the house.

Mark walked over and sat down on the steps next to her, shrugging. "Kids these days." They both looked in the direction of the door.

"He's a good kid. Sort of reminds me of you at his age." Sallie hit his shoulder playfully.

"I did have a great older sister."

Sallie changed the conversation. "Dad mentioned you got promoted recently. Are you in charge of a division now?"

"Well, 'in charge' is a little high-sounding, seeing as how the department has very firm policies about everything."

Sallie detected some irritation. "Tell me what you do."

"I'm a liaison to the schools. Part of an anti-drug community program to keep children clean and drug-free. Mostly, I work with junior high kids. Everyone seems to have an opinion about what I should be doing."

"Oh? Like what?"

"Some school people seem to think we're too hard on the kids."

"What do you think?"

"I think we've gotten too soft. Kids shouldn't be making decisions about what to do at their age. They need old-fashioned structure and discipline. There's not enough discipline at home or school."

"Maybe kids have different pressures on them now than when we were young."

He looked over at her and opened his mouth to speak. She glanced back and carried his gaze. *How can we decide what to do about Dad if we don't even know how to have a simple discussion? I'm not going to be the first to give.*

Shifting his body, he turned to stare at the street. "As far as I can see, the pressure is on the parents who overindulge their kids, running them here and there with an overloaded schedule, giving them whatever they want. Things should be simple. I like simple."

"Yes, don't we all wish life could be simple?"

Her brother turned away, ending the conversation. Sallie was left with an empty feeling. *Is it me or did I miss something? Oh well, if he won't tell me, I just won't worry about it right now.*

Sallie called Anne on Sunday night, bubbling with news.

"It happened just like you said, about looking for synchronicities. Usually, when I go to my nephew's games, I sit in the stands behind his dugout. Last week, something just told me to sit on the other side. I thought it was because I was embarrassed by my brother's shouting. Guess what, though? You were right!"

Anne smiled at Sallie's enthusiasm. "How was I right?"

"I met this lovely woman named Nonna. Her grandson plays shortstop for another team, and she's just like my idea of what a grandmother would be." Sallie's voice rose as she told Anne the story of meeting the Parker family and the dinner she had shared with them. Halfway through the conversation, her voice took on a note of shyness as she told Anne about Robert asking her to lunch.

"Anne, you know how I feel about first dates. Well, there I was in his office and…" She hesitated, searching for the right phrase. "What went through my mind was that he was going to like me more than I'd like him. And I guess I just didn't want to deal with it."

"Hmmm," said Anne. "I wonder. Perhaps it's because you might also like him."

"I don't think so. He's a nice guy and everything, I just have so much going on. I don't want to deal with another relationship issue."

Before Anne could respond, Sallie continued, "Not to change the subject, but I've got some other news. I've been asked to submit a guest column for one of the *Courier's* magazines! It'll be about home decorating, gardening, all the things I know."

"Sounds good. What're you going to write as a sample?"

"I was thinking of an article about how to decorate a home to attract better offers when you want to sell. You know, sort of a 'how to stage a house' article."

"Sounds great," responded Anne. "So, what's going on with your family?"

"Oh, well, where to start?" replied Sallie, her enthusiasm waning. "There have been some tense moments, to say the least. The same game where I met Nonna, the Panthers lost by one run and my brother was really angry and started in on Brian. It reminded me completely of how my father treated Mark when he lost a game as a kid. It's as if we as a family are repeating the same mistakes and there's no way to change it."

"You know, it doesn't have to be that way."

172

"Something tells me you're right," said Sallie, reflecting. "Yet I find myself looking up at the stars at night and wondering at the vastness of the universe and how I fit into it all. Why am I here in this place with this family right now? Sometimes I just want to live on an island all by myself."

"You don't really want that."

"Something calls to me, Anne. I have this nameless fear. It's as if I've forgotten something and I need to remember. It's all I can do to keep myself under control sometimes."

"Well, perhaps control isn't what you need."

"What's the other choice? Being out of control? That's not me. It's just that I'm not being heard. It's like I'm an outsider."

"How does that make you feel?"

"Wait, there's more. I agreed to make dinner for my father a couple of days a week. Now he's begun to rely on me and so has my brother."

"Oh," Anne responded with a surprised tone. "How do you feel about that?"

"I'm not only his chief cook now, Mark also has the expectation that I'm here to stay as Dad's caretaker. I'm back in my childhood."

"That doesn't sound good. So, how do you feel?"

"There's still more," said Sallie. "Mark's still adamant about putting Dad into this new retirement home in town. I think what's coming next is that I have to move in with Dad or else."

"Oh my goodness," Anne said, drawing out each syllable. "How do you feel about all this?" Her voice was slow and insistent to get Sallie to listen to her words.

"Thus far, we're at a standstill. However, I think Dad wants the same thing."

"How do you *feel*?" Anne repeated herself, this time more emphatic.

"How do I feel?" Sallie finally heard the words. "Well," she paused, considering what she knew to be true. "I feel…" She hesitated again, as if learning a new skill, then spoke quickly. "I feel very frustrated as it brings up my fear of having to do what others expect and not necessarily what I want."

"Oh, Sallie, that's good, being able to figure out how you feel."

"The frustration reminds me of what Mike did and the fact that he couldn't trust me to let me be part of his process. Now, my brother is doing something similar. I get angry. There's this lump in the middle of my body, like a baseball, and I want to tear it out of me and throw it at him. Bean him on the head to get his attention."

"Don't be bitter. Mike had his own insecurities that had nothing to do with you."

"Yes, but he made me his co-conspirator, so to speak, without even giving me the opportunity to weigh in, to be part of the decision. Just like my brother's doing."

"Just be patient. I'm sure you'll work this out for the best. Have you considered that you're just going through the anger stage and this too shall pass? You're smart and know how to figure things out."

Sallie sighed, yet perked up from the compliment. "I don't want to be around my family because I get so insecure. You say I need to respond to my feelings and not directly to my brother and father." Her voice became fierce. "I get caught up in the drama. I hate it, yet am uncertain how to change. I also feel like if I run away from this, just like with the situation with Mike, it will forever haunt me. I've entered a new world and don't know what to do."

"It's not necessarily a question of knowing what to do," Anne counseled. "It's more a question of letting your intuition guide your way."

"What do you mean? How can I do that?"

"Well, what I sometimes do when Joe and I are having an argument is to excuse myself—just go into another room. That way, we both have time to cool down and get our feelings sorted."

"That might help." Sallie's voice was hesitant. "I'm still having these dreams that leave me feeling like something will go wrong if everything is going right. I don't want to get settled into anything that might become permanent."

"Remember our talks about trusting yourself, about listening to your heart?"

"I still find it challenging to think that everything happening to me is perfect."

"Sallie, what I mean by perfect is everything is appropriate to the moment by moment in which you live your life. Can you give yourself a little slack and just trust?"

"I guess so."

"Just let things flow. Remember the yin and yang of life. Sometimes you have to push for what you want, and other times you have to relax and just let things come to you in time."

"Thanks for the reminder," Sallie said, grateful to have such a wise and patient friend. "Love you. Have a good week." She signed off from their weekly chat in an optimistic mood.

Sallie's Journal—June 22nd

I desire to get clear on my purpose for being back in my hometown. I am still attached to my family's words and their attitudes. I vacillate between being independent and confident of my path, and thinking I have to live within the world of their expectations.

My mind tells me there's another choice and their way doesn't have to be my way. Yet I'm drawn to them in an emotional dance of unexpressed thoughts and remembrances.

Around them, I have these deep-seated feelings come up and it's all I can do to keep them contained. I am afraid of what I might do if I allow myself to express how I really feel.

I recently met the Parkers, very different from any family I have ever known. Nonna is the matriarch. Her real name is Firenze Maria

Paparelli Parker. She came with her family to the United States from Italy in the late 1930s as a young child, when it was turning Fascist and war was imminent.

Her father worked on a wine estate in Italy, and the family settled in the Santa Barbara area where they worked for the Parkers, an old California family who'd been making wine since Prohibition ended.

Nonna grew up with the Parker children and married Robert Senior, the youngest son. After the children were born, they moved to Southern California to develop a market for selling the family wines. Nonna's been a widow for many years.

Iris is part of a writing group and has asked me to join, so my tentative beginning of a journal becomes even more significant. This all seems serendipitous, yet I know it is part of the unfolding of my life.

My diary begins in the middle of my life. Pieces stretch back to my beginnings and parts stretch ahead to my dreams of the future. I have discovered I have always lived in the future, in my daydreams, because that is where I felt safe.

I realize that for me to reach in a new direction, I must live in the present, finding the link between my dreams and my future. My desire is to discover the person I truly am, not the person I have thought myself to be. I'm beginning to see that I've been defining myself through the eyes of others and now must discover who I am through my own eyes.

I also met Robert and have become uncharacteristically shy around him. We were in high school at the same time and I don't have any recollection of him; however, he tells me he was quite geeky then and I would not have noticed him. Very similar to me, he has dated rarely in the past ten years.

I had a dream in which I am with my parents in their house and someone wants to hurt us. We cannot leave the house.

I beg my parents to change the locks on the house. They tell me the bad man returned all his keys and is unable to get in. I don't believe them. I am paralyzed by fear and I cannot do anything.

My parents tell me what to do and what to eat. They put me in a harness device with straps like a jacket around my chest, attached to pulleys and strings that are going out from my body to a huge machine. I realize the machine emits an electric shock. My father is telling me to behave or he'll pull the lever that elicits the shock. My fear is palpable, insistent, and pervasive.

CHAPTER TWELVE

Sapphie: The Angel of Peace

From a distance, Sallie heard the motorized sound of gears squealing and people screaming gaily as the outline of an old fashioned carnival rose against the midnight sky. As she got closer, she saw a searchlight sending luminescent cones of pink, turquoise, blue, and purple into the sky, as if announcing a Hollywood premiere.

As she approached the midway, she spotted someone who looked exactly like her standing before an arched gate.

"Come!" her twin yelled. "Hurry, we must get going. It's so much fuuunnn!" She stretched out the word as she held out her hand to Sallie.

Sallie reached out and instantly they were off, running together down the midway. They raced past the sideshow, the games of skill, a booth where taffy was being pulled by steel fingers, spinning rides, and the brightly lit Ferris wheel. On they ran until they came to a sign marked "The Hall of Mirrors."

"Wait," yelled Sallie. "Who are you?"

"Why, I'm your other half," her twin answered. "That part you deny and hide from others, and even conceal from yourself. I'm your unacknowledged self."

"What?" Sallie stuttered. "What are you doing here? Where am I? And where are we going?" The questions came quicker than she could think.

"Why, look around and see! We're at the carnival. And it's time to see yourself." With that, she disappeared into a large round tent.

Sallie followed with trepidation. As she entered, her twin pulled her close. Sallie shrank from the large circle of tall mirrors that filled the space.

Sallie knew about fun house mirrors and how they could distort one's image, making a body look short and squat, or tall and extremely thin. In one, body tops would be distorted, and in another, a bottom would look elephantine.

To her surprise, this house had mirrors reflecting her emotions, each one showing someone in her life that represented an attitude. Some people were adversarial, while others were accepting of her. She hesitated as her twin beckoned her to the center of the circle of mirrors.

She saw herself reflected in a long line out toward infinity in one mirror's silvery glass face. She shuddered as she saw a possible future that could be hers if she continued her current course of action. Mesmerized, her eyes widened as she focused on her image.

Her twin tugged on her arm. She turned reluctantly to gaze at the plethora of images reflected in the mirrors. She saw her father in one, then Mark in another, then Mike, and Nancy, Robert, Iris, and Nonna.

As she turned in a slow circle, she spied aspects of her soul in the eyes of each reflected person and how they viewed her. Her father's fear of her hit Sallie squarely in her chest. Mark with his attitude that life came too easy to her left her stunned. Mike was content in his assurance that he had acted properly in all his endeavors. She saw Nancy's certainty that she held the key to Sallie's happiness in her philosophy of womanhood. Nonna reflected the acceptance of her just as she was. Robert demonstrated sensitivity to her femininity, and Iris reflected her own hopes for a happy ending.

The last mirror, though, revealed a harrowing sight. An inhuman grayish-black lump, like a shriveled gigantic prune, filled the glass. Staring at the shapeless image, Sallie began to make out a semblance of a face. The mass moved to communicate with her.

Suddenly, the walls fell away and the cones of light that had covered the carnival transformed into an angel. Sapphie descended lightly over Sallie, encompassing her in a swirl of intensity that lifted her soul upward into a placid merging with this peaceful angelic presence.

Glowing swirls of pink, blue, purple, and green engulfed Sallie as Sapphie's angelic aura unfolded. It reminded Sallie of the air of a summer evening spent in a wide-open meadow under a spacious canopy of stars, when the wonder of nature brings a joy beyond imagining. Sapphie exuded a soft gentleness that caressed Sallie into a deep state of ultimate peacefulness.

Sapphie's words registered deeply in the center of Sallie's soul. "That unsettling image is your other half that you carry around on your back. You've been unwilling to stop and turn to look at it. The more you reject that side of you, the larger, lumpier, and more grotesque it becomes. Stop a minute and acknowledge the pieces that you think make you so unlovable."

Sallie peered into the mirror with a grimace. "It is as if I will come undone and all that I am will be negated if I don't keep up the appearance of being good, kind, helpful, and loving. I don't want others to see anything bad in me."

"That is all a pretense, which disavows half of who you are. The more you reject the side of you that you consider to be negative, the more it grows."

"If I work on being good and minimize that part of me, then maybe it will go away and I will be the person I really want to be." Sallie's voice was plaintive, seeking agreement. Sapphie waited for her to continue. "I just don't want others to see me like that," Sallie finally acknowledged, barely audible.

"Sallie, you cannot truly know the light of life if you do not respect and acknowledge the dark. Tell me, how do you feel about the darkness of night?"

"Oh, I love it!" Salle answered enthusiastically. "I enjoy the night curling up around me and shutting out the harsh glare of day. I love going to bed, with its dreams and faraway journeys that give me hope for a better day tomorrow."

"That is how I want you to consider the parts of you that you do not like."

"You want me to like the dark parts of me?"

"Not only like. I want you to express them outwardly. What are some of the parts of you that you don't like that you might want to embrace?"

Sallie reflected a moment. "Like how I think something is wrong with me and I am unable to make it right?"

"And?" Sapphie asked, her voice patient.

"Well, I might be too much of a perfectionist. My insecurity makes me controlling because I think that's the only way to get what I want." She hesitated, waiting for Sapphie's approval, but gasped as she realized the importance of what she had said. "Is that what you mean?"

"Yes, that is a start. You partake in a deep grief endemic to Western culture, so deep it does not even register on the surface of your life. Grief arises from an expectation that you have about your behavior and that of others," said Sapphie.

"I sometimes sense I will do something wrong and others won't want to know me, which paralyzes me from doing anything. Then I get excited and start something new. When it goes wrong, I see the cycle starting over."

"That is the grief of which I speak, which is a deep part of your life. It starts as a numbness, a denial of your essence, and then surges into a yearning and searching for someone or something to fill the void. This brings alternating currents of hope and despair as you find that nothing can fulfill that which is insatiable. Then, unsatisfied with what you are, your anger responds, yielding a growing despair that becomes deeply embedded into the fabric of your life."

"I just want to be accepted."

"Consider the price you pay when you negate your soul and very reason for being."

"It hurts when someone rejects me."

"Sallie, you hang onto past hurts as a form of revenge upon yourself that becomes a self-fulfilling prophecy causing emotional pain. Yet, this revenge only mirrors back to you and turns itself inward becoming the mirror of judgment."

"I often wonder where the judgment starts, whether it's me or it's others," she pondered.

"So, which is it?"

"Are you saying I'm too judgmental?"

"When you look to others to define who you are, you judge yourself. This keeps you from your own life's mission. If you don't judge yourself, no one else can judge you."

"How can I stop?"

"Your role at this time is to turn the mirror of judgment into one of unconditional forgiveness," responded Sapphie gently.

"What do you mean?"

"Everyone who is significant in your life has given you a gift and a challenge. It is up to you to find the gift and use the challenge to grow. Look around you. Think of the people reflected in these mirrors and what they represent. For example, what is the gift and challenge from your father?"

"I'm not certain." Sallie paused to consider her answer. "I know I persevere and follow my dreams even without any evidence to support them. I guess if I had gotten everything as a child, I might quit easier. The downside is that I don't trust that others will meet my needs."

"That's a valuable assessment. Now, how about your brother and sister-in-law?" asked Sapphie.

"Hmm," Sallie said. "I'd say they give me a sense of family, and even with our ups and downs, we'll work things out. The real issue is their judgment that I'm not okay and I need to be someone different than who I am. Is that what you mean?"

"Yes. Now, how about the Parker family?"

"That's easier. Nonna makes me feel loved and Iris is like a long lost sister. My femininity seems to come out more around Robert than any man I've known before. When I'm around them, I begin to believe I can manifest my dreams, yet I also get nervous about surrendering and just letting things flow." Sallie stopped, unsure of her words. When she continued, she spoke in a slow, even tone. "Perhaps I'm afraid to surrender and just let things flow."

Sallie bowed her head at the impact of what she had said, then looked excitedly at Sapphie. "This is all new to me. I'm not certain what it all means."

"They are only reflecting back to you that which you need to experience," responded Sapphie.

Sallie thought a moment and then smiled, her eyes alight with a revelation. "So, in thinking how others are judging me, you're saying that what others think about me is more about them than it is about me?" queried Sallie.

"Exactly. Look inside before you judge what others are saying. Be thankful the people in your life are willing to carry your anger, fear, and the issues that are a part of your life. It takes a lot of love on their part to be that reflection for you."

"Wait a minute. You're telling me that when someone gets mad at me, it's because I am mad at them?"

Sapphie patiently continued, "Consider that they are reflecting your anger. Perhaps you are not angry with them directly. It might be they are simply there to assist you getting in touch with your emotions so you can release them."

"Oh, so the attitude I have toward them is the same as what I have toward myself, or just how I'm feeling in general," mused Sallie. Then, thinking further, she added, "And, in forgiving them, I can forgive myself."

"Yes. Through thanking them you are set free. Forgiving is 'for giving' yourself and the other a gift. It is a gift of surrender—the surrender of what you are currently so that you can become something greater."

"You mean when someone does something that makes me angry, I need to thank them?"

Sapphie smiled and nodded, aware that her charge was absorbing this message. "Resentments can be changed into their opposite through surrender," she said. "Surrender is a spirit of detachment that accepts that which is unacceptable. It is an act of expansion into the nature of the divine, a giving up of the will to release further energy."

"What must I do?" Sallie was eager to learn.

"To engage in the act of surrender, realize that everyone did the best they could at the time and everything is appropriate to your life and your mission. Empathy will come as you look deeply at others and realize they suffer too. Most of all, embrace who you are and stop shaping yourself to the expectations of others.

"As you learn from the mirrors of trauma, you will have new reflections in your life that will represent further lessons, particularly those of joy, love, and happiness. You're already beginning to see those characteristics in the Parker family. You will become comfortable with your new feelings as you learn to accept yourself as being worthy.

"There is no difference between anyone. I am in you and you are in me. There is only one living being. I am the Angel of Peace and thus have I spoken since ancient times. If, within your body, your thoughts and feelings make peace with each other, you will move mountains."

Sapphie's voice was soft and her touch gentle as they explored the lesson Sallie had been resisting. "Remember your Oneness with Spirit and with all things. Know that you are love and you are loved. Live accordingly. Be at peace with your spirit."

Sapphie took Sallie in her arms and embraced her with the warmth of eternal love until she finally surrendered to the peace of the All. As Sapphie slowly transformed to light, her final words filled Sallie with a sense of her true nature. "Surrender what is to what could be."

PART VII
Compassion

Darkness and Light are both of one nature,
different only in seeming,
for each arose from the source of all.
Darkness is disorder.
Light is Order.
Darkness transmuted is light of the Light.
This, my children, your purpose in being;
transmutation of darkness to Light.

The Emerald Tables of Thoth

.

CHAPTER THIRTEEN

The Mirror's Reflection

Sallie awoke earlier than usual with a surprising alertness. The beautiful Southern California sun pierced through the curtains of her open window, extending an invitation to come out and play.

She heard a chorus of birds clamoring for attention, chattering like a group of teenage girls talking about boys. Stretching as she gazed at the dawn light, the words "make peace with yourself" seemed to echo softly in her ear. This was one of those moments where she felt suspended in time, a sense of harmony permeating her consciousness.

An everyday routine now filled her time. Most days, she would call her father or stop by his house in a dance of renewing their acquaintance. Their conversations, sometimes tense, were peppered with only superficial minutia of their lives, when what Sallie craved was intimacy.

"Tell me about your life," she would ask. And he would recount stories of her and Mark's early years, memories already part of her recollection, when what she desired were new insights into their history.

"What about before we were born?" she would ask.

And he would answer, "Oh, my parents came from England and I was born here, an unexpected late surprise. I joined the Army when I was sixteen, lying about my age, and met your mother in Germany after the war. Then you were born."

Other days she would ask, "What about your memories of when you were a child?"

"Oh, I don't know," he would say. "You have to remember it was the Depression, then the war years, and life was hard." After repeated requests, she learned to limit the discussion to baseball, the news, and what they were going to eat that day.

Today's chore was her father's office. Sallie stood in the doorway, surveying the mess. She could hear her father's shouts in the living room and pictured him leaning forward in his chair, yelling at the television while Vin Scully, the Dodgers' announcer, called the game.

On a shelf mounted behind the desk were old baseball memorabilia her father had collected over the years. There was an old Dodger Blue cap, a Don Drysdale Blinky Blue Collector's Pin, and a Dodgers mug. His most prized possession sat in the middle on a stand—a baseball signed by the Dodgers World Series team. Sallie picked it up and heard his voice telling her that he was taking Mark to one of the Series games. "You know I'd like to take both of you, don't you?" he had said.

She heard her answer, still hollow in her mind. "It's okay. I don't want to go anyway."

From the living room, his shout brought her back to the present. "Come on now, bring him home! Let's tie this one."

The Dodgers must be down a run, Sallie thought. Buoyed by his excitement, Sallie joined him into the living room. "Who're they playing?"

"Arizona," he said as she sat down next to him, a companionable pair united in their mutual love of the game. The inning ended with a strike out.

"Darn!" her father yelled, muting the sound during the commercial break.

Sallie held up a paper. "I found this notice from your bank saying you need to update the beneficiary on your IRA. I can't find the paperwork."

"I sent it in."

"Did you make a copy for your records?"

"I didn't need to. Besides, it's my affair." He glared at her. "Why do you care? Do you want to see if I named you?"

"I'm just putting your papers in order," she said, her voice rising in exasperation.

"They're in order," he insisted gruffly.

"I'll just keep this separate until I can get it resolved."

He turned back to the game, turning the sound back on. "Just don't throw anything out."

She started to leave the room, then stopped and turned back. "I could take care of this for you. It might be easier if I got Power of Attorney to speak on your behalf without you being there. Banks are notorious about not talking to relatives without one."

He waved a hand to silence her, his full attention on the game. "Whatever you think is best. Just don't throw anything out."

Robert was waiting in the parking lot next to his office as Sallie drove up and pulled into a spot. He opened her car door. "Right on time. Traffic can get iffy so it's good to get an early start."

She handed him an easel pad as she stepped out of the car. "For recording our session," she said.

They walked over to Robert's late-model Lexus sedan, where he opened the passenger door for Sallie. Walking around the car, he put the easel in the back seat and slipped behind the wheel. "Looks like you're pretty organized."

"Oh, I don't know."

"You're not nervous?"

"Not exactly. It's just I don't know these people and wasn't expecting to be the Chair."

Robert eased the car into traffic and turned toward the freeway. "Well, let me tell you what little I know about them."

"That would help."

"Alice was an English teacher for many years before becoming a counselor. Now she's the new principal of Lincoln Junior High. Jim teaches History at MLK Junior High, an inner city school that's very low income. He came from the same background and is very dedicated to his students. Rhonda has been a volunteer in the Santa Monica School District since her children were young. She's an amateur artist and knows the importance of balance." He looked over at her and pointed to both sides of his brain. "You know, left brain, right brain."

Sallie nodded. "Being creative is as important as knowing the ABCs."

They continued their conversation and pulled into the school parking lot sooner than expected. Sallie noticed how comfortable she was talking with Robert. *He puts me at ease. Maybe we can become friends. Just friends, though.*

Alice showed them around the school as they moved toward the meeting location. "Summer school's in session in the morning, but everyone's already gone. The campus empties quickly at the end of the day."

They arrived at the old art classroom that would serve as their conference room. "The arts have gotten lost in the quest for academic excellence. We have a roving teacher who comes in twice a week. Not enough, in my opinion. Here, you can get settled. I'll find the others."

Sallie set up the easel and put an agenda out for each person, as well as some research information she had gathered on several existing arts programs.

After everyone had arrived and exchanged introductions, Sallie asked the group to tell why they were participating in the group. She looked toward Rhonda to start.

"I've got some artistic leanings myself and have worked in my children's school throughout their school years. We had a very successful arts program, and I'd like to see that expanded to lower-income students."

Jim spoke next. "When I was in school, I had a mentor who understood the importance of giving kids outlets to their creativity. Even though I teach history, I often have my students draw something related to what we're studying. I find it helps them retain what they learn."

Alice nodded in agreement. "At my last school, we had a pilot program where an arts teacher paired with an English and History teacher to create a similar program to what Jim does. We found our students had higher achievements in their core classes when their thinking was expanded through exposure to creative outlets."

Robert said, "My goal would be to encourage budding artists to pursue their art."

Sallie nodded to all. "We've got a good mix of purposes. I know my fascination with art began when I took an arts appreciation class in college. I think a well-rounded education can help everyone in their life."

As the group got more comfortable with each other, ideas began to flow, and Sallie wrote them on the easel pad. Rhonda wanted to develop a slide show of the various art eras, while Alice suggested the creation of a studio where students would have access to an art teacher both during and after school. Jim agreed with Alice and wanted to purchase art books and supplies for each school. Sallie suggested doing something with the Los Angeles County Art Museum and their docent program.

Alice laughed. "Seems we like ideas that might cost more than the schools could afford. After all, the arts program has been dropped mostly because of budgetary constraints."

"Well," said Sallie, "at this time, we should still put everything on our list for study."

Rhonda spoke up. "I've done some volunteer work with the County Art Museum. They always want to budget share and they're fairly expensive."

Sallie looked around at the group, who nodded their agreement. "Well, let's put it on the list with the proviso that the budget fits."

Jim spoke up. "I'd rather do something experiential within each school than something purely intellectual with the county. These kids have enough mental anguish just keeping up with their core studies."

Alice nodded. "I agree with Jim. Also, I'd like to add a training program for non-art teachers to our list."

By the end of the meeting, each committee member was assigned to research ideas and costs for an item they had discussed. Sallie's assignment was to follow up with the museum.

Arriving early to scout a good table on the front patio of Ida's Eatery, Sallie was looking forward to her lunch date with Iris. In the brief time they'd known each other, Sallie felt they had established a real connection.

She heard Iris approaching from across the street and turned to see her walking in that odd gait of hers, like the rat-tat of a woodpecker. Iris loved high heels. They made her slender ankles turn so nicely, she said. She wore them even when a more comfortable shoe would have sufficed, and their impractical height caused her to tilt slightly forward from the waist, as if her legs were unable to keep pace with the rest of her and her mind needed to arrive ahead of her body.

Iris saw her and waved. Sallie admired her put-together quality—a tailored, almost preppy style with a femininity that wasn't fussy. Perhaps it was the pearls she wore with her classic cotton blouse and crisp green skirt. They gave her a grace that belied her practical façade. She seemed to be two people; Dr. Iris, with her gray eyes focusing directly on you from behind her stylish glasses, and her alter ego, Princess Ella, with the Pollyanna, Someday-My-Prince-Will-Come persona.

Since they had first met, they had become constant acquaintances, still looking for commonalities that might turn them into good friends. During lunch, they browsed the edges of many subjects: Iris' summer writing class at UCLA, Sallie's new writing career, baseball, and the rivalry between Tim and Brian. Iris liked to share her experiences. She collected words like Sallie collected cookbooks, each poring over entries to make sense of their respective lives.

"What's the word of the day?" Sallie asked.

"Drum roll, please," said Iris, simulating one on the table edge with her fingers. "Today's word is 'filicide,' parents who kill their children."

"Oh!" Sallie's interest was piqued. "Literally or figuratively?"

"Originally it was probably literally, back in the 15th century when the word came into its usage. Today, it's another story. It's like the death of individuality in a figurative sense," responded Iris. "You know, a cultural thing."

"Where did you find that word? More importantly, how do you intend to use it?"

"We talked about it in class today." Iris feigned a slightly intellectual snobbishness in her voice for effect. "The subject was the original *Frankenstein* story by Mary Shelley. We were given an assignment to write about the effect of filicide on our lives. What do you think?"

Sallie blinked, caught off guard. No reply came immediately to mind.

Iris leaned in conspiratorially. "I think we all are."

"All are what?"

"Killed in some way by our parents."

"I'll have to think about that one. It's too morbid for such a beautiful day," Sallie said with a shake of her head, hiding the emotions welling up at the mere thought of the effects of filicide in her life. "You're all dressed up. Looking to impress someone?"

Iris simply grinned, an odd crooked smile full of secrets.

"Is he available?" Sallie saw by the other woman's reaction that she had hit the mark.

"No ring on his finger. Other than that, I'm not talking." She laughed with a shrug. "And how about you," Iris paused for emphasis, "and my dear brother?"

"What? He's just helping me out," Sallie responded, fidgeting under Iris' scrutiny.

"I wouldn't be so sure."

Sallie squirmed and turned toward the front door of the restaurant. "I wonder where our waiter is."

One wall of cupboards in her father's kitchen was now spotless and organized, save for the pairing of the plastic containers and lids that looked to be a lost cause. Sallie absently wiped a stray hair from her forehead with the back of her wrist as she surveyed her progress. The sounds of the baseball game drifted in from the living room, occasionally punctuated by her father's voice. Lost in her thoughts, Sallie jumped as the back door flew open and Mark bustled in.

"Hey," said Sallie. "I wasn't expecting you."

"I usually bring lunch a couple times a week," Mark said, putting a grocery bag on the counter and pulling out a couple of sandwiches.

Sallie peeked at the labels. "What'd you get?"

"Dad likes roast beef. I don't know what you're into these days, so I got their vegetarian special."

"Sounds good." Sallie unwrapped the sandwiches and sliced them, arranging them on plates with some condiments from the refrigerator on the side.

"Brian played a great game the other day," Sallie said as she worked.

"Yeah, only a couple of mistakes."

Sallie shook her head and smiled. "I enjoy watching him, though. He reminds me of you."

Mark looked astonished. "Oh." After a slight pause, he said, "I guess," before quickly changing the subject. "His batting average is close to .600."

"Amazing. I didn't realize these kids could hit that well."

"Yeah, surprising." There was quiet between them. "Are you staying long?" Mark finally asked.

"Hmm, I'll just be here for about another hour. I'm on a project hunt with Nonna this afternoon," Sallie answered.

"No, I mean staying in Los Madre."

"Oh," she said, wondering why he was asking. She answered carefully, "I'm not certain. I'm just playing it by ear for now."

"You've been spending a lot of time with Dad."

"I'm having a good time bringing his garden back to life."

Sallie looked closer at him to see if she could read his unasked questions from his body language.

"What are your plans?" Mark finally asked.

"I'm taking Dad to the game later today, if that's what you mean."

Mark looked impatient. "Well, I've got to go. I'll just look in on Dad. See you later then." Then just as quickly as he'd arrived, he was gone, leaving Sallie wondering what was unsaid between them.

Since her return, their conversations had only touched the surface of their lives and the facts of their surroundings. Sallie had hoped to rekindle what they'd had in childhood, yet so much was left unsaid. She was beginning to recognize that what she craved most was family and connection.

Sallie marched into her father's office and put her hands on her hips. Time to get down to business. There was another pile of mail on the corner of the desk that needed review, and she made a mental note to get to that project today. She had found some unpaid bills during her original cleaning of the room and wanted to make certain that didn't happen again.

The room was small, just an alcove in the front of the house, opposite the porch. When it had been her brother's bedroom, there was barely space for a single bed, desk and chair, and the wardrobe that had been his closet.

The only piece of furniture left from that era was Mark's wardrobe, and she had decided that today was the day for cleaning out its contents. Her brother had used a large bulletin board to display posters and other relics of his high school years. It still covered the wall with its original keepsakes, and she expected the wardrobe would contain some of Mark's old belongings as well.

Opening the door, she was surprised to find dusty boxes filled with the paperwork of a lifetime—old and recent tax returns, business letters, and military documents—all filed in yellowed manila file folders labeled with her father's schoolbook perfect script. Each box was catalogued and titled by year, with records going back to her early childhood.

She lugged each box from the cabinet, riffling through them to see if there were any clues to her parents' shrouded history. All she found were musty documents with frayed edges; nothing that couldn't be thrown out. Starting to put them back, she noticed another box in the back of the closet marked "Old Files."

It was smaller than the other boxes and covered by dark red canvas. She removed the lid to find vintage brown leather gloves, a pair of spectacles, and three small books written in German. They were antique leather-bound with gold lettering on the covers. One appeared to be a stenography textbook, another a work of fiction, and the last was an English-German grammar book.

Sallie picked them up one by one and opened to the frontispiece, looking for an inscription. Not finding any, she put the books down next to the box and reached inside for a crumpled envelope. Inside were a dozen or so photographs, small black and white pictures with lacy edges, slightly out of focus.

Her hands began to tremble as she placed the pictures side-by-side on the desk to examine each one closer. They were filled with exuberant young men and women of the late 1940s. Their faces were bright and joyful, as if they were making up for the lost time and vanquished comrades from the earlier part of the decade.

She studied a picture of her much younger father and another man. They were both in uniform and leaning against a counter, standing with their ankles crossed, holding steins up to the camera as if toasting the photographer.

Sallie found a picture of her mother and another woman the same age in shorts and fitted blouses. They stood straight with their arms around each other, smiling boldly at the camera.

Another showed a group of eight seated around a table with the remains of dinner before them. She frowned, looking closer to identify her mother and father in each picture. Some photos appeared to be of strangers.

She came upon another picture that made her frown grow even deeper. Her mother, wearing a light-colored suit and a small hat with a veil, stood next to the man from the bar photo. On either side of the couple stood her father and the woman who had been entwined with her mother. They were all smiling, champagne glasses held aloft for the camera. *It looks like a wedding celebration. Yet, why aren't my parents standing together?*

She reviewed each of the pictures again and could not find any in which her mother and father were together. Sallie picked up the wedding photo and walked into the living room, where her father was dozing lightly in his chair. His head jerked up as Sallie sat down next to him. "Just resting my eyes," he mumbled.

"When were you and Mom married?"

"You already know—New Year's Eve," he said, his brow furrowing. "What's this about?"

"What year?" Sallie's voice was harsh.

David stared at her and then looked away, not able to keep eye contact. "I don't remember. It was a long time ago."

Sallie tossed the picture onto his lap. "Who is this man?"

David studied the picture, and then glanced at her. He hesitated a minute to put his thoughts in order. "Where did you get this?"

"I was cleaning your office. Who are these people?"

"It's just your mother and me with some friends of ours from Germany."

"Then how come you and Mom aren't standing together? It looks like she's with this other man."

He put the picture on the table next to his chair. "No, it's just the way we wound up in the picture."

Sallie peered at him, considering his words. "It looks like a wedding celebration," she pressed.

"No, it was some other celebration. We were all good friends."

Sallie gave him an incredulous look. "That's not good enough." When it was clear he would say no more, she grabbed the picture and stomped out of the room. *What is he hiding?*

Back in her dad's office, Sallie threw the picture in the box, slammed the lid down, and shoved it to the back of the cabinet. *Why am I here?*

Closing the cabinet, she turned around and leaned against the front, going through the chain of events that had led her to this room. I wonder how Fred is doing on my license. Locating her cell phone, she noticed a missed call from Fred. *What synchronicity! Perhaps he's been successful and I can get back to my real life.* She dialed his number, thinking of Carol and Gail and how great it would be to be back in action with them.

When Fred answered the phone, Sallie said, "Saw your call just as I was thinking about you. Any news?"

Without any preamble, Fred started, "I've had a conversation with one of the outside attorneys the State uses for special cases."

Sallie interrupted, "Is this a special case?"

"No, I just didn't want to talk to one of the staff attorneys and I know this man. He's a good guy and might be helpful to us."

"Okay." She tried to quash the hint of skepticism in her voice.

"Apparently, the State is looking to make an example of people who embezzle funds."

"What does that mean?"

"You might be caught in their crosshairs."

"Is there anything you can do?" she asked.

"I've got some friends in the Real Estate Office. Let me see what they say.

"Do you have to tell them about me specifically?"

"No, I'll do a hypothetical. Not use your name. The guy I'm thinking of calling is not the attorney assigned to your case."

"Okay, great. Go ahead," she said. "What else could we do?"

"We could request a hearing where you would appear in person. Generally, everything is done through snail mail or email. However, if you request a hearing, they're usually accommodating."

"Do you think it would be helpful?"

"Well, I've seen it go both ways. Sometimes, yes. Sometimes, no. And I know you'd have to come a long way. It would be held in Sacramento."

"I could do that. I'm basically here on a temporary basis. My thinking is to stay here until I can go back to work. Do they give you their decision at the hearing?"

"Not usually. It does comes pretty quick, within a week or so."

Looking out through the door toward the living room where the game was still in full swing, Sallie sighed. "I'd like that. I might be finishing up down here pretty soon anyway."

After they signed off, Sallie plopped down into the chair, assessing the clutter on the desk in front of her. *I'm almost done here.* Her mind began to spin out. *What about everything here? Dad? What about Nonna? What about… Stop it right now. Don't even think about any of that.*

Turning her focus to the task in front of her, Sallie methodically put everything on the desk away with an air of finality. She never wanted to touch her father's mess again. Brushing unseen dust from her hands to eliminate her frustrations, she stood. *I need to put this behind me, at least for the moment, and go meet Nonna.*

Nonna liked to keep her hands busy with her "projects," as she called them. They ran the gamut of handcrafts, from crocheting and knitting, to sewing and even tatting—small lacework done with a shuttle. Following up on Sallie's interest, Nonna had determined it was her mission to teach Sallie to knit.

"Knitting is a good way to drift off into a reverie," Nonna had told Sallie. "It's what I think you young people mean when you say you're meditating. In the knitting and purling, following the pattern, you can get lost from your daily life, and new ideas can come to you. My projects have helped me through many of my personal crises. Give it a try," she'd suggested.

Today's outing was their first yarn shopping expedition. Meandering through The Knitting Basket, Los Madre's nationally known knitting store, Nonna touched each yarn as they wandered down the aisles. Sallie trailed behind her, overwhelmed by the vast array of colors and textures.

"Start by using your fingers to touch the yarn and feel its essence." Nonna enticed her by handing her a ball of yarn. "There's a sensual quality to yarn that tells you how it wants to be used." Sallie took the yarn from Nonna and cradled it in her hands. "Close your eyes and tell me how this yarn speaks to you," encouraged Nonna.

Sallie ran the yarn between her fingers. "Well, it's soft, almost like warm skin. Each thread is thin and smooth. It's like… I'm not certain. It's just very soft. If I had to describe it in one word, I would say gentle."

"Good. Each of those threads is called a fiber, and the ones you're touching have some cashmere in them that gives that softness," explained Nonna. "Now, what might you make with this fiber that would feel good on your skin?"

"Perhaps a lacy, lightweight shawl," Sallie responded like a schoolgirl with the right answer.

"Perfecto," replied Nonna. "You catch on quick."

They wandered through the store, examining the yarns and talking about their characteristics and how best to use each one. Finally, with Nonna's guidance, Sallie selected a light-weight yarn with variegated colors of orange and black, reminding her of her favorite baseball team. "I can even wear it to a Giant's game," she told Nonna as they picked out a pattern for a simple scarf. Sallie was buoyed by the idea of beginning something new.

As they were finishing their purchases, Nonna asked, "By the way, would you and your family like to join us on the Fourth? The town puts on a great celebration."

Sallie was taken aback, unsure of whether she could deal with both families getting together. "I'm not certain if there are any plans."

"If it's okay with you, I can call Nancy and we'll take care of everything."

"Okay, I guess," Sallie acquiesced. Nonna and Sallie said their farewells outside the yarn store and headed off in separate directions.

Walking slowly down the block, Sallie struggled to recall past Fourth of July celebrations and wondered how her family and the Parkers would get along. Suddenly, her toe caught on a crack in the sidewalk and she stumbled, putting her hand out against a tree to steady herself. When she looked up, she was disoriented. *Did I get turned around? Where is that new parking structure?*

A passing woman noticed her befuddled expression and stopped. "Are you alright? Do you need help?"

Sallie shook her head. "Just lost my bearings for a moment. Thank you for asking."

She turned back in the direction from which she had come. *I think I'm going the wrong way.*

"If you're looking for the new parking structure, make a left at the corner." The woman pointed the other way. "It's just a block and a half down, on the right." Sallie thanked her and regained her awareness of the surroundings.

Sallie rounded the corner quickly, nearly plowing into Robert. "Oh! Hello." She took a step back and tried to regain her composure. Other than their joint work on the Arts Committee, she hadn't talked to him much on a personal level since their meeting in his office.

"Hey, hi. What a coincidence. I was just thinking of you. How's your dad?"

"He's fine." She returned his smile.

202

"Well, say hello for me." There was an awkward moment of quiet and Sallie looked up the block. Robert rushed to add, "I'm helping a friend of mine, Amanda, organize an art exhibit opening on Thursday. She's a photographer. I thought you might like to go. It'd be a chance to meet some people."

"I don't know," Sallie wavered.

"I understand. You have to take care of your dad. Just give it a thought. You might enjoy it."

"It is a nice thought," she admitted.

"You know, I could ask Nonna if she would like to stay with your dad."

"Oh, no. I wouldn't want to intrude," Sallie quickly responded. "I'll see what I can do."

"I could pick you up."

"I could meet you there."

"Let me know. It's the Magnus Gallery on Third, Thursday, 5 PM. You'll enjoy it."

One wall of kitchen cabinets left to go. Hands encased in rubber gloves, Sallie teetered precariously on a small stepladder, peering into the back of a high cupboard as she scrubbed the shelf. The contents were on the counter below her, sorted into various categories.

"What are you doing?"

Startled, she jumped and bumped her head. She almost lost her balance as she turned to see her father staring at her from the doorway. "You scared me."

He looked away as she stepped down from the ladder and began to move baking dishes from one side of the kitchen to the other. "You sure haven't changed."

She whirled around and gave him a challenging look. "What do you mean?"

"You always had to have everything in perfect order."

"Me? You were the one who pushed us to perfection," she practically shrieked at him.

"Maybe your brother, yes. He had talent." David pulled a glass from the cupboard and turned to the sink to get some water. "No, you did it on your own."

"He had talent?" Sallie's voice rose in anger. "What does that mean? And what do you mean it was me? I got perfect by trying to please you." Realizing what she had revealed, Sallie turned away, not wanting to betray the hurt in her eyes. "I mean, you always wanted things just so."

"The house was never my domain. I left it up to your mother. And then to you." He walked out, as if his were the final words on the subject.

His words echoed in her head. *So, my brother had talent, did he? And I was the one who wanted everything perfect.* She began to put things away, purposefully allowing them to clatter and bang together, as if in making a lot of noise she could chase her father's words out of her head.

As she tamed the kitchen and put everything away, Sallie's anger gave way to resentment, then an aching sadness. She took a deep breath, then went to the living room and sat on the couch next to her father. Noting her fierce look, he picked up the remote and turned off the television.

"I think we should talk," she stated, her voice carefully measured.

"About what? I don't have anything to say."

"I thought we could set up some rules."

"There you go, 'rules.' I don't need any rules around here. This is my house."

Sallie stiffened and took a deep breath. "Let me start over. Perhaps we could talk about what we each need from our arrangement." She paused until he looked over at her. "I'll start. I need to feel appreciated."

"I don't need anything."

"Perhaps then we could talk about what I need."

David's mouth set in a hard line. "You have such a strong will. It's gotten you in trouble before. When are you ever going to learn? In my world, women were homemakers."

Sallie bit back an angry response. "What if a woman wants more?"

"Just as defiant as always," he said, shaking his head.

"I only wanted the same that men get by right," she said, her voice fierce.

He looked at her as if seeing her for the first time. His voice was quiet. "I thought I was helping you. I just wanted to shape you for the job of a woman."

"It was as if you told me I wasn't good enough for your world and I had to prove I was."

"No, I was only afraid you'd be unhappy, like your mother. She never felt like she fit in. I just wanted you to fit in."

Sallie answered quietly, "And I just needed to be accepted the way I am."

His voice reached across the space separating them. "I accept you," he said quietly. She looked up and found him gazing at her with a caring look in his eyes.

"Can we just say we're going to pay more attention to each other?" she asked.

"I'm willing to give it a try," he said, watching her. "I just want to stay in my home."

They looked at each other as if each had gained a new perspective on the other. Sallie stood up and walked toward the kitchen, glancing at the clock. "We need to start getting ready for the game. Don't want to be late for Brian."

Sallie quickly got ready and headed into the den while she waited for her father. As she picked up a pile of mail and began sorting it, she

205

yelled toward the hall, "Dad, are you ready yet?"

"Almost, honey. I'll be right there," he called back.

Finished with the stack, she stepped over to the wall cabinet and picked up the last photo taken of the four of them before her mother got sick. She looked closely at her mother, straining to recall her touch.

David came up behind her and looked over her shoulder, reaching for the picture. "You remind me of her, you know," he said as he handed it back.

"Do you ever think of her?"

"Every day. You look just like her. I noticed it when you became a teenager. It was hard on me."

Her eyes widened at his confession. She had never expected to hear this from her father. *Is he actually opening up to me?* Maybe there was hope for them yet.

Sallie entered the large, open space dominated by immense modernistic paintings. Frowning, she stepped back out onto the street and looked up at the sign for the Magnus Gallery. A young woman scurried from the back. "Wait, don't go."

Stepping back into the gallery, Sallie said, "I'm here for the opening."

"They're in the upstairs salon. Let me take you there."

At the top of the rise was a more intimate space. A dozen or so people were clustered in tight groups around a table set with small plates. A bar was set up in the corner. Photographs with dark shadows and heightened contrasts covered the walls. Robert saw her and hurried over.

"You look great." His smile was infectious. "So glad you could make it."

"I shouldn't stay long."

"Come meet the artist."

206

Robert ushered her over to a young woman with black hair, pale skin, and dark make up, talking with a couple about one of the photos.

"The contrast between the highs and lows is so significant," the well dressed middle-aged man said as he pointed to a picture of what appeared to be a naked woman's body lying on a couch in shadowy relief against a white background.

The young blonde woman standing next to him added, "I agree. They seem to shout, 'pay attention to me!' "

"Yet, it's difficult to tell who she is; the shadows around her are so predominant," the man said.

"It's a metaphor for our dark side, hidden yet demanding," Amanda explained.

As Robert approached, Amanda excused herself and turned to him. "Hey, Robert. Thanks so much for your help in putting this together." She looked toward Sallie. "And, who's this?" She raised an eyebrow toward Robert.

"Amanda, meet Sallie."

Sallie put out her hand as she pulled slightly away from Robert. "I'm new in town and Robert's just showing me the ropes."

"He's good at that."

Sallie gave her a warm smile and looked toward the pictures on wall. "Your photographs are intriguing. I'd like to know more about your creative process."

"I'd love to tell you about it."

The three of them wandered through the exhibit with Amanda and Sallie in quiet conversation. Sallie stopped in front of a blurred picture of what looked like a woman in white caught like a deer in the headlights.

"Who is your model? Your relationship to her seems so intimate, as if you know all her best and worst qualities."

Amanda gave a hardy laugh. "I should." Sallie raised an eyebrow. "They're me."

207

"What?" Sallie scrutinized the picture further.

"Yep. The long exposure creates an atmosphere of mystery, don't you think?" said Amanda.

Sallie smiled and looked closer. "It's quite a neat effect."

Amanda shrugged. "They're meant to call attention to the parts of us we don't like to share."

"There's a vulnerability about her, yet it's also as if she's protecting herself by living in the shadows," Sallie observed.

"I started this project several years ago after a pretty traumatic period in my life. Working on my art was my attempt to make sense of a bad experience."

"Did it help you?"

"For me, it's an ongoing process, like peeling away the petals of a flower."

One of the organizers of the event came up and motioned to Amanda, who turned to Sallie. "I need to go. It was wonderful to meet you." Amanda gave a slight bow and headed off to greet another guest.

Robert, who had been quietly listening to their conversation, took Sallie's arm as they continued looking at the photographs. "So, what do you think?"

"They look more like abstract paintings than photographs." Sallie was intrigued.

"Yes, isn't it brilliant?"

They strolled until they came back to the first picture. Sallie observed the naked woman. "Most photographs usually capture images more realistically," said Sallie. "Hers are different, aren't they?"

"Amanda has always been interested in the hidden aspects of the personality, those parts of us we deny."

"It looks like a woman's body, yet it's vague. I guess that's her point. It's sensuous, yet dark and forbidding."

Robert looked intently at the photograph, then turned to Sallie. He spoke in a quiet, intimate voice, leaning toward her ear. "Well, I would say it's a sensuous woman, one who says 'don't come too close or you might be burned.' Just enough of a challenge that a certain kind of man would like to discover the softness behind the prickles."

Sallie turned toward him. His face was only a breath away, close enough for a kiss. She held his gaze for a moment and turned back to the picture, the corner of her mouth twitching up slightly. She tilted her head toward him. "What if the prickles are all there is?"

Robert leaned toward the picture, his head almost touching hers. "Every woman has a soft side. It's up to a man to discover it. Perhaps she's the kind that only shows it to one man. He'd be a very lucky guy."

Sallie turned away to hide a smile. "What if she doesn't know if she has that side?"

"Well then, it's up to him to uncover it."

A woman hurried toward them, interrupting their quiet conversation. "Robert, the caterer would like a word with you."

The moment broken, Sallie saw the opportunity for a graceful exit. "Look, you're really busy. I told Dad I wouldn't be too late. I better go."

"This will just take a second. A few of us are going out to dinner later. I had hoped you would join us."

Sallie hesitated. "Perhaps another time. I really need to go… but thank you. For the invite." She squeezed his arm and made her way out into the night, willing herself not to look back.

Nancy's kitchen counter was covered with the signs of their handiwork. On weekends with games, Sallie and Nancy's comradeship extended to picnic lunches for an odd assortment of twelve-year-old boys.

Sallie's hands were white with flour as she gently kneaded the dough for a peach cobbler. Nancy bustled around, multitasking as she fried chicken and diced ingredients for a potato salad. Her specialties, simpler than the gourmet fare Sallie liked to craft, came from her experience, rather than the latest celebrity cookbook.

Nancy chattered away on a variety of subjects, all connected to her role as wife and mother, her words a stream of consciousness reflecting her personality.

"Brian is really excited about the game today. He's doing so well. We can have the picnic afterward in the park next door. Mark's going to pick Dad up. We can meet them at the park. We have to be out the door by 11:30."

Sallie let her mind wander. Nancy's perky energy and boundless enthusiasm sometimes made Sallie wonder if she were real. Was she ever sad, depressed, or angry? Nancy was definitive by nature, as if she had figured out everything there was to know about life; no further questions needed.

Sallie assessed her sister-in-law with a mixture of awe and nervousness in her gaze. *She has a good heart*, Sallie thought, as she recognized a sisterly love for her. Nancy was content with her life, certain that everything she did was right, and all women should be staying at home and taking care of their families. This made Sallie apprehensive about opening up, not wanting to be judged for her view of life. *I'm different than she is, yet we share many things in common. There seems to be no reason for this disquietude plaguing me.*

Nancy interrupted her reverie. "Do you cook a lot?"

"I enjoy it. My cooking time, in the past, was often limited by my work, though."

"What kind of things do you cook?"

"I like making complex dishes, where there's a base of ingredients which get cooked and then the result gets used in another dish," Sallie responded. "Like making a stock from scratch and then making a soup using the stock as a base."

"Oh, I don't do anything that fancy. I'm just a basic cook. Mark likes his meat and potatoes. He says it goes with the territory. He's just a simple man. I match to him. I like liver; he doesn't. We don't eat it."

With a small laugh, Sallie said, "Everyone is an individual with their own tastes and ideas about things, especially food."

"Oh, yes, we each have our role. I believe, though, a woman's role is to take care of her man. There must be one who makes the final decision. Mark is the leader in our family."

"Don't you ever want to do something for yourself?"

"Oh, Mark doesn't dominate me, if that's what you mean. I just like doing what my man wants. I want him to make all the decisions for us."

"I'm not certain I could get used to that," said Sallie thoughtfully.

"Listen, my father left when I was nine. One day, he just didn't come home from work. I didn't know why. My mother just went into a trance and we never discussed it. To this day, I still worry that it was my fault. I vowed I'd do whatever it took to make my marriage work.

"Mark is the only man I have ever known, and my marriage is the most important thing in the world to me. I admire him. He's strong and decisive. I was so proud of him getting promoted to lieutenant and having responsibility for the drug program. He's good with kids. He's a good provider and he takes care of us. I tell him so. He treats me like a queen. I wouldn't change my life for anything."

This was a fresh view of her brother that Sallie hadn't considered. She pushed it to the back of her mind for further reflection at another time. "Alright, the cobbler is going in the oven. Where's your honey?"

Nancy pointed toward a cabinet.

"I'll get the lemonade ready for the boys."

Once she had prepared a fresh pitcher, Sallie headed out to where Mark was taking Brian through his pre-game drills.

"Eye on the ball, eye on the ball!" Mark yelled, throwing grounders, one right after the other, not letting up. "Keep up the pace. Don't let up!"

Brian stumbled and missed a ball.

"Focus! You've got to focus!"

"Mark, that's enough!" Sallie cried out from the porch as her nephew stumbled again.

Mark stopped and strode over to Sallie, looking sideways at Brian as he went by. "That's enough, son. Go in and get ready." He waited until Brian had passed them and gone into the house.

"I don't like you telling me how to handle my son, especially in front of him. You're undermining my authority."

Sallie walked down the steps until she stood right in front of him. "I remember when Dad used to take you through those same drills and how resentful you were."

"This is different. Brian has talent. And a scholarship will get him into a better college."

Sallie gave him a wry smile. "That's what Dad said about you."

"And you should stay out of things that are none of your business," Mark snapped and headed into the house, slamming the screen door behind him.

Sallie followed him into the house. "Wait, Mark, please."

He turned. "Look," said Sallie. "I didn't mean to upset you."

"We've got a game today. This is how I get him ready, and it's been successful."

"Yes, I know. Can we let it go?"

He shrugged. "I've got a job to do. Let me do it."

"Peace?" She held out her hand.

Mark relaxed and took it. "Peace."

A holiday mood drew Sallie from her sleep and she rose early with a mixture of trepidation and excitement about the day's events. Years had passed since she had been to a Los Madre Fourth of July celebration. Nonna had guaranteed that Sallie would have a good time, promising the festivities had only grown more elaborate since she had last attended.

Nancy and Nonna had wanted their families to spend the entire day together, so Sallie had instructions to meet at the pancake breakfast first thing in the morning to start the day's festivities. Sallie's job was to pick up her father and meet them at the square.

"Oh," Nancy had said over the phone, "and bring a salad for the picnic. And some blankets. And also some of your honey lemonade." And the list went on.

Sallie filled the order, picked up her father, and circled the town plaza, searching for parking. Robert waved and jogged over to meet them as they settled into a spot.

"Hey," he said, motioning toward the festivities energizing the town as Sallie helped her father out of the car. "Looks like the beginning of another fine celebration."

"Hi," Sallie replied, then turned to her father. "Dad, this is Robert Parker. I've told you about him and his family."

David straightened up as tall as he could and put out his hand. "Pleased to meet you, son."

"Likewise, sir," Robert responded, recognizing David's military background from his posture. A quiet lull infused the triad, each uncertain what to say next.

"Well," began Robert, talking quickly in an effort to bring some gaiety to the group, "I hope you're hungry. This pancake breakfast can really fill you up." He motioned toward the basket Sallie was starting to take out of the back seat. "Leave everything. Just bring your appetite."

The trio walked across the plaza to where the local Kiwanis Club spearheaded the Annual Pancake Breakfast. Robert spotted Nonna and Nancy at one of the long tables, waving wildly to get their attention. They were the last to arrive and the rest of the family was in line for food.

"Ah, there they are, with places for all of us," he said, steering them through the crowd beginning to line up for breakfast. An area of the park was roped off and filled with huge grills, now overflowing with pancakes, ham, bacon, and eggs. The festive mood of the day was kicked off with the enthusiasm of the volunteers and their teasing of all who came through the line.

"Ah, here's our Mayor!" A tall man in a red, white, and blue striped apron waved a spatula in the air as a petite, dark haired woman smiled and held out her plate. "What's going on at City Hall?" he ribbed with a jovial laugh. "Got any plans for that vacant lot over at Marshall and Second?"

There was laughter everywhere and Sallie finally relaxed as she saw her family and the Parkers begin to merge and converse. Nancy and Nonna had orchestrated the seating arrangements with Tim and Brian at one end, Mark next to Iris, Maria and Sam, and their children seated with David. With only two chairs left, Sallie and Robert easily found their seats at the other end.

"Well, that was simple." Robert shrugged. "What do you think?"

With a quick smile, Sallie responded, "I guess you're right." She looked down the table to her brother, who smiled at her, the sharp words of their recent dispute forgotten in the festive atmosphere of the day.

"You were expecting a war, perhaps?" Robert quipped, an easy smile on his lips.

After breakfast, the highlight of the day was the Fourth of July parade. The high school and two junior high bands were interspersed with some vintage floats, one of which included Miss Los Madre.

Sallie was delighted to see that her favorite part of the parade, the March of the Animals, was still a main attraction. All the town children brought their pets and marched around the square. Dogs of every size and description paraded alongside bunnies in wagons and cats on leashes. Hamsters in cages were pulled by their miniature owners, and even a pet snake made the march, in its glass cage, of course.

The parade always ended with members of the local firefighters union riding in their vintage 1934 fire engine, which had been the original fire protection when the community was first incorporated.

After the parade, the entertainers and artists took over, with music blaring from speakers on a giant stage in the middle of the park, a dance platform at its base, and arts and crafts booths surrounding the outer fringes of the square. The Olde Thyme Dixieland Band started the day with music from an earlier era. Sallie, Robert, and David sat down on a park bench to listen.

Maria and Sam headed with their children over to the Children's Corner, sponsored by several of the local pre-schools in town. Tim and Brian declared themselves too old for kid stuff and said they would meet everyone later after the baseball game as they disappeared in whispered collusion. Nonna and Nancy decided to save a table for the picnic later in the day and gathered up all the gear to get it organized. Mark wandered off with them to carry the ice chest.

"I haven't been here in years," said David. "That old time music sounds good."

Sallie smiled and gave his arm a squeeze. "I'm glad you're enjoying yourself. Let me know if you get tired. I can always take you home for a nap and pick you up later."

"I'm not that senile," he answered with a quick retort, then gently patted her arm. "I'll be okay. Don't worry about me. I'll go watch the bocce tournament later. They still have that, don't they?"

"Oh, yes," replied Robert. "It's a big deal every year. You should play yourself. It's a great game."

"I tried it when I was younger, right after I retired. There's a lot of competition here and some pretty good players," said David. "Anyway, Sallie tells me you have your own business."

Robert nodded and began to tell him about it. Sallie let them talk as she felt a calmness infuse her body. *Everything is going to work out just fine.*

From across the street, Sallie saw Frank waving at her. She rose and waved back, walking to meet him as he jogged over.

"Hey, Sallie, that was a great column you wrote—exactly what we want. Your style is what I call 'down home.' I like it. So does Kent. We want to run it next week. See how it goes. See the response." His voice was animated. Sallie's heart surged with excitement. "What do you think? Will you give us permission?"

"Oh, yes." She could barely contain her enthusiasm. "I would love that."

"Well, there's two opportunities—my weekly, and Kent's magazine. I'd like to see how a weekly column might work. Then, if it works for you and me, we could add the magazine. What do you think?"

"A weekly column?" For the first time, Sallie realized the extent of her commitment. *Well, I could always write from Las Rosas. I don't need to be here to write.* She gave him a wide smile. "Sounds good."

"Come by my office next week. Need you to sign our standard contract for freelance writers. Oh, by the way, we'll need a name for the column. Think up something and let us know. Well, got to run. Glad I ran into you. Enjoy the festivities." And with that, he was gone.

Sallie danced back to the bench with a spring in her step and a big smile on her face, executing a two-step as she approached them.

"Well, what gives?" asked Robert. "You look like you just won a prize or something."

Sallie beamed and nodded. "Bingo! The *Courier* is going to run my column on real estate." Turning to her father, she added, "I don't know if I told you, Dad." She gave him the details of her first publishing effort, ending with, "I need a name for the column before next week."

Robert smiled. "Hey, that's great. Let's brainstorm something later. We've got some good heads between us. We'll come up with something. Congrats." Robert stood up and gave her a big hug.

David squeezed her arm. "That's the ticket. Now, how about that bocce tournament?" He got up quickly from his seat without the full

216

support of his cane and his feet started to slip beneath him. Robert reacted swiftly, reaching out to support him before he fell.

"Just a lightheaded moment, that's all," David said, as he planted his cane firmly and stood straight, supported by Robert.

Sallie rushed to his side. "Dad, are you okay?"

"Certainly," he said, shaking off her concerns. "Now, let's go see about that tournament."

He headed off without further ado, leaving Sallie to catch up with him. She whispered in his ear. "Let's not tell Mark about this, okay?"

The bocce court was quiet when they entered. Two teams were playing, each with four players. The three of them sat down on a bench a distance away so as to not disturb the game.

David whispered, "See that guy over there, the one with the ball?" He pointed toward a balding, stocky man who was intent on his target. "Ex-military, name of Mac. Watch."

"What should we be watching?" asked Sallie.

"See that small ball?" He pointed toward a ball in the middle at the far end of the court. "That's the jack. The idea is to get your ball closest to it."

Mac threw his ball, his face contorted in a look of deep concentration. His ball found its mark, knocking away a competitor's ball and rolling to a stop closest to the jack. He punched the air in satisfaction and turned to another man with a triumphant look on his face.

"That's Emmett," David explained. "They've always got something going."

They watched as Emmett made an unsuccessful attempt to knock out Mac.

"They're so competitive. There never seemed to be a point in trying to catch up to them."

"Isn't there a beginning group somewhere you could join? Seems like a good way to make some friends."

He shrugged and put his finger to his lips to quiet her.

They watched in quiet anticipation until Mac's team won after an intense last minute play. Cheers went up from the players and their supporters around the court.

Leaving the bocce tournament, they went in search of the picnic site, where they found a table laden with food. Robert helped David to a seat on the end as Nonna fussed over him. "You must be starved," she said. "May I make a plate for you?"

David nodded, looking on with approval as she loaded it with generous portions of American classics. "You women did a good job on the food. Nothing beats some good home cooking," he complimented the chefs.

Nonna sat down opposite him. "Seems a shame we hadn't talked before, after seeing each other at the grandkids' games."

Sallie and Iris filled their plates and sat on the blanket, where Robert joined them. As they ate, Iris and Robert kept up a constant banter, teasing each other. Full and happy, Sallie took up her knitting, listening and interjecting a comment now and then.

Iris looked at her brother, who tilted his head toward Sallie. Taking the hint, she said, "I think I'll get some of those cookies you made. I've been eyeing them for some time."

"Help yourself," said Sallie.

"I've already had several and can attest to their deliciousness," Robert confessed.

After Iris left, Robert turned over on his stomach and put his chin on his hands, watching Sallie knit. "You know, I'd like to get to know you better."

"And you know I've got a lot of responsibilities. I'm not looking for a relationship."

"How about just being friends?"

Sallie put down her knitting and looked at him. His face was expectant, yet genuine. She realized he wasn't trying to pressure her into something she didn't want. "A friend would be good."

"Well, then, may I ask you a professional question?"

Sallie nodded.

"I've been looking ahead," he paused to choose his next words carefully. "That is, to my retirement some day. I might want to grow some grapes."

"Grapes?"

"I've got the family wine business in my blood, remember? I was thinking about the Santa Barbara area."

Glancing toward the setting sun, Sallie packed up her knitting. "What would you want me to do?"

"I'd like your professional assistance in finding some land. Perhaps represent me in a purchase."

Sallie looked around to see if anyone could overhear them, then said in a quiet voice, "I can't represent you right now."

He gave her a questioning look. "I thought you were a real estate broker."

"I'm not familiar with Santa Barbara real estate. However, I could help you find someone."

Not the answer he wanted, Robert switched tactics. "Well, would you accompany me to offer advice?"

Sallie hesitated. The look in his eyes was so sincere that she found herself smiling despite her reservations. "Yes, I'll go with you."

His triumphant smile was illuminated by a colorful burst of light as the fireworks show lit up the night sky. They lay side by side, admiring the bright trails and sparkling shapes until at last the celebration was over.

"That was a nice day," her father told her as they drove home in the darkness. "I enjoyed meeting your friends. Your grandmother, my mother, came from a family like that. She used to talk about her big family in Italy. I always wondered what would have happened if my parents had gone to Italy to her side of the family instead of coming to

219

the United States to my father's family."

It was the first that Sallie had heard about her family in Italy. She held her breath, desperate for him to continue. When he remained quiet, she gently nudged, "What else can you tell me about your mother's family?"

"Oh, that's about it," he said and sank into a reverie.

Sallie glanced sideways at him, deciding whether to probe him further, releasing a breath she didn't know she was holding. *Please tell me more,* she willed.

As if hearing her thoughts, he reached across and patted her hand. "That was such a long time ago."

She put her hand on his. "I'd just like to know more about my ancestors."

Sallie smoothed her blouse as she watched the quiet street from the front window of her bungalow. Despite her initial reluctance, she now found herself filled with a heady mixture of nervousness and excitement about her impending trip to Santa Barbara with Robert.

This would be the longest period she had spent with him in one sitting. Once she got in his car, there would be no way out. Still, she relished the feeling of being back in action and planned to use her professional expertise to set the tone for the day.

She frowned as a vintage red Corvette pulled into the driveway. *Who could that be?* She grabbed her real estate file and headed outside to investigate, stopping short when she saw Robert jump out the driver's side door.

"Ready for a fantastic day?" he asked as he walked around the car to open the passenger door for Sallie.

Caught off guard, she recovered quickly. "Definitely." She stood back to take in the sight, her eyebrows arched as her eyes flowed over the curves of the car. "And, pray tell, whose is this?"

Robert shrugged with feigned nonchalance.

"It's cherry." Her eyes glittered and she let out a low whistle, tracing a finger along the hood as she walked around the front. "Someone's obviously put a lot of work into it."

"It's mine," he confessed, his voice thick with the pride of fatherhood.

"Yours? What about the Lexus?"

"Can't a guy have two cars?" Robert grinned, relishing the moment. He tilted his head toward the door. "Try her out."

Sallie slid into the passenger seat, admiring the immaculate classic interior. Robert closed the door for her and walked around the car to take his place in the driver's seat. He turned the key and revved the gas. They exchanged a smile as the Corvette purred.

"Do you like it?" Robert asked.

"Like it? I'm drooling. There's got to be a story here. Tell me."

"Dad was good with old cars. He could put together anything you could drive. This was the last project we worked on together. He taught me everything I know and gave me a passion for vintage cars."

It must be nice to bond over a shared project like that. "Well, she's a beauty, no one can deny that." Sallie shook her head.

"You look surprised."

"I guess I just wasn't expecting this."

"Impressed then?"

"Maybe," Sallie admitted.

Robert laughed. "Well, if you give me a chance, you'll find I'm full of surprises."

Sallie gave her companion an appraising look. *Somehow, I believe him.*

Robert put the car into gear and eased out the driveway. As they drove out of town, Robert nodded toward the files on Sallie's lap. "Whatcha got for me?"

Sallie opened the folder, pointing out the properties she planned to show him. "There are only a few properties available with enough land to meet your needs. I've made some appointments."

"I also want to show you the area I really like. It's slightly west of most of the wineries. More coastal."

Sallie nodded. "I believe one of the properties is coastal." She pulled out her phone and looked up directions. "Looks like it'll take us about an hour and a half to get there."

"That is, if the Force is with us."

Sallie leaned back in her seat, watching the road and feeling a sense of comfort. She was in her element, slipping easily back into the familiar role. A pang of nostalgia tugged on her chest as her thoughts wandered back to Las Rosas. *At least this trip will keep my skills sharp for when I return to my job. I wonder how Carol is doing.*

Robert interrupted her reverie. "I know you like baseball. What about movies?"

"My favorites are the old movies from the '30s and '40s." Sallie sat up and looked toward Robert. "How about you?"

"I like all movies. Old movies, new movies, what really matters is good characters. Blow 'em up action is not my style. Who's your favorite actress?"

"I love Barbara Stanwyck. She had style."

"And a favorite leading man?"

"Oh, probably Cary Grant. He had such charm. And that accent…" She got a faraway look in her eyes. "There's just something about the classics."

"I know what you mean. Montgomery Clift is one of my favorites. He was so intense. And Spencer Tracy sure knew how to steal a scene."

"Sure did. Loved him in anything with Katherine Hepburn."

"What's your favorite Hepburn/Tracy moment?"

"Hmmm." Sallie took a moment to collect her thoughts. "I loved it when she was holding her own in the company of men. The ending to *Woman of the Year* was smaltzy. I'd say *Adam's Rib* would be my fav.

Hepburn's character was a take charge kind of woman who didn't compromise her values."

"Always a plus." Robert winked at her.

Their conversation continued in the dance of getting to know one another until at last they settled into a comfortable silence. Sallie glanced at her cell phone and was surprised to see they were now only half an hour out from their destination. She marveled at how at ease she felt in Robert's presence, laughing to herself as she wondered why she had been worried.

"Do you mind if I put on some music?" she asked.

"Be my guest," he said amiably.

She turned on the radio, scanning through channels until she landed on a station playing the final chorus of one of Fleetwood Mac's classics.

Robert nodded approvingly. "I knew you had good taste."

Sallie smiled and tapped her fingers on her skirt as the familiar strains of Van Morrison's "The Mystery" began to play.

Robert began humming along, first under his breath, gaining volume as the verse built into a crescendo. As the chorus hit, Sallie jumped and nearly hit the car roof as Robert burst out singing in full voice. She couldn't help but laugh at the enthusiasm behind his slightly off-key rendition.

He grinned at her. "Come on, I know you know the words."

She blushed, yet his energy was infectious. She began to hum along quietly, unsure at first, until she found herself singing the melody out loud as he shamelessly butchered the harmonies. As the song came to a close, they smiled at each other and laughed.

"You know, he's going to be at the Bowl this month."

"I've never been to the Hollywood Bowl."

"No, really?"

"I left to go to college up north and haven't really done a lot in LA as an adult."

"Well, I can remedy that, if you'd like to go."

Sallie gulped. *He's asking me for a date. I'm not certain I'm ready to date him. He's so disarming. But what if I get hurt? What if he gets hurt?* "It's hard to turn down a chance to see Van Morrison in person," she admitted.

"It's a deal then."

"Not a date, though?"

"No, just a couple of friends checking out the LA music scene." Robert looked up at the exit sign. "Hey, I better pay attention to the directions. This looks like our exit."

Robert turned off the freeway and drove for a couple miles until he turned onto a small paved road leading into the thirty-two-acre site. As they approached the driveway, they saw the realtor, Jane, standing next to her car, waving at them.

After introductions, Jane got down to business, reciting the particulars of the property.

Robert glanced in all directions and nodded. "Looks promising. How many acres in vines?"

Jane consulted her printout. "Looks like sixteen, a combination of Malbec and Chard."

Sallie looked over her shoulder at the pictures. "Let's go see the house."

They walked into the Craftsman-style structure and could see all the rooms from the front door. "It's a little small," Sallie remarked, looking at Robert to see if he agreed.

"Could be used as a granny unit." They walked back outside and Robert pointed to an area studded with oaks surrounding an open space. "Looks as if there's a good site on that knoll for a larger main house." He turned to Jane. "This one has promise. Let's keep looking."

"Let's take my car," said Jane. Robert nodded, opening the passenger door for Sallie.

The next property was open land, about forty acres. When they got out of car and walked a few feet into the property, Robert pointed toward the west, where there was a small view of the water. "I like this property because of its location near the ocean." He turned to Sallie, pointing to a hill north of them. "The area I had in mind is just over that rise. This is close enough. With the ancient beach and diatomaceous earth, plus foggy nights and warm days, this is near perfect for both Chard and Pinot."

"I didn't know you were that knowledgeable on grape growing."

"Runs in the family." Robert beamed from her compliment. "I could lay the property out to my specs. Disadvantage is the time, money, and effort spent in putting it all together."

Jane and Sallie watched as he picked up some dirt and ran it through his fingers. "Good soil." He shook his hand, letting the soil fall to the ground. "Let's see your last listing."

Driving further inland, they rounded a curve and came upon the third property. Sallie caught her breath. Before them was an idyllic view of oaks with vineyards curled up a hill toward an old-fashioned farmhouse. Jane pulled over to the side of the road, picked up her spec sheet and read the description. "Forty-five acres, fifteen planted in Cab."

Robert's eyes were bright with excitement. "Looks promising. I like the fact that some of the land has grapes."

"And the house is the original farmhouse from the 1930s," Sallie chimed in, smiling at Robert.

Inside, the home was fastidious with original details still in place, including built-in bookcases, ornate moldings, and hardwood floors.

"Look at these built-in bookcases. It still retains its old charm." Sallie ran her hand over the oak frame and the walls. "And the old lathe and plaster walls."

"The oak floors look original."

Jane consulted her papers. "The entire house is original." They walked toward the kitchen, where Sallie looked out the window into a backyard garden. She ran a hand along the farmhouse sink. "Even the kitchen hasn't been changed."

Right behind her, Robert touched the stove and gave her an intimate smile. "It even has an O'Keefe and Merritt from the '30s. Kate and Spence could have cooked a meal here."

Sallie laughed. "That they could. Lots of charm, just needs a little face-lift. Not too much, though. Not enough to take away that charm."

Jane came into the kitchen. "Sallie, got a question for you." Sallie turned to her. "I know you're a real estate agent up north. Would this be a shared commission?"

Sallie stiffened and leaned back, her hands white-knuckled on the sink behind her. "Well, I don't… It might be… We'll just have to wait and see." Both Robert and Jane gave her a questioning look.

When Sallie didn't elaborate, Jane looked at the file in her hands. "Alrighty then. Let me see if I've forgotten anything about this property."

Their tour of the properties complete, Jane dropped them back at Robert's car and promised to follow up with Robert by phone on Monday. As they settled in for the long drive home, Sallie asked, "If you were to buy one of the properties, which would it be?"

"Hmmm. Probably the one with the old farmhouse."

"That one is nice." Sallie relaxed into the seat, a daydreamy smile on her face.

Passing through the small nearby town on the way to the freeway, Robert slowed down. "What a cute little community."

Sallie leaned forward to get a better look through the windshield. "It has some of the same charm as Los Madre. Looks even smaller."

Robert pointed out his window as they passed an aging marquee. "Look, they even have their old theatre. It looks as if it's still in operation. Our old theatre hasn't shown movies in over a decade."

She nodded. "Surprising that there can be that many movie buffs in a rural area like this."

"Perhaps it's the main entertainment."

She chuckled. "That might be it."

They were quiet for a minute, each lost in their own thoughts about small town life.

"This place sure brings back old memories." Robert's eyes remained on the road ahead of him, yet his gaze seemed to look into the past. "When I was about ten, I had a couple of friends, Mickey Flanagan and Tommy Blake. We were a bit mischievous, always trying to outdo each other. Well, Mickey had an older sister who worked at our movie theatre. Did you ever go?"

"Yes. Sometimes my friends and I would go to the Saturday matinee. I'd buy lemon drops because they'd last through the whole movie. My mouth was certainly puckery by the end of the day." They both laughed.

Robert went on, "Well, Mickey's sister would sneak us in the side door every Saturday and we thought we were hot stuff, getting in free to the movies." He glanced over at her. "Bet you never got into the movies free."

"No, I didn't even think about doing that. It's not like it was really expensive back then."

"You're right. It wasn't. For us boys, though, it was the thrill of being illicit. Well, anyway, one day we got caught by old Mr. Snipes. You remember him, the sourpuss manager of the theatre?"

Sallie nodded. "I do. You didn't want to cross him; what a cantankerous old man." She looked over at him. "What happened?"

"Well, my dad came and got us. Told Mr. Snipes he'd take care of everything. And he did…" He paused for effect.

Sallie looked at him expectantly. "And? What did your dad do?"

"It wasn't what he did. It was what he didn't do. He didn't raise his voice. He didn't give me a whipping, although I probably deserved one. He just talked to me, sorta like I was an adult. He told me about character, about integrity, about always being the person you want to be, where everyone could know everything about you."

"Really." Sallie reflected on this new insight about Robert and his father. *His dad must have been very loving.*

"It was an interesting time for me. Before that, Dad had been very distant, as if he carried secrets and he didn't want anyone to know anything about him. Our family changed and he finally started to open up to us." He patted the Corvette's dashboard. "One of the best parts for me was bonding with my dad over cars. Because of that experience, I've always felt that good can come from what looks like bad."

"He sounds remarkable."

"He was." Robert was quiet for a moment. "How about you? Any childhood mischief you'd like to share?" he teased with a quirky smile. Keeping his eyes on the road, he let Sallie fidget in her seat.

"Well, I can't think of much." She went quiet.

Robert didn't respond, letting the silence fill the space between them until Sallie couldn't deny the urge to fill it.

"Okay, I thought of something. Geometry. Mr. Ferguson. You remember those theorems, and how each had to be memorized exactly line by line?" She looked over at him. He nodded. "Well, one week I didn't have enough time. There was too much to do at home. And so," her voice got quiet, "I cheated."

She looked over to gauge his reaction. Robert gave her an encouraging smile, his face open and free of judgment.

Sallie took a deep breath and continued, "Well, one of the boys in class ratted on me and told Mr. Ferguson. But, and I have a soft spot for him because of this, he didn't believe the kid and stood up for me."

The car got quiet for a minute. "What did you do?" Robert urged softly.

Sallie opened her mouth to respond, but was cut short by the shrill ring of her cellphone. She frowned as she glanced at the caller ID. "Hold on, I have to take this. It's Nancy."

Nancy spoke quickly, as if to lessen the impact of what she was saying. "David fell. Mark took him to the hospital." Her voice sounded calm, but it was full of tension.

A jolt of fear iced its way down Sallie's spine and lodged in the pit of her stomach. "What happened?"

"Mark didn't have time to say much. I think it was the edge of the rug. You know, next to the couch between the dining and living room."

"Was he lying there for very long? How did Mark know?"

"Luckily Mark asked him to carry his cell phone with him all the time."

"I'll be there as quickly as I can." She hung up the phone and turned to Robert. "It's Dad."

"What happened?"

Sallie's face was grim. "We need to get to St. Mary's." Her mind raced with dread for her father. Their previous conversation forgotten, the car was quiet for the rest of the ride.

Robert pulled up to the entrance of the hospital and let Sallie out. "I'll park and find you," he called after her as she jumped out of the car and rushed toward the lobby.

David had been moved out of the emergency room and into a private room, where Sallie found him gesticulating wildly at Mark as she walked in.

"Come here, Sallie, help me out, please," he implored as she strode to his side and took his hand.

"Are you okay, Dad?" Sallie asked. "What happened?"

"Listen, I want both of you to listen to me," his voice was demanding, like the man of Sallie's youth. "I know you both want what's best for me. I just want you to know I'm still in charge of my life."

"But, Dad—" Mark started.

David interrupted, his voice fierce, "Take the damn rug out of the living room if it'll make you feel any better. I just tripped on the edge. Don't make a federal case out of it."

He reached out to Sallie, putting his other hand on top of hers. "Help me out here."

Before she had a chance to respond, a doctor came in and introduced herself as a geriatric specialist. She wanted to examine David and asked the two of them to step out of the room.

Sallie and Mark moved out into the hall. The mirror on the wall opposite the door revealed a grimace on Sallie's face. As she evaluated her reflection, she unconsciously moved a hand to her hair, pushing it out of her eyes. *Is that really me?* She stepped across the hall, judging her image. *I look just like my family. My mouth is set just like my brother's.*

Mesmerized by her reflection, Sallie's eyes took on a blank expression and she was no longer seeing her image. Rather, she had the sense of something she was supposed to remember, like being pulled down a long dark hallway. A shiver of recognition went through her body.

She turned to face her brother. He stared at her accusingly, his face contorted in anger. "See what I mean?"

Sallie's relaxed her face slightly, willing a non-committal expression to hide her emotions. "And we have to go to extremes to find a solution?"

He glared at her and she held his gaze. They both turned away at the same moment. Sallie crossed her arms and leaned against the wall, feigning a relaxation she didn't feel. She struggled to evoke the unknown memories the mirror had stirred. *I think I've done this before.*

Her brother turned back to her and pointed his finger, his voice rising as he spoke. "I've been here. You haven't. I know what he needs. You need to respect my opinion."

Sallie turned her head slightly and looked at a spot on the ceiling about a foot away from Mark to see him with her peripheral vision. Still wanting to retrieve her lost memory, she suddenly dropped her hands as the anger drained from her body. She walked over to her brother and lightly touched his shoulder.

"I know you want what's best for him," she said, her voice low.

Just then, Robert arrived and the doctor came out of the room and approached them. "We'd like to keep him overnight for observation. However, he appears to be in good health. His heart is strong for his age. There's some weakness in his legs that would be helped with some low level exercise. I suggest you get him a walker. A short walk every day would help."

Mark turned to Sallie. "Are you willing to stay with him at home for a while?"

Sallie nodded without hesitation.

"Alright. That's a short-term solution, at least. Let's go tell Dad."

Mark headed back into David's room. Sallie nodded to Robert to follow.

David pulled himself up straighter in the bed as they entered, searching their faces for a clue to his fate. "So, what's the verdict?"

"Well, they can't find anything wrong with you," Mark admitted.

David puffed his chest. "Just as I said."

"However," Mark said, "we do want some changes."

David scowled. "I don't want you telling me how to lead my life," he said in a harsh voice.

Sallie reached over and patted his hand. "Listen a minute. It's not that bad. I'm going to move in with you for a short time."

His face brightened. "Why didn't you say so? That's what I've wanted all along." He took her hand. "Now, when can I get out of here? I can't sleep in a hospital. Need my own bed."

"It's just one night, Dad. We'll be here to pick you up tomorrow, bright and early."

David looked disappointed, but he nodded. "See you tomorrow then," he grumbled.

As Sallie and Robert left the hospital together, he noticed her uneven walk. "You're limping. Is anything wrong?"

Sallie pulled herself up. "Nothing's wrong. I just have one leg slightly shorter than the other."

"Funny, I've never noticed it."

"I'm very practiced at controlling it."

"You don't have to control yourself with me." He put his arm around her as they walked toward the parking lot. Without thinking, she leaned into his embrace, finding comfort in his quiet support.

Sallie stood at the doorway of her childhood room, thinking back to the last time she had slept there. *The bedspread is still that same old green chenille I hated. I don't know why I hated it. Maybe because I wanted yellow and Dad didn't let me go with him to pick it out.*

She laid her overnight bag on the bed and her laptop on the desk, looking around for an outlet. *Oh, geez.* She rolled her eyes. *There's only one plug in the room. How did I ever get by? Well, I'll just have to start a list. I'll need a power strip.*

Walking across the hall to the house's only bathroom, Sallie ran her fingers across the original bright green 1930s tile. *Maybe Dad liked green.*

The room was small, with an old-fashioned pedestal sink that matched the color of the tile, a toilet, and a bathtub with shower curtain. She opened the medicine cabinet to find it stocked with her father's toiletries. Noticing the familiar Old Spice shaving cream can, she pulled it out and squirted a small amount on her finger, closing her eyes as she breathed in. The aroma filled her senses, stirring childhood memories of watching her father shave with that old straight razor he liked so much. *That smell hasn't changed. I always thought it was the essence of being a man.*

She put the can back in the cabinet and looked at three prescription

232

bottles on the bottom shelf. *That's not a lot for someone his age.* One she recognized as an antibiotic. She shook the bottle. Empty. The other two included an antacid drug and a pain medication. *Boy, he must be pretty healthy.*

She looked around for a place to put her cosmetics. Settling for the top of the toilet tank, she laid down a small towel and arranged her products in neat rows on its surface. *I could get a small cabinet. Or perhaps a basket.* She mentally made a note of the size that would fit in the space.

Sallie reviewed the day as she brushed her teeth. After picking David up from the hospital and helping him settle in, she had invited Mark and Nancy over for a welcome home dinner. Conversation at the table had been light, almost artificially cheery, as if no one wanted to think beyond the festivities of the evening. *Where do we go from here? Something's got to give.*

Her thoughts snapped back to the present as she heard David's voice calling her name. She walked down the hall and stood in the doorway to his bedroom, peering in to see his face barely illuminated by the bedside lamp. "Do you need anything, Dad?"

"I need to use the bathroom," he said, his voice defensive.

"Let me help you." She walked toward the bed.

"I feel fine," he continued with the same harsh tone. "I didn't break anything. Just need to get my sea legs back."

She smiled at the image as she helped him from the bed and down the hall, where he pulled away and closed the bathroom door firmly in her face. "I can take it from here," he barked.

Leaning against the doorjamb, Sallie waited outside, her eyes closed as she strained to hear any sign of distress. Instead, she heard the sound of his urine against the bowl of the toilet.

When he opened the door, she smiled at him with compassion, holding out her hand to help him back to bed. He gave her a look of panic at the invasion of privacy and pulled his arm away. "I'm okay. I don't need any help," he said in a severe tone. Turning abruptly, he moved slowly toward his bedroom, one hand on the wall. Sallie followed a short distance behind, her arms outstretched to catch him if he fell.

As he got into bed, Sallie stayed at the doorway, arms crossed. "May I get you anything before you go to bed? Perhaps some tea?"

"It's too late to drink," he said, not changing his tone.

"I guess I wasn't thinking," Sallie stuttered.

"You sure do have a lot of things, don't you? The bathroom's filled up. Are you going to fill up the rest of my house, too?"

His words were like a slap across the face. Sallie stood in silence for a moment, too shocked to respond. Her father reached to turn out the light, as if to dismiss her. Regaining her composure, she walked up to the bed. He put his arm down.

"Dad, please, don't start anything. I don't want this any more than you do."

He looked at her and nodded, "You're right. I shouldn't have said anything."

Knowing his words were the closest he could come to apologizing, Sallie patted his hand. "We'll talk more in the morning." She switched off the light and returned to her room. *How is this going to work out? Will I ever get back to Las Rosas?*

Laundry was her favorite chore. A certain peace descended on her as she ironed and folded the clothes, placing them neatly into lavender sachet-filled drawers. Sallie stood in front of her father's dresser, organizing his things so that everything could be easily found.

She leaned over and pulled out the bottom drawer, putting it on the bed. In it was mostly winter wear lying there in a jumbled mess. She had purchased some lining for the drawers and was starting to put down a sheet when she noticed something small in the back. She picked up a small hinged cedar box and analyzed the intricate carving on top. It looked very old and depicted a scene from the German countryside.

Holding it gingerly, she sat down on the bed and put it in her lap, running her fingers around the edge, as if she could gain a memory from the past just from her touch. Lifting the lid, an old-fashioned tune spit out a few notes before fading away. Sallie turned the box over and wound the key, again listening to a tune she could not place.

Inside, on a velvet tray, were a few pieces of costume jewelry—a pair of pearl earrings, a marcasite pin, and a single strand pearl necklace. She carefully placed the items on the bed, lingering over the pin. *I wonder if my mother liked marcasite as much as I do,* she thought, realizing these items must have belonged to her.

Lifting the tray, she found a letter. Touching it gently, her eyes misted as she recognized her mother's tiny, neat handwriting. She opened the letter and began to read, only lifting her head as she heard her father's voice.

"What's that music? And what are you doing in my room?" he barked accusingly, looking from her to the box on the bed.

"I was putting your laundry away and straightening the drawers," Sallie said, her voice cold.

Seeing the letter in her hand, he blew up. "You had no right to go into my things!"

"You mean, my mother's things. Don't you think they're mine by right?"

"I was going to give you the jewelry," he said grudgingly.

"What about the letter? And what did she mean, 'I accept your offer for the sake of Sallie?' "

"It didn't mean anything," he answered quickly, covering up his confusion. "I was being transferred back to the States and she was uncertain about leaving Germany."

Sallie narrowed her eyes, not certain she believed him.

Sunday night had arrived, yet still Sallie hesitated. She hadn't talked with Anne for a couple of weeks. Going over all that had happened during that time, she rehearsed her answers. *Robert. It's going to be all about Robert and I don't know that I'm ready to say anything. Better to stick with the facts.*

Sallie dialed Anne's number. As soon as her friend answered, Sallie apologized and launched into her excuse. "So much has been going on. I don't even know where to start."

"You're forgiven if you start by telling me what you did a couple of Sundays ago that was more important than our call," Anne said, a laugh in her voice. "You sounded conspiratorial when you called to say we couldn't talk."

"Oh, that," Sallie lowered her voice to a whisper. "Well, I went to a Van Morrison concert."

"And I suppose you didn't go alone," Anne coaxed her friend.

"You'd be right. I went with Robert."

"And, do you suppose you'll finally admit to having had a date with him?" asked Anne.

"Hmm. Not really. We went as friends," said Sallie.

"What gives, girlfriend?"

"Oh, the concert was great. And yes, I did enjoy his company, if that's the question."

"Precisely. Anything else you want to tell me?"

Sallie hesitated a second. "I'm not reading too much into anything."

Anne noticed a sound of dejection in her voice. "As long as you're paying attention to your feelings, that's all I ask," she said, trying to draw Sallie out.

"Yeah, I am. I think," responded Sallie, vaguely aware that she had heard those words from someone other than Anne. *I'm not used to listening to my heart. Right now, it's confused. How can a heart be confused?* "Did I tell you about the Santa Barbara trip?"

"What Santa Barbara trip?"

"Oh, he wants to buy wine property and asked for my help as a real estate professional. Of course, I told him I couldn't help him."

"You told him about your license?"

"Not exactly. I would have needed to work with someone local either way. I don't have the expertise in that area."

"Okay." Anne drew out the word.

"We found three properties and he might want to buy one."

"Did you have a good time?"

"It was nice. Better than I expected even," Sallie admitted. She recounted the details of their long drive and their shared interests. "But then, on the way home…" Sallie's words became halting. The other end of the line was quiet and Anne heard a shudder escape Sallie's lips as if she were beginning to break down.

"What's happened?" Anne asked gently.

"Oh, Anne, I've moved in with my dad."

"How did that happen?"

"Let me go outside," Sallie said as Anne frowned on her end.

Sallie walked out into the night and moved away from the house, sitting down on the grass at the back of the yard. Between sobs, her faltering voice detailed the sequence of events that led to her moving back into her old bedroom.

Struggling to gain control, Sallie hiccupped. "I haven't even told you what I found out about my mother. You see, there's this letter and my dad is not giving me a believable answer."

"It definitely sounds as if you are going through what is called 'a dark night of the soul,'" Anne said compassionately, not asking too many questions. "I know you can work it out. Remember, though, if you don't surrender to its message, things can get worse."

"I feel as if I've heard that before," said Sallie, breathing deeply to calm herself. "I just want to do a good job."

"What's wrong with just being who you are?"

"I don't think I like that person."

"Ah, the truth comes out."

"You're no help," Sallie said with a snicker.

"That old mirror of judgment has raised its ugly head," said Anne.

"Wait, what did you say?" Sallie frowned, struggling to recall something lurking just beyond the edge of her conscious mind. "It's as if I've heard that before too."

"Maybe it's your guardian angel speaking. You know, sometimes they have other people—even strangers—tell you something you need to hear."

"Wait," said Sallie. "Something about a gift and a challenge. What does it mean?"

"The way I've learned it is that everyone who is important in your life gives you both a gift as well as a challenge, and it's in figuring out these gifts and challenges that you come into balance with your relationships."

"How do you know so much?"

"Experience," responded Anne. "It teaches us what we refuse to hear when things are going well. Sometimes we humans just don't pay attention any other way."

Sallie was quiet for a moment, letting the warmth of friendship settle around her, then said in a quiet voice, "You always know the right thing to say. Thanks. I don't know what I would do without you."

Their conversation wound down and Sallie signed off with a sigh. *It's great having a best friend who understands me and accepts me as I am,* she thought as she walked back into the house and collapsed into bed.

Sallie's Journal—July 20th

I haven't written in almost a month. I have so much to say, yet I cannot express things and I'm not sure if I want to record what is happening anyway.

I am having a war within myself between my rational and feeling natures and am about to be consumed by those parts of me I don't like. I feel I will burn up and be only a shell of who I really am if I start to give in to my feelings.

I want to live my life within my own parameters and not out of a need for approval from anyone. Right now, I'm not even certain there is a common thread with my feelings. Why is it easier for me to be who I am around the Parker clan?

I'm starting to sense some dreams, deep amorphous wanderings, as if I am a million miles away at night, somewhere in another universe. I awake in the morning without any memory, yet my body aches as if I have been in school all night and worked as I have never worked before. I have a vague remembrance of someone trying to cut off my hands.

Words come into my brain—singular ideas—and I have no reference point in which to place them. I think of my family and a numbness pervades my chest, turning into a deep pain that will not go away until I allow myself to feel, really feel, the pain I have denied all these years.

I look in the mirror and see my father in my eyes. I look at my brother and want to reach out to him as we did when we were children. I want so much to go to them and express the deep sense of love I have for them.

I also want to get as far away as I can from the confinement I feel since I moved in to take care of my father. I don't want to be here, yet it takes a great effort just to leave the house. I especially don't want to talk to Robert. What is wrong with me?

In my last conversation with Fred, he said that his attorney contact recommended asking for a public hearing. It's up to me to request one. Yet here I am, having agreed to live here. And for how long? I left for one day with Robert and look what happened. What could happen to

Dad while I'm up in Sacramento? And what would I say in a public hearing anyway? That I'm a loser who doesn't even know what she's signing. Yet, if I don't go, I won't get my life back. This was always meant to be temporary. Yet, where's the end point?

Yearning for something outside myself, I am incarcerated and unable to venture forth. Fear invades me. Then, I cannot get out of here fast enough and I get in my car and drive for what seems like hours. Lately, I've found myself at the beach sitting in the car, watching and listening to the sound of the waves, continuous, never changing, mesmerizing me with their tempo.

The only respite has been my new column with the Courier. Even though I was a writer for the newspaper in high school, most of my writing since then has been sporadic. Just odds and ends here and there. Then, my journal. Now a weekly column on real estate that pushes me beyond my capabilities.

I never considered I could make a life of writing. Now, I'm being encouraged wherever I go. I even ran into an old high school classmate and she had seen the column and liked it.

Dream: I am in a hotel room looking out from the third floor window onto the promenade stretching out the front door with its wide pedestrian walkway. I see Robert at a distance, walking purposely toward the building. Somehow I know his accommodations are on the floor beneath me.

I am a mess, yet I want to see him anyway, so I leave the room and start down to the second floor to find him. There I see a woman who is talking to a group of people. She has a message for me. She tells me I need to get in touch with Athena and do a ceremony to ask for her help. I ask her who Athena is and what I need to do. She tells me Athena is the ancient goddess of wisdom and war.

CHAPTER FOURTEEN

Mairye: Angel of Unconditional Love

"Once upon a time, there lived…" Sallie heard her mother's voice as if from a great distance.

"Mommy, where are you?" she cried out into the blue-black India-ink world that surrounded her.

An echo shouted at her from all directions at once. "I am here."

Sallie turned in a circle, hands outstretched into the darkness, panic rising in her chest. Snippets of conversations and images of her childhood arose before her.

"Mommy, I need you! Please don't leave me," she screamed, her body trembling in terror. She hugged herself to calm her fears, curling into a shaking ball on the ground as she sobbed like a forlorn child.

"Once upon a time, there lived a princess." It was her mother's voice again. Sallie closed her eyes and waited for her to continue. "The princess was very beautiful, much like you, little kitten."

Her mother used to tickle her when she would say those words, and

Sallie waited to feel her mother's touch. Instead, the voice continued the tale. "Her parents told her never to leave the castle because there were dangers and she could get lost and be unable to find her way back home. As the little princess grew up, she would look out the window of her bedroom at the world beyond the fortress. The tall leafy trees would sway with the soft whispers of the wind and call to her. 'We live in a forest of possibilities with endless opportunities for your delight,' they said. 'Come play with us.'

"They would tell her of the spirits that lived in the woods who knew every kind of flower and lived with abandonment. Just as every day her parents told of her duty within the confines of the castle, so too she listened to the forest tell her of the joy she would experience if she were to venture forth and play."

Sallie remembered what happened in the story. As the princess grew up, it wasn't enough for her to live with her riches in the castle. She wanted to experience all that life had to offer, and so she ventured forth into the forest. *I'm that little girl, and now I'm lost.* She listened for her mother's voice. "Mommy, tell me what to do now!" she shouted.

Another voice, soft yet firm, answered her. "You cannot go back to the castle the way you came. That path is now closed to you. You must find the universal mother." The gentle words loosened the clamp of terror encasing Sallie's body as the voice infused her with a newfound courage.

Sitting up, Sallie looked around as her eyes adjusted to the murky environment. Surrounded by thick trunks of trees overhung with shadowy branches, she found herself on a bed of ferns next to a narrow path that was outlined by sharp pointed rocks.

At a crossroads, she saw paths converge from three directions into a circular space. In the center was a sundial sitting on a pedestal. Her curiosity spurred her to stand up and go over to peer at it. *Curious that a timepiece that relies on the sun would be in this dark place,* she mused.

A thin sliver of moonlight shone through a parting of the trees, illuminating the device. The flat piece that usually showed the hours of the day was instead a shiny black mirror, and its elevated gnomon cast a shadow pointing toward the left pathway. Sallie stared down the dark road showing no hope of success. She glanced in the other two directions and saw inky shadows move across them as if to bar her way.

Somewhere high above her head an owl hooted, telling her that he would lead her through the darkness. Sallie looked up and listened, somehow understanding the message of his cry. She cautiously followed his call, walking down the narrow winding path with tentative footsteps, alert to his message of nourishment and wisdom. As she went along, Sallie felt her body become lighter, as if she were shedding burdens from the past. The owl continued his encouragement, showing glimpses of an emerging future.

The owl's hoot grew faint and Sallie raced to catch up, tripping on a tree root that rose up unexpectedly in front of her. The forest was still. Not a leaf moved. Sallie peered around the inky darkness to get her bearings. Her fear had abated and her curiosity was aroused as she waited to discover what to do next.

Off the path, a new moon illuminated a circular opening in the forest. She stood up and moved cautiously in its direction, touching the trees for support as she felt her way over the tangle of vines that covered the ground.

In the center of a grove of ancient redwood trees was a tiny wayside chapel, barely large enough to hold a dozen worshippers. Sallie hesitated at the heavy, carved wooden door. Suddenly it swung open and an invisible nudge pulled her into the pitch-black darkness. She stood inside the door as the coolness of the ancient stones filled her with their primeval energy, solidly anchoring her connection with Mother Earth. She halted to allow her eyes to adjust to the tenebrous environment.

Darting her eyes around the tiny space, she willed her pupils to open so she could identify her surroundings. In a far corner, a soft light emanated from a small statue. She followed the passage made by its beam to a Black Madonna, arms outstretched with palms downward in a pose of welcome and acceptance. Carved from obsidian, her face was completely black and her head was covered with a mantle of midnight blue.

As Sallie knelt before the icon, its voice began to flood her heart and waves of emotion overwhelmed her body as she heard the statue speak to her.

"You have allowed your world of form to have more significance for you than the world of your heart." Her voice was compassionate, as if she knew Sallie well. "In the long ago past, all the souls that have existed in your world made the decision to descend into matter so that you could see its effects. Now, worn out, you feel you have lost your way.

"I am Mairye, the Black Madonna. I have been the hidden feminine, the one who has remained deep within the earth through these past long ages of denial. I have lived underground, in repose, hidden from those who wished to destroy me because they feared the part of my energy that has the power to annihilate.

"That power also resides in you, and because of this force, you have accepted subjugation. I am contained in you, and it is my wisdom you fear, for you know you have the power to eliminate all who obstruct your path. Now is the time for you to come to terms with that strength and to resurrect me in your heart so that you may become a beacon to others.

"There are many ancient myths of warrior goddesses who went on rampages, destroying mankind when she was displeased with his arrogant behavior. Later, subdued, she became the all-mother figure of benevolence. Yet, this aspect, never far from their memory, caused ancient man to fear the possibility contained within the feminine for further destruction."

"I've had that rage come over me," said Sallie, stiffening as she resurrected the feeling inside of her. "It's as if the sun is obliterated and I am a dragon, spewing fire from my mouth." She hesitated. "With my family, I want to be the dutiful daughter and so I hide rather than allowing anyone to see the effects of my strong feelings."

The Black Madonna nodded. "You must experience that rage in all its fury. Yet that sense of destruction must be combined with its counterpoint, compassion."

Mairye stepped down from her perch, growing to her full height as she approached. She took Sallie's hand. "Come with me," she said as she led Sallie behind the altar to a narrow set of marble stairs descending deep into the crypt.

At the bottom of the steps, they came to a flowing stream bubbling forth from deep within the earth. Mairye gestured for them to sit on the bench nearby. Sallie watched as the Black Madonna turned her palms toward the water and a brittle silver-white light began to emerge from its depths.

"That is the energy of Mother Earth, rising from the darkness of the planet. I greet these feminine earthly energies and bring them forth to rise up to meet the downward spiraling golden energies of Father Sky." With that, she raised her hand and let the current to rise into the air. "From this symbiosis, a transformation will occur that allows for the birth of a new consciousness in the heart of all who walk the earth." Mairye turned and gazed directly into Sallie's eyes. "As you gain compassion, you will also have the ability to assimilate and transmute this energy."

Sallie reached out to touch the rising plume, allowing its force to permeate her body. Mairye continued, "This force within your planet has existed from the beginning and will live until the end of time."

Sallie watched in awe as she felt the energy imbue her body with the power of its solidity of purpose. "I have never felt this combination of power and compassion before," she said. "It's as if I can accomplish anything I want, yet it is so gentle as if to make certain what I do honors everyone."

Mairye nodded. "That is the source of true feminine power. This is a voice that has been muted, yet still speaks out in your myths and legends, your dreams and daydreams, and your sense that something is amiss. Past suppression of this voice has led to anger, sadness, and fear."

"I can feel those old emotions right in here," she said, her hand on her chest. "It is as if they are stuck and won't be dislodged."

"Inner confusion, chaos, and despair are reflected back by the outside world, which is centered on self through greed, accumulation, and individuality. By understanding the depths of your rage, the unacceptable becomes acceptable and fear is turned to trust, becoming the light born out of darkness."

"I want to have the same power as men. I want to be equal in their world." Sallie's voice was passionate.

"Your responsibility is to the spiritual life of your community, as guardian to the mysteries of life, a combination of soul and matter, shadow and light, and the interplay of both in the realm of the world."

"If I have to get mad, so be it. Anger can be good if it creates change."

Mairye nodded her acceptance. "There is a great wealth of emotion that you must now bring to light so that it may be transmuted to the gold-silver union of the mother and father," she said, putting her hand on Sallie's heart, allowing them to meld in an embrace.

"Without the feminine," she continued, "the masculine loses its empathy. Without the detachment of the masculine, the feminine loses clarity. In the tension of this opposition you will find a new matrix that will provide direction to your soul's evolution."

"How does that relate to my desire to be equal?"

"Like a mold filled with clay and then fired to hardness, you have been imprinted by that which surrounds you—your family, friends, education, and culture. You believe that this person, this Sallie who has been created, is the real you. You begin to see yourself and your needs, desires, and imperfections through the eyes of others.

"That is the world of form. To see your spiritual essence, you must look beyond the mask that peers back at your from your mirror." Mairye directed her gaze toward the pool of water before them. "Look at your reflection," she commanded. "What do you see?"

Sallie stared at her image for a moment and said, "I see my imperfections and the deficiencies I want to change and improve. I want to make myself perfect so I can be admired and liked and help change the quality of life for women in the world." Sallie looked up at her, pleading for acknowledgment.

"Within your sense of perfection is integrity, yet it is also coupled with stubbornness." Mairye's voice was firm. "You believe in your way, a way that comes from your conditioning. You accept it as truth and then you fit your surroundings into that view of the world, like putting a square box into a round box of the same size. You want to force it. This is not the feminine way, and it contributes to the imbalance of your true nature." Mairye gave her a look that bore into her soul. "Look further. Look into your eyes to see your soul within to find the true radiant being you are."

Sallie's eyes widened and she pulled back, afraid of what she might see. The Madonna's eyes burned fiercely into hers. "Look, I say!" As Sallie turned once again toward the dark water, she stared into her eyes, searching to find the depths of her being.

The voice beside her was soft. "See the truth of who you are."

A sob escaped Sallie's throat as she gazed into her eyes and began to see the true perfection of her soul. Her hand reached out with compassion to touch the image in the water.

Mairye nodded and softly said, "When you know your own light, then you will more clearly recognize the light in those who are around you."

"I am confused," said Sallie. "I don't want to dominate or be dominated. I want equality."

"Men and women have similarities, as they also have their differences. In their similarities must be found this equality you seek, yet in their differences they can each make a rich contribution bringing balance to the changing world and to each other. Every man must find the feminine within, as every woman must discover her masculine aspects. However, it is not a question of one being superior and the other being submissive. The feminine aspect is receptive, not passive. You must recognize the distinction."

Sallie looked at her with a mixture of awe and respect. Mairye continued, "You gain the wisdom of the earth when you confront and transform fear, betrayal, and uncertainty. It is a paradox. Just as all colors disappear in black, so all that holds you back must disappear into the wasteland of your rage. At the other end of that fully realized fury is the voice of compassion."

As Sallie's consciousness began to withdraw from the crypt, she heard a voice resounding in her head, repeating itself so as to imprint its message on her very being. "I am the Black Madonna. I represent the essence that a woman must be, do, and have, which uses her unique talents to exalt her individuality. I am the woman who stands in her own authority, determines her own destiny and says yes to it, even though what she claims might not get the approval of others.

"I am the woman who is strong in the ways of the feminine, and who does not compromise herself to the ways of the world. I am the woman who does not allow others to shape the decisions of her soul. I am the woman who says yes to a new vision of power, one that does not seek to dominate and bend others to her will. I am the woman whose authority is a command of herself and the mastery of her skills. I am the woman whose power is based on competence and interdependency."

Her final message rang loud and true. "You must learn to love even when you experience nothing to love."

With a swirl of energy Mairye was gone, leaving Sallie sleeping deeply with a peaceful smile gracing her face.

PART VIII
Manifestation

I heard a thousand blended notes,
While in grove I sat reclined,
In that sweet mood when pleasant thoughts
Bring sad thoughts to the mind.

To her fair works did nature link
The human soul that through me ran;
And much it griev'd me my heart to think
What man has made of man.

Through primrose-tufts, in that sweet bower,
The periwinkle trail'd its wreathes;
And 'tis my faith that every flower
Enjoys the air it breathes.

The birds around me hopp'd and play'd:
Their thoughts I cannot measure,
But the least motion which they made,
It seem'd a thrill of pleasure.

The budding twigs spread out their fan,
To catch the breezy air;
And I must think, do all I can,
That there was pleasure there.

If I these thoughts may not prevent,
If such be of my creed the plan,
Have I not reason to lament

What man has made of man?

William Wordsworth, 1802
Lines Written in Early Spring

CHAPTER FIFTEEN

Descent into the Underworld

The day had been built upon irritation—the dirt clods thrown at her car by the unruly ten-year-olds, the truck that cut her off in traffic, the sharp tongue of the grocery clerk, and the condescending attitude of the manager at the high-end boutique. They were all little things that might appear to be minor issues, yet taken together, they yielded an inward fury, like water that goes from warm to boiling in short order. Unwilling to face the feelings coursing through her body, Sallie found herself in an obstinate insistence of wanting what she wanted.

Her inner desire for control of the events surrounding her was aroused to a stubbornness that pushed her to the edge. As she talked on the phone to a clerk regarding adding her father to her cell phone account even though they had different addresses, her voice was strong and determined. "Don't tell me you can't do it. I know you can. It isn't illegal. Just say it. You just don't want to do it."

Hearing the woman begin to repeat company policy for the third time, Sallie's reservoir of patience ran dry. "Let me talk to your supervisor," she snapped. "I'll wait." Despite her insistence, even the conversation with the supervisor concluded without success.

Throwing her cell phone down on the bed, Sallie put her head in her hands, sinking through the emotional layers of her life. And there it was, at the bottom of the stack—pure unadulterated rage. Beyond her measure to contain, it washed up like bitters in her throat and she gagged at its insistence. She wanted to vomit the angry words she had suppressed and throw them at all those who had ever wounded her. Yet, who were they and where were they, these people against whom she now raged? *They lived in the past and are no longer here. I know that now.*

The rage turned to anger, and then to frustration. The tears of release stuck in her chest. Gradually, the grief permeated the rage, its tiny fringes coursing through her veins, tearing apart the miles and miles of arteries that kept her body together.

I am dissolving. Right here. I can no longer hold this grief inside me, especially in front of my family. Dinner at Mark and Nancy's tonight. No way. I'm better off canceling. In my current state, feeling as if the whole world is conspiring against me, I would probably tell everyone what I really think of them. On the other hand, perhaps I need to tell them what's on my mind. That's what Anne tells me, anyway. Yes, and she also says to make certain I am beyond the wild edge of the anger. Sallie's thoughts were chaotic, not allowing her to see any resolution to the clamor.

She shut the door to her room, snapped her blinds shut, and lay down on her bed, enveloping herself with a coverlet as she examined these new feelings. Her chest, rigid and immobile, was growing tighter, as though a tourniquet were squeezing her body. Realizing she was holding her breath, she took a deep inhalation, almost choking on it. Slowly, as she continued to breathe deeply and bring energy to her heart, the muscles in her body unwound one by one.

The grief that she had long held at bay at last permeated the cracks between her cells, washing upon her and leaving her adrift like an endless sea with waves curling on her soul. Pounding unceasingly, they crashed as breakers do onto sand during a storm. As she surrendered to their insistence, they began to recede and eventually became gentle emanations that soothed her body. Sallie fell into a light sleep.

In her dream, she could not tell the time of day. It was both night and day at the same time. She was floating in the middle of the ocean. The sun beat warm upon her body, while the moon shone its bright beams upon her soul.

Sallie awoke as the light from a waning sun beamed through cracks in the blinds onto her bed. *I must go. I just barely have time to get ready.* She jumped up out of bed and hastened out the door.

Her father was already pacing in the living room. "I thought you'd sleep forever," he said gruffly as she grabbed the keys and started toward the door.

"Let's go before we're any later," she replied, not wanting further discussion.

The atmosphere in the car was tense. Sallie wrapped herself inside an artificial calm, not wanting to betray the havoc of the thoughts and feelings coursing through her. She sat ramrod straight, concentrating on her driving.

"You could move in permanently. It would be easier and you wouldn't have to pay any rent," her father started up again.

Keeping her eyes straight ahead, Sallie focused intently on the quiet road as if it were a freeway crowded with aggressive drivers. "We've already been through this. Now's not the time to discuss it. We're late. Let's just get there."

Dinner was a quiet affair with Nancy chattering to fill the awkward void. To Sallie, it was as though there were other conversations lying on the table that no one wanted to pick up. Until there was resolution of their unsaid issues, their lives would be at a stalemate.

Still pivoting around the edges of her anger, Sallie was particularly quiet, only answering questions put to her directly. *Tonight is not the time to open these doors. I just need time to sort through my feelings before acting upon them. Sort through my feelings. Did I just think that? Am I ready to feel my feelings?*

After dinner, David got up from the table and motioned for Brian to follow him to watch the game. Sallie started to rise to clear the table and help Nancy in the kitchen, but stopped when she noticed Mark hadn't stirred from his place at the table.

"Dad says you're going to move in permanently." Mark looked directly at her for the first time since she had arrived that evening, leaning in to scrutinize her response.

Sallie blinked quickly. "I…" The words stuck in her throat as her thoughts rebounded, like a handball bouncing off first one wall, then another. "I never said that," she finally said firmly, her voice flat.

"He has that idea, and well, frankly, that would be okay with me," said Mark. He crossed his arms leaned back in his chair, tilting onto its back legs.

Sallie took a deep breath before answering. "It's just that I'm not used to living with someone." *Oh, what's the use? I love my dad. This just isn't what I want to do.*

Sallie spoke quickly to avoid being cut off before she could finish her thoughts. "I've done some research about alternatives for his care. He can hire someone fairly inexpensively to come in to fix meals. I checked with the County Social Services Agency. They have a list. Or there's always Meals on Wheels. And there is a newly opened Senior Day Care program at the Community Center." She stopped abruptly, not knowing how to get her point across.

"He's a creature of habit who likes his privacy," said Mark in a very matter-of-fact tone. He brought the chair down hard and leaned forward. Sallie stiffened.

"The Senior Day Care can provide stimulation. He'd be around people who have similar interests, which might open a totally new door for him." She knew the words sounded hollow. They seemed to move past her brother without him taking notice.

"Well, what about you? Why shouldn't you move in with him? You can save money. Besides, what are you doing for money anyway, now that you're not working?" queried Mark, his voice becoming insistent. "That's the only way I would consider him staying at home permanently." He crossed his arms as if to indicate his was the final word.

Sallie stared at her brother. Their eyes locked until she had to turn away. She rose from the table and joined her father watching the game, a false smile on her face for her father's benefit. The television announcer replayed a clip of the runner scoring that had just put the Dodgers ahead.

Closing her eyes, she let her mind drift over the conversations of the past few weeks with her family. As she relaxed, she held her brother in her mind's eye and was drawn into Mark's consciousness, seeing herself as he perceived her. She was shocked at his attitude toward her.

Why, he thinks I've had it too easy and have always gotten what I wanted. He stayed behind to be the good son, and now it's my turn. That is so far from my perception of myself. How could I ever explain who I am to him? How sad it is that we let our different perceptions of who we really are come between us.

Sallie opened her eyes and looked absently at her father. "Are you ready to go? I have an early morning." He stared at the television and she stood without a glance. "Come on. We can listen to the rest of the game on the radio."

Sallie fidgeted in the passenger seat as Iris wove through the crowded south bay traffic toward Luisa's house for the weekly meeting of the Tuesday Writers Group.

"I'm a little nervous," Sallie admitted. "You all know each other so well from your UCLA class. I feel almost like an intruder just tagging along like this."

"Oh nonsense, Sallie. We've wanted some fresh blood for the group for some time. When I told them about you, they were excited for you to join us. You're a perfect candidate for the TWIGs."

"But I don't have the background like you all do. I haven't taken a writing class since high school."

"So what? All we are looking for is like-minded people who want to expand themselves through writing. That sounds like you, doesn't it?"

"I suppose so," Sallie agreed, her nerves settling. "Tell me a little about them at least."

"Well, Todd loves creating sci-fi worlds with interesting alien characters. Luisa is a more romantic writer; she loves Jane Austen. Danielle is a no-nonsense feminist and her characters are grounded and real. And Pete, well, he has the most vivid imagination. You won't believe the characters he makes up."

"They sound so knowledgeable about what they're doing."

"We're all just works in progress. I love the topic Luisa proposed for this week. 'To wish was to hope, and to hope was to expect.' A good *Sense and Sensibility* quote, don't you think? Did you have a chance to write something?"

"I did and was surprised at what I wrote. I'm a little nervous about sharing it."

"You'll be fine. This group is easy. We only give positive comments that encourage growth in a constructive way. We were taught those are the kind that allow expansion of our ideas and creativity."

Iris pulled up to a townhouse complex and punched a code into the keypad to open the front gate. "Hey, we even get front row parking," she said, as she slid the car into a visitor spot in front of a neat, gray two-story home. "We're right on time. Come on!" Iris flashed Sallie an encouraging smile.

As everyone settled into seats in Luisa's comfortable living room, Iris introduced Sallie to the group and each member welcomed her. Luisa passed drinks and homemade cake around the circle. "Don't worry," she assured Sallie, "we'll go first so you can get a sense of what we're about."

By the time it was Sallie's turn, she had relaxed into the liveliness and humor of the group. As she read, she gained confidence in what she had written.

Shame on You

"Shame on you," the mother said to the child.

The child looked at her with eyes wide open, wondering what she meant.

"You mustn't do that."

Do what? The child thought.

"You mustn't behave like that. It isn't seemly. It's not appropriate for a little girl your age. Sit down, cross your ankles, pull your dress down, act like a lady."

Am I a lady? The child wondered.

Later, the child came running up to her mother and threw her arms around her. "Stop that," the mother said. "Can't you see I'm busy? Go play with your dolls. I have to get dinner on the table."

Once, she had questioned her mother. "Why?" the little girl had asked.

"Because I said so," the mother had remonstrated. And so the girl stopped asking.

"Be like the other children. They're not running around," the mother said.

Am I different than the others? The child worried.

258

And so, the child became very anxious, then fretful, then demanding.

The mother said, "What's gotten into you? You're not the sweet little girl that I love." This made the little girl very anxious and she spent her time rocking her doll, wondering what to do next.

"Don't embarrass me," the mother told her.

What did I do? The child speculated.

"Didn't you hear what I said? Stay out of the kitchen. I just mopped the floor. Go outside."

What am I to do outside? The little girl wondered.

"You know better than that. Act your age."

What is my age? The child considered.

When she went to school, the child was told to sit still and do her work. When she came home, her mother said, "Oh what a good girl you are—you got all A's on your report card."

And so the girl began to work hard to get A's all the time so she could hear her mother's praise. She learned to sit still even more and to do more work; she learned to listen to what others told her and to only do what they said.

And the more she did, the more that was expected of her.

"It's not like you; a B on your report card. You usually get all A's."

It was an Honors class; it was really hard, the girl thought.

As she grew older, her responsibilities increased. "You have to earn your keep around here. Come home right after school to help me."

What about seeing my friends? The girl questioned to herself.

When she became a teenager, there were even more rules.

"You're too young to date," her mother told her.

When will I be old enough? She wondered.

"Be a nice girl; save yourself for marriage."

What if I never get married? She thought.

"You're too pushy. It isn't ladylike," the mother said.

What did I do? The young woman questioned.

When she graduated, her mother said, "We've done everything we can for you. Now you're on your own. You have to figure out what to do with your life."

How can I do that? The young woman wondered.

When Sallie finished reading, she took a deep breath and looked up at the group. She was surprised to find them looking at her intently, totally involved in her story.

"Well, thank you for sharing, Sallie," Luisa started. "What a great story. Good structure. A beginning, middle, and end. That's not easy in such few words."

"I agree," said Pete. "Sounds as if you've taken personal feelings and put them into a story that doesn't preach."

Todd nodded. "Your past experience comes through in a non-judgmental way. Sounds as if you've been writing for a long time."

Danielle stood up and paced the room. "Well done. Stories like that get me riled up. We've got to do something to make changes in the world so women don't have to live to different standards than men."

Iris chuckled and waved her hand. "Oh, sit down, Danielle. We don't have to solve the problems of the world on Tuesdays." They all laughed.

Luisa lifted the cake plate. "Seconds, anyone?"

Story sharing concluded, the mood was light as the group burst into animated chatter covering an array of topics, from favorite authors to town gossip. Sallie was swept up in their enthusiasm, laughing along as one of the gang.

As they walked back to Iris' car after the meeting adjourned, Sallie felt unusually ebullient. "What a great group. I really appreciate the feedback they gave me. Particularly Danielle. I felt as if she really saw me."

"She's got a rebel spirit, that's for sure."

"And Luisa, telling me she was impressed with the structure. And Todd saying that I sounded as if I'd been writing for a long time... it made me feel like I could really be a part of your group."

"I know what you mean," said Iris. "That's why we only allow positive comments. I feel energized and want to write more after our sessions."

Sallie nodded. "Writing this has allowed me to touch hidden chords of my life. Getting encouraging feedback is helpful."

"Everyone enjoyed your writing today and having you as a part of our group. I think you add another dimension to our writing," said Iris with a smile. She gave Sallie a shy look, not wanting to be rebuffed. "Tell me about your story."

"I'm not certain where it came from," Sallie said. "It's as if I have all these things bottled up inside with no place to put them."

"Sounds familiar."

"That story isn't something that really happened to me, yet it feels true to my life. I sometimes feel as if everything I do is wrong and has no real meaning."

Iris nodded. "I feel the same. I often have the vague feeling there's something I should be doing, but I can't quite figure it out. It's disquieting, like I can never feel really comfortable with my life."

Sallie nodded. "Yeah, that's a good way of putting it."

"I'm so happy you joined us. It gives us more in common. And time to share an enjoyable evening," said Iris.

Sallie gave her a warm smile and hug. "Thanks for including me. You're like the younger sister I always wished I had."

There was always time for a knitting lesson at Nonna's. Sallie had finished her first scarf and was now working on a simple pullover top. Friday nights had become dinner with the Parkers for her and her dad. They were sitting in that quiet time between the preparation of the meal and the arrival of the guests, working on their projects while her father watched the baseball game in the family room.

"Your house is such a happy home, Nonna." Sallie smiled as her heart opened with love toward this giving woman. "I really enjoy being here." She looked around at the warmth and charm of the lived-in room. "You have the ability to accept everyone and make them feel important. How do you do it?"

"Oh, it's not that difficult," started Nonna. "I just look at others from my heart and feel who they are. Then I just encourage them." She stopped her knitting and looked around the kitchen, appraising what needed to be done.

"That's such a nice philosophy," replied Sallie. "Were you always like this?"

Nonna's eyes softened, remembering the past. "When my family was in Italy, we always had a lot of relatives around," she said. "When we came here, we lived on the Parker Ranch, where my mother was the cook. There was always a crowd—the Parkers, all the ranch hands— and it just seemed we always had to get along with a lot of people. We just worked together."

"I would've liked to have seen that." Sallie sounded wistful. "I'm very happy to be a part of it now. You have such wonderful children."

"Oh, they have their faults. I just love each of them for who they are. I'm a lucky woman," she replied, and then went on with a matter-of-fact tone. "I know them. Robert wants to make everybody happy. Iris loves children, her son and her students. Maria, she's a good wife and mother. You just learn to let them be who they are."

Sallie's emotions overcame her and she breathed in sharply to quell the tears that had started to well up in her eyes.

Glancing in her direction, Nonna noted her reaction and put down her needles. "How about we share a glass of wine as we wait for the others?"

Sallie nodded. "That sounds good."

Nonna fetched a couple glasses and poured the wine. "Would your dad like a glass also?"

"A beer would be more to his liking. I can get it." Sallie opened the refrigerator, cracked open a beer and took it to her father in the living room. Returning to the kitchen, Sallie sat down next to Nonna and took a sip of Chianti.

"How do you feel?" Nonna asked.

Sallie frowned and looked at her, uncertain of the question. "What do you mean?"

"It's simply a question about feelings," Nonna said.

"I really can't say." Sallie looked at her with a puzzled expression.

"Well," started Nonna, "look into your body and scan it with you mind, sensing where you have pain."

"Pain. Oh, pain. I'm fine. No pains, none at all." Her answer was too quick.

Nonna reached over and touched Sallie's hand, making her jump in surprise. The touch was soft, yet penetrating, and Sallie had to swallow her immediate impulse to jerk her hand away. *What does this mean?*

Nonna kept one hand on top of Sallie's and moved the other underneath to clasp Sallie's hand in hers. This gentle contact did more to Sallie than many thousands of words. The warmth spread through her fingers, up through her arm and into her chest, radiating through her body, causing her to gasp from the tingling sensation. She looked at Nonna and her composure cracked at this spontaneous act of love. Her body loosened its tension.

"Life is messy," Nonna said. "It leaves a trail of unfinished business. It's the opposite of gathering all the issues up into a pile and tying them with a big beautiful bow. People escape. Ideas escape." Nonna began to stroke Sallie's hand, sandwiched between hers. A small gesture, yet Sallie focused all her energy into the motions, watching Nonna's tiny vein-lined hands as they massaged hers. An unconscious habit of Nonna's, soothing as she might quiet a fussy baby.

"You have a strong will. Much needed in the world. You are needed."

Sallie's voice was quiet. "Everything I've ever done has been to get his love. My success in the world pales. He just doesn't acknowledge my efforts."

"Have you considered that perhaps he does love you?"

Sallie shook her head. "He doesn't show it."

"Perhaps he doesn't know how."

Sallie set up a meeting with Marilyn, head of the docent program at the Los Angeles Museum of Art, and asked Robert to attend with her. Marilyn was one of a group of society matrons from West Los Angeles who volunteered at LACMA. Short, slender, and neatly attired, her manner was clipped and efficient. Someone less confident of her own accomplishments than Sallie might have been intimidated.

Marilyn's large office was shared with several other volunteers. The desks were neat, with papers and files tucked into overhead cabinets. Marilyn smiled as they sat down around her desk. "Interesting timing," she said, the pen in her hand poised next to her head. "Our board has been talking about a community project and the schools are one of the areas I've been investigating."

Robert spoke first. "We're just getting started and are looking to initiate something fairly simple."

Marilyn turned to Sallie. "As I said on the telephone, there would be a need for some cost sharing. Our budget is, of course, limited at this time." She turned back to Robert. "Over time, if it works out, we'd be willing to consider covering most of the program costs."

"We understand." Sallie was visibly excited about the enormity of the project. Such a venture could bring the Children's Action Group to the attention of the museum's donors, perhaps even garnering more funds for their cause. She ignored Robert's look.

"Let's go to the museum and talk about some of the art we might use." Marilyn appeared eager to get to the heart of the proposal.

They went to the building housing American artists. Marilyn's heels clicked on the hardwood floor as she moved quickly through the wing, followed closely by Sallie and Robert.

"One of the things I most like about exposing children to real paintings is that it shows the grandeur of art, the fact that it's bigger than who we are," Sallie said. There was no response from the other two, as if she were talking to herself. Looking at the paintings on the wall, she went on, "Art is timeless and brings a point of view of another time into our lives that we might not have in any other way."

Marilyn glanced back at her and nodded. "It's a perspective that would have been lost to us without the artist who took the time to record his sense of his world." She paused until Sallie fell in step beside her, then continued, "I thought we could talk about the various epochs of American art and see which artists you might want to consider for your students."

They spent an hour perusing the gallery, animatedly discussing the value of the artists and the pros and cons of such a program. As they were leaving, Marilyn said, "I'll talk to the Museum Director to see what kind of budget we're discussing. I think a 50-50 split might work for us." She turned abruptly and walked away.

Leaving the museum, Sallie radiated energy and talked excitedly about their visit. Robert walked quietly beside her without response. Looking over at him, she said, "I'm very pleased with our meeting. What did you think?"

Robert answered in a low tone, choosing his words carefully. "I'm surprised by your enthusiasm since it's probably more expensive than what we've discussed in our meetings."

Sallie calmed her voice to match his seriousness. "We don't know yet what it might cost. And we did agree this was something we should consider."

"Well," Robert's voice was precise, "the main objection to this idea was the concern about its cost. We need to ascertain from Marilyn what our cost might be before we get too excited about specifics of a potential project." His standards were clear and simple—integrity, consistency, and loyalty, the top triumvirate of his existence.

Sallie measured her words. "I just thought it would be a good idea to explore the possibilities so that the committee would also get excited too, and then…" She stopped. *This is the first time he's ever challenged me. Have I overstepped?*

She put a hand on Robert's arm and turned to him. He stopped and looked at her. Having his full attention, Sallie said, "My motto has always been to think bigger than what is in front of me. That way, as each step is completed, there's always another one 'waiting in the wings,' so to speak."

Robert nodded, "I understand. However, we need to focus right now on what we can do, and let the future take care of itself."

Sallie acknowledged his wisdom, "Should we take this idea off the table?"

"Perhaps we can just present it to the committee as an afterthought for future consideration."

Sallie nodded, trying to quash the conflicting thoughts racing through her mind. She still felt a strong urge to push for her ideas, despite Robert's guidance. Surely in the past she would have. *I've never been good at working out differences in opinion. Maybe it's time to try something new.*

Sallie sat on the floor of her father's den, surrounded by an explosion of bank statements, newspaper clippings, and various other forms of paper detritus. The bottom drawer of her father's desk had been stuck, and when she had yanked on it, the entire compartment flew out, sending her backwards with the drawer in her hand and the files all over the floor.

Balancing file folders precariously on her lap, she sifted through the papers, looking at the titles and filing them in the appropriate place. Sallie's eye caught the word "ORIGINALS," all in caps, stamped on an old yellowed document sticking sideways out of the bottom of a stack. She pulled it out, discovering three certificates paper-clipped together with part of her name written at the top.

She frowned as she inspected the top page, which appeared to be her birth certificate. Her first and middle names were printed as they should be, yet her last name was incorrectly labeled "Benson." Separating the papers, her hands began to shake as she saw the words "Adoption Certificate" at the top of the second document. Here, her name was listed as Sallie Jane Whitaker. The third page was a marriage license with David and Hannah's neat signatures at the bottom.

She sat there stunned, taking a moment to make sense of what she had found. *This can't be. Yet, it makes sense. No wonder I've always thought something was wrong. Now I know why he doesn't love me. I'm not even his child.* Pain began to course through her chest, and anger seared her thoughts. *How dare he withhold this from me?* Her thoughts shifted and she felt a sense of betrayal rising in her body. *And my mother? Why wouldn't she have told me?*

Sallie stood up and strode into the living room where her father was watching the game. She stood in front of the television, holding the papers in front of her. She threw them toward him and they landed on the floor at his feet. David turned off the game and leaned over, picking up the papers and fingering through them without meeting her glare.

"I was six months old when you and Mom were married." Her voice was shrill and accusatory.

"I loved her," David said, his eyes still on the documents.

"I knew. I just knew." Sallie began pacing in front of him. "I've always known something was wrong." She sat down and stared at him, her gaze piercing.

"We were best friends, Charlie and I. We did everything together." His voice was halting, remembering events from so long ago. "Your mother was an orphan—lost her family in the war. She worked on the base. We both loved her. She chose him. I was best man." His voice choked and he coughed. "He was killed right after you were born—an auto accident."

Sallie was speechless. She began to punch one fist into the other.

"When he died, I stepped in. I had wanted to marry her from the beginning. She wanted to do what was best for you." His voice became dry. "I loved her," he repeated. He looked away, then back at her. "Then I got transferred back to the States. She didn't adjust. She just shut down. She seemed to resent everything. Everything except you. She loved you."

Feeling as if her body were moving in slow motion, Sallie turned away from her father and ran from the room, flying out the back and letting the door slam hard behind her. She looked around the yard as if she had arrived in a strange land, then stumbled toward the back of the lot, finally falling against the fence and pawing at the ground as if she wanted to sink into the earth and be lost forever. She sobbed as she gasped for air, unable to see through the tears in her eyes.

The days went by in a haze. Each morning, Sallie would wake early, fix breakfast for her father, then leave the house before he awakened, leaving him a note. Most days, she went to her cottage where she hibernated, writing her column and making impossible plans for her future. When she knew the Dodgers game was on, she would return with lunch and dinner for her father, sneaking in and out so as to not have to speak to him. She returned to her dad's house late each night after he was already in bed.

She still kept up her schedule of sessions with the TWIGs, baseball games with her nephew, and another task force meeting. She maintained an aloof air, such that no one around her knew of her distress.

One morning, after weeks of this routine, the buzzing of Sallie's cell phone woke her from a dead sleep. With bleary eyes, she squinted at Anne's name on the digital display. Sallie felt a pang of guilt. Her despair had turned her away from even her best friend; it had been weeks since they'd spoken. *Why is she calling at 6:30 AM? What if it's an emergency?* She hesitated and finally put Anne on the line.

Sallie put a neutral tone to her words, whispering into the phone. "Anne, you're calling early. Is everything okay?"

"What is happening? We've been so worried about you." Anne's voice was a cross between concern and anger at her for not calling. "You haven't called or answered my messages."

"I've been challenged," Sallie said, choosing her words carefully.

Sensing something in Sallie's tone, Anne's voice softened. "Are you ready to tell me? If not, I'll call back later."

"Oh, Anne, I'm so sorry. Let me call you back later. I'm not even up yet." She ended the call and got up, meeting her dad in the hallway.

He gave her a guilty look, grappling for words as if he didn't know what to say. "You can move out if you want."

Her anger bubbled up. "Is that all you can say? After everything? After your lies and deceptions? That's all you can say?"

David reached out to her. "It's not all. You've been…"

She pushed her hands toward him as if to push him away. "Just leave me alone."

He shrank back. Sallie saw the pain in his eyes and put her hands over her heart, trying to press away its throbbing. "Later. I'll… Just later." She turned back into her room and shut the door, lying on her bed to assess her situation. *I… I feel… I feel, what word can I use… I feel sad… and angry… yet there was something about the way he looked.*

Later that morning, back in her own place, Sallie called Anne. "Apologies Anne, for not calling."

"What's up that you can't talk to me?"

"It's just… everything's such a mess."

"Well, if it's not about Robert, catch me up on him."

"Oh, that's an issue too," responded Sallie, the tiredness in her voice coming through.

"Is it about your arts committee?"

Sallie gave a sigh. "Well, I got this idea. You know me. So I did a lot of research."

"That sounds like you. Nothing wrong with that," said Anne amicably.

Sallie recounted the story of her meeting with Marilyn and Robert's concern about the cost of doing a joint project with LACMA. "Robert was nice and all, a perfect gentleman. I don't believe he's ever given anyone an angry word. He was firm, in a good way," she finished.

"So, what happened?"

Sallie sighed. "Well, after I found out the budget, I went back to the group and asked them what they thought about adding this kind of program to our agenda. Consensus was that it was a little too much to start and might be appropriate after we have an initial plan in effect. The good news is I caught myself before I got into too much trouble."

"I'm proud of you," said Anne with enthusiasm. "Sounds as if you learned something about yourself and working with others. Congratulations, this is a milestone. Have you patted yourself on the back?"

"Not really."

"Well, have you had a real date with him yet?"

"Oh, Anne, I don't even know what a 'real' date is."

"I guess what I'm saying is, do you acknowledge that you do like him and he likes you?"

"Not really. It's just that it doesn't matter, compared to…" her voice trailed off.

Anne responded to her despondency. "What about your family? And your dad? Do they still want you to move in permanently with him?"

"That's just part of the issue. There's more." Sallie sounded deflated, her words barely audible. "You see, it turns out I'm adopted," she finished.

"Wow." Anne was quiet. "How did you find out?"

"I found the certificate in his office." Sallie's voice faltered. "He didn't even tell me himself."

"That must have hurt. But it's good news, don't you think?"

Sallie didn't answer right away. Anne's response had brought her up short. "That's not exactly what I expected you to say."

"Well, you've always had the sense something wasn't right. And it has kept you from feeling a part of your family. And you always thought it was your fault," said Anne, carefully laying out her case. "As I see it, your father is human, just as we all are. And didn't you say he told you that he really does love you? Perhaps you've always just misunderstood his actions."

"That's not the way I see it." Sallie gulped. "Anyway, there's no reason for me to stay here anymore. I've decided I'm coming home. I don't belong here."

"Oh, Sallie, you know how much I would look forward to seeing you," said Anne. "Just make certain you're doing it for the right reason."

"There's nothing for me here. Just as I've always thought. I don't fit in."

"What about your license?"

"Fred is still working on it. I might have to go to Sacramento for a hearing. Or something else. I don't really want to explain right now."

"It sounds as if you're having some internal conflict."

"Yes. Can we talk later?"

"Of course. Just don't let it go so long. I thought I was your best friend."

"Oh, Anne. You are. I just don't know exactly how to explain what's going on. Please give me a little more time."

"You got it," Anne agreed, and they signed off.

Sallie's Journal—August 14th

Everything good that ever happened to me always seemed to include something that was tragic. My life is like playing "Mother May I"—take two steps forward and then a slap, two steps backwards; or one giant step forward, and then, slap, slap, slap—three baby steps backwards. As a result, it seems as if I'm rooted in the same spot, like the plants in my garden.

I find myself enraged because my mother and the man I thought was my dad have lied to me. Also, I am grieving the loss of my real father even though I never knew him. I have always felt as if I didn't belong and I wonder if somewhere within me I somehow knew.

Dad says that he knew me from birth and he held me and loved me as much as my real father did. Charles Stephen Benson, that was his name.

My real name is Sallie Jane Benson. When I write that name and look at it, it's a person I don't even know, as if half of me is a stranger to the other half—connected to someone who did not exist to me until recently. My body tingles with strangeness, as if I don't even know who I am. There seem to be pieces of me that are lost, perhaps forever.

I wonder what he was like. I look at his picture and he and my dad look so young and so much alike. I wonder why my real father had to die. Who were my grandparents? What happened to them? Did they ever know about me? Do I have cousins? Dad does not remember.

He thinks my real father was from somewhere in the South and that he was part Italian. It was a bond they shared and what probably brought them together. It's as if they were mirror images of each other and Dad could have been my real father. Yet, he's not. My mother chose my real father first and now they're both gone. I'm an orphan.

I need to find the gift and the challenge my adopted dad gave me. He made me want to prove him wrong, that I was just as competent as my brother. I guess that would translate to perseverance. I don't give up easily. The challenge would be not to judge myself too harshly and to trust others.

There is also the issue of Robert. I'm uncertain how I feel about him and about the future. I don't want to think about getting any more involved here than I am if I'm not going to be staying here. Besides, he might not like the real me. I'm not even certain who the real me is.

When I am passionate about something, I become forceful. Perhaps I think I will not get my point across. My strength and power can overwhelm others, and my anger seems to keeps me distant from them. I believe I hold myself to a higher standard, yet it appears my methodology is suspect.

I think it's time to move back home. I'm hopeful I can get my license back, even if there would be a fine.

Dream: I am taking a class. At the end of the second day, I tell the teacher I want to learn and she hasn't taught me anything. I am enraged and can barely hold myself back from killing this woman. Unable to contain myself and screaming at her for her incompetence, I follow her to my mother's home and begin to choke her, almost killing her. My mother is there and she invites me into her house. It is all pink and filled with angles and stairs. There are platforms separating the spaces with fences around them making them inaccessible. On these platforms are all different kinds of chairs.

"You must put some stairs over here so we can get into your house," I tell her.

"It's just as I want it," she tells me. I leave the house disgusted and see my father and another man who looks just like him. I wave to talk to them and start walking in their direction. They both turn away and walk down two separate roads.

CHAPTER SIXTEEN

Ogoawa: Spirit of Abundance & Prosperity

Sallie's eyes opened to a Technicolor world, awash in colors with a clarity normally reserved for a cartoon creation. She had gone to bed in black and white and now awoke to a world of magic, where every color vibrated with a diaphanous glow, making the lines that separated each piece of the landscape sharp and definitive.

She was lying in a bed of grass. This was not like the short carpet of lawn mowed in suburbia every weekend; rather this grass had long tendrils that curved gently upward and sprayed sideways in arcs as a light draft of air moved gently through it. When Sallie raised her arm to discover where she was, the grass under her body bounced back to its mounded tufts, making her body feel weightless.

Around her, Mother Nature presented a royal court where each flower, plant, and tree awaited her word, all declaring her the "Princess of the Land." Taking in the splendor of her surroundings, she noticed little dots of sparkling light that flickered like fireflies. Not able to look at them directly, she glanced sideways out of the corner of her eye to see winged fairies with garments matching the brilliant colors of the landscape.

Tiny pinpoints of light surrounded each of these miniature sparkling beings, and Sallie discovered the same shimmering light emanating from every pore of her body, like a multi-hued rainbow dress glistening in the air. A wide-eyed Sallie watched the tiny beings dance with such exuberance and grace that she felt part of the great show of nature.

The rhythms of the wings of the tiny creatures created a musical resonance that infused her body, causing waves of new feelings to course through her veins. She couldn't identify the new sensations, as if they were obscured with gauzy fabric. As the music swept through her soul, she heard lyrics that were not quite decipherable to her mind. She cocked her head to the side, listening more carefully. *What is this song?*

She heard the notes clearly as they resonated through her senses, causing the atoms of her body to line up in unison with the nature elements surrounding her. Their form of music was different than any she had ever heard. The sound expressed itself as more than singing, a form of chanting perhaps, yet even more.

She could discern the space between the notes, and it registered deep within her, opening up her heart to a new feeling. She clapped her hands with joy and danced in rhythm like a small child. The words individually made little sense, yet taken all together they had the power of the whole, causing her thoughts to disappear and giving lightness to her soul.

Suddenly, one of the tiny beings fluttered over and landed on a large moss-covered stone nearby. Sallie had to use her peripheral vision to see her companion clearly.

The diminutive fairy answered Sallie's unasked question. "I am Ogoawa, the Spirit of Abundance and Prosperity. I am a Nature Spirit— a deva for the plants and animals and all that lives and breathes in the universe apart from humans."

Sallie smiled as she opened her arms to the intensity of the flowers in the garden. "This is like a vision of the ideal garden I see in my mind," she said to Ogoawa. "It is the image I have when I look out and dream how I want my surroundings to look."

Ogoawa nodded. "When you look at nature, all that you see is a profusion of life. The dreams you have of your garden are the same as the dreams you have of your life, all part of the plan you chose to manifest. Just as the seed knows the flower it will become, somewhere within you is the knowledge of all that you are."

"The beauty makes me want to laugh, and dance, and sing," replied Sallie as she waved her arms toward the expanse around her.

"You are like those flowers," Ogoawa continued, "blooming in their perfection, without concern as to whether their color or shape is better than another's. Plants delight in putting on a display of their foliage, showing you the abundance of the natural world for you to emulate in your life."

Sallie savored the words coming from the tiny winged fairy. "They bring me such joy."

"That is the happiness that comes when you live in the moment and see yourself as a flower in the garden of life," smiled Ogoawa. "This is you seeing yourself as perfect just the way you are and allowing that perfection to blossom into all you do."

"That sounds all well and good," countered Sallie, sitting at attention, "yet living my life on a daily basis is another matter. Things just come up."

Ogoawa replied, "What is important is to look at the 'how' of these things, not the 'what.'"

"What do you mean?"

"Your response to the events creates your daily life. Look at the events that come up in your life as simple exchanges of energy. When your energy emanates from the seat of anger in your belly, a charge is sent out that blocks you from experiencing the full truth of the situation."

"I'm not certain I understand," Sallie responded with a frown.

"As a child, you were taught to be quiet, sit still, not to cry or express your feelings—in essence, not to vibrate the spirit that you are. As time went on, life and space began to close in and you had less and less personal freedom. The denser you became, the slower your emotions could vibrate and attract things to you."

Sallie hesitated for a moment, tilting her head. "Is that what is meant by filicide, the killing of our children?"

Ogoawa's wings vibrated an affirmative answer to her question. "You were controlled, trapped and compressed until you lost your spiritual power and the ability to vibrate enough to hold that creative space open."

"Like losing pieces of me," Sallie said quietly, almost to herself.

"Exactly. When you do, it becomes more difficult to attract success into your life. Recovering your true sense of yourself is the way to reclaim your spiritual power. Free your feelings and your thoughts will follow the path to true prosperity."

"What do you mean by true prosperity?" Sallie asked.

"True prosperity is having a point of view that you are perfect just the way you are and there is work awaiting you that no one else can fulfill. Through your passion, fully realized, you will find the full richness that brings contentment—the secret law of prosperity," replied Ogoawa.

Sallie's eyes lit up. "I think I am beginning to find my passion. I have begun to write a column for the newspaper and I have been encouraged to write a book. Is that what you mean?"

"Yes. When you are expressing what makes you happy, you create a pulsation that gives movement to and propels your creations. In your creations, new ideas and attitudes arise that in turn intensify your vibration, activating the principle of magnetic attraction, which further draws your desires to you. You were born with a spiritual power to express yourself, and your emotional vibration holds that space open."

"And it feels good. I get excited when I write." Sallie's voice became excited as she spread her arms wide and turned in a circle. Putting her arms down, she became thoughtful. "Yet there are other areas of my life that aren't exactly working very well right now." Her voice wound down and she frowned.

"Creating your life is not an act of forcing others or the world to give you what you want. More, look to attune with your soul through intention, then let go of control and relax so that your desires can come your way in a more effortless manner. Commitment to your vision helps you stay on the path. One of your strengths, Sallie, is your persistence. Now, it might be said that sometimes this manifests for you as being pushy."

"Yes, I know. I have been told that before," said Sallie with a smile, not as offended as she had expected.

"If you'll notice, when babies cry, they put every ounce of themselves into their wail. Just like those babies, putting all of your energy into your desires will bring you satisfaction. You will be an example to others, who may decide to follow in your footsteps. Fulfill just one longing and you will realize the potential of all unfulfilled dreams."

Sallie listened intently to all Ogoawa said and knew the truth of the words. She sat back, contemplating. Quietly, she said, "I know, though, I still have anger inside me. Yet, at the time I am angry, my mind seems to have a will of its own and I get caught up in its energy."

Ogoawa touched Sallie's forehead and said, "Let me show you what you can do when these intense emotions overtake you. Remember, you want to free your feelings so that your thoughts will manifest right action in your life. Let us try right now. First, sit quietly. Take a deep breath and become aware of your feelings."

Sallie sat back and breathed deeply, searching inside her body for the feelings that were prominent. She found tightness in her chest and she explored its pain, acknowledging the rage that had filled her. Suddenly, her body jerked and tensed in response to her unrequited fury.

"Ah, that is good," said Ogoawa. "Now, I want you to find the deep longing inside yourself for whatever you dream."

A quiet sigh slipped from her lips and a barely perceptible smile crossed her face. "I dream about being part of a loving family, where I know I am valued and people want me in their lives."

"Now," said Ogoawa, "follow that idea as if it were a beam of light you are riding out into the universe. Get the sense of what it would be like to have that family and let it permeate your entire body, every cell, and then expand outward and create a bright golden disk around you, as if you were encompassed by your own personal sun." Sallie nodded as the energy of light covered her and took hold.

"Next, let the level of your longing intensify until it is almost beyond what you can hold, like a small ball in the center of your body that will burst into a million bits of energy, a supernova exploding in space." She watched as Sallie's chest began to rise with an intake of breath that she held for what seemed like a long time.

"Now, let your body move in concert with what it feels. Begin by letting your senses take over. Start making sounds, and move your body in a dance. The vibration of sound and the movement of your body will allow the energy from the explosion to release into the universe. Let yourself go into the sound and the movement until your energy is vibrating fast enough to ignite the disk and burn it up."

A noise came out of Sallie's mouth, beautiful and clear like an opera singer in training. She, who felt she could not carry a tune and had no sense of rhythm, was now singing with a clarity she had never known before. She stood up with eyes closed, dancing spontaneously with grace and precision, at one within herself, like a tuning fork had been turned on in her brain and was resonating at the perfect pitch to bring her body into harmony with her soul.

As she spun around, Ogoawa danced around Sallie's body with the same rhythm. Sallie opened her eyes, a wide beatific smile lighting up her face.

"And lastly, Sallie," Ogoawa went on, "the most important thing of all is to give thanks for all you have. Gratitude is the prayer of prosperity. The power does not lie in the words; it is in the intention of your heart that conveys the message across time and space.

"Prayer is an attitude; a way of looking at life with a reverence for all that exists. You can say, 'Praise the Lord,' or recite a mantra many times, or say a simple prayer of gratitude, such as 'thank you, thank you, thank you.' All words lead to the same source through the intention of your heart."

"In spite of everything happening right now, I'm very thankful for all I have," replied Sallie, nodding in agreement. "I know I am blessed."

"Trust your eternal self to guide you. Ask Spirit to hold you and show you the way. Get into it. Like a baby crying, give your all. In you being who you are just as you are, you will manifest your dreams."

"You make me believe I am capable of doing all that I dream," said Sallie.

"You can do all you desire, and more," Ogoawa promised. "As you emerge on the other side of your anger, your attitude will change. You will be full of energy and joy. You will see your life more clearly. If your body has been numb and asleep, it will wake up. The more you are willing to release and open to receive your true nature, the more energy will fill you. This increased vibration will magnetically attract all you need for true prosperity."

"I have a sense of that energy of which you speak when I am writing," said Sallie. "I do feel more alive than I've felt in the past few months."

"You are beginning to see what I mean," replied Ogoawa. "Seek red, seek green, seek sound, seek beauty, seek in every living thing the vast potentiality that is life. Know, trust, release the past, and believe in your highest good. Send out loving thoughts to all those you encounter. Know everything is profitable to your soul.

"These are the thoughts I send to you, Sallie. You do well with the dreaming of dreams and need to trust yourself and your presence more. For I know these things, as I am of the fairy kingdom and I live within the exuberance of Mother Nature. I know only abundance and fullness as everything I need is provided to me. I choose to live in the richness that exists in the world around me and to be the life I am here to perform. I live in who I am at all times and all I desire comes to me."

"Perhaps that is why I love working in my garden," mused Sallie, a faraway look in her eyes as she brought an image of her garden into focus in her mind. She tilted her head to get a closer look at Ogoawa. "You know so much about my nature. I desire to learn to live as you do."

"I leave you with this message: Enough pain, enough wounding. The hurting is over. You do not have to do anything to be lovable. Just as Spirit is, you also are. You are perfect the way you are, which does not mean you will not make mistakes. It means that, in your humanity and the boundless nature of your soul, even your mistakes are perfect as they are part of the plan you chose to manifest."

PART IX
Transformation

God and I in space alone
And nobody else in view.
"And where are the people, O Lord," I said
"The earth below, and the sky o'erhead
And the dead whom once I knew?"

"That was a dream," God smiled and said,
"A dream that seemed to be true.
There were no people, living or dead,
There was no earth, and no sky o'erhead
There was only Myself – in you."

"Why do I feel no fear," I asked,
"Meeting You here this way?
For I have sinned I know full well,
And is there heaven, and is there hell,
And is this the Judgment Day?"

"Nay, those were but dreams," the Great God said,
"dreams that have ceased to be.
There are no such things as fear or sin,
There is no you – you never have been –
There is nothing at all but Me."

Ella Wheeler Wilcox
Conversation

CHAPTER SEVENTEEN

Beginning Anew

Sallie's voice sounded as if she were miles away listening to someone through a couple of cans connected by a string. Sitting with Mark and Nancy at their dining room table, she felt separate from herself, as though she were eavesdropping on someone else's conversation, yet she was the one speaking.

"I can't live with him anymore," she said. "Anyway, I need to go back to Las Rosas. That's where my home is."

Mark glared at her, confused. "What happened?"

"It's just not going to work out, that's all," she responded, not meeting his gaze.

"You have to tell us more." Nancy reached her hand across the table, aware of the faraway look in Sallie's eyes.

She ignored Nancy and met Mark's stare, her eyes ablaze as she drew herself back to the present. "We've led different lives, you and I. You had talent. I didn't."

"But you had the guts to leave," Mark responded. "I didn't."
Neither wanted to be the first to back down.

"Where do we go from here?" His eyes narrowed, straining to read between the lines.

"I guess we go check out Shady Acres. Go and sign him up," she said matter-of-factly. "Oh, also, his office was a mess. I've been working on it. Since I'm leaving, perhaps we should go over things together."

Mark shrugged. "Okay. I'll make the appointment. My schedule is free tomorrow afternoon."

"I'll meet you at David's home."

Mark and Nancy looked at her and then at each other, not understanding why she had called her father by his name.

Sallie pushed down the final box of papers into the overflowing recycle bin. *There. I'm almost done. At least the room will be neater and Mark will be able to find what he needs.*

Walking into the den, Sallie surveyed the results of her handiwork. *The room looks so much better,* she thought, as she went to a last stack of magazines. The first magazine she picked up was the latest issue of *Los Madre Living.* "So much for my writing career," she said aloud, as she turned the magazine over and noticed again the labyrinth ad on the back. Sallie grimaced. *That's the third time I've seen this labyrinth. I had wanted to go check it out before I left. Oh well, not this time.*

"Wow!"

Sallie jumped up and spun around, startled by Mark's voice coming from the doorway. "How'd you get him to let you throw anything out? I've tried to no avail."

"Oh, most of it's still here—in that cupboard." She nodded toward the old wardrobe. "I only threw out things that were outdated."

"By the way, I set our appointment at Shady Acres for Friday morning."

"Good," she replied, a note of efficiency in her voice.

"What are you two doing?" David said from the hallway. "Where are my newspapers? My magazines?" His voice began to rise in anger.

Sallie rolled up the magazine in her hand and used it to point toward the desk. The most recent ones I put in your desk drawers, right there. I only threw out the really old ones."

He turned to her and yelled, "I told you not to throw anything away! I kept them for a reason!"

Sallie rolled her eyes like a petulant teenager. "The place was so disorganized. How could you tell where anything was?"

"I can't even trust you to clean my office."

"I couldn't trust you with my life," said Sallie, her voice quiet now.

"I took care of you when there was no one else. You and your mother would have been alone."

Sallie squeezed the magazine more tightly in her hand, preparing to fire back, when Mark interjected, "What ARE you talking about?" He moved between them as if he were refereeing a boxing match.

Sallie stared at David. "I'll let you tell him." She inhaled deeply to gain her composure and turned away, marching toward the door. Mark gave his father a questioning look, and David shook his head and waved his hand as if to say "some other time."

Sinking into the office chair, Mark put his hands to his forehead and let out a deep sigh. Glancing down, one of the papers on the desk caught his eye and he frowned as he picked it up. He looked up quickly and called, "Sallie, wait."

She turned back to him, her look challenging him to try to stop her from leaving the room.

He waved the paper in the air. "What's this?" he asked. "It says 'Power of Attorney' and it has your name on it."

Sallie turned to face him directly, putting her hands on her hips. "I was working with the bank on Dad's affairs and they wanted it in order to talk to me without him being there."

Mark stood up and came around to the front of the desk. "And you didn't consult me?"

"It seemed a simple matter."

David looked from one to the other. "What're you two talking about?"

Mark waved the paper toward him. "Well, it seems as if your daughter now has control over your financial affairs."

David looked back at her accusingly. "I never said to do that."

"We discussed it. You agreed."

"Then I didn't know what you were doing."

They both looked at her in shock and anger.

"Obviously I don't belong in this family," Sallie said as she left the room and stormed out the front door, slamming it behind her.

Sallie stopped her car at the curb in front of Nonna's house and bent over to peer out the window at the darkened residence. She cautiously walked up and knocked on the front door, then stepped away, as if she might lose her nerve and bolt. The outdoor light came on and the door opened. Nonna, still dressed, peered out.

When she saw the crestfallen look on Sallie's face, she opened the door wide. "Oh, child. What is it? Come in. Come in." Nonna reached out to her and Sallie let herself be taken into Nonna's motherly embrace.

"Are you busy?" Sallie whispered, breaking down into sobs of despair.

"Oh, child, not for you." Nonna led her to the couch where they sat until Sallie's sobs began to subside and she was quiet. Nonna's voice was tender. "Are you hungry? Have you had anything to eat today?" She leaned closer to hear Sallie's murmured response.

Sallie's expression was blank, as if she didn't understand the question. "No, I guess not. I don't know."

"I have some *pasta e fagioli* soup I made today. It'll do you good."

Sallie forced a smile and raised her tear-lined face. "You really do believe you can solve all the world's problems with a dish of food, don't you?" Sallie looked down. "I'm not certain I can eat."

"Well, you never know until you try." Nonna gave Sallie a motherly smile and gently led her to one of the bar stools. After bustling around the kitchen for a few minutes, Nonna returned with a steaming bowl of soup. "Just start with one bite and eat what you can," she said, wiping her hands on a towel.

After taking a couple of bites, Sallie put her spoon down. In an almost inaudible voice, she said, "My dad's not my real father."

Nonna came over and sat down next to her, placing a warm hand on Sallie's arm. "That must have been hard on both of you."

Tears flowing down her face, Sallie nodded. "I just don't know what to think." Nonna was quiet as she went on, her words barely audible through her tears. "His name was Charlie Benson." She pushed the soup bowl back, put her head on the table and began to sob inconsolably.

"Oh, my child, how difficult for you." Nonna stroked her hair and let her cry until the wave of emotions subsided.

Finally, Sallie raised her head and looked at Nonna. "Why didn't he tell me?"

"Perhaps he didn't know how."

"What do you mean?"

"Men, particularly those his age, don't always know how to express their feelings," Nonna said. "I remember my husband, Bob. He loved his family and showed it in his own way, but he wasn't able to tell us. It caused a lot of trouble when the kids were young."

"Why?" Sallie asked, the grief in her eyes open and raw. "I just don't understand."

"Something happened to these men in the war. They came home

apparently whole, yet they were different. They didn't want to talk about what they'd been through. As a result, they closed off some part of themselves and quietly went about their duty. They took care of their families, yet only showed part of who they were."

"That's like my father, exactly."

"It extracted a great price from them."

Sallie frowned. "I never thought about it like that before."

"I found that by accepting my husband with love and compassion, and looking for openings to help him express his feelings, he was able to reconcile with his children before he was gone. You know, we weren't always this close as a family. When he was nearing the end, he was finally able to show them his love. His death was the real catalyst for our family coming together in the way you see us now."

"Oh, Nonna, I don't want to wait until he dies," Sallie cried out.

"You don't have to, my child. You have an opportunity now, if you choose to take it, to help him forgive himself for what he considers his failings."

"I've never thought Dad would consider himself as having failed."

"We all do until we're forgiven," Nonna said quietly.

Sallie looked at Nonna. *She is such a loving person. She can see the good in everyone. Perhaps she can see me.*

"Nonna, there's something else. Something I haven't been able to tell anyone outside of my office at home."

"What is it, child?"

"My real estate license was suspended right before I came down here." She looked to Nonna to see if she understood.

"Oh my child, that's a real challenge."

Sallie gulped and nodded, tears rising in her eyes. She blinked them away.

"Can you talk about it?"

She exhaled slowly, searching for the words. "I did something illegal. But I didn't know I was doing it."

"That must be trying for you. You don't have to tell me the whole story. Just say how you feel."

Sallie giggled a little, then laughed. "That's what my friend, Anne, is always saying. Just feel your feelings."

"That's how things are healed—things we think are failures."

"I didn't know, Nonna." Sallie's face twisted. "I just didn't know."

"Then why don't you just say that."

"It will look like I'm a failure. Like I didn't know what I was doing."

"No, child, it will just look like you made a mistake."

Sallie looked up sharply. "What? What do you mean?"

"We all make mistakes. It is in acknowledging them that we are able to learn and grow."

Staring across the room with an unfocused gaze, Sallie took in Nonna's words.

"You don't have to decide now. Just think about it," Nonna counseled.

Love shining in her eyes, Sallie smiled despite herself. "You always know what to say, don't you?"

First thing the next morning, Sallie called Fred. After his usual terse greeting, she opened, "Have you done anything about a hearing?"

"Hasn't quite been timely to bring up the subject. Why?"

"I had another thought, if you're interested."

"Of course I am."

"Well," she hesitated, took a deep breath, and then blurted, "I could…" She stopped, unable to continue.

Fred didn't respond, making her feel as if she had all the time in the world to gather her thoughts.

"I could tell them what actually happened, from my point of view." Her heart was pounding in her ears, but she pressed on. "I could say I

290

didn't know what Mike was doing, that I signed blank documents and was remiss in not paying closer attention."

"Are you sure you want to do that?"

"What other choices are there to get my license back? It would disclose my naiveté, yet would be genuine."

"Yes, it would be genuine. Are you ready to do it?"

"I…" she hesitated. The answer was either yes or no. If she couldn't say yes, it was a no. *Can I really admit I made a mistake? That I can look foolish? That I'm less than what I hold myself to be?*

The questions tumbled through her mind, falling aside like petals until only one remained. *Can I forgive myself?*

"Yes."

Sallie walked toward the entrance to Shady Acres where Mark was waiting. Focusing on keeping her gait even, her eyes searched his face for clues to his state of mind as she approached. The last words she had said to him, yelled in anger, echoed through her mind. *Maybe I don't belong in this family.* She wondered if he agreed.

He spotted her and walked toward her, holding out his arms. Tentatively, she welcomed his hug and put her arms around him, letting go of her tension as she relaxed into his easy embrace.

"Hey, Sis," he said. "Let's see if this will work for Dad."

They both turned toward the building, their shoulders touching, evaluating the premises through their father's eyes.

"Well-kept landscaping," said Mark.

Easing into business mode, Sallie nodded. "Looks high end." Her tone was crisp and efficient.

"Looks as if the building is in good shape too. Impressive."

Sallie nodded as Mark opened the door for her and they entered the open lobby. To one side was a small attached office where a secretary monitored the comings and goings of residents and guests. Upon asking for the administrator, they were told to look around the facility while she was paged.

The living room was spacious, with several seating areas and two widescreen televisions at either end of the room. Tables for four peppered the large dining room. Sallie made a quick count. "Looks like there are about a hundred people living here. That's a lot."

Mark nodded as he picked up a name tag from one of the tables. "Looks like it's assigned seating."

A team of four was preparing lunch for the residents in the spotless kitchen. Sallie nodded at the workers and turned around as a neatly dressed silver-haired woman approached them.

"Good afternoon. I'm Wylma Biggs, the manager here," she said, extending her hand. Her voice was warm and encouraging as she showed them around the rest of the facility, keeping up a running commentary of the amenities available to the residents.

She showed them one of the apartments with a small living area, bedroom, and bathroom, and pointed out the safety features that allowed each resident to be monitored twenty-four hours a day. "This is one of our larger units. We also have studio apartments, if cost is a factor. Right now, we only have one of the one-bedroom units available, so you should make your decision soon before it's taken." They nodded, letting her talk without much interruption.

After reviewing the library and activity room, Wylma's phone beeped and she quickly took it off her belt and checked the read-out. She looked up and gave them both a motherly smile. "Would you excuse me for a minute?" They both nodded. "Why don't you look around and I'll meet you up front to go over the costs and other details?" She turned and strode toward the office.

Wandering down one of the halls, they heard sounds of a baseball game in progress. "Oh, Dad would like that," commented Sallie.

They followed the sound and came to an apartment with an open door where a man, looking much like their father, was watching a

Dodgers game. They glanced at each other and nodded in agreement; they could see David in the same position.

"Dad would get along just fine here," Sallie said as Mark knocked on the door and poked his head inside.

"Hi," he said. "Excuse the interruption. Would you mind if we ask you a couple of questions?"

The man waved them into the room. "Come on in."

"How's the game going?" Sallie asked.

"Dodgers are down a run. They have the big guns coming up next inning though." He muted the television. "How can I help you?"

Mark introduced both of them and said, "We'll only take a minute. We're looking for a place for our father and wondered how you liked living here."

"Food's okay. Company's good."

Before they had a chance to ask any more questions, an orderly walked inside. "Mr. Bernard, it's time for your exercise class. Doctor's orders."

"There's just one more inning," Mr. Bernard said in a plaintive tone, begging for a reprieve to finish the game.

"Exercise class begins in one minute." The orderly's voice was pleasant and light, yet insistent. There was no other option available. "You can't miss it." Mr. Bernard looked crestfallen as he solemnly turned off the game and shuffled after the orderly.

As they walked back toward the front, Sallie and Mark exchanged a glance.

"Did you see how upset the old guy was?" Mark asked.

"I don't know if I can do this," said Sallie.

"Neither do I."

They hurried out of the building and sat down on a bench outside. "Besides, how would he even afford it?" Sallie asked.

"He'd have to sell the house."

"There'd be no going back."

"That's the downside," Mark admitted.

"No wonder he's resisting it," said Sallie.

A sense of their old closeness as children surfaced and the years fell away. Mark reached over and put his hand on top of Sallie's. He looked her in the eye. "Dad told me about your father. It doesn't matter to me. You're still one hundred percent my sister."

Sallie stared back and sighed. "What happened to us?"

Mark shook his head. "I'd like to get to know you again."

Sallie was quiet, uncertain whether she would be heard. Hesitantly, she said, "You know, sometimes you act just like you're my father. It invalidates me."

"You have a forceful personality that can be overwhelming," said Mark. "It's as if it's your way or nothing."

"I just want you to listen to me," she replied. "It's not an either-or conversation."

"Well, sometimes it feels like it is."

They sat in silence, each wondering how to find the path to reconciliation. Finally, Sallie said, "Perhaps we could use a little shorthand with each other, something to indicate when we're feeling pressured."

"What do you have in mind?"

"Perhaps you could say to me something like…" She thought a moment. "Something like 'lighten up.' "

He let out a loud laugh. "Sounds good."

Sallie smiled as she looked down at the ground. Turning to him, she said, "What would you like me to say to you?"

"Hmmm. Maybe you could ask me if I'd like to hear a suggestion."

She nodded and looked at him, a playful smile on her lips. "I could do that. Would you like to hear a suggestion now?"

"Sure."

"Let's get some lunch. We should go to that new Thai place that just opened."

He gave her a pat on the back. "Lighten up, Sis."

When Sallie and Mark got back from their visit to Shady Acres, David grumbled to them about not being allowed to go along with them.

"After all, it's my life you're planning," he said. "The least you can do is to let me see where I'm going."

"Don't worry, Dad," Mark answered. "It's not for you."

David looked visibly relieved. He sat down in his chair as Sallie and Mark sat on the sofa. He looked at both of them. "What are the plans then?"

Sallie nodded to Mark to start. "We thought it would be a good idea to have a family conference."

"Let's just get one thing straight," said David, wagging his finger. "I like my life the way it is. I can't say I like either of you interfering."

"We know that," Sallie said.

"And another thing," he looked directly at Sallie, "I'm not sure I want you living here."

"We can all agree on that," said Mark with a chuckle.

"Well, there's got to be some other options." David looked between them.

"There's a day program for seniors with a shuttle that picks up in the morning and brings you home in the evening," said Sallie.

"It would make me—I mean us—feel better if you got out more," said Mark. "At least a couple of days a week."

"Just so I don't miss my ball games."

"Oh, Dad, I went by the place. They've got several TVs. You can see your games," said Sallie. "And with other like-minded fans."

"My biggest concern is when you're alone at home," Mark explained.

"There's an organization that hires out part-time people to keep tabs on seniors," said Sallie. "I know you've never wanted anyone to stay here."

"If it would make you guys feel better, then maybe. As long as they don't touch any of my stuff or throw anything out."

"No one's going to throw anything out unless you give the okay, Dad," said Mark.

"We'll definitely make certain of that," seconded Sallie.

"I know you both want what's best for me," David's voice was emotional, "and I want you to know what's best is for me to stay here." His voice became quiet. "With some changes," he added.

As their new plan fell into place, Sallie moved back into her small cottage. She still continued to visit her father on a daily basis, often staying and cooking dinner.

David began to talk about the past, telling her stories of his war service and his work in southern England and Germany, servicing the engines that kept the planes aloft. Small stories emerged about his comrades, including some who had fallen, and he seemed to release some of the grief he had carried throughout his life. He told her of his life with her birth father, Charlie.

Pictures that had been kept for years unshared began to surface. David found an album in the back of his closet and he and Sallie were sitting on the couch turning the pages when Mark walked in.

"What are you guys doing?" asked Mark.

"Do you remember when we all went to Hawaii on vacation when you were about six?" Sallie asked.

"Some of it," he said and leaned over the back of the couch to better see the pictures.

"I was stationed in the Midwest. You guys had never seen the ocean," said David.

"Here's a great picture of Mom," Sallie said, pointing at a picture of

Hannah in a bathing suit with sunglasses and a wide smile. "She laughed all the time on that vacation. That's what I remember the most."

"You guys couldn't get enough of the ocean and wanted to spend every waking moment at the beach," David said, pointing to the two of them playing in the water.

Mark inspected their faces, deep in focus as they built a sandcastle. "You were so intense, Sallie. Catch that look on your face." He chuckled and Sallie smiled. "Mom always made us put our shirts on over our bathing suits."

"She didn't want you kids out in the sun very much and was always putting lotion on you so you wouldn't get burned."

"We really got tan," Sallie said, her eyes going soft. "By the end of the week, she called us her 'little Hawaiian munchkins.'" She reached a hand back for Mark. "Do you remember?" He squeezed her hand in response.

"There's that needle rock," Mark said, pointing. "We walked in that rain forest."

"You pretended we were lost and had to live forever in the jungle," Sallie laughed.

They went quiet, each awash in their own memories.

David broke the silence. "After that, I got a transfer to Southern California so we could live near the ocean; you guys loved it so much."

"That was my favorite vacation ever," said Mark.

"It was the best," agreed Sallie.

It was one of those rare occasions in which anyone who had been watching would have thought they were a close-knit family. And, indeed, today they were.

The last game of the year had finally arrived and it was the bottom of the ninth, two outs, with the Police Panthers and Benny's Bruins playing for the championship. The game was tied 6-6. The nervousness of twelve-year-olds in a close baseball game energized the parents as they yelled their support from the stands.

Each team had held the lead at one point. With two outs, it all came down to Brian. A strike whizzed across the plate. Brian looked over to his dad, who nodded. The next two pitches were down and away, barely off the plate. "Good eye!" someone in the stands yelled.

The next pitch was straight down the middle. Brian swung, twisting on his ankles as the ball snapped into the catcher's mitt. Brian glanced again at Mark, who held his arms high as if hitting a ball. Brian nodded and raised his bat to match his father's stance.

As the next ball flew toward him, he swiveled his hips and hit it hard. The sound carried to the stands, where screams erupted and passersby stopped to see what was happening. The ball arched over the left-field fence high above the head of the center fielder. The players rushed out of the dugout as Brian rounded the bases, heading for home. As he crossed the plate, his teammates smothered him, jumping up and down in excitement. With this victory, they were the champions of the league.

Throwing herself into the spirit of the moment, Sallie jumped up shouting, then looked apologetically at the Parker clan, who also stood up and cheered.

Nonna looked at her with a smile. "It was a good game. The winners need to be congratulated."

Sallie turned to her father as he rose to his feet and she threw her arms around him. "Look at that, Dad. Brian is just a great all-around player. You must be proud."

Her father sported a big grin as he answered, "That's the ticket. Just like his dad."

Robert took David's arm. "Let's go congratulate our boys. After all, they're both champs."

Sallie walked her father to his front door, each of them savoring the events of the day and the sense of family it had brought.

"How about having a beer with me?" Her father asked as they entered the house.

Sallie raised her eyebrows. *A beer. What's he going to bring up now?*

"Sure, sounds good to me." She headed for the kitchen and the pilsner glasses.

"That's the ticket. I'll take mine in the bottle."

Sallie poured herself a glass and found her father in the den looking at the old pictures. "Let's go sit in the living room," she said. He reached over and picked up the baseball from the shelf.

David sat on the couch and Sallie sat next to him, handing him his beer. He took a swallow and put his bottle on the side table, turning to her and clearing his throat.

"After your mother died and you became a young woman, you looked so much like her. It made me sad. I..." he faltered. The words tumbled from his soul unspoken, yet Sallie heard the message. She squeezed his arm gently.

"Here, I want you to have this." He handed her his cherished signed baseball. "I know how much you love baseball. I've saved it all these years for you. I wanted the right time to give it to you. I had given up and thought I'd missed my chance."

She knew this was the highest honor he could pay her. Sallie could barely respond, a catch in her voice betraying her emotions. "You'll never miss your chance with me."

"It's just I could only get two tickets," he said quietly.

Sallie looked deep into her father's eyes. *He's had disappointments too. He loved deeply and wasn't loved the same way in return. Yet, he was willing to be vulnerable, to live his life in the most naked way.*

She knew of the possibility of being rejected, and with it the likelihood of becoming bitter. *I have, in the past, declared I would not let it happen to me. Perhaps, it is in just such vulnerability, though, that our souls are nourished.*

"Oh Dad, I never blamed you."

Her words seemed to lift a burden from his shoulders. He sat up straighter and smiled, returning the love in her eyes.

With an hour to go until the print deadline, Sallie's ancient laptop had just about had enough. Dismissing the latest error message and recovering her document, Sallie closed her eyes and bargained with unnamed forces. *Please just let me get this column done and then I'll call Mark and deal with this issue. He knows computer stuff.*

An hour later, her column successfully submitted, she got Mark on the phone. Getting right to the point, Sallie said, "My old laptop is about to bite the dust. How would you like to help me pick out a new computer?"

"Sounds like fun," he said, sounding pleased she had sought his expertise. "What kind of errors are you getting? You might be able to fix the issues with a fresh OS install."

"I think it's time to upgrade completely. This tiny hard drive just isn't cutting it anymore, and I'd really like a faster machine. I haven't been in the market for years and I'm not sure where to start."

"Don't worry, Sis. I'll show you the ropes."

Browsing the local superstore, they were talking much as they had when they were children. It was the happiest she had felt in her brother's presence since she had arrived home those months ago, and Sallie basked in the glow of the camaraderie that comes when siblings are aligned.

Sallie took his arm and squeezed it. "It's fun to shop with you."

Mark smiled at her. "It's good to be with you, too." He hesitated, deciding whether to go on. "Remember when I wanted to get that pen set for Dad for Christmas? I had made some money, but it wasn't quite enough for the ones I liked."

"Yes, I remember." Sallie smiled at the memory of that twelve-year-old boy, anxious to fit his desire to his pocketbook.

"You came through for me then, just like a big sister, giving me the money to get the one I wanted. I don't recall what you got Dad that Christmas or whether you had to settle for less. I just know you helped me do what I wanted. I don't think I ever thanked you."

"It was a pleasure. I enjoyed being a big sister to you," replied Sallie, surprised at his admission.

They continued to stroll down the aisles, looking at the computer choices.

"Here are the laptops. They're a lot lighter than they used to be, and you can get the new wireless technology embedded so you don't need as many accessories. Let's look here at these notebooks." Mark was more talkative than usual as he steered her toward a vast array of computers, asking questions as they went.

"I would really like a good-sized monitor if it's a laptop, plus I'd like one of those wireless printers," said Sallie, considering her options. "Also, do you have time to help me set it up and get started?"

"Sure do. I've got all day for you," he replied congenially.

By late afternoon, Mark had taken Sallie through all the bells and whistles of her new computer and printer.

"This is great! Perfect for all I want to do," exclaimed Sallie. "Thanks so much." She turned to look at him. "I really enjoyed spending the day with you."

"I enjoyed it, too."

She reached over and put her hand on his. "Before you go, I want to acknowledge you for your commitment all these years to Dad."

"It's not like I didn't want to. He's Dad, after all."

"I just want you to know that I appreciate you taking the responsibility. I know sometimes it must've been a burden. You're very responsible, and you have a beautiful family. You've done so much for them."

"Thanks," Mark responded, suddenly quiet. "You've done a lot this summer, too. Thank you for that."

"I've really enjoyed it." Sallie started to say more, then hesitated, afraid a conflict might arise. Finally, she went on. "Caring for Dad has really changed me. I'm finally beginning to see the world in which he was raised and how it affected how he treated us. I can see how you and I each had a different perspective growing up, and how that led us to take different routes to resolve our lives."

"I just want things to be simple," her brother admitted.

"Simplicity is not my primary motivation. Resolution is more important to me. Finding an outcome that meets the needs of all involved."

"What about 'honor thy parents?' " Mark said quietly.

"I honor him by looking at what he wants and giving it to him, if possible," Sallie said.

"I just want to make certain he's safe and taken care of."

They looked at each other, seeing their contradictory points of view for the first time.

"I really do want to help, you know," she said, a sincere ring to her voice.

"I know you do." Mark acknowledged her contribution.

"I like checking in with him every day and making certain he eats well."

"I just get worried about what will happen in the middle of the night if he gets up and falls or something and can't get to the phone."

"I know. I'm concerned about that too," answered Sallie.

Mark continued, "And I know he doesn't want a stranger to stay with him at night."

"What about those devices that are used in retirement homes? I'm not certain what they're called. They're like wearing a watch. Perhaps we could hook one of those up so he would have a lifeline to get to us?"

"Yeah, I've heard about them," said Mark. "Would you look into it?"

He looked at her as she sensed a new energy between them. *He really is asking for my help.*

"I would love to," Sallie answered, giving him a hug.

Sallie sat with Robert on the seaside deck of Alberto's Restaurant, looking out over the ocean as the sky turned a pale orange from the descending sun. They had just finished dinner, with their conversation ranging from local Los Madre politics to national issues, with stops in between for best movies and favorite wines.

There had been an easy rapport between them, and Sallie relaxed into their banter. *I feel happy,* she thought, as if it were something unusual. As the waiter took away their used dinner plates, a quiet descended between them. Sallie looked away from Robert's intense gaze, letting a lock of hair slant across her forehead. Her eyes darted quickly toward him and then away, not wanting to ask what he was thinking.

"You'd like to love someone like me." Coming from his mouth, it sounded as if it were the simplest truth in the world.

She reached across her face to push the hair aside, all the while covering her eyes to hide her thoughts. She had purposely refused to let the possibility of a deeper relationship penetrate her façade. Not wanting to look into his eyes, her gaze sought the colors of the garden planted just below the deck. *The gaillardia looks surprisingly effective against those hollyhocks.* The juxtaposition of the red heat and cool, pastel colors, though strong and asymmetrical, resounded with her. *Perhaps I'll try that combination in my garden.*

He continued in a low voice. This was a new path for him, and he was careful not to push her too hard. "You seem to be afraid to let a man love you. Why?"

A lot of little things. I don't really understand men that well. They seem so self-absorbed, almost addicted in their desire to dominate. I don't see many models of men I can admire. I just don't trust them, at least not with my heart. Confusing thoughts raced through her mind.

When she finally spoke, her answer was so soft he almost missed it. "I don't know." Her non-committal statement was meant to gain time rather than to say what she felt.

"You're a strong woman, Sallie. I like that about you. You are definite in what you want. I don't want a stereotypical homemaking woman, especially if it's not you. Being anything except who you are handicaps you. I wouldn't want that. I like a little spice in my salsa." His voice was emphatic with a quiet timbre, a slow smile covering his face.

Sallie looked at him sideways to read his facial expression. *So, I'm like a spicy salsa.* The thought made her smile in spite of herself. *I want to want someone. Yet who is this man? I could tell him about my marriage. I could say a lot. I believed in that white picket fence life once and it didn't work. Can I really trust him? The only way to find out is to tell him my story. Where to start?*

She took a deep breath and leapt. "I was married once. My husband couldn't or wouldn't hear my point of view," she started.

As she began to open up, all of the old feelings she had pushed down for so long began to rise anew. She tensed, recalling how she had first told him in quiet tones who she was, the blues and greens of her being. He did not get it, so she yelled it in violent tones of red and yellow. Then, she'd turned her frustration inward until she arrived at the edge of a cliff, veering dangerously on the jagged edge of becoming catatonic.

She knew that going over the edge would remove the pain, her frustration at being a non-person in his eyes. Yet, she also knew, in a quick instant, that she would forever lose all that was beautiful and wondrous about her life. So she had stepped back from the brink and vowed to find a path she could tread on her own terms. It might have mistakes; it might have its own serrated edge, its own disappointments. Still, it would be her life. She had left the marriage with a vow to never let another commandeer her soul.

That was more than she could express at this moment, so she finished simply with, "I resolved that having no husband is better than having one who wants to bend me to his will." Keeping her eyes low while she spoke these private thoughts, Sallie now looked up and met Robert's gaze. There was a compassion there that was new to her.

He leaned forward and touched her hand. His voice was soft as he assured her, "You will always have a choice with me. You can always say no. I want to love and cherish you, not control or tell you how to lead your life."

Robert's words sunk deep within her heart, and Sallie realized the importance of what he had just promised.

That's it. It comes down to a choice. Whether I can say, "No, I don't want to do that," or "yes, I want to." If I have that choice, then I can know I am loved and treasured. If I must do what another person tells me to do, then I will not feel appreciated and cherished, and I will have lost my essence. Can I trust this man?

As if to answer her unasked question, Robert said, "It's not about putting your trust in another. It's about trusting yourself on your path and being willing to take a risk with faith in your own life. It's not up to me to change your mind about men. You must decide if you can accept a real flesh-and-blood man to love you… or do you want to spend your life by yourself?"

A long week had passed and Sallie was looking forward to talking with Anne. Their conversation began with an update about Las Rosas politics. As Sallie listened, she realized she had become separate from the details of the town and she saw her life there as a long time ago. *I am beginning to identify more with events and people here in Los Madre.*

"Anne, I have something to tell you," began Sallie.

"Oh, this sounds ominous," answered Anne. "What can it be that's so serious?"

"I think I like Robert."

"Oh, that." Anne laughed. "I've been expecting it for some time."

"You have?" said Sallie querulously.

"Yeah, I figured it out. It's good. Just take things a day at a time and let things just happen," responded Anne.

"Yeah, well, this is me, you realize. That's not quite my style."

They both laughed.

"Hey, so the Giants are really doing well this year. Now, I don't want to jinx them, but if they go to the playoffs, how about you and Robert come up for a game?"

"Wow," Sallie said, "that would be great."

"We want to meet him."

"He says I'm like spicy salsa." She chuckled at his comparison.

"Well, actually, you are."

"I am? Really?"

"In a good way, of course. We've always liked our salsa spicy."

"Thank you, Anne." Sallie paused, considering her next request. "Do you think my dad could come too? I know he would really like it."

"Of course. I would love to meet your father."

They laughed and joked a little longer, then Sallie's tone turned pensive. "Remember our talk about guardian angels?"

"Sure."

"Well, how do you know it's your guardian angel talking to you? How do you know it just isn't your own mind?"

"For me, it's because I learn something I didn't know before," said Anne. "It's new information."

"Do you think we have more than one?"

306

"I think we can. Maybe they're specialized, just like us. Then we would need one for different parts of our lives."

"I keep hearing this phrase over and over in my brain, 'Remember the Oneness.' Do you think that's my guardian angel talking to me?"

"Could be." Anne smiled to herself.

"I feel as if a whole new world is opening to me," said Sallie. "There have been so many changes in my life. Perhaps all this is happening to me at the same time because I've ignored my inner self for so long and now I'm paying attention."

"It doesn't matter when you do it," said Anne. "Just that you do."

"In the midst of the pain, there was also something else—sort of a juxtaposition of something exciting waiting to happen beneath the discomfort. I had tremendous clarity, as if I were being led through a cave blindfolded so that I could open another way of seeing—a third eye, so to speak. I felt as if someone were talking to me, telling me I had to change, yet also leading me and pointing the way. I thought life would get easier as I grew older. Now I know it only seems easier because I stood still and didn't grow. Not any longer," she said, emphasizing the words. "I want to expand who I am in all ways, not just my material world."

"You've come a long way," said Anne.

Sallie's Journal—September 29th

I am seeing for the first time in my life that I can just be myself, faults and all. I am grateful for this, as I now know that everything that has ever happened to me makes up who I am today. This feeling is very powerful and freeing.

I have begun to discover the shape of my destiny, and that I can just be who I am and not worry about other people and what they think, a very freeing idea. In the past when I have felt happy, I worried about it disappearing, believing I did not deserve happiness. When I was a child, I would focus on what I did not want to happen or the worst that could happen, thinking that if I thought about what I really wanted, it would be chased away. Now I know the truth is just the opposite. We attract what we think, say, and where we put our focus.

This happiness appears sustainable as it keeps moving to a higher level. Not a higher level like being manic versus being depressed. This is a stability I seem to maintain by slowing down and not rushing.

I am very thankful to everyone whom I have ever known for the contribution each has made to my life—my family, friends, enemies, both alive as well as those who have gone. I am grateful, as I know everything that has ever happened to me makes up who I am today. I am very thankful for it all.

Dream: I am coming out of the library with my beloved dog from childhood when I see my former husband's face in the window. I go outside where he is waiting for us. We begin talking and laughing while holding hands. We are back together, yet are not ready to tell anyone. We get separated and I cannot find him.

I pick up my dog, who has a bone in his mouth. When he was alive, he would never let me near him when he was chewing on a bone. This time, he lets me carry him—careful, however, to keep his mouth and bone averted. It is too delicious for him to share with me. We find my former husband again, who apologetically tells me we will not be together as he has pressing obligations.

I awake with a tremendous sense of love for these two souls, both of whom I had grieved deeply for their loss.

This dream brings me peace about my love for those who have departed from my life; they still exist as a part of me. The love I had for them and they for me exists forever. Their presence sustains me.

CHAPTER EIGHTEEN

Serapis: An Ascended Master

In the middle of a grassy clearing stood the Healing Center, a large octagonal-shaped structure of poles covered with a silver opalescent fabric like a circus tent. Each of the poles was decked out like a Maypole, with brightly colored ribbons fanning out from the top. The shades on the eight sides could be rolled up at dawn to open the interior to the healing energies of nature, and at night unrolled, sustaining the silent energy of the therapy.

The Center was located at the end of a dusty road in the heart of a jungle area, far away from any town. Vegetation crowded the surroundings, making a dense pattern of foliage in multitudinous shades of green. A single narrow path curved through the countryside, linking the Center with civilization many miles away.

A long line of people twisted into the distance, talking in low voices as they waited patiently in the warmth of the day for their turn with the Healer—he who could look at a person or touch them and instantly know what was needed for their healing. His cures were not just of the body; they were also a healing of the mind, emotions, and spirit. The air around the compound hummed like the drone of bumblebees, a drowsy resonance that lulled Sallie into a contemplative peace as she viewed the diversity of humanity around her.

The wait seemed interminable. The lazy sun had traversed the sky and was ready to depart in the west when Sallie finally reached the head of the line. With apprehension about what she would be told, she took her seat before the Healer, gazing into his eyes as he appraised her.

His compassion enveloped her, making her feel as if she were the only person he had seen that day. His voice, soft as a mother's caress, told her, "You must find the Sanctuary of Truth located in the Ascension Temple. He is waiting for you there."

Sallie panicked, wondering who "he" was and exactly what it all meant. Before she had a chance to articulate the questions tumbling through her mind, the Healer pulled a small object from within his robe. "Take this key," he instructed, placing it in her palm.

She frowned, examining the strange item. The key was unlike any she had seen before. Instead of a notched flat surface, it was a three-dimensional pyramidal shape, carved from labradorite. Sallie studied the grayish-blue feldspar; it appeared ordinary until she looked deep within the stone and saw waves of mountains and clouds with bright diamond-like spots above, like a starry night. She felt as if she were peering into the far reaches of the universe.

"Find four objects," the Healer continued. "Each of these objects represents one of your four bodies—the physical, emotional, mental, and spiritual. Then look for the Door to the Sacred. This key will open its secrets. Now, be on your way."

Sallie touched the four sides of the pyramid-shaped key and looked into its depths as the Healer's words echoed in her mind. *Find four objects, each representing my four bodies. Look for the Door to the Sacred. What are the four objects? How will I find this door?* Realizing she would learn no more from the Healer, she set off down the path.

She wandered aimlessly, pondering the meaning of the words until she came to an open space in the jungle where the trees rose up at least a hundred feet. A stream of light sparkled on a large, flat table rock in the clearing before her. She walked over to it and sat down, feeling its warmth with her fingertips.

As she contemplated her task, Sallie looked around and picked up three small pebbles, absently rolling them around in her palm before shaking them in her hands and throwing them on the rock like dice. As they rolled to a stop, she was hit with a revelation.

Why, these three rocks represent the physical universe, so I guess they could represent my physical body. Oh, what fun! A feeling of joy arose in her body as she was inspired by the idea of playing within this unknown realm to find her answers. Sallie put the stones in her pocket.

Now what? My emotional body is next. Perhaps my feelings could be represented by my dreams. The more she thought about what might symbolize this body, the more confused she became. Finally, she began to walk around again, enjoying the exotic sounds of the jungle. Hearing the swooshing of rushing water, Sallie realized she was thirsty. *I'll get a drink while I contemplate my task.*

Following the sound to a tributary, she dipped her cupped hand into the stream. As she came up with a handful of water, the tiny droplets turned into silvery ribbon streamers that were held together by a pearl ring. Sallie put the ring on her finger and feelings of love coursed through her body. This gesture reminded her of her dream of a loving family, which was beginning to manifest in her life. *Why, this could represent my emotions,* she realized.

Turning back to the path, Sallie's focus became sharp in her observance of the world around her. *What is next? My mind? What would represent my mind? Perhaps it would be something that cuts through my misperceptions of this world and those who inhabit it,* she mused.

She stopped in front of a large plot of sword ferns, standing alert and on guard as if they could read her thoughts. *Why, a sword fern would fit that criterion.* She asked permission, then picked one and waved it around like a sword. Giggling, she wove it into the strands of her hair like a feather stuck into a headband.

The last body is my spirit. Sallie looked around for a jungle denizen that would represent her soul. Suddenly, the breeze picked up and she heard the distinctive screech of an eagle coming from the heights of the trees.

"Look up," the eagle cried, dropping a feather into her open hand. "Use this to lighten your spirit so that you too can fly. Journey toward the setting sun until you come to a flight of stairs with three steps. At the top is the door your key fits." And with that, he opened his wings and took flight as the gently stirring breeze lifted him gracefully above the trees.

Contemplating the two-toned feather in her hand, Sallie looked upward and thanked the eagle spirit, then turned toward the west to resume her journey. As she came to a small opening between the trees, she spied three marble steps rising out of the jungle like the ruins of a prehistoric temple. Not seeing a door, Sallie wondered at this discrepancy. Remembering the eagle's words, she walked over to the steps, each very steep. Taking three giant leaps, she found herself at the top, peering at the empty space for the door.

Suddenly, an outline appeared out of thin air. When she looked more closely, she discovered it matched the shape of the bottom of her key. Instinctively, she matched the two flat bottoms together, pushed the key in, and turned. The key instantly connected with its opposite, creating a star tetrahedron that spun into an upright position and began to rotate in a clockwise direction. The whir of the spinning formed a second star tetrahedron, which began to rotate in a counter-clockwise direction, creating counter-rotating fields of light.

Sallie watched wide-eyed as the star tetrahedrons grew larger until she was encased inside. She found herself floating weightless inside the rotating shapes of light, and she laughed with a childlike joy that expressed her exhilaration.

The landscape changed around her and she discovered herself inside a large square temple. Twelve white pillars supported the four sides, with open air above. A man dressed in a white robe walked toward her. He had a circlet of gold spun around his head like a crown, from which the white flame of ascension rose. His face appeared very young, with piercing green eyes under dark, thick eyebrows. A neatly trimmed beard covered his square jaw.

"I am Serapis Bey, here to assist with your ascension into higher levels of consciousness. I am an Ascended Master, one who has lived life on Earth just as you, yet I have fulfilled my mission and ascended back to Divine Source, reuniting with Spirit. My task now is to hold the energy field that will allow you to do the same and ascend to the higher dimensions.

"Each of the four gifts you acquired represents a purpose in your life, a mastery that is necessary for you to have the final gift of ascension. The stones represent your destiny, the water is your perseverance, the sword fern your courage to live with justice and in service to others, and the feather is the love you hold in your heart and send out to others on your path.

"The star tetrahedrons represent the equilibrium of the opposing laws of your dualistic world—the law of spirit and the law of matter—and is called a Mer-Ka-Ba. It is a vehicle of light that, when it comes alive in you, allows expansion of your spirit and body to the next world of consciousness. When this field awakens within you, an electromagnetic change occurs, resulting in a disc of energy that comes out of your spine and expands around your body.

"The key you used, when connected to its other half, allowed you to expand your consciousness to reach this temple. Just as you have begun to resonate with your soul's purpose, so also are you and every person on your planet part of a larger mission that involves bringing the spirit of the Oneness into manifestation."

"I'm not certain how I can do that," said Sallie, frowning.

"As you love and honor others, you allow the flow of love from Spirit to enter into form through you. The more you acknowledge that force in you, the more your awareness expands. Love allows your world to transform into its higher counterpart. You do this by balancing your body, mind, emotions, and spirit, and raising your vibration to connect with the ascension flame."

"What is the ascension flame?" asked Sallie.

"Look around at this temple. Do you see only one space?" As Sallie nodded, Serapis continued, "There are other rooms overlaying this one, and as you learn the lesson of each, you will receive a key that will unlock the temple built on top of it, which remains unseen until you are ready to ascend to the next level. Here, let me show you. Notice first the color of this room."

As Sallie perceived the whiteness of the marble, he continued, "The lessons here are brotherhood, trust, courage, joy, hope, and love. When you master these lessons, you will see the lock that will take you to the next temple. Your key will then unlock that door. Here, I will show you how. Just as you did before, take the key in your hand and look until you find its match."

Sallie saw the triangular shape emerge from the nothingness. "Now put your key into its opening," Serapis instructed.

Sallie inserted the key, and again the two pyramids merged and became two star tetrahedrons. They expanded until she found herself surrounded in their light, vibrating as before. A new temple with the same dimensions and characteristics emerged, except this one was a different color.

Returning to the Temple of White, Serapis continued, "As you master the lessons for each color, you will ascend to the next through a stream of love that will lift your energy to a new world."

Awed by what she had seen, Sallie said, "I'm not certain I understand all of what you mean."

"Earth and all its inhabitants are going through a transition to the next level of consciousness, which is one of love and connectedness to all living things."

"Am I a part of this? How can I participate?" queried Sallie.

"All souls alive on Earth today, as well as Gaia herself, have as their mission to participate in this expansion. To make this transition, you and everyone else must live in love and be conscious of yourself as part of a bigger picture, as part of the community of life, as being part of the Oneness."

"I have never thought that my life included being part of a mission with a bigger plan," said Sallie. "I am willing to participate though, if you can tell me how."

"Everything you perceive and everything that comes to you in your life can act as a teacher. The scriptures, literature, communion with others and with nature, all can bring to you an alliance with your soul. As you gain clarification of your purpose in life, you become a participant with others on the same path in the journey home to the heart of Spirit."

"What must I do?"

"I reiterate what you have heard before. Stay on your path. Be alert to all you meet there. Honor your process and that of others. Observe your mind observing your world. Pay attention to your feelings, for they are important and come from your soul. Your mind uses them to create your world. Yet, perhaps your mind doesn't know everything. So trust your sense of things."

With that, her surroundings blurred and Sallie was back in bed, dreaming peacefully.

PART X
Light

Then I said, "I covet truth;
Beauty is unripe childhood's cheat;
I leave behind with the games of youth."
As I spoke, beneath my feet
The ground-pine curled its pretty wreath,
Running over the club-moss burrs;
I inhaled the violet's breath;
Around me stood the oaks and firs;
Pinecones and acorns lay on the ground;
Over me soared the eternal sky,
Full of light and of deity;
Again I saw, again I heard,
The rolling river, the morning bird;
Beauty through my senses stole;
I yielded myself to the perfect whole.

Ralph Waldo Emerson
Each and All

CHAPTER NINETEEN

The Labyrinth

A strange wisp of anticipation fluttered through Sallie's chest as she approached the small labyrinth outlined by flat slate stones in the middle of the grove. Overhead, the canopy of tall trees surrounded her like giant beings of light, allowing the dappled beams of sunlight to shimmer softly on the space at her feet. Sparkling dots, like those from a disco ball upon a dance floor, created a moving pattern that added clarity to her journey. The noise of the world beyond the trees was muted and the quietness of the area imbued her with its soft gentleness.

Sallie paused at the beginning, as if taking a step upon this twisting path would change her life. Nonna's instructions replayed in her mind: *Focus on a question you would like answered.* Her thoughts flitted among the myriad possibilities.

What is my purpose? Where do I belong? Focus! What is my focus?

She closed her eyes, seeking the calm clarity of knowingness. When it got right down to the bottom of her soul, the question she needed to know from the inside out was, *am I lovable just the way I am?*

Her hesitation disappeared as she placed her foot upon the path. At first, her vision seemed to vibrate, a dizzying lightheaded feeling that left her woozy. Then she focused on the path in front of her. The ground was covered with a carpet of small bits of broken twigs, bright patches of green, various weeds, and other unknown specimens of cover.

She stepped gently between them, not wanting to bruise their tiny leaves or fragile stems. Then she disappeared into the depths of foliage, observing the lighthearted play that nature made with all the plants, rocks, and trees moving and interacting with her.

The atmosphere was still, yet carried a gentle wave of air around her face. Lifting her eyes up to the denseness of the tree cover above, she let the light of the sky descend upon her shoulders. The circular path wrapped back on itself and she appeared to be returning to where she started. Then it abruptly turned again, taking her to the outer edge of the ring, where she found herself in a different quadrant. Here, the path narrowed until it was only as wide as one footprint and she had to put her arms out slightly to maintain her balance.

Suddenly, there was a barrier in front of her. A pile of branches covered the path and she had to pick her way carefully through the obstruction. Stopping a moment, she looked back and thought—*this is so much like my life. I've gotten through other obstacles and I'm still here.*

Buoyed with a tiny glimmer of hope, she resumed her walk. In and then out, Sallie spiraled endlessly as the path took her around through the segments of the circle. She sensed a communion with the unknown nature spirits that inhabited this glade. With each step, she descended deeper into the mysterious reaches of her soul, looking for her essence.

She passed a dead stump, its distorted carcass a pale imitation of the tree's former grandeur. *The caretaker should remove this stump. The twisted shape detracts from the beauty of the site.*

Coming to the center of the labyrinth, a low, flat rock beckoned her to stop and meditate upon her circumstances. Sitting, she closed her eyes, her mind a blank.

I give up. I've always wanted to know and plan each moment so that I could control the future. My life is a mystery and I now give up my desire to know its outcome. I've always wanted to win. As a result, I became what I most disliked in my father—controlling and forceful with others.

She sighed, acknowledging that small voice within. Suddenly, a vision appeared in the center of her consciousness with a clarity that surprised her. A tiny version of herself, dressed in a cheerleader outfit with an "S" for "Sallie" on its sweater, gave a rousing shout. "Two, four, six, eight, who do we appreciate? Sallie! Sallie! Sallie!"

She laughed out loud. *What an image in the middle of this quiet solitude.* Her heart soared. A new peace descended upon her.

Then the moment evaporated, as moments do. She would carry the memory of that moment to reconstruct when she was, once again, lost. It would have to be enough.

Leaving the center of the circle with a surge of excitement, she passed the dead stump again. *I know why you're here. You're the part of my past that is dead in the moment. Yet, you still are a part of what makes me who I am. I thank you for your contribution. You are, indeed, beautiful and do belong preciously in this surrounding. Death is a part of life, and I must leave the old behind to receive the life that is waiting for me.*

Despite the Dodgers clinching the National League West division, the Giants still managed to earn a seat in the postseason as one of the Wild Card teams. Sallie and her dad watched the games with anticipation and a friendly rivalry, each cheering their team as they raced toward the World Series.

When the Giants won the National League Championship Series,

Anne called, screaming with delight. Her earlier invitation for Sallie, Robert, and David to attend a game was again extended and Sallie was thrilled to accept.

They would drive Sallie's car because it was the roomiest in the back seat. The day before they were set to leave, Sallie popped into her dad's bedroom as he shuffled around collecting clothes and packing them neatly into his suitcase.

"Do you know what you're taking?"

He looked up at her, perplexed. "I only have Dodger blue in my game wardrobe."

Sallie gave him a hug and a hearty laugh. "We can always go to the Dugout Store and get you some orange and black."

"Blah." He pretended to throw up. "No can do." His voice was emphatic, yet there was a twinkle in his eyes that she acknowledged with a knowing smile.

"Okay, okay, I get it. Can you do dark blue, almost black?" She opened his sweater drawer, and rummaged through his options, pulling out a dark grey cardigan. "This will be fine." She held it up for his approval.

He grabbed it from her, added it to the pile in his suitcase, and then turned to give her a direct gaze. "I'm looking forward to meeting your friends. And going to another World Series game, this time with you." He emphasized the 'you.'

She smiled and touched his sleeve. "Me too, Dad."

She heard the buzz of her cellphone in her bedroom. "Excuse me a minute, Dad." She hurried down the hall and grabbed her phone. Her heart leapt as she saw the caller ID. *Hope the news is good.* She stubbed her foot on the rug in her bedroom and caught herself, barely maintaining her balance. Catching her breath, she dropped onto her bed and hit the "accept" button.

"Fred?" She could barely get his name out and licked her lips to try to wet her parched mouth.

"Good news, with a little bad news," Fred's voice was ebullient.

She sat up taller. "Good news first."

"You have your license back."

She gave a yelp, causing her dad to call from his door, "Everything okay, honey?"

Jumping off her bed and peering out her door, she gave him a thumbs up.

"You wrote a good letter. The proper amount of apology with a good dose of honesty. I think it helped."

"Now the bad news."

"There's a fine. Not too big, but big enough to send a message." He told her the number.

She plopped flat on the bed, her legs dangling to the floor, feeling as if all the air had drained out of a balloon inside of her. *It's only money.* Her voice became calm and centered. "I can deal with that."

Her mind raced, considering the implications of this news. *It's all behind me. I can still have everything I wanted.* She sat up, feeling invigorated. "Fred, I want to thank you for your service. I don't know what you did to make this happen, I just know you did something special."

"All in the line of duty. And you're welcome. You deserve it."

"Thanks, Fred. You're on the Christmas list forever."

He laughed. "What's that get me?"

"You'll have to wait and see."

Sallie hung up and lay full upon her bed, staring at the ceiling. *I can go back to Las Rosas with my head high. I'm vindicated. I can have what I want there with Carol and Gail, my perfect life.* She sat up and leaned against her headboard, looking around her childhood room. *Yet, my father's here, my brother, my family. Robert. Home. What does that word mean? Home. Where is my home?*

Sallie's hand trembled as she put the key in the lock and opened the door to her home in Las Rosas. *Strange, I feel as if I'm breaking into someone else's place.* Behind her, David stood on the porch as Robert unloaded their luggage from the car. She smiled at the precise layout of the room before her. Everything was in its place. *Almost too sterile*, she thought with a smile.

"Dad, you'll be in my room," she said, as she pointed down the hall toward the master bedroom.

"I don't want to take your bed," he protested.

"Now, Dad, I want you to be comfortable," she said as she turned to Robert and nodded for him to take David's luggage to her room. "Just let me spoil you." She smiled at him. "Let me show you around."

As she took his arm, she took a new look at the home she had cherished, feeling mixed emotions at the thought of leaving it. *A new life.* Her thoughts began to tumble and she took a deep breath to center herself. *This or better. I can create something just as perfect as this again.*

Sallie pointed toward the tall secretary desk in the corner.

"Remember that? I got it from your sister's estate." They walked over and she opened the top, pulling out several photos.

"Here are some of my favorite pictures of us from back in the day." They stood close together, heads almost touching as they looked through the stack.

"That's the ticket," he said as he fondled the edge of one of the well-worn photographs.

Robert returned and looked over their shoulder. "What's this? Not some old naked childhood pictures on a shaggy carpet?"

Sallie looked up at him and laughed, "No, none of that here." She handed him the pictures and he leafed through them.

"Tell me," he said with sparkling eyes.

"Okay, okay." She took back the pictures and with a quick motion, began to thumb through them. "Mostly, they're from our childhood. Here's my mother, this is our vacation in Hawaii, here's my graduation…" She gave a brief synopsis of each photo, then rapidly arranged them in a pile.

"All right, that's it. Later, we'll go through them more slowly," Sallie said, a bit self-conscious as she replaced the pictures in their slot and closed the desk. "I haven't shown you the garden."

As Sallie turned toward the back of the house, she heard a light knock.

"Yoo-hoo!" Anne called as she opened the door and stuck her head inside. "Anyone home?"

"In here!" Sallie called, smiling as Anne and Joe came bustling in, excited for their reunion.

"Welcome back," Anne said as she hugged Sallie.

After introductions, Sallie said, "I was just going to show them the garden."

"You just want to know if it's still as pristine as you left it," said Anne.

They all laughed as Sallie blushed. "No, no, really. I just wanted to show the garden."

"We know you."

"Okay, whatever you say." She turned and ushered them toward the back door.

"Wow. A new Sallie in our midst?" asked Anne playfully, raising an eyebrow.

"Don't count on it," Sallie responded with a laugh as she led the group into the yard.

The garden swept her away with the perfection that is nature. Walking down the path, Sallie looked from one plant to another, admiring the completeness of the whole. She saw the alyssum she had left as a seedling in the pathway, now grown to its full size. Smiling, she bent down and ruffled its edges.

Sallie felt some trepidation the next morning as she approached her old office. From the outside it appeared unchanged, save for the new sign hanging in front of the building. *The Caldwell Group. Impressive. Carol must be holding her own.*

Taking a deep breath, she pushed open the door and entered the familiar old lobby. Upon seeing Sallie, Julie jumped up and ran around her desk to give her a hug.

"Welcome back! We're all so excited you're here."

Sallie smiled. "I missed you, too."

Heading down the hallway to Mike's old office, she found Carol and Gail deep in conversation. They both looked up and rushed toward her, hugging her and talking simultaneously.

"So good to see you," said Carol. "We just found out you got your license back!"

"Yes, Fred is a magician. He got me reinstated with only a small fine. I'm not quite certain how he did it. I expected the worst."

Carol looked at Gail, giving her a frown. Gail shrugged and turned to Sallie, saying what they both were thinking. "Is that all we're going to get? After all this time? After all we've been through together?"

"Details. We want the details!" said Carol.

"Look, it was no big deal. I just told the truth," Sallie said lightly.

"Uh huh, and…" Gail coaxed.

Sallie looked at their expectant faces. *These are true friends. It's just not easy to tell them how I felt like a victim, nor my role in owning up to my imperfections.* With a smile acknowledging their importance in her life, she began, "Okay. You want the long version or the short version?"

"The long version," they both said in unison and then laughed.

Sallie told the story piece by piece, going through the specifics and explaining her feelings along the way and what it took for her to accept her failings. She ended her explanation with, "Telling the truth was what it took for me to find forgiveness, for both myself and Mike."

Carol reached over and gave her hand a squeeze. "I know what you mean."

Gail jumped up. "Well, is this the day we've been waiting for or not?"

"Yes," said Carol. "We've got more to discuss."

"Before we start, how about tea for everyone?" With nods from both of them, Gail left to get some tea.

Sallie looked at Carol comfortably slouched in Mike's old chair. "You look good sitting there," she said. "And you look at home. What's happening?"

Carol fidgeted. "I don't know where to start. I feel as if I've come back to life in a way I didn't know as Mike's wife. I'm not sure I can explain it."

"I know exactly what you mean. This business can be exhilarating."

"Yes, that's it."

Gail returned with refreshments.

"Uh oh. Why so quiet? Is everything all right?" Gail looked at Carol. "Have you told her?"

"Told me what?" Sallie asked, her eyebrows raised. "That you want to keep the business?"

Carol's eyes widened. "How did you know?"

"Just a guess."

"Actually, I do want to stay, with you as a partner."

Partner. The word I've waited to hear all these years. It was as if the conflict within her that had been seesawing back and forth came into focus. *Two good choices, yet one leads to my future, while one leads to the past.*

"Thank you for the offer," Sallie reached across the desk and took Carol's hand in hers. "I'm flattered." She saw the hope in their eyes.

Gail blurted out, "Then can I get out the champagne now?"

"You can," she felt her decision solidify inside, "but for a different reason. I have other plans. Let's toast to new beginnings."

"How'd you score two more tickets?" Sallie asked Anne as they wound their way through the crowd on the mezzanine, looking for Section 138.

"Oh, it took some finagling." She gave Sallie a mysterious grin. "Let's just say we know the people in the area around us really well. After all, we've had the same seats since the park opened."

Sallie turned to look for her dad. He was walking between Robert and Joe, talking animatedly about the ballpark and how it reminded him of the old stadiums back in his day. She smiled. It was good to see him in his element.

There was a full house of almost 43,000 fans jammed into AT&T Park for the first game of the World Series. Their team had been spectacular in the playoffs, and expectations were high for the outcome of the match.

As they settled into their seats, Sallie asked her dad what he thought of the day so far.

"Well, it's not the Dodgers, but I think I can handle it. After all, it is a World Series game," he said, giving her arm a squeeze.

"Enjoy the day, Dad. You deserve it."

The game was never in doubt. With their ace on the hill, the Giants led the entire game, winning with a final tally of 7-4 as the enthusiastic crowd screamed with ecstasy.

Amber rays pierced the sky as the sun started its descent at the end of the crisp fall day on the coast of Marin County near Sallie's home in Las Rosas. Robert and Sallie walked along an empty beach, weaving in and out of the small waves that lapped the sand.

As they walked with the wind at their backs, Robert asked, "What are your dreams for the future?"

Sallie's eyes went hazy as she thought about how to answer his question. "Hmm, I have to think about it. What about you?"

"You always want me to answer first, don't you?"

Sallie laughed in tacit agreement with his observation. "Well, will you?"

"I'd like to have my own family. I'd like to come home from work at night to find someone special waiting for me."

Sallie looked down at the sand and bent to uncover what looked like a shell. She stood up, empty-handed, and brushed the sand off her hands. *Somehow what he says doesn't bother me as much as it did a few months ago.*

He looked over her shoulder toward the west. "It'll be chilly when the sun goes down. We'll have to hurry and eat before it gets dark."

Sallie followed his eyes to a watercolor sunset filled with vibrant shades of orange and purple, and then turned to look him directly in the eye. "Wait. Do you want an answer?" she asked.

"Of course I do."

"I'm not certain I can be what you want. However, just like you planning this day, making me feel special, I want this feeling. I want to go down that road with you. I'm ready."

Robert took her in his arms and kissed her. "That's all I want to hear."

They hurried toward where their blanket and gear was spread near the water. Robert started the fire and lay down on the blanket next to Sallie.

"It's been a great week," Robert said. "And your team won the World Series!"

She laughed. "What a fitting finale. I can't believe the season is over already."

"Do you think you can change your affiliation now that you're officially going to be a SoCal resident?"

"You mean to the Dodgers?" she said, an incredulous look on her face. "And give up my team and the bantering with Dad? Don't even go there."

"I didn't think so." He grinned, then his look turned pensive. "You have a beautiful home. I imagine it's going to be hard to leave."

"Thank you. It's been my passion, fixing it up."

"Are you going to miss it?" His voice was quiet.

Sallie gave him a tender look that lingered as she answered his question. "Of course. It will always be part of me. Yet, new adventures lie ahead. You know how I've been doing research on the various home designs of Southern California for a book project?" He nodded. "What I would like to do is organize the book by architectural design, and then combine detailed information on each respective style with a complete rundown of the appropriate remodeling options to maintain the integrity of the original design using what's available today."

Robert smiled. "Hmm. Good plan. I've seen some real disasters where people update their homes with little compatibility between the old and the new. I'd think such a book would do well."

"Well, I've had a new thought this week. I'd like to sell my home in Las Rosas and buy one in Los Madre. It seems to me there must be a lot of homes like my father's—you know, ones that have never been changed. As they're sold, they're going to need to be updated, and my idea is to buy houses, fix them up properly, and then resell them. That way, my book could include real life situations where the remodels work."

His eyes lit up. "What a great idea!" He reached across the blanket and grabbed her hand. "I'd really like to help you make that a reality."

A memory flickered across her consciousness. "I just remembered something I've always wondered. Perhaps you're the person to ask."

"Shoot," he said, waiting for her to continue.

"I've spent some time researching how Los Madre got its name, and no one seems to know."

Robert shrugged. "It means 'The Mother,' doesn't it?"

She nodded. "That's what it means. It's just that 'Los' is a masculine article. It's as if the founding fathers of the town wanted to squash the mother and make her into their image."

"I don't think it's that," he said thoughtfully. "At least not consciously. If I had to guess, I'd say it's more a lack of understanding of the power of language." He gave her a solicitous look. "And, it appears as if someone didn't know their Spanish."

"Things like that have always made me really angry." Her tone began to rise. "As if men are trying to dominate women."

"I'm listening," he said gently.

"I always felt as if I had to do more and do things better just to be considered equal to a man." Her voice was forceful. "And, even then, I wasn't totally successful. Just look at what happened with Mike."

Robert reached out and took her hand in his, stroking it to calm her resentment. "I know things aren't always equal in our culture and you're probably right. There is something else to consider, though."

She looked at him as he composed his thoughts.

"We guys don't always have our act together," he said, a soft smile taking over his face. "Sure, there are a lot of thoughtless people out there…" He hesitated and then his face broke out into an impish grin. "I like to think that what Mike did was good."

Sallie was taken aback. "How can you say that?" She glared at him.

"Well, we never would have met if you hadn't lost your license…"

"And I would have continued doing what I've always done— working harder without getting the family I wanted." Sallie realized the gift hidden in the disappointment.

He nodded. "Perhaps it is a perfect world after all."

She smiled at the irony of her life. "I guess my anger also made me insensitive." Her voice was quiet as she made the confession. "You're such a giving person, Robert." Sallie reached across and touched his arm. "It's one of the things I like most about you."

"You're worth the extra care."

Sallie breathed deeply, trying to compose her thoughts. "It might take me some time," she said slowly. She absently began to take food out of the basket and arrange it on the blanket between them.

"That's okay," he said, taking the slice of cheese she offered him and picking up a cracker.

"I know I'll always be dealing with my need for perfection and control. Just because I gave it up today…" her voice trailed off. She glanced out toward the sea.

"Look at me." Robert's voice was soft. She turned back to face his gaze. "And, I'm stubborn, and sometimes I isolate myself and forget to tell others it's not them. Sometimes I want to please people too much, and, oh, what are my other faults?"

Sallie laughed softly. "I guess you're right. We both have plusses and minuses."

"As long as we're alive, we will have our challenges," Robert said. "Would you rather live with your faults alone, or work on them in the company of others?"

"Good point," responded Sallie, a lighter tone to her voice. "I guess, though, I'd want to know that you'd desire to resolve whatever differences we might have."

"Just one question. What do you think about living in Santa Barbara wine country?"

"As long as I can be myself. And, speaking of Santa Barbara, I never answered the question you asked me at the end of our trip."

"Yes, I know."

"Well, the answer is no, I didn't tell Ferguson I had cheated."

He raised an eyebrow.

"I couldn't. I just couldn't have him think bad of me. Only, I never cheated again."

He gave her a radiant smile. Taking her hand in his, he looked into her eyes as he gently kissed the tips of her fingers, one by one.

"You know I love you, don't you?"

Sallie glanced down at their entwined hands and then looked directly into his eyes. With a catch in her voice, she answered, "I thank you and want you to know that you give me courage to walk into the unknown. And for that alone, I love you." She took a sharp breath as her fingers tensed slightly in his.

"Do you want to know when I knew we were meant for each other?"

She gave him a quizzical look.

"When I discovered we both liked éclairs."

"Now, wait a minute. I like profiteroles. They're quite different from éclairs."

"Oh, and tell me how they are different. They're made from the same ingredients—just put into a different shape."

"No way. While they may appear the same, there are remarkable differences. Profiteroles are generally small and round, one bite of deliciousness, and drizzled with hot fudge sauce, not the chocolate glaze that's on éclairs."

"Yet, if I offered you an éclair," he said, reaching into the picnic basket, "would you turn it down?"

Her eyes opened wide. "Let me at it!" She laughed as Robert brought out an éclair, took a bite, and handed it to her.

"Thought so," he mumbled with his mouth full.

Sallie's Journal—December 21st

I have purchased a home in Los Madre and have begun a new garden very different from my old one. This garden is more disorganized than my past creations, a rambling affair with twists and turns, displaying none of the order and neatness I demanded in the past.

I like each season of the year and the changes they bring to my garden. The results of my efforts with my plants match the change that has occurred in my life this year.

I particularly like the winter garden. The perennials are gone, dying back to the bare dirt. There is an elegance to the bareness of the view. It reminds me to lay bare those parts of myself as I get to the root of who I am and the purpose of my soul.

Plants do not worry about what to do with their lives. They remember their purpose and live only to show the world their joyful beingness. Each year my perennials go dormant, only to gather new energy and reemerge in the spring, displaying their magnificence.

There is a perception of soul in my garden—the dirt under my fingernails, the tiredness at the end of the day when I cannot move a single muscle in my body and I limp inside the house to collapse in a heap. I have an incredible sense of accomplishment, tied as I am to the earth and all of life going about on my hands and knees in my jungle. What a difference from my garden in Las Rosas, where I paid someone else to have this joy.

I trim my roses back to bare branches and remove the leaves, as this is Southern California and they must be forced into dormancy. The twisted branches remind me of myself. When I trim, I take away branches that cross each other. I shape the plant to an openness in the middle so that light can enter into its innermost core. I trim each branch at an angle, just above an outward facing leaf node, so the plant will grow with bowl-shaped branches.

As I prune, I can see the beginning of next year's roses, just tiny, barely discernible protrusions on the canes that will emerge in a couple of months as they expand to the brilliance of who they are. My red rose will still be red, and my yellow rose will show its yellowness. There are still a few roses left on the bushes from last year that I pick to enjoy. I see them now as more than just a decorative addition to my home. I see them as individual pieces of a whole.

I am also an individual part of the whole and I fit. I fit in the world. And it is my world, with its highs and its lows, its triumphs and moments of despair. I fit with a family where it does not seem like I belong, and with friends who feel like family. I look out and see the world from my heart, not just from my head. I am learning compassion for others, and, mostly, I am gaining it for myself.

I am learning of my magnificence and the purpose of my soul. I can almost hear my guardian angels cheering. I can now see them beckoning me to my future. They tell me that, as spirit, I can identify with myself even as I move forward in my life into the unknown. I can only be who I am and be the purpose I am here to be. I go into my garden to discover the color that I am and learn to be that color.

Dream: In my dream, I am lucid, awake and living my everyday life. I am walking in my house, and then I spread my hands out like wings. I stand on my tippy-toes and just allow the air to lift me. Like an eagle, I begin to fly. Suddenly I am floating above the room and rising toward the ceiling. "It's easy," I shriek with a laugh. "I know I can do this when I'm awake in my other world."

Then the walls expand and the ceiling becomes a skylight several stories high. As I approach the glass, it appears as if I'm going to hit my head and I cringe, waiting for the impact. Instead, I find myself floating through an opening, clear and unfettered. I am exhilarated by the idea that I can float through this impenetrable surface. I fly ever upward, like a hot-air balloon, steadily rising, soaring free and loose. I am happy.

Then I awake with the calm knowledge that I could repeat my flight in my everyday world, if I just put my soul in charge of my life. These are the times when I know my everyday life is the dream world and my nocturnal wanderings represent my real existence.

CHAPTER TWENTY

Islea: The Guardian of Light

The cloud-like atmosphere above Sallie's head was thick with fog that looked like giant mushrooms with their tops overlapping each other. It was so eerily quiet and dense she could only make out a few inches in front of her as she walked a path that seemed to disappear into the mist. Sallie looked down to find her way. *Where am I? I cannot even see my feet or the path upon which I am walking.* She blinked several times to adjust to the grey light.

Somewhere, she heard a voice, lyrical and sweet. "You have the tools—use them." Sallie looked around to find the source of the voice.

"What tools?" she shouted into the haze to dispel her fear. Then she stopped, realization dawning. *I do have the tools.*

Sallie began to recount other lessons of trust and knowingness, of will and destiny, of forgiveness and surrender, of wholeness and ascension. Now, with an anticipation of the completion of her mission, her feet stepped out with purpose. *I can find my way, even in the darkness and oppression of this fog.*

Sensing again the presence of the voice, Sallie turned toward the sound of wings beating with gentle vibratory flutters, like a humming bird.

"I am with you." The voice spoke in a soothing tone that reached into her soul. "Look for the bridge that will take you to the tunnel of light, and thereupon, to the Place of Truth. All you have done so far has been to remember the destiny that has lain dormant in you, and now you are looking for the way home to Source, from whence you came. This is the place of Oneness, where there is no hate, no fear, and no judgment."

"How do I get there?"

"You have already begun," Islea responded softly. "Your awareness of the Oneness has drawn closer as you have listened to your heart and heard the sound of your soul. Now, listen for the song that will expand your remembrance of who you are." Islea's voice went quiet.

Sallie closed her eyes and listened to the silence, straining to hear what she had never heard before. She caught a note and then another. And, finally, Sallie heard the song—a tune without lyrics that told her in its melodious unfolding all she needed to know about her true home, the place that held the truth of who she was, and the purpose of her life on Earth.

As she allowed this melody to sweep over her, Islea breathed light into her and the fog lifted. Sallie found herself on the edge of a very steep cliff. Her brow furrowed. "I thought you said there was a bridge."

"There is. Look inside with your soul eyes to discover that which your mind thinks is impossible. See this bridge so that you can pass to the other side of the chasm."

Sallie responded with a halting voice, "I don't know how."

"Hmm. That is just a thought you have and an inaccurate one."

"It is what I see with my eyes."

"Ah, there you go, believing what you think you are seeing. Use the magic in your heart to send out streams of light into the darkness and anchor them to the other side. Keep sending out these beams until you create a bridge, and when you know it is firm and strong, you can step onto it and walk over it to the tunnel of light."

As she followed Islea's instructions, a bridge appeared that spanned the abyss. Sallie's eyes widened as she saw the results of her new thoughts. "How did I do that?"

"You created something that before you considered to be impossible because you had the thought that you could do it and then believed."

"Amazing." She stood a little straighter. "I can do what I think is impossible." Still with some trepidation, she stepped onto the bridge.

Islea continued, "As you walk, you will see loved ones and others you know, some of whom have crossed the rainbow bridge ahead of you and await your soul when you have completed your tasks. Smile to all and acknowledge their contributions. Send them the love they need for the completion of their own missions. I will meet you ahead in the Place of Truth."

As Sallie walked, visions appeared before her: David, Mark, Nancy, Mike, Anne, Robert, Nonna, and Iris. She smiled and nodded to each of them for the progress they had helped her make, as well as the work they had accomplished on their own respective journeys. Her heart leapt with joy as she recognized her mother, and she reached out to receive Hannah's love.

Her ancestors greeted her next, thanking her for remembering them. She could see their hearts expanding as she sent them healing waves of energy. As she continued, Sallie saw all of the spirit guides that had been with her throughout her journey. They sent their thanks and told Sallie of their delight in working with her, as she was necessary for the fulfillment of their mission in the eternal dance of union back to the Oneness.

At the end of the bridge, an arch appeared over the path with a sign, "Place of Truth," resplendent with bright, glittering jewels of sapphire, ruby, and emerald. Islea appeared, surrounding and enclosing them both in a beam of translucent light.

"I seem to remember you," Sallie said, looking at her angel guide with wonder in her eyes. "It's as if I've waited a long time to see you again."

Islea acknowledged her words with a nod. "I have returned to provide you encouragement as you continue your mission on Earth. Now is the time for you and all who currently reside on your planet to remember the truth of who you are.

"In the past, the world has only taught you who you are not. You live in two worlds, the dualistic reality of your everyday existence and a non-dualistic realm. They need to exist side-by-side equally. You do this when you connect your brain to your heart. This raises your awareness to the next level of consciousness.

"Around your heart, there is a toroidal field of energy. This donut-shaped torus surrounds your body, Earth, your solar system, the galaxy, and the universe. It can be likened to a gyroscopic two-ended trumpet standing on end. Rather than a hole like a donut has, however, this torus folds in upon itself, continuously flowing in a bidirectional manner, in through your head and feet. When you live in fear, it is quite small, giving you a feeling of separation. As you bring unconditional love into your heart, this field expands, connecting you to others and to the divine spark that makes you unique."

"In my life, there are times when I feel that connection to others and times when I feel all alone," Sallie responded. "I just know my shortcomings."

"Your consciousness creates your reality, just as the outcome of a scientific experiment is affected by what the researcher believes. To change your experience, you must look to your thoughts, words, and actions as they influence what comes your way. Just as you built a bridge of light today in your non-dualistic dreamtime, you can take that energy into your everyday dualistic existence."

"I have known about my thoughts creating my experience. Sometimes, though, I forget as I get caught up in the moment and the challenges of just being human and interacting with others."

"You will know the Oneness of all life and find peace when you feel the connection between yourself and the divine light within others. When you look at others, see the truth of who they are in their souls through your soul eyes. It is for you to be aware of their divinity so that you might see yours."

"Will you help me learn how to do this?"

Islea nodded and said, "Let us rest in the Place of Truth and practice. First, close your eyes and place your hands right below your heart at the top of your rib cage. Sink your thoughts deep into the center of the planet and visualize your heart beating in resonance with Mother Earth. Allow that earth energy to rise into your body and swirl up and around through the torus spinning around your heart. Now, visualize the sky energy of the universe descending into your body and swirl it through the torus in the opposite direction. Feel these two flowing energies merge and expand as you bring unconditional love into your heart. Allow the love you feel to envelop you, expanding your consciousness, and let any dissonant energies dissolve.

"Tell yourself: I am Spirit. I know my truth. I create the design of my life. I live my full potential. I have the memory of my knowing."

As Sallie breathed in, she felt her divine spark reaching up, as if it would lift her into the sky. "I know I can fly," she said. It was a simple statement of the truth in her heart.

"You can. It is the flight of your soul, and it comes through the Light—the light that calls forth the truth. Love unconditionally with an open and vulnerable heart, pray to know the design of your life, join in the toroidal bubble of light with those you love, and spend time dreaming and just being, always yearning for your true home."

"Will you and all my guides continue to be with me?"

"We are always with you," Islea assured her. "It is for you to call on us."

And, with that, Islea wished her well on the next phase of her journey, then slowly dissolved, leaving Sallie encircled in a rainbow of light.

EPILOGUE

Sallie's Journal—December 31st

Change is very much a part of existence on Earth. Yet, when it comes to me, I act as if it is an aberration, and I go kicking and screaming into a new way of life that is always different, and usually better, than my previous reality.

My life is an everyday venture of highs and lows, positive feelings followed by waves of hopelessness. That it requires some transformation on my part has not eluded me. Gaining insight from my dream world has given me courage to reach beyond my limited expectations.

I know a positive attitude is imperative to create the intentions I desire. I know affirmations work. I have an impression of my personal will intertwined with a sense of my destiny. I know all that anyone could tell me about living a thoughtful life. Yet, the hours, days, and months go by, filled sometimes with despair and longing for a life that might be. I will always wonder if I am living my greatest potential.

Moments of great clarity, those times when I can see for miles in all directions of my life, suddenly open to me. Then the everyday world intrudes and little seeds of doubt begin to undermine my confidence.

Negative thoughts are the worst enemy of any intention. A new goal is like a seedling that must be tenderly nourished and nurtured in order to grow. For a goal to transform from its dreamtime origin to the material world, it must be supported by a sustained pattern that is unwavering in its belief in the original, clear thought. Whenever a shadow of fear, doubt, or negativity enters my mind to cloud my vision, I look back to that first moment of clarity to sustain me, like taking a window cleaner and wiping away the cloudy film of pessimism ruining the clear reflection of my path so that my dream can be transported into my everyday world.

In times of transition, anxiety pervades to my core as I see that I create unwanted events by my negative thought patterns. I must remember that thoughts are very powerful and negative ones have the power to impede progress. To reach the goals I am seeking, I must cross the bridge of uncertainty and fear that lies across every river of change separating my current life from a better future.

Somewhere, though, in the day to day, I find an aptness in all the feelings I have, and I know my life is perfect just the way it is, with the positive and negative, ups and downs, and the ins and outs of all my feelings. I travel my path in fits and starts, gaining a measure of trust bit by bit. I learn from all I observe around me, including the messages that seem to have come to me from the deepest reaches of my imagination. I remain hopelessly in love with my life, as I listen to the sound of my soul.

Acknowledgments

Over the many years it took to get this story to the reader, there has been a community who can lay claim to having their fingerprints on this book. Thank you…

To long-time friends, Linda, Lynda, and Janice,
may we have many more years together.
Your friendship provides stability.

To my writing pals at Relax and Write,
may we all achieve our destiny.
Most particularly to Maia, leader of the clan.

To my writing partner, KC Moffatt,
your insights are deep and empowering and
your editing skills are awesome.

To the beta readers,
your comments and support enhanced the final version of the story.
A special thanks to Linda and Brett for your detailed notes.

To all those whom I have met throughout my life story,
whether you be friend or foe,
you have contributed immensely,
for without all the experience of being human,
we are incomplete.

And, to my business partner, Eric,
your support provides stability.

Join the conversation at thesoundofmysoul.com

About the Author

Like many novels, this one had its genesis in an experience that became a turning point in my life. For many years, I'd harbored the secret dream of writing a book, so one day I sat down and began to write a story that had some parallels to mine. Early feedback was discouraging. The story just didn't work. Many drafts later, Sallie's story began to solidify as it became more and more distant from my life. It truly became a work of fiction.

Despite its divergence from my own experiences, Sallie's world provided a playground in which I could pay homage to memories that continue to bring me pleasure. The high school teachers that Sallie describes were modeled after my own. Mrs. Lindsey was my favorite, and she imparted a love of literature that continues to this day.

The angel messages came from afar, as if unseen helpers whispered in my ear as I slept or daydreamed. A name would come into my head, like Mairye, with the unusual spelling, and Eudarge, a name I heard at three in the morning and had to turn on the light and write down so as to not forget it with the dawn. Through their messages, I became open to the opportunities for growth surrounding us all.

It is my hope that this story resonated with you and helped you take another step along your own path. As you open to new messages from your guides, I encourage you to share your experiences on my website and join the conversation.

Contact me at patti@thesoundofmysoul.com
Visit my website: pattiwilliams.com

Made in the USA
San Bernardino, CA
29 November 2016